BEAUTY IN BLOOM:
Homeopathy to Support Menopause

BEAUTY IN BLOOM:
Homeopathy to Support Menopause

Eileen Nauman, DHM (UK)

Cover artwork: Ruth Owens
Typesetting: Louella Holter

ISBN 0-9634662-7-5

Published by

Blue Turtle Publishing
PO Box 2513, Cottonwood, AZ 85326

DEDICATION

To women around the world who deserve better than hormone replacement therapy in experiencing their wonderful and liberating natural cycle, called menopause!

and

To my women Navajo clients on the Navajo reservation who willingly embrace homeopathic medicine, It'taweena Ah'Zee, as a natural complement to their belief that the body can heal itself with the help of natural cures from Mother Earth. Yahtehay!

ABOUT THE AUTHOR

Eileen Nauman, DHM (UK), is a classically trained homeopath who has practiced for 30 years. A graduate of the British Institute of Homeopathy in England, she is also a member of their faculty. Currently, she is on the core faculty of the Desert Institute School of Classical Homeopathy in Phoenix, Arizona.

Owner of Blue Turtle Flower and Gem Essences, she conducts provings to show their curative effect on people and animals. Moderator and owner of an alternative medicine list on the Internet, she creates a classroom atmosphere of introducing people to homeopathy, flower and gem essences, and other healing modalities.

A worldwide lecturer on many topics, she is the author of more than sixty fiction books and eight non-fiction books. In her spare time, she resides near Sedona, Arizona with her husband at her home which is known as La Casa de Madre Tierra, The House of Mother Earth.

CONTENTS

ACKNOWLEDGEMENTS

A book of this scope is never written alone. I want to thank Rosemarie Brown, MSW, for her research work that this project entailed. Without her, it would have been a Gordian Knot to unravel alone.

And thanks to Melissa Assilem, a renowned British homeopath who is one of our great leaders toward women reclaiming and owning their own bodies.

INTRODUCTION

I started peri-menopause at age 40. Suddenly, my life was transformed by terrible night sweats, where I felt as if a fire was sweeping up from my feet and engulfing my whole body. As these internal (and infernal!) flames roared through me, I would break out into such a heavy sweat that my bed sheets would be soaked through. For someone who had never sweated much in the past, this was extremely upsetting. And there seemed no end in sight!

Soon, another "symptom" joined the night sweats—hot flashes by day. Just when I least expected them, my upper chest and face would flush, and within minutes, I'd feel dampness under my armpits and would begin worrying about ruining my clothes.

It didn't take long for the homeopath in me to declare "enough is enough!" I analyzed my symptoms and came up with the homeopathic remedy, Folliculinum, a non-drug form of natural estrogen that has helped many women breeze their way through menopause. It worked for me, too. Thanks to Folliculinum, I never had a hot flash for the time that the remedy was working with my vital force and constitution.

During my 30 years as a practicing homeopath, I've treated hundreds of women, and every case reinforces my respect for this subtle, yet powerful form of healing. The results have ranged from satisfying to the near miraculous!

Sofia, a woman in her mid-forties, called me one day in a panic. She was bleeding uncontrollably from fibroids she'd acquired in her twenties. Now, she was moving through menopause. "You must help me," she begged. I quickly checked her symptoms and came up with a wonderful remedy that helps women with menstrual and menopausal bleeding: Kali Muriaticum (Kali Mur.). Her daughter ran to the nearest health food store and bought the remedy in a 6X potency. I told her to take one tablet every five minutes and to call me in an hour.

I was quite sure that, if the bleeding didn't stop, she was going to be bound for the emergency room and probably have a DNC. Happily, Sofia called me an hour later, utter relief in her voice. "After I took the third tablet," she reported, "my bleeding slowed down so much, it seemed like a regular period." The clots and heavy bleeding were gone—and never returned.

Within these pages are stories of women whose lives changed when they tried homeopathy. Some of them had been suffering with symptoms of drug and hormone therapies. As soon as they stopped taking the pills, their bodies immediately began to heal, their symptoms disappeared, and a stronger, healthier person emerged.

If homeopathy is so effective, why doesn't everyone use it? Many people do! In fact, for centuries, since the late 1700s when Dr. Samuel Hahnemann discovered homeopathy, it has been practiced widely throughout Europe and Asia. In 1850, homeopathy came to the United States. By 1900, one out of every five doctors were homeopaths.

Then penicillin was discovered, and the American Medical Association (AMA) lobbied vigorously to promote this "cure-all." Homeopathy took a back seat to conventional or allopathic medicine among physicians until the 1980s. Since then, there has been a tremendous resurgence of interest in homeopathy. Today, hundreds of practitioners cannot keep up with the demand for their services.

The arguments for using homeopathy are certainly impressive.

* Homeopathy gently and naturally stimulates the organs and systems of the body to help it rebalance and heal itself.
* Homeopathy has no adverse side effects, no allergic reactions, and no addictive influences.
* Homeopathy works with the body's natural defense system. Drugs, on the other hand, often damage vital organs defending the body against these "foreign" invaders.
* Homeopathic remedies are a fraction of the cost of drugs. Some are used only one time to get the desired results!

Allopathy, or conventional medicine, may be the automatic answer to "What can I take to feel better?" but it isn't necessarily the best one! In fact, drug taking always involves risk. First, the medicine offered might not be appropriate for the patient. All too often, a doctor will "try out" a drug to see if it works. The patient is, in fact, a guinea pig—sometimes with unpleasant results.

Second, because the drugs are usually in synthetic form, the body reacts to these invaders by rejecting them. Therefore, very large doses are given to destroy the symptom. When this finally occurs, the patient is declared "cured." But, in fact, the condition may reappear after the drug is stopped, or it may return months or years later in another form.

Third, because large toxic doses are used to make the symptoms disappear, the patient's organs may be damaged. Has your doctor ever told you that liver damage can occur with high drug doses? Because the liver is closely associated with the immune system, large amounts of drugs stall the liver's ability to keep us healthy. Particularly these days, with a number of immune-system diseases rampant, it's certainly advisable to avoid taking drugs whenever possible.

Fourth, drugs given as vaccinations can overwhelm the body's natural defense system. And while the immune system is being attacked by the vaccination, the condition it is supposed to "cure" may come back. For example, millions of children injected with the measles vaccine may now get measles again. Why? The original vaccine did not prevent recurrences, as hoped.

Fifth, when drugs are used to eliminate (and suppress) a medical condition, the disease may hide and return with a vengeance, or show up a year or two later in another form. Take Dawn, a young woman of sixteen whom I recently saw at the Navajo Reservation. Dawn had gotten a mild case of acne across her forehead, cheeks and chin when she was fifteen. When she was given drugs, the rash disappeared for three weeks, then returned worse than before.

Dawn, now afraid of an even worsened condition, insisted she was finished with the white doctor's medicine. I agreed with her and gave her a single dose of Arsenicum Album 30C. A month later, Dawn proudly showed me her smooth, newly healed face. She no longer had to hang her head from embarrassment.

When a woman becomes menopausal, she is poised on the brink of a great adventure. It can prove to be either exciting or terrifying, depending upon some choices she must make. Suddenly, she's facing the Big Decision: should she take Hormone Replacement Therapy? This is not as simple as the family doctor might imply. If she takes hormone replacement therapy, which is strongly promoted by the medical profession, she might avoid heart attack and also osteoporosis, if she has a genetic predisposition to the disease (it is not a symptom of menopause!). But HRT has proven to be a risk for uterine and breast cancer. It's like asking a woman if she wants to jump off a bridge, or walk in front of traffic. Not much of a choice, is it?

Homeopathy offers an alternative to this difficult choice. Within these pages, women will learn how homeopathy can help them achieve their objective of perfect health—yes, perfect health—without hormones, without drugs.

Because this particular book project was very close to my heart and I was going through menopause, I decided at age forty-eight, as I entered the time frame when most of us get our menopause symptoms, to not take anything homeopathically for it because I wanted to be able to talk from a point of experience about menopause. You read in so many books that some women, for example, get insomnia. Well, what causes it? What is it like? I wanted to find out. I did not know if I'd get this symptom (I did) and as a result, I have a wonderful understanding of it.

As you go through the various chapters, I will add my own personal experience and I hope, in doing so, that it will alleviate many of your concerns and worries. At age 53, I feel wonderful despite these symptoms that come and go. Pretty soon, I will be through menopause completely. I hope that the information in this book will make your transit through this marvelous time easy and carefree!

CHAPTER 1

WHAT HOMEOPATHY IS AND HOW IT WORKS

CAN HOMEOPATHY HELP ME THROUGH MENOPAUSE?

Yes! Remember, menopause is NOT a disease; rather, it is a natural transition that every woman's body experiences. Homeopathy naturally stimulates the body to treat itself. And because menopause is not an illness, it is actually one of the easier conditions to treat—successfully.

One of the main reasons I decided to write a book of this scope arose from a personal experience. When I was 45, I suddenly developed depression. I woke one morning and felt as if someone had pulled the plug on my emotions. I felt emotionally bankrupt—without one genuine feeling—except for a hollow emptiness that I found horrifying.

A first, I thought: *Oh, it will go away in a few days.* But those "few days" turned into 3 weeks! During that time, I felt a loss of connection between myself and my husband Dave, to whom I'd been married for 19 years. I also lost my enthusiasm for the foods I love to eat, and for my beloved mother and grandmother. All I felt was a deep emptiness inside. This occurred in July, when beautiful, violent thunderstorms criss-cross Arizona. No one loves storms more than I, but when they arose, I looked at them through empty eyes, without one emotion.

In those weeks, I had lost the will to live. I became a couch potato, content to sit and do nothing—just the opposite of my normal self. One day, Dave sat down with me and we began to talk. I told him that I felt as if I were losing more and more of myself to this deep, bottomless pit where emotions and feelings did not exist.

Suddenly, a light went on, and I muttered, "I wonder if this is caused by menopause?" Years before, I'd had some night sweats and hot flashes, and had cured them with a homeopathic remedy.

I went into my office and turned on my computer, popping in a software program designed for homeopaths. Then I typed in all my symptoms. The remedy that came closest was Sepia—one of the three major remedies for menopause! I felt a thin ray of hope, went to my pharmacy, and took one dose.

I became very sleepy shortly after taking the remedy, and I laid down in the afternoon. I must have slept for 3 hours. When I awoke, all my lost emotions were back! I sat on the edge of the bed in tears, realizing that what had hit me was the very depression I had heard about from my menopausal clients.

Within 24 hours of taking the remedy, I was back to my former energetic self. I embraced life again: I love to walk, ride my horse, and enjoy my husband—my best friend. I could again marvel at the thunderstorms rolling into our canyon and the brilliant rainbow that always follows. I resolved that, because of my own frightening experience, I had to do something to help other menopausal women with similar symptoms.

CAN HOMEOPATHY HELP IN EVERY PHASE OF MENOPAUSE?

Absolutely! Not every woman will become depressed, as I did. (Only 26% of us will, according to a large study—lucky me!) Most women will experience hot flashes (about 40% according to this study), and a smaller number will experience night sweats. In the chapters ahead, I have listed the various symptoms that we may experience during menopause. There are homeopathic remedies for all these conditions, thank goodness! We need not be frightened or controlled by the medical establishment, nor need we assault our bodies with drugs or hormones while we go through a *natural* event. Instead, we can utilize Mother Nature's remedies, which help our bodies make the adjustment with grace and without stress.

One of my dear friends, B.T., a chiropractor, complained that she was an emotional mess. She was in her early forties, pre-menopausal, and extremely weepy. "I'll cry at everything, Eileen," she said. "I feel as if I'm on an emotional roller coaster that just won't stop."

I took B.T.'s case and prescribed Folliculinum 30C. Within 48 hours, she got off that roller coaster. Now, she could take care of her clients without having to dodge into another room, shed a few tears, and dash back to finish treating them.

As you go through this book, you will discover where you are on your own menopausal path. You will find people's true stories illustrating how homeopathic remedies have helped them—and can help you—naturally, without drugs or hormones!

And perhaps just as important, I've gone through my own symptoms of menopause. At age 53, I've experienced depression, hot flashes, night sweats, heart palpitations, lowered sexual desire, restless legs, allergies, and insomnia. As a result, I can speak with some authority on this, and hopefully, alleviate your concerns. All of these symptoms are temporary and can be worked with via homeopathy, or perhaps flower essences, upon which you'll find information in later chapters of this book.

Our personal arsenal of choices contains many ways, many "healing tools," that are natural. Although this book has mostly a homeopathic slant, it also provides information on flower essences, as well as some key vitamins and minerals that may make your menopause years "no sweat"!

WHAT IS HOMEOPATHY?

It is a complementary form of medicine, practiced around the world, that is based on the Law of Similars. The Greek word "homeo" means similar and "pathos" means disease; similar disease or "like cures like." Homeopathy utilizes medically active substances at infinitesimal potencies, which makes it safe, non-habit forming, non-addictive, non-allergenic, and without side-effects.

Let me give you an example of "like cures like" so that you can understand homeopathy in action. Everyone, with few exceptions, has been stung by a bee sometime in their life. Everyone has felt that sharp, burning pain from the sting itself. Then, the skin raises, turns bright red and there's lots of heat surrounding it. The skin will usually feel itchy, too. In a more scientific explanation, your body is dis-eased by the sting. We choose a homeopathic remedy that parallels the symptoms of the sting, and introduce it, like an artificial disease, into your body. Because the potentized remedy is stronger than the sting, the body or vital force gets the signal that something is wrong, reorganizes itself and its systems, and focuses its energies on healing the symptoms introduced by the remedy. In doing so, the actual bee sting is cured, too.

The vital force is our intrinsic energy that is within and outside of us. This includes our physical, emotional, mental, and spiritual states. This force helps us in our daily lives and becomes invaluable when we fall sick. Homeopaths are trained to perceive this vital force and are able to measure this life energy in each of us, to help us get well.

Let's get back to the insect bite. Our homeopath will consult a special reference manual called a Materia Medica, which contains 1,400 FDA-approved remedies. The one that most closely matches the symptoms of swollen insect bite is Apis Mellifica. This is crushed honey bee, and is the remedy used for a sting that matches the symptoms of this potentized remedy. We would give you one medicated sucrose pellet and within minutes, the symptoms of the sting would disappear.

We've introduced an organic, potentized remedy, at an infinitesimal potency, into your body. Your body has responded to this remedy and voilà! You have cured yourself of a sting with all its accompanying symptoms. The most exciting thing about this process is that your body's own natural healing force creates the cure. There are no after-effects, and the body does not become dependent on drugs.

IS THERE PROOF THAT HOMEOPATHY WORKS?

Yes. The first type, which is anecdotal and not scientific, is your experience with a homeopathic remedy. Simply ask anyone who has benefited from a homeopathic remedy when in distress. I remember one highly dramatic case I helped with while attending the Lakota Indians' Sundance ceremony in South Dakota in 1991.

Bob, a paramedic who was also attending the event, called me by walkie-talkie to tell me that a family of four was in acute distress. They were having an allergic reaction to the lime dust spread over the Porta-Johns. Their throats were swelling closed, and Bob was afraid that if help didn't come soon, they would suffocate. I raced to their tent, where Bob pointed out a 50-year-old woman seated on a chair, leaning over with her hands on her throat. She was wheezing, her face was gray, and I knew that she was not getting enough oxygen. Reaching for my high-potency homeopathic kit, I took out an appropriate remedy and pushed a couple of pellets into her mouth, telling her she would be all right.

I then looked over at the husband and oldest daughter. They were both breathing harshly, but were in better shape than the mother. The baby, a beautiful little girl, played quietly on a quilt on the floor between us. She didn't display any symptoms at all. Bob, in the meantime, was hovering over the mother. I'm sure he was thinking that he'd have to cut a hole in her throat to allow breathing if this remedy didn't work.

I gave Bob the proper dosages for the husband and daughter, and a smaller, preventative dose for the baby. Within 5 minutes, the older woman's harsh breathing had evened out. Her hand left her throat, and the gray color began to leave her face. Within 15 minutes, her allergic reaction was gone.

Twenty minutes later, everyone was fine. I walked back to my truck with Bob at my side. He shook his head, saying that he couldn't believe his eyes. He'd been a paramedic for 10 years in Seattle and thought he'd seen it all.

WHERE DO I GO TO GET HELP FOR MENOPAUSE?

In the appendix section, you'll find the names, addresses, and phone numbers of national homeopathic associations. For a small charge, the National Center for Homeopathy will send you a directory of homeopaths in your area. You might have to travel a bit to get to the right practitioner. But it's worth it. The freedom to breeze through menopause without hot flashes or drugs makes that trip a small price to pay!

HOW IS A HOMEOPATHIC REMEDY MADE?

We have FDA-approved homeopathic pharmacies all over the United States, and we have the HPUS, the homeopathic pharmacopoeia for the United States—our guidebook that tells us exactly how to produce a remedy. Let me lead you through an example. Our homeopathic remedies come from three sources: the animal, vegetable, and mineral kingdoms. They are made of flowers, plants, roots, trees, insects, and minerals, to mention a few sources. Almost everyone, especially mothers, are familiar with Ipecac, which we keep in our household in case one of our children accidentally becomes poisoned. We know that if they do, we will give them Ipecac, an herb that will immediately cause vomiting. Let's use Ipecac root as an example of our understanding of how a homeopathic remedy is made.

The Ipecac root is gathered according to the HPUS, which may state that it must be dug up at a certain time of the year. We then take it to our pharmacy, wash it, sterilize it properly, and macerate it; or put it into a machine to tear it up and break it down. We then add a certain amount of ethyl alcohol (also known as 'grain' alcohol) and water and place the macerated root into a gallon jar. We let this sit for a certain period of time to let the alcohol pull all of the nutrients and chemicals out of the root.

At a specified time, the entire contents is strained. The Ipecac root is thrown away and what is left is known as a "mother tincture." This comprises the constituents—the vitamins, minerals, and chemicals of the Ipecac—now suspended in a fluid of alcohol and water. Another lab assistant will be preparing a number of vials in the meantime.

To keep this simple, we will make an "x" potency, which means that there is 1 part of the mother tincture to 9 parts of alcohol and water. When these are measured out, the vial is corked and then "successed." The bottom of the vial is struck against something solid, but not so hard as to shatter the vial. This succussion or jarring is done 100 times. We then have Ipecac 1X.

When the contents are succussed, the energy contained in the molecules of Ipecac are released. The more jarring that occurs, the more energy is released. The lab assistant will then take a small amount from this first vial of 1X Ipecac and place it in a second one that contains the same amount of alcohol and water. You can see that by doing this, we are putting less of the original mother tincture in the second vial. This vial is succussed 100 more times and we end up with Ipecac 2X.

Depending on the potency needed, we can do this upward to 3X, 4X, 5X, and so on. When we have the potency desired, we spray the contents of the vial over sucrose (sugar) pellets; they are thus impregnated with the Ipecac, which has been homeopathically prepared.

IS THERE A GENERAL HOMEOPATHIC POTENCY FOR REMEDIES SOLD IN HEALTH FOOD STORES THAT I CAN BUY?

Yes. Let's take a closer look at a common, over-the-counter potency that is sold in better health food stores, called a "30C." The C (which stands for 100) means that the mother tincture remedy was made of one part of substance and 99 parts of alcohol and water. The 30 means that the remedy was then diluted 30 times (and successed 100 times with each dilution). The higher numbers represent more potent remedies because the energy released by succussion increases with each dilution.

You may find lower potencies on store shelves, such as 3X or 6X, but generally speaking, FDA laws allow health food stores to sell up to a 30C potency. Anything higher should come directly from a homeopathic practitioner.

CAN A 30C POTENCY HARM ME?

A 30C potency is considered a moderate potency, and is used in the United States because of its gentle and persistent action. In some cases, it can cause an "aggravation." In homeopathy, an aggravation is an intensification of symptoms that you already had before taking the remedy; they may intensify after taking the remedy. An aggravation can last a few moments or hours. If it goes on for more than 24 hours, consult a homeopath immediately.

For example, when you take a low potency, such as 30C, your body's response would be a gentle stimulation of its natural defenses. But if you used a much higher potency, such as a 200C, you could get too much "bang for your buck"—or an aggravation. For example, if I took a 30C potency for hot flashes, they would lessen or completely disappear over a period of hours, with no negative physical reaction. But if I took a 200C potency, I might have more intense hot flashes for a period of time before they disappeared—which is highly uncomfortable.

Ideally, you should contact a homeopath in your vicinity and ask her or him about any possible use of any remedy you find in this book. Get their professional opinion. Then, if the homeopath approves, you will be under their guidance, which is best. To self-medicate with a homeopathic remedy, even at a 30C potency, is not the best of all conditions. If nothing else, if this book inspires you to find out who your local homeopath is, then you are well on your way to better health.

IT SEEMS TO ME THAT YOU'RE USING LESS AND LESS OF THE HERBAL SUBSTANCE. AT SOME POINT, IF YOU MAKE A HIGH ENOUGH POTENCY, IS THERE ANYTHING OF THE HERB LEFT IN THE LIQUID?

In mathematics, which is not my forte, there is a theoretical calculation known as Avagadro's number. Avogadro, an Italian physicist, postulated in 1811 that equal volumes contain equal numbers of molecules. By his theory, a 24X or 12C homeopathic potency has NO MOLECULES left in the liquid. That is true—insofar as his hypothesis goes. However, Dr. Jacques Benveniste, a world-renowned homeopathic researcher from France, proved that water continues to contain a MEMORY of that remedy, regardless.

That is why we call homeopathy "energy medicine." With potencies above 24X or 12C, we are dealing with submolecular materials that continue to retain the memory of the remedy. As we continue to dilute our remedies, there is less and less of the actual substance in the liquid. At that point, there are no molecules of the original substance left in the liquid. This is what makes it infinitesimal. No one can explain WHY it works after the molecules are gone. I'm sure in the years to come, there will be a sufficient scientific explanation and we'll have instruments that can prove this phenomenon adequately. Until then, we must rely on faith, anecdotal case histories, and scientific research. No one can SEE gravity; all we can do is measure its effects upon us. Homeopathy falls into that category.

IS THERE EVIDENCE THAT HOMEOPATHY WORKS?

There are two kinds of evidence that medical scientists consider proof. One is anecdotal evidence, which means that doctors or health practitioners have consistently observed a healing effect of a certain drug or treatment in their practices, but no clinical studies have yet been performed to prove exactly how it works. Nonetheless, if such a treatment is known to be safe and effective, doctors will not hesitate to prescribe it. An example is the popular drug Retin-A, which has been scientifically studied and proven for use only as a treatment for acne. Because anecdotal evidence shows that it works for wrinkles, it is used by thousands of people who haven't seen a pimple for years.

The second kind of evidence, which is most respected by the medical establishment, comes from scientific studies. The best are called "controlled, double-blind" studies. In this kind of research a large group of people who are treated with the drug being studied are compared against a similar, untreated group. The untreated group is receiving a placebo, or pill with no active ingredients. A third "control" group receives nothing. This prevents subjects from guessing the effects of the treatment or drug, and results in more objective proof.

For homeopathy, there is evidence of both kinds. You'll get plenty of anecdotes by simply asking anyone who uses homeopathy. After people have used a homeopathic remedy, they have seen its often near-miraculous results. In my 30 years of practice, I've seen homeopathy work just like this in thousands of cases. But there are scientific studies, too.

IS THERE SCIENTIFIC EVIDENCE THAT HOMEOPATHY WORKS, THEN?

Yes. The *British Journal of Clinical Pharmacology*, March, 1989, published results from France showing that a homeopathic remedy was effective in treating flu symptoms. The 487 people who took part in the double-blind study didn't know if they were using a homeopathic remedy or a placebo. The end result showed that twice as many clients using homeopathic medicine recovered within 48 hours, compared to patients who were given a placebo.

Lancet, October 18, 1986, published results of a double-blind study from the University of Glasgow (Scotland) showing that a homeopathic remedy significantly reduced symptoms of hay fever in patients.

And the *British Journal of Clinical Pharmacology*, in September, 1980, published a study showing that 82 percent of patients with rheumatoid arthritis experienced a significant improvement in symptoms, compared with 21 percent who took a placebo.

These studies are solid, but why aren't there more? Because homeopathy honors the individual in all respects. It is very tough to devise a statistical return that will show the effectiveness of homeopathic remedies because, for example, everyone's "headache" is different. Headaches can start at the root of the nose, at the temples, at the rear of the skull, or on top of the head. The pain associated with a headache is not general, either. If you ask your friends to describe the pain associated with their headaches and compare them to your own, you'll see how varying the symptoms really are! Further, headaches occur for differing reasons: some are from stress, and others are from high blood pressure, dehydration, too much sun, and so forth. Hence, every headache may need a different remedy.

To try to devise a test of homeopathy that is acceptable to the prevailing scientific establishment is tough because our conventional (or "allopathic") system of medicine generally takes the stance that one kind of drug can treat almost everyone's headache, stomach ache, or flu. Homeopathy believes instead that everyone's headache is different; therefore a different remedy is needed for each of these individual headaches.

Now you can appreciate our problems in trying to convince the medical establishment! We rely heavily on the millions of people who use homeopathy to prove that it works. But the best proof of all will be your own experience, when you try it yourself.

WAS HOMEOPATHY EVER POPULAR IN THE UNITED STATES?

Absolutely! Homeopathy was brought here to us in 1825 by several doctors who studied in Europe. They taught their colleagues, and schools were slowly established. By the mid-1800s we had homeopathic medical colleges, including the New England Female Medical College, which was the first medical school in America to admit women.

By 1900, we had 22 homeopathic colleges and one out of every five doctors in the United States was a homeopath. Unfortunately, there was a move toward a mechanical model of the body and disease, and homeopathy lost ground—not because it didn't work, but because homeopaths, by nature, weren't politicians—and the American Medical Association, the allopaths, were. By 1910, only 15 homeopathic colleges remained. By the end of the 1940s no courses were taught in America.

Homeopathy was also pushed into the background of America's medical history with the discovery of penicillin and the use of drugs or shots that would give instant relief. That, and the discovery and use of vaccinations, all pushed homeopathy further from the minds of the millions who had used it and been cured by it.

Interestingly enough, when we had the Spanish Flu Epidemic of 1918, when 22 million people died worldwide of this virus, some fascinating facts emerged to show that homeopathy was still a better medicine. Several homeopathic remedies were used by homeopathic doctors to save lives during this devastating flu epidemic. The allopathic doctors relied on their crude drugs. There were 500,000 deaths in the United States alone from this epidemic. Afterward, Dean W. A. Pearson of Philadelphia and Hahnemann College collected data on 26,795 cases of influenza treated by homeopathic physicians with a mortality rate of 1.05 percent, whereas the average old school (allopathic) mortality was 30 percent.

Because of vigorous and aggressive politicking by the AMA, homeopathy was pushed out of the picture via Congressional acts and laws, and would have died a certain death in America if not for the "lay" homeopaths—the ordinary people who had been patients of homeopaths, and who picked up the torch and carried it forward. If not for the lay public, who continued to not only use homeopathy, but teach it to those who were interested, homeopathy would not be enjoying the resurgence it has today. From 1940 to 1980, the lay public not only kept homeopathy alive, but gave it a second chance.

Now, since 1980 and into the present, homeopathy has become the "darling" of the complementary or alternative medicines in our country. And the effort of the lay homeopaths should never go unsung. We have MDs, DOs, and NDs taking courses and going to newly established homeopathic colleges. Homeopathy is strutting its stuff once again, and proving it where it counts—with the people.

Homeopathy is grass roots medicine. It is about people caring for people. It's about knowing that all things are connected and that natural medicines are not only kinder and gentler, but can give profound, equally miraculous help to someone who is ill.

WHO USES HOMEOPATHY?

In the United States, the poorest to the richest people utilize homeopathy. Because it is inexpensive, it is within reach of anyone who desires to use it. There is no slide rule to say that a certain part of our population is drawn to it. Rather, people discover homeopathy because the allopathic, traditional medicine system has failed them, or they have run out of money to continue drug treatment.

People who are interested in their health, who would rather use something other than invasive drugs that would give them side-effects, cause allergy reactions, or in some way inhibit a true quality of life, are the ones who check out homeopathy. Once they've tried it, few ever return to drug treatment. Or, they use drugs more sparingly.

I know mothers who absolutely refuse to have their babies immunized because they see the deadly spiral of children from past generations getting sicker and sicker at a younger age. This wasn't so before the advent of vaccinations, and they don't want their children's immune systems compromised with a series of shots from the moment they're born and throughout adolescence. So, they turn to homeopathy to strengthen their children's immune systems—naturally, and without the side-effects of vaccinations.

There is mounting evidence that too many vaccinations are making a person's or child's immune system too sensitized and that is why children are ending up with allergy and asthmatic conditions whereas before the Vaccination Generation, allergies and asthma were practically unheard of!

For instance, the DPT shot, which comprises three vaccinations in one, was routinely given to every baby. Unfortunately, over the last decade, there is more than anecdotal evidence that this DPT shot causes epilepsy. A lot of mothers don't want to trade off the DPT shot for epilepsy in their child. So, they research alternatives, and homeopathy is certainly a viable answer.

Another example is the Navajo people that I care for up on their reservation. They dislike and distrust "white man's medicine." In their realm of thinking and seeing the world, they would rather use homeopathy because many of the products are herbal in origin, and in their world, their medicine people use herbs all the time to cure people in ceremonies. Further, they intrinsically understand "energy" medicine like homeopathy, because they believe that all things have energy in and around them. So, it's quite easy for them to make the choice between homeopathy and allopathic drug treatment at a hospital.

CAN HOMEOPATHY TOTALLY REPLACE ALLOPATHIC "TRADITIONAL" MEDICINE AS IT'S PRACTICED IN THIS COUNTRY?

No, not entirely. Homeopathy has its limits of jurisdiction, just as EVERY form of medicine. Fortunately, homeopaths recognize these limits and refer patients if homeopathy is unable to help a condition. For example, it cannot replace surgery when it is needed. It can, however, delay or even prevent surgery in some cases. There are also homeopathic remedies that can be given before or after an operation that enable people to heal faster, and leave the hospital more quickly.

There are other factors that may not make homeopathy the treatment of choice. One of them is age. The older population (70+) is tougher to treat, often because their vital force may be low or weak. Because homeopathy has limited effects on a weak, faltering vital force, drug intervention may have to be used instead. A homeopath can assess your vital force and your potential to use homeopathy.

Homeopathy is also ineffective when an organ is beyond mending. For instance, homeopathy is not able to "fix" cirrhosis of the liver, although the liver is a regenerative organ (the only one in the body). If you have suffered a heart attack, homeopathy cannot replace or fix the dead muscle tissue. What it can do is support the circulatory system and heart, along with diet, to prevent another attack.

Generally speaking, however, homeopathy can help everyone to varying degrees. Even if a person has a life-altering disease, homeopathy can make a positive difference. Let a homeopath determine if you're a candidate for homeopathic treatment.

WHAT HAPPENS WHEN I GO TO A HOMEOPATH?

First, speak to the homeopath by phone and see if there is good rapport. If you don't feel good about the phone consultation, then seek out another homeopath until you find one that is right for you.

At the homeopath's office, you'll find that the "taking of your case" may run from one to many hours. This will be in sharp contrast to the usual 15-minute history taken by an allopathic physician. Your homeopath will take the time to question you about many different levels of yourself. You may find some of the questions funny or seemingly irrelevant to menopause. However, your homeopath will be looking at you as a WHOLE person who has spiritual, mental, emotional, and physical needs.

At the end of the case-taking, the homeopath will probably give you a remedy to place under your tongue. These may be a few white sugar pellets or a dilution of water, alcohol, and the remedy. The homeopath may tell you to take your remedy home and take it later that day or night. Then, you'll be given a follow-up appointment 4 or 6 weeks after taking the remedy to see how well it's working.

I like to vary this slightly in my practice. I will tell my client to take the remedy home with her and take it just before she goes to bed. Then I ask the client to call and check in with me 48 hours after taking the remedy. If I have chosen the right remedy, there are going to be minor signs that it is working to help her.

Some conditions or people may be slow to respond and a homeopath is lucky to see any movement or change for 6 weeks. So, be patient after taking the remedy; your menopause symptoms will slowly, subtly change, without you really being aware of it.

When you check in with your homeopath at 4 or 6 weeks, you may or may not receive another remedy; it's not unusual if you don't. Regardless, another appointment will be set up for you 4 to 6 weeks later.

Generally speaking, I have found that it takes 3 months to "clear a case" of menopause complaints. There may be some exceptions to this rule, but you should be free and clear of any menopausal symptoms within 6 months of homeopathic treatment in normal circumstances.

IF I HAVE QUESTIONS ABOUT HOMEOPATHY, WILL MY HOMEOPATH ANSWER THEM?

In most cases, yes. Many have brochures and pamphlets to give you a more in-depth explanation. Homeopathy is a highly complex form of medicine and the homeopath doesn't always have the time they wished they had to answer all of your valid questions. Some homeopaths have a receptionist or lay homeopath who can answer your questions; others do not.

Another way to seek more information is to write or call the National Center for Homeopathy (see appendix). Also, if you're fortunate, there may be a homeopathic study group in your area. The National Center for Homeopathy is an educational nonprofit corporation with hundreds of affiliated study groups around the United States. You can call them and find out if there is a study group in your area. The president or leader of such a group will be exceptionally helpful and enthusiastic in answering any and all of your questions!

I'M INTERESTED IN UNDERSTANDING THE DIFFERENCE BETWEEN TRADITIONAL ALLOPATHIC MEDICINE AND HOMEOPATHY

Allopathic (or conventional) medicine as practiced in the United States treats a condition based on the structure of chemical changes presented. They may look at the patient's background, or try to determine why the structure 'cause' appeared in the first place. In other words, they are trained to look only at the pathology or problem presented. This does not include your state of mind, your emotions, or an event (root cause) that might be connected with your dis-ease, which may have a direct bearing on it. A homeopath does consider these aspects of you and your case. When an allopathic doctor "diagnoses" the problem, it is usually treated with a synthetic drug given in large, continual doses for a certain period of time. Pills will be prescribed for a number of days. At the end of that time, the pathology or problem should be gone. The cause, however, may not be.

The problem with drugs is not that they are synthetic; rather, it is that the drug is not a 'close fit' to the symptoms. Further, the drugs may be toxic and won't heal the dynamic problem that is creating all of the symptoms. But the drug does take away the symptoms and people think they are healed—and they are not. A good example is a woman with a yeast infection who is given drugs. While she takes the drugs, the symptoms are gone. When she stops taking the drugs, the symptoms come back. Why? Because the drugs are not addressing the dynamic in our vital force that is sending out this array of symptoms.

Homeopathically, you would come in and get your case taken. There is no "diagnosis" in homeopathy; instead you present a compilation of many, many symptoms. We look up the group of symptoms in a special book called a Repertory, and find the single remedy that most closely matches your particular, individual set of symptoms. You will be given an initial dose of that potentized remedy just one time along with instructions on when to take it again. That might be several hours later, or days or even months later, and only your homeopath can determine the frequency of dosage for you. They are able to do this by retaking your case every 4 to 6 weeks and when they see a shift in your symptoms, there may be another dose given.

The remedy, which in reality is an artificial disease, is more powerful than the set of symptoms you are currently experiencing, and the body generates enough resistance to eliminate the new symptoms and your old condition.

Homeopathy uses infinitesimal doses of a potentized remedy, given only once, to set the body's natural response into action. Allopathy hammers away, day after day, with a synthetic drug that the body regards as a poison, which does not enlist the help of the body's own responses in any way. When a person takes a drug, it may often suppress the symptoms. Later, the cause of the problem, which was not dealt with, may create another set of more serious symptoms.

WHAT IS SUPPRESSION?

Let me give you an example of suppression. Many babies are now experiencing otitis media, middle ear infection. The course of antibiotics eradicates the symptom, but relief is temporary. The ear infection comes right back after the round of antibiotics, which means the drug didn't cure it, but rather, suppressed the condition for a while. And it becomes a maddening circle of drugs, money, and a child's discomfort and parent's angst. The drug does not cure the condition.

Babies also may be given cortisone at an early age, and after cortisone has suppressed the earlier, less dangerous skin condition, they often develop asthma 1–5 years later. Of course, the pediatrician may not see this happen, and by the time he does, he's telling you to take your child to a specialist. Many times, drugs will suppress a condition and drive it more deeply into the body, and it re-emerges years later, in a far more deadly form. In some instances, it does not, because the person's vital force is strong enough to combat it and throw it off. Allopathic doctors are not trained to think holistically or to recognize suppression. Homeopaths are trained holistically to recognize when suppression has occurred.

The correct homeopathic remedy DOES NOT suppress a condition; rather, it CURES. This is known as the Simillimum. The wrongly chosen remedy, however, can suppress your condition, just as an allopathic drug does, which is another reason to see a homeopathic practitioner for your menopause symptoms and not try to treat them on your own.

THAT'S REALLY SCARY. I'VE TAKEN A LOT OF DRUGS IN MY LIFETIME. AM I A SITTING TIME BOMB WAITING TO EXPLODE?

Yes, it is a scary concept, and homeopaths see suppression all the time. The good news is that in most cases, the suppressions can be eliminated through case-taking and an ongoing constitutional homeopathic treatment program that can last 1–3 years. You see, it took you decades to get in the state of health you are presently experiencing, and homeopathy will take a few years to get you back into a balanced state of health and free from symptoms.

Menopausal symptoms are usually treated acutely and you may see relief from your symptoms in a matter of a day or less; so don't confuse constitutional homeopathic treatment with more immediate homeopathic treatment and relief from this type of symptom.

You don't need to worry yourself about getting some awful disease. Most people's vital forces are strong enough to handle the drugs, but in some cases, especially where there is a weak vital force, there can be serious health impairment. Your homeopath can judge this and then create a healing plan via a remedy, to get you onto safer ground.

IS THERE A TIME WHEN DRUGS SHOULD BE USED INSTEAD OF HOMEOPATHY?

Yes. For instance, I had a call from a client recently and it was obvious over the phone that she had pneumonia. She hates medical doctors and hospitals and turned to homeopathy because it's user friendly and natural. I told Judy that I would take her collection of symptoms over the phone, repertorize, and find a remedy to hopefully halt that pneumonia in its tracks. Her husband came over and picked up the remedy. I told Judy to call me in an hour; if she wasn't obviously improved in that hour, she was to get to the emergency room for immediate treatment.

With more than 1,400 remedies in our pharmacopoeia, a homeopath can be wrong about which remedy to use. They are only human, and as such, can error on the choice of remedy. However, in most circumstances, the right remedy is found by the second or third try. In Judy's case, her pneumonia had struck her so hard and fast that I knew I didn't have time to try a second or third remedy if I had chosen incorrectly. I wasn't about to let my client suffer at my hands. Fortunately, the remedy I chose for her was correct and within 24 hours, she was up and around, without the pneumonia symptoms. It took us 3 days of intense, close work with one another to clean it up completely, but it was done without drug intervention.

There is a right and wrong time to use homeopathy. A homeopathic prescriber knows which occasions are going to need allopathic intervention. The bottom line is this: your life, your health, is first, and what the medical philosophy is shouldn't count—your survival does. Another example is that if a client steps on a rusty nail, I automatically tell them to go to an allopathic doctor and get a tetanus shot. I then give them a homeopathic remedy after the shot, but basically, tetanus is something that doesn't always respond well to homeopathic treatment.

Luckily for us, menopause symptoms DO respond beautifully to homeopathic treatment, so we don't have to go the allopathic route of hormone replacement therapy—HRT.

WHAT HAPPENS AFTER I TAKE A HOMEOPATHIC REMEDY?

Eighty percent of those who take a correctly prescribed remedy will begin to experience a lessening of their symptoms. This can happen gradually over several weeks, or as quickly as within a few hours—it depends on the individual's vital force and the remedy chosen. Some remedies are fast acting, while others are exceedingly slow. This is why the homeopath usually sets up the next appointment 6 weeks away from the time the remedy was taken.

Twenty percent of those taking a remedy may experience a very fleeting aggravation—the intensification of symptoms discussed earlier. The aggravation may last seconds, minutes, or up to a few hours or even days. For example, let's say you always get hot flashes in the afternoon. After taking the remedy, your hot flashes may become more intense, longer, and more uncomfortable for a few hours or a day afterward. The aggravation IS uncomfortable, I won't deny that; I've experienced it myself. However, an aggravation is actually a good sign that the correct remedy was chosen; so this is good news.

With some people (a very small percentage), an aggravation may go on for more than the expected time. If this happens, you should get in touch with your homeopath right away. There is no sense in suffering! The homeopath may antidote the remedy and choose another remedy, which usually will not create an aggravation in you. Sometimes the remedy chosen matches your set of symptoms so closely that it creates long-term aggravation. The homeopath will then antidote it and choose another remedy that isn't so close to your set of symptoms and then you won't experience aggravation.

WHAT IS HERING'S LAW OF CURE? AND HOW DOES IT AFFECT ME?

Homeopathy has a very clear healing path. It's called Hering's Law of Cure. Homeopaths discovered more than 250 years ago that when they gave a remedy to a client, there was always a very definite, clear sign of cure. This curative path rarely wavers or fluctuates from person to person—it's almost always the same pattern. Dr. Constantine Hering, one of our great homeopaths, who brought homeopathy to this country in 1850, brought this collection of curative path insights and observations together and it has since then been known as Hering's Law of Cure.

When a person takes a homeopathic remedy, a number of curative paths will begin:

1. The remedy will stimulate the body to heal the most important organs first and work outward to the least important. What this means is that if there is a problem with your heart or brain, they will be worked on and "fixed" first. The body has it's own hierarchy of what will keep it alive. If the heart or brain stops, then it is dead. A remedy stimulates the body to begin to heal itself, and if there is any problem with these particular organs, they will be repaired first. The least important organ to the body is the skin. Your homeopath will be delighted when you come into her or his office complaining of having a skin rash 6 weeks after initially taking a remedy. This is a good sign that the remedy has healed from the most important organs to the least important—your skin. Happily, this skin rash will disappear within a few days or weeks, on its own, and is nothing to worry about.

2. The remedy will work from the top of your head first, and will move down your body to the tip of your toes. Cure has a very specific direction, usually: from the top down, so to speak. (I have seen some cases where it will start elsewhere, like the chest or the extremities, and then it moves up to the head and begins its unaltering downward path to the toes.) If, after taking a remedy, you get a headache, and then, the next day, you experience a pain in your left arm, and then a minor ache in your right knee, this is the remedy working in tandem with your body to create balance and health once again, within you. Interestingly enough, any little fleeting aches and pains you may get will be transitory, so don't worry.

3. Every ailment or sickness that you've ever experienced, that didn't totally run its cycle in your body, will be repeated in order of the most recent to the oldest. I've coined a new term for this: "retracing." You see, when we get sick (and this can mean an emotional trauma, just menopausal symptoms, a cold or flu, etc.), the body may or may not be able to completely cycle the set of symptoms from your body.

For example, you might have had a terrible cold that went on for 7 days. You went to an allopathic doctor and he gave you antibiotics and it cleared up. Or, it seemed to clear up. When you take a homeopathic remedy, you may experience this nasty cold—but it certainly won't be as long, as intense, or as deep as the original cold. The remedy helps the body to cycle out what was left after this cold was suppressed by the antibiotics you took. In essence, this part of the cure is the most important because it gets rid of whatever is left of ANYTHING you've ever had—be it physical, mental, spiritual, or emotional dis-ease.

Retracing can be short or long, depending on how your vital force has handled all of your symptoms over the years. If you start to get snatches or bits of illness that you had before, this is an excellent sign of cure; it is the correct remedy and you don't need to worry; these symptoms are fleeting.

Your homeopath can help you up and over these periods when you are retracing. I use flower essences (similar to Bach flower remedies, only I make my own) if it is an emotional or mental symptom. I may also suggest the use of aspirin from time to time, too. As a classical homeopath, I don't like to "mix and match" other remedies to take care of these fleeting retracings. Aspirin, by and large, does not suppress, so I do use it in my practice when necessary. Above all, no one should suffer if there is something out there to ameliorate it or help you through this phase of your healing. Ask your homeopath what kind of contingency plans s/he has if this happens in your case.

CAN ANYTHING I EAT OR DRINK ANTIDOTE MY HOMEOPATHIC REMEDY?

Yes, there is quite a list. See the appendix for details on specific items that will antidote your remedy. One of the biggest is coffee, and it doesn't matter whether it's "real" coffee or decaffeinated. There is an oil in the coffee that will antidote your remedy. Another big one is camphor, usually in the form of eucalyptus, or from mothballs. Mint, which contains camphor, is a big one, too. Most people brush their teeth with a mint toothpaste, and this will antidote the remedy. It is better to brush with baking soda. Besides, baking soda gets rid of gingivitis, so this is an extra bonus.

Another area of possible antidoting is dental drilling. The spinning of the drill creates a frequency that may instantly antidote a homeopathic remedy. So, if you are slated for dental work, get it done first, and then take the remedy afterward. Of course, if you crack a tooth or develop tooth pain, go see your dentist right away. It's better to get these taken care of rather than worry about antidoting your homeopathic remedy. Novocain is also known to antidote a homeopathic remedy.

Right now, aromatherapy is big—and any strong oil or essence (or even counter perfume!) placed on your skin, or simply being in the room where it's kept and inhaled, will antidote your remedy. If you get a massage, just use an oil without fragrance or strong odor. Ask your homeopath if your remedy can be antidoted by anything other than the list in the back of this book. Some remedies, such as Hepar Sulph, are easily antidoted by drinking vinegar in any form—even in salad dressings! Crotalus Horridus is antidoted by drinking any beverage containing alcohol.

Homeopaths don't like to keep giving you a remedy every time you antidote it. A great deal of caution on your part must be maintained, along with the responsibility to make sure you stay away from items that will antidote your remedy. Some homeopaths will refuse to re-dose you if you've antidoted. These remedies strike your vital force, and to keep striking it isn't good for your health, either. So, there has to be some "watch dog" attention paid to this list so that you don't antidote your remedy.

Another area that may disrupt your remedy is any other form of "energy work" such as Rolfing, acupuncture, hands-on-healing, Reiki, chakra balancing, and so forth. Even electric blankets or electric heaters to warm a water bed are out! They too will antidote a remedy.

Sometimes, no matter what you do, something new will come up and antidote a remedy. One of my clients, a singer, was working in his room, setting up for another gig, when an extremely high, intense shriek from one of the microphones filled the air. He called to tell me that within 5 minutes, his asthma symptoms had started to return! So, he took another dose of his remedy, and the asthma symptoms went away. This was the first time I'd heard of a piercing sound rupturing a remedy, but it makes sense because the remedies are high frequencies of energy—and any other source of high frequency sound could, in essence, antidote it. And, there is the possibility that the fright from this sound antidoted his remedy. Any powerful, sudden emotion can do it, too.

If you think you've antidoted your remedy, get in touch with your homeopath. A gradual return of some of your old symptoms will be the signal that it was, unfortunately, antidoted.

ARE HOMEOPATHIC REMEDIES DANGEROUS?

They can be if you are self-prescribing. For instance, many homeopathic remedies sold over the counter do not put on their label a warning: "Stop taking the remedy as soon as your symptoms go away." And they should.

To take a homeopathic remedy for weeks on end will cause a 'proving' in you. A proving means that all of the old symptoms you got rid of initially, with the remedy, have come back—and there may be more symptoms than originally! You will feel far more miserable than you did before you took the remedy in the first place.

The best course of treatment is to find a homeopathic practitioner where you live. This information is provided in the appendix. Do not try to dose yourself. Go to the professional and avoid this potential situation.

Good reading to you—and a natural, gentle, drug-free menopause!

CHAPTER 2

MENOPAUSE: IT'S NOT A DISEASE— WHY TREAT IT LIKE ONE?

I'VE HEARD SO MANY SCARY STORIES ABOUT MENOPAUSE THAT IT'S HARD FOR ME TO SEPARATE TRUTH FROM FICTION. IS IT A DISEASE?

Most certainly not! Menopause is a NATURAL part of your life cycle—as natural as puberty. (Remember your first menses? Your acne? Your raging hormones as a young teenager? That was puberty.)

Puberty is simply a turning on of several hormones in our endocrine system to change you from a girl into a woman, to fill out your breasts, start your menses, mark your entrance into womanhood, and give you the ability to conceive children.

Menopause is at the other end of this spectrum. It is the turning down (not off) of certain hormones so you are no longer capable of conception.

CAN YOU GIVE ME A DEFINITION OF MENOPAUSE?

The words menopause and climacteric are often intermixed, but they shouldn't be. If we look at the Greek meaning of menopause, it means "monthly stop." Climacteric in Greek means "rung of the ladder." Or put in more modern terms: another step in our life cycle as women. The first step is puberty, and the second is menopause. Menopause means the end of having a menstrual cycle and the end of being able to conceive a baby. This lasts from 1 to 7 years, although the usual is 2–5 years. It means the ending of our periods and that we're no longer fertile. This occurs, generally speaking, between the ages of 48 and 52. The counterpart to menopause is menarche, when our first menstrual cycle began.

The climacteric lasts 15–20 years and during this phase, our ovaries and hormones go through many changes. The ovary function slows down and it eventually stops producing and expelling eggs. The production of hormones—which helped to create the lining in the uterus that held the egg expelled by the ovary during our fertile years—declines. Climacteric signifies the hormonal shifts we go through and the time during which our ovaries and hormones decline and go through transition. This occurs between ages 40 and 60, and lasts, generally speaking, 15 or 20 years.

SO REALLY THERE ARE PHASES WE'RE GOING THROUGH ALMOST SIMULTANEOUSLY?

Yes, at least for awhile. These separate functions overlap, usually between ages 48 and 52, and may move forward simultaneously for 2 to 7 years. Menopause is a part of the climacteric process. By strict definition, pre-menopause means your periods are regular and you're exhibiting no changes of any kind. Menopause begins between the ages of 48 and 52 and includes the following: Our menses cycle becomes shorter, and we no longer have them monthly (also known in the medical world as peri-menopause). We can go 2 or 3 months without a menses, and when we do have one, it is only 2 or 3 days in length, not the normal 5 or 7 days. This change in our menses length and regularity is accomplished by the declining levels of hormones in our body, which eventually will lead to a complete halt of the menstrual cycle. At that point, we bid goodbye to menopause and continue in our climacteric phase.

During this time, we will experience not only physical changes, but emotional ones, as well. This isn't a threat to instill fear in you. Read further for the common signs of menopause.

WHY DO DOCTORS CONSIDER MENOPAUSE AN ILLNESS WHEN IT'S NOT?

Medicine is oriented toward disease and regards changes in women's bodies as problems to be solved. To most allopathic doctors, a woman at midlife is considered sick. Aging is a normal event, yet suddenly, menopause and the ending of our menstrual cycle is seen as an illness!

Because we're going through this change, the climacteric, the medical machine unfortunately views us as not only diagnosable (we now have symptoms), but worse, treatable with drugs.

To the pharmaceutical companies around the world, this provides limitless expansion of different drugs to treat different symptoms of what was once considered a natural process. Climacteric was pretty much ignored by everyone until the massive population of Baby Boomers came along.

MY DOCTOR HAS MADE ME FEEL AS IF THERE'S SOMETHING WRONG WITH ME. I FEEL HEALTHY AND FINE EXCEPT FOR SOME OF THESE SYMPTOMS OF CHANGE. WHAT'S GOING ON?

Doctors, right or wrong, their intent genuine or questionable, begin to use words such as sag, drooping, dried up, or weakening, when we reach menopause. If we're not educated, these comments can scare the daylights out of us. The stigma of menopause can be attributed to Dr. Robert A. Wilson. He created the erroneous idea that menopause is a disease, not a natural cycle in a woman's life, when he wrote that the "tragedy of menopause often destroys her character as well as her health." He advocated that we women could be saved from this "disease" by taking estrogen "from puberty to grave."

Wilson wrote the book *Feminine Forever* in 1966; it boasted that estrogen was a fountain of youth for women. Between 1960 and 1970, we were bludgeoned with publicity and marketing hype on this drug with more than 300 articles appearing in, of course, women's magazines. But Wilson went on to create keywords designed to be derogatory toward women, making us feel that if we didn't go on estrogen replacement, we'd end up divorced, alcoholic, and addicted to drugs. Pure poppycock. If that was so, why didn't our mothers and grandmothers before them become addicted to drugs, get divorced, or turn alcoholic? Wilson and his disciples so staunchly repeated these threats so that we would buy the drugs. He doesn't have the research statistics to back up his unfounded "threats."

You've all seen the ads on television about women getting osteoporosis along with our menopause! These false messages are unforgivable! Osteoporosis is a true disease, unlike menopause, which is a natural cycle! *Osteoporosis is not part of menopause*!!!! Yet the ads make us think that it is, and we run screaming, in terror, to our doctors, who are only too happy to shove hormone replacement therapy at us as a fix-it measure for all the above conditions. As eager as they are to help, somehow they forgot to tell us that it raises the stakes for getting breast and uterine cancer—big time!

Unfortunately the so-called menopause industry is pointedly targeting mostly white, middle-class women for HRT. After all, we're the Baby Boomer generation. Right now, we are the largest population of women in history experiencing menopause. I'm sure many in the menopause industry see billions of dollars in front of them, but we women should be suspicious. We should educate ourselves, ask questions, and not allow ourselves to be stampeded like some brainless herd filled with fear, into taking drugs that do nothing but hamper our natural, normal processes.

WHAT ARE THE COMMON SIGNS OF MENOPAUSE?
(No woman gets all of these symptoms—we just get a few of them!):

1. Hot flashes or night sweats
2. Insomnia (due to hot flashes)
3. Hair growth on the face
4. Bone or joint pains; leg, arm, or foot cramping or numbness
5. Headaches, congestive or migraine types
6. Depression
7. Mental confusion, nervousness, irritability, loss of concentration, forgetfulness
8. Hair thins, falls out, or breaks or splits easily
9. Urinary incontinence or frequent urination
10. Dry skin, sensitivity or crawling sensation on skin surface (formication), bruising of skin surface, varicose veins
11. Sexual libido comes and goes
12. Allergies
13. Menses cycle becomes irregular and finally ceases; there may be spotting from time to time
14. Excessive bleeding or "flooding" from time to time
15. Digestive upset, nausea, particular cravings or aversions to foods
16. Breasts may become tender, may swell
17. Tiredness in general on the mental, emotional, or physical levels
18. Heart palpitations (associated with hot flashes)
19. Vaginal dryness or thinning of the walls
20. Weight gain or loss

WILL I GET ALL THESE SYMPTOMS?

That's the good news—you won't. Some women breeze through menopause without any symptoms, or just two or three of them. For instance, my total symptoms have been 3 weeks of depression, hot flashes, and night sweats. I took Sepia at one time and then, later, Folliculinum—both are homeopathic remedies—and they stopped the symptoms. Now I'm breezing through menopause symptom-free!! And so can you!

The best way to predict future symptoms is to talk to your mother and grandmother. If your mother had hot flashes, more than likely you will too. Or, if she had joint pains in her knees, you might experience that, too—all temporary, of course.

HELP ME UNDERSTAND ABOUT ESTROGEN. AM I LOSING MY ABILITY TO MAKE ESTROGEN?

1. Each gender is born with a certain level of estrogen and testosterone. You will lose some estrogen—but NEVER all of it.

2. Males have more testosterone and females more estrogen. That is what gives them their muscling and strength.

3. Each gender has a "fixed" immovable level of estrogen (in men) and testosterone (in women).

4. We reach our individual "pause" beginning at age 40, it really starts moving at age 45, and truly starts changing around age 48, when the estrogen levels in women begin to slowly lower. Testosterone levels in men also begin to slowly lower.

5. However, the "fixed" levels in each gender (testosterone in women and estrogen in men) don't move—they stay where they are!

6. In women, this is WHY we start getting hair on our face here and there (some more or less)—because as the estrogen recedes (it never goes away—so don't panic), the testosterone level remains the same—which is WHY women become more outspoken, more aggressive perhaps, certainly more assertive, and more confident, more of everything the guy has been all of his life—only now, it's time for the greatest Cosmic joke of them all—gender role reversal! A woman who was a woman for 45 years will now become more male-like in the last half of her life.

This is, in part, why women, during menopause, become leaders instead of followers. They go out and create their own cottage industry or corporation, they become confident (you can literally feel it seeping into your bones over a year or two's time), they become assertive and walk out of bad situations or environments, and create better ones for themselves. We become highly independent (those who don't like us that way say we are rebellious—but that ain't so); we are more assertive and even aggressive in reaching our goals or creating visions of the future as we see it. And a woman may no longer want to be "mother"; she turns into herself, her inner being of unfulfilled dreams and wishes, and wants those aspirations for herself. (And the joke here is that the testosterone level is there, more exposed, more of it in our bloodstream, feeding this desire to manifest many wishes, hopes, and desires we couldn't before because we had a mothering role to play, as well as raising children and keeping a house.)

7. In men, this is WHY men begin to sag here and there (potbellies). Without all that testosterone their muscles don't "hold" like before—we women know this one, right? They become "softer," they lose that aggressive testosterone drive, that type-A modus operandi, that hard-hitting assertiveness that carried them so well through their first 40 to 45 years of life. Because the testosterone is reducing in them, and their estrogen level is remaining fixed, men become more in touch with their emotional structure, their ability to feel, express their feelings, and feel emotion (whether they like it or not—it's going to happen). The Cosmic joke here is that they become more female-like because they have got comparatively more estrogen circulating in their bloodstream now, because the higher testosterone level is no longer there to counteract it. Most men, at least patriarchal ones (not matriarchal ones) fight this because all their lives they have been brainwashed by this patriarchal stereotype not to feel, not to cry, not to do all the female things that we women have done all our lives.

So, when this situation manifests, some men, unfortunately, panic in one form or another. They leave their wife and a marriage of 20-some years, they choose a woman 20 years younger, they start a new job to try and recapture their old testosterone days—on some level of themselves—and this is very subconscious. Some men are grasping at straws from the past because they feel these changes coming on. That's the negative of this situation. The positive is that the man, for the first time (at least under patriarchy), has a chance to begin to integrate his feminine energies and expressions within himself—if he'll do it. But it takes a very strong man who is confident in himself to do it—because to not run and be part of the "herd" of males in patriarchy is brutal on this courageous kind of man.

If he can stand the heat from the herd, then he will turn into himself on his own wonderful inner journey of completeness and integration of his female energies, just as we women, during our menopause transit, will integrate our testosterone and male energies within ourselves. Many men turn to far more creative endeavors at around age 45–49. A good example of this was my husband, David. He retired after being a civil engineer for 20 years and what did he do? He took up stained glass—he makes beautiful stuff! And now, he runs an art gallery!

It can be one of the most exciting changes in our lives, regardless of our gender, but it takes an attitude to make this transformation from cocoon to butterfly mode!

DO MEN GO THROUGH A SIMILAR CHANGE IN LIFE TO WOMEN GOING THROUGH MENOPAUSE?

Great question! The answer is an unequivocal "yes." There is no question that, as a homeopath, I've see men go through what I term "malepause" just like women go through "menopause."

CAN HOMEOPATHIC REMEDIES HELP ME WITH MENOPAUSE?

Absolutely! This is the best news yet! We have homeopathic remedies for *every* symptom of menopause listed above. This book describes these symptoms and matches them to the appropriate homeopathic remedy. This could mean that you won't have to even consider hormonal drugs to deal with some of these symptoms, thus minimizing the chances of putting you at risk for breast or uterine cancer.

HOW CAN HOMEOPATHY HELP?

The most important thing to keep in mind is that homeopathy works in concert with your body and its many and varied functions NATURALLY, without adverse side-effects. It is non-toxic and safe when dispensed by a homeopathic practitioner. It does not cause cancer, as HRT drugs can do.

If you'll turn to Chapter 1, there is a definition of what homeopathy is, how it works, and how it can help guide us through menopause.

IF I'M HAVING HOT FLASHES, WHAT SHOULD I DO TO FIND HOMEOPATHIC REMEDIES THAT ADDRESS THIS?

Turn to Chapter 8, "Your Skin," and you'll find a number of homeopathic remedies that directly address hot flashes. Whatever your signs, leaf through this book and find out what can help. Of course, you should always take this information to your nearest homeopathic practitioner before taking a remedy, and get the benefit of their experience and judgment. If you don't know where your nearest homeopath is located, just go to the appendix, look up the National Center for Homeopathy, and call them. They have a directory of homeopaths in the United States to guide you to the closest practitioner—it's that easy!

CAN I GET PREGNANT DURING MENOPAUSE?

Yes, as long as your ovaries continue to expel eggs and they are nestled in the lining of your uterus awaiting fertilization by sperm, you can get pregnant. Even though your menstrual cycle may be waning and becoming shorter, that doesn't mean that you can't get pregnant—because you can!

Women are born with a certain number of eggs in their ovaries. When the supply of eggs is exhausted, the ovaries no longer release them for fertilization.

Until there is full cessation of your menstrual cycle, which can take, generally speaking, 2–5 years to accomplish, you are capable of pregnancy during the menopause phase. After the menstrual cycle has finally, completely stopped, then you can no longer get pregnant because the ovaries no longer have any eggs to expel. No eggs, no pregnancy!

WILL MY WEIGHT CHANGE AS I MOVE INTO MENOPAUSE?

Yes, it will. Most women gain about 10 pounds, which lovingly hugs our hips and abdomen. Some gain as much as 15 to 20 pounds. This extra fat then becomes a 'bank' that stores extra estrogen created by the body, so that in later years we'll still have some to feed us hormonally. This extra fat is really good news for us, even though we all hate the idea of adding it on!

I used to weigh 155 pounds. At five foot, nine inches tall, I can carry that weight very nicely. At about age 43, I noticed that 10 extra pounds kept trying to creep up on me. At first, I was stymied because I hadn't changed my eating habits and I was getting a good amount of exercise raising and riding horses. I was frustrated until I finally figured out what was going on. At age 50 I went up to 180 pounds, which was simply too much. When I realized that this extra fat is to my advantage because it's going to store the estrogen, I had less problem accepting it in one way. In another way, that much weight (an extra 25 pounds) was making me feel heavy and unhappy. I decided to go on the Zone way of eating and have maintained, through consistent watchfulness, around 160 pounds.

WHAT ABOUT NATURAL ESTROGENS? CAN HOMEOPATHY BE COMBINED WITH THESE TO HELP ME THROUGH MENOPAUSE?

There is a food group known to contain phytosterol, which is considered a natural source of estrogen. As an example, the wild yam produces a form of natural estrogen. Many herbs contain these phytosterols: alfalfa, black currant, dandelion, ginseng, and licorice, to name a few. Wild yam cream is now sold over the counter to combat a drying vaginal tract with some short-term success. It is not a long-term consideration because it is a vegetable estrogen and the receptors don't fit, exactly, human equivalents, so the benefits are less and less over the months that it is used by the woman.

If a woman wants to use these INSTEAD OF homeopathy, she should do so only after she educates herself and talks to her health care practitioner about them. Unfortunately, some of the phytosterol herbs, such as ginseng and Dong Quai/Dang Gui, have been shown to antidote a homeopathic remedy. So, a woman has to make up her mind ahead of time as to what form of natural treatment she wants to pursue.

In my practice, I haven't seen a woman yet who exhibited menopause signs and couldn't be helped with the correct homeopathic remedy.

I was, quite literally, raised on herbs by my parents in the 1950s. We were very, very poor. My family could not afford either the doctor or the attending prescription, so I know the first-hand value of herbs in not only acute, but also serious chronic illness.

Having experienced herbs and homeopathy during my menopause, as well as listening to other women's experiences, I can say that homeopathy is much simpler, in some ways, than taking natural estrogen-bearing herbs. For one thing, you take a homeopathic remedy ONCE. If you take an herb, you have to take it continuously, every day. (I don't know about you, but I'm not a pill popper. I HATE to take any kind of pill.)

Second, most herbs do not CURE a condition; they only palliate it. This means that what is out of balance in our body is not corrected; only the severity of the symptoms is lessened for a period of time. The only time it can cure is when a woman's symptoms parallel the symptoms the herb can cure. Homeopathy CURES every time.

Third, in some cases where the menopause signs are severe, the woman may have to OVER DOSE on the herb(s) to get the right amount of phytosterol to stop her menopause symptoms. Overdosing on some herbs may have long-term harmful side-effects. Homeopathically, you take a remedy per the instructions of your practitioner, and that's it. If you are under the care of a classically trained homeopath, there is no chance of overdosing and there are no side-effects from it.

Homeopathic remedies are much easier to take than herbs bearing natural phytosterols. However, as always, your health is in YOUR hands and I would urge you to go out and educate yourself if you're drawn to the herbal route of treatment as opposed to the homeopathic one. Just be sure to have a health practitioner who is an herbalist who knows about the herbs you're considering so that you don't accidentally overdose.

WILL I BECOME LESS FEMININE BECAUSE OF MENOPAUSE?

I asked my grandmother, Inez Cramer, who died at 99 years old and who lived with us for those last 6 years of her life, if she still felt "feminine" at her advanced age. She looked at me with her watery blue eyes. They suddenly became very focused and intent as she considered my question. Her thin mouth puckered. She straightened up a bit (mind you, she was mobile and she had all of her faculties) and scowled. "How could you ask such a question, Eileen?"

I sheepishly shrugged and said, "Well, you've been through menopause, and I'm going through it now. You're on the other side of it. I was just wondering how you felt about being a woman—before and after menopause?"

Her hand, which was crippled with some arthritis, tightened around the cane she used to get around with. "You youngsters are sure making somethin' out of nothin' about this menopause thing!" she spouted, indignant.

"Probably so, Grandma."

"Why, in my day, it came and went without so much as a fare-thee-well!"

"I know."

"I'm still alive, aren't I?"

I grinned and suddenly burst into laughter. I watched as her weathered, beautiful face lost that imperious scowl and her blue eyes softened as she regarded me. "You sure are, Grandma. I always did say you were a tough old buzzard."

She chuckled and sat back in her favorite chair. "So you're worried you're going to lose your femininity by going through menopause? Is that it?"

Grandma never failed to amaze me with her startling and very clear insight.

"Well," I stumbled, "I'm not worried about it. It's just that I've had to counsel a lot of my women clients about this in the past and I was just wondering, since you're almost a hundred, how you felt about it."

With a shake of her head, she muttered with defiance, "Femininity isn't something you gain or lose by goin' through life! It's about how you're feeling about yourself as a WOMAN. Menopause has nothing to do with this. Never did. Who put that thought into your head?"

"Oh," I said, raising my brows and looking up at the ceiling, "you see the ads on television and in the magazines."

Grandma Cramer snorted vehemently. "Hogwash. That's all this stuff is. Always was." She jammed the cane down on the floor to make her point. "In my day (she was born in 1897) there was no such worry." She reached forward and poked me with her index finger on my shoulder. "Women are closer to the natural cycles than any man will ever be. If a woman listens to her heart, to herself, she knows menopause isn't no big deal. Why, I actually enjoyed it."

"Yeah?" I baited with a grin.

Primly, she looked around for a moment and then slanted a glance in my direction. "It just makes life easier, that's all. The kids are raised and gone. You don't have to worry about getting pregnant. You can travel more ... do the things you always dreamed of doing but couldn't."

"What did you do, Grandma?"

"John (my grandfather, John Cramer) and I traveled all fifty states," she said proudly. "All fifty. Can you imagine that? After menopause, the money wasn't going out for kids' clothes, food, or schooling. The mortgage on our home was paid off. We finally had money to travel with." She smiled fondly in remembrance. "We had a wonderful time from the time I was 50 to 70 years old."

My grandmother was widowed at the age of 75. She came to live with us at age 90 and it was a very happy arrangement for everyone.

I don't feel any less feminine at age 53 than I did at 20. I think that femininity, besides being genetic (female), is a state of mind and emotions. Some of my homeopathic clients have felt as if some of their femininity has slipped away, as they transited through menopause. In those cases, the women believed the ads in the papers and on television, that if you couldn't look 20 and be slender, you weren't a 'real' woman.

I feel that we will all learn about the 'other half' of what it means to be feminine and a woman by moving through this third phase, this climacteric phase of our lives. My Grandmother Inez, at 99, was a formidable woman. I loved her fiercely. My mother, Ruth, is over 80, and she is equally strong and vital. I have two wonderful role models in my life who constantly, on a daily basis, remind me of what it is not only to be feminine, but to be a fully rounded, confident woman.

I don't believe that menopause needs to make us feel like less of a woman or less feminine. I believe that all of the ads on television and in magazines are designed to drive us to pharmaceutical drugs to try and look younger. I find that tact offensive and insulting. My grandmother wore dresses as well as slacks. She still had her hair permed; her gestures were always as graceful as a ballerina. To me, she was the epitome of femininity as I know it—and I want to be exactly like her.

THE ADS ALL PROMISE THAT WE'LL LOOK YOUNGER IF WE TAKE ESTROGEN OR HRT. IS THIS TRUE?

I can only speak for myself on this topic. Natural aging is going to happen no matter what we do to try to stop it. Taking estrogen or a combination of estrogen and progestin, which is known as hormone replacement therapy (HRT), will give us softer skin and may slow down the aging process to a degree, but inevitably, we will age—with or without it.

The cost of going on estrogen or HRT drugs, to me, isn't even a choice I'd consider. Why would I want to risk a 70 percent chance of getting breast cancer within 5 years of taking these hormonal drugs, just to capture a few more years of so-called "beauty"?

We all age. Everything slides "south" with age. Everything slows down, including our metabolism. We shift gears, shift our sights, and shift our priorities to other spheres of our lives. This is a natural part of aging. It doesn't have to be horrible or debilitating. I like to think of us as a fine wine; age brings out all of our wonderful qualities and nuances. I believe that our "third age," the menopausal years, are the years in which we find our freedom. These years are the time to pursue goals, dreams, or activities that were unavailable to us earlier because of family responsibilities, or because our careers had us tied to a time clock.

I would not trade 5 years on HRT for breast cancer in order to have this so-called "beauty." Studies have shown that, inevitably, when you get off of these unnaturally high doses of hormone drugs, you age anyway and you lose a tremendous amount of bone mass as a result of postponing the aging process, which makes your bones unnaturally brittle and can set you up for osteoporosis later on.

We can't stop aging, nor should we try. What we want to do is alter our state of mind about aging and stop listening to all those ads that constantly tout youth and beauty as the only things worthy of a woman. A woman's beauty is really inside of her. If anything needs to be fixed, it's our mental and emotional attitudes about ourselves—about how we see ourselves.

That is why I titled this book "Beauty in Bloom," because I can stand on the other side of menopause and tell you, unequivocally, that this natural process is going to make you feel different—better—and life will become far more exciting for you from a personal and spiritual standpoint.

CHAPTER 3

HORMONE REPLACEMENT THERAPY (HRT)—WHY IT SHOULD BE A WOMAN'S LAST CHOICE

WHAT IS ERT AND HRT?

ERT, which stands for estrogen replacement therapy, was one of the top-ten drugs sold in the United States in 1975. Robert A. Wilson, MD, touted ERT as the fountain of youth. Those who took ERT did find that there was less incidence of osteoporosis, and that, in regards to menopause, hot flashes and vaginal atrophy lessened.

But there was a negative side. A number of independent research teams declared that the use of estrogen for more than a year would cause endometrial cancer. That same year, the FDA warned women that the estrogen dosage should actually be a quarter of what was being prescribed! The too-high doses caused the endometrial lining in the uterus to build up, layer upon layer. Uterine cancer followed.

Without the necessary progesterone to force the sloughing off of these layers of cells, women were ingesting a cancer time bomb. Sadly, women were acting as guinea pigs to test this hormonal drug, and only after several women contracted uterine cancer was the red warning flag raised. You'd think that we'd have gotten a little more coherent with the birth control pill sales rap that was handed to us in the 1960s.

Needless to say, sales of the hormone drug dropped off dramatically, so the pharmaceutical companies scrambled to come up with a replacement. They lowered the dose of estrogen and added synthetic progesterone, known as progestin. This new formation became known as HRT or "hormone replacement therapy." Taking both hormones was supposed to mimic the body's normal menstrual cycle. Women going through menopause, who were supposed to stop having their period or menses (a natural occurrence), were now having one every month—and would continue to have one so long as they took these hormonal drugs!

The sad ending to this true story is that, in the *New England Journal of Medicine*, June, 1995, it was reported that women who were on both hormones for 5 years had a 70 percent incidence of BREAST CANCER!!!!

Ladies, ERT and HRT are deadly. Who, among us, wants cancer? And at what cost? If you want your menopausal symptoms alleviated, look to natural, non-cancerous homeopathic remedies instead, and continue having the quality of life you enjoy—and deserve.

ERT is currently being phased out in favor of HRT, but with such statistics, HRT is no safer than its counterpart. Right now, in this country, misinformed physicians are dispensing HRT thinking that it's safe for a woman—when it is not.

IS THERE A GROUP OF WOMEN WHO SHOULD NEVER TAKE HRT?

Yes, there is. Here's the list:

* If there is a history of breast cancer in your family (mother, sister, grandmother).
* If you or a family member have varicose veins.

* If you have a history of stroke, blood clots (phlebitis), or thrombosis.
* If you or a family member have ever had sickle cell anemia.
* If you have ever had gallstones.
* If you have ever had liver or kidney disease.
* If you have ever had high blood pressure.
* If you have ever had diabetes.
* If you have unusual vaginal bleeding that has not been evaluated by your physician.
* If you have ever had any circulation problems.
* If you have had any other estrogen-related disease such as PID (pelvic inflammatory disease), endometriosis, fibroid tumors of the breast or uterus, or recurrent cysts.
* If you have ever had epilepsy or seizure disorders.
* If you have ever been obese and had irregular bleeding.
* If you have a family history of heart disease.

The above symptoms will be intensely aggravated by HRT, perhaps becoming life-threatening in some instances, and women who fall into these categories should not consider ERT or HRT as a viable course of action.

I suggest that any woman with these symptoms should see her homeopathic practitioner. In some cases, these problems can be cured. In others, they might not be cured, but at least there will be palliation and a significant lessening of the amount of drugs currently being taken. This alone could dramatically improve your quality of life!

WHAT ARE THE SIDE-EFFECTS IF WE TAKE HRT?

It encourages abnormal growth of fibroids. Normally, fibroids in the breast or uterus go away during and after menopause. If you are prone to fibroids and you take this drug, the fibroids will remain after menopause. If you aren't, you may get them anyway. For some women, fibroids are part of their natural history, genetically (20% of our population is prone to fibroids or FBD, fibrocystic breast disease). Most get rid of them, thanks to menopause. But who wants to take a hormonal drug to keep them?

Headaches, especially the migraine variety. Many women taking ERT or HRT have constant, miserable headaches. In fact, 22 percent of them, according to one study. Headaches are debilitating and you can do without them. You have too busy a day and too many things you want to do with your life to be hampered constantly by headaches. Not only that, you don't want to become a "pill factory" and take over-the-counter drugs to make the headache go away. Why not get to the source of the headache? Go for the root cause and eradicate IT, instead. Stop taking HRT. Then, no more miserable headaches!

Weight gain is a promise for 60 percent of us who take HRT. With more estrogen, the body will make the food you eat into fat cells. There's a normal 10-pound weight gain starting in our forties, but do you want a lot more???

Edema or water retention, bloating of the abdomen or breasts. One study showed that 41 percent of women on HRT suffered this unnecessary symptom. Fluid retention is a side-effect of HRT. Then, to get rid of it, doctors want to put you on diuretics, which compounds the problem. Who wants to become a drug factory? Aren't you tired of being a guinea pig? Aren't you tired of having unnatural drugs in your body and having doctors tell you how to make your body run when your body has a natural intelligence of its own—without drugs?

Diuretics are well known to be hard on our kidneys—sort of like flogging a thoroughbred that's already run a mile, but we want it to run full speed ahead for another 10 miles. The drugs force the kidneys to work beyond their engineered capacity. Why beat up our kidneys? Why stress our whole urinary and renal system, when it's a hormonal drug causing us to blow up like balloons? Let's get rid of the cause, then we won't have to take a "counter" drug to get rid of the water that's making us look like doughboys.

Water retention created by these hormonal drugs is particularly hazardous to any woman with a history of asthma, epilepsy, heart disease, kidney disease, or migraines.

Discoloration of the skin. It may turn yellow due to jaundice (liver dysfunction). Dark spots, known as melasma, may appear on the skin. Itching is another possible side-effect. Remember when you were pregnant and your skin may have been off color? You can welcome all this back if you go on HRT.

Lowering of the voice. Who wants to sound like a man!?

Loss of hair on scalp. This drug can double the rate of hair loss during menopause. Some women with thick hair can afford to lose much more, and will be all right—but what about the women with naturally thin hair, such as blonde or light brown colored hair? When HRT is stopped, the body rebalances itself—naturally—and the highly noticeable hair loss will stop, too. If there is some hair loss, homeopathy can help you retain what you've got—naturally.

Continuation of your period. I don't know about you, but I'm looking forward to no more periods. Menopause is one way of giving our ovaries, our reproductive equipment, a well-earned rest. Asking them to continue, especially when the body wants to shut them down, is decidedly tinkering with Mother Nature—and we'll be the loser if this happens, in more ways than one—extra, needless periods and a good chance of breast cancer. If we drug our bodies, we continue to flog the very system that wants to shut down, because it is going on beyond its natural capacity.

Nausea. As if you were pregnant once again—and 14 percent of us will experience this symptom. Who needs it? Nausea will haunt our daily activities. If I had that to look forward to, I'd say: No thanks!

Breakthrough spotting can be an indicator of something more serious going on in your uterus and it should be checked by your doctor. Who needs spotting at awkward moments to cause us embarrassment? Who needs a period when we aren't supposed to have one in the first place?

Breasts sore or swollen because of drugs that force the body to hold more water than it needs—42 percent of us will have this symptom. Who needs this constant discomfort? Personally, I had horribly sore and tender breasts before I was introduced to homeopathy. Fortunately, the right remedy (Pulsatilla), based on my set of symptoms, put my body back into natural balance. I stopped having this painful problem, but many women on HRT continue to have breasts so sore that it hurts to move, jiggle, or even put clothes against them.

B-6 deficiency is created because of the hormonal drugs. This seems like an innocuous statement, doesn't it? Think again, ladies. Here are some of the B-6 deficiency symptoms, created when we lack this B vitamin, which acts like the little "engine that could" in our body, thanks to hormone drug interference: Diabetes, hypoglycemia, low blood sugar, water retention, hypochromic anemia, skin disorders such as seborrhea, crusty patches on the face and scalp, redness, and acne, swelling of the hands and feet, cramps, and painful nerve disturbance of the fingers and hands. Without enough B-6 in our body, riboflavin (B-2) and B-12 cannot be assimilated properly. The B-6 problem is compounded when these other two B vitamins cannot go about their business in our body.

So, in essence, discouraging B-6 in our normal metabolism not only sets us up for the deficiency symptoms listed above, but also encourages deficiency symptoms of B-2 and B-12. Messing with the mighty B-complex in our body is scary to me. Taking a B-complex vitamin isn't going to CURE this problem if you're on HRT. HRT stops the chemical breakdown of B-6. If you take a B vitamin pill, that too, will be seized upon and destroyed by this drug.

The power of HRT to destroy B-6 is so pervasive that doctors will rush to put you on a diuretic. Without B-6, toxins, poisons, and fluids cannot be urinated out of the body. Diuretics, which are also drugs, are brought in to counter this particular side-effect of HRT.

So, if HRT can inhibit B-6, what are we setting ourselves up for later on? Diabetes? Hypoglycemia? Anemia? It's like playing Russian Roulette—only this time, no matter what we do, we're going to shoot ourselves with an HRT "gun" and damage our own body's stability by destroying the vitamins needed to maintain good health.

The cornea of the eye will curve and change, causing vision difficulties. Our vision is our most precious gift, in my opinion. With age, all eyes deteriorate to a degree—with or without menopause. I would not want a hormonal drug injuring my eyes. How important are your eyes? Important enough, I hope, to look to homeopathy and avoid HRT, because homeopathy will not injure your eyesight.

Depression and, in some instances, a higher rate of ***suicidal thoughts or actions***. A study shows that 21 percent of us will have this side-effect. I know, first hand, the effects of endocrine drugs in this area. When I was on birth control pills for 2 years, when I was young and ignorant and believed anything doctors told me, I was almost pushed to the edge of suicide. I knew there was something wrong with me, so I went into a hospital voluntarily and had every lab test known to womankind. I also went to a psychiatrist to see what was WRONG with me. My 3 days worth of lab tests came back normal and the psychiatrist said there was nothing wrong with me—except that I kept having suicidal thoughts.

How bad did it get? So bad that one weekend, I went out in the woods with a pistol to shoot myself in the head—all thanks to a nasty reaction to taking hormone pills for 2 years. Fortunately, my will to live—even miserably—was stronger than my desire to die. After that, I finally figured out, on my own, that the ONLY remaining culprit was the birth control pills I was taking. So, on Monday I called up my male gynecologist and asked him if it was possible to be suicidal on the drugs. He said, "Oh, yeah, it is." Relieved but angry, I got off the hormone drugs and my suicidal urges went with it, never to return. That was 30 years ago, but that one experience set me on the course I'm on today as a homeopathic practitioner and a strong advocate of drug-free solutions for women.

I wonder how many women on HRT are in depression, either acute or chronic, or if they're having suicidal thoughts like I did on birth control pills back in the 1960s? There is little difference, chemically speaking, between birth control pills and HRT—they use the same drugs, only in different dosages. I strongly urge any woman who has become depressed or suicidal since being on HRT, to GET OFF THE DRUG IMMEDIATELY and seek homeopathic help.

Life is challenge enough for all of us without HRT adding another deadly brick to the loads we all carry.

Vaginal yeast infections can become a nuisance that turns into an unrelenting plague. Vaginal discharge can cause a constant stain on your undergarments. Being on HRT and having a period as WELL as excessive fluid discharges the rest of the month is like being on a napkin for the WHOLE month!

Who needs yeast infections? Take HRT, and you're a candidate for this, on top of everything else. Life's too short to have to stop and itch all the time. When the delicate inner balance within our body is upset, no amount of douching can destroy the yeast infection. The problem must be eliminated, not masked.

The medical "solution" will be to place you on antibiotics. Does it make sense to be taking antibiotics for something that can be stopped before it starts anyway—by not being on HRT?

ERT raises triglyceride levels, which can lead to heart attack or stroke. Alas, women are often unwitting guinea pigs for the pharmaceutical companies. ERT not only causes alarming breast and uterine cancer, but it also shoots our triglycerides up through the ceiling. This makes me wonder what HRT, which also is being tested on us women as if we were guinea pigs, will do? No one knows yet.

Allergies can suddenly appear if you are allergic to the synthetic variety of estrogen you are taking! The drug can cause itching, tongue swelling, and rashes. Any woman who gets any of these symptoms should get OFF the HRT bandwagon immediately. Allergy reactions can be mild, or deadly. If your tongue swells up, so can your throat. When the throat starts swelling shut, you can suffocate. This is called an anaphylactic reaction—and it is deadly. HRT is not worth dying for, is it?

Abnormal clotting of the blood. These clots can lodge in organs or in the blood supply. This can result in a stroke, a heart attack, or pulmonary emoblus (cutting off the blood supply to your lungs).

Dizziness, nervousness, or anxiety (19% of us will get this side-effect), cramps (18% of us will have this, too), insomnia, fatigue, changes in your sex drive, changes in your appetite, acne, and additional hair growth (usually on the face) are some of the more adverse reactions. Who needs them?

I'VE BEEN TOLD THAT BY TAKING ESTROGEN OR HRT, I WILL STAY YOUNGER LOOKING. IS THIS TRUE?

An informal survey, by Drs. Barbara and Gideon Seaman, revealed that estrogen users did not look more youthful; they only *thought* they did. The doctors saw no difference in these women who were on estrogen, but the women believed themselves to look more youthful. So, it goes back to the age-old dilemma of "we see what we want to see."

It's much like buying a new dress; we feel prettier in it, or more confident. In reality, no matter what clothes we wear, we are still ourselves. If a woman goes to an expensive spa and has deep facial cleaning or mud packs or whatever, she believes herself to look younger or more beautiful than before. In reality, it's the same face with the same features—and the same beauty.

Adding to the problem, the pharmaceutical companies, and some doctors, are also subtly and not-so-subtly implying that if you take estrogen or HRT, you will look younger.

Youthfulness is subjective at best, and the television and magazine ads touting ERT or HRT push this particular "button" in the psychological realm for all of us. To give you a stark example of this, in one magazine, an advertisement shows a white, upper middle class, gray-haired, good-looking couple, happily standing arm in arm on a large sail-boat (presumably theirs). Does this natty appearance and luxurious lifestyle result from taking HRT? Another shows a couple, not so natty, but looking very married. The doting wife clings to her brawny husband, both of them looking pleased with themselves. Next to them, large type captions: "Mentrium (a combination of hormones and tranquilizers) treats the menopausal symptoms that bother him most."

Unfortunately, these ads define us in terms of physical attractiveness, financial well-being, and whether or not we have a husband and can keep him happy. These ads tell us that these criteria are valuable enough to convince us women to take hormones. I find them offensive and insulting.

In my own practice, I've watched the before and after effect on women clients who have come to me on ERT or HRT. I get them off these hormonal drugs. In my observation, they looked better off the drugs than on them. I saw their eyes clear up, becoming more sparkling and more alive with energy. I saw their sallow and yellowed flesh tones go away. They became flushed and pink with life once again. These observations aren't subjective on my part; these are obvious physical changes.

In my practice, all of the clients who were on HRT and have gotten off of them have reported that they were glad to be off the drugs. They felt less fatigued and felt as if their lives had been given back to them. They've reported more vitality and more energy. And, in my view, they don't look older for getting off HRT. In fact, I saw no change from youth to cronehood by being on and then getting off HRT. I saw the same faces. They had neither aged nor become more youthful while on or off the estrogen.

To these clients, the difference was dramatic. They were amazed at how much better they felt after getting off the HRT. None of them said they felt older or looked older. Based on my clinical observations, I feel that, because they got off the hormonal drugs and felt immediately better, the youthful promise became far less important to them.

Conversely, according to the doctors who created this study, Barbara and Gideon Seaman, women who exercised, watched their diet, and continued to have an active role in life, were "deceptively young in appearance."

What keeps us younger looking as we age isn't a drug containing estrogen or progesterone, it is how we maintain ourselves. Exercise and a proper diet are important to our vitality.

BUT MY BODY IS SLOWING DOWN. WHAT CAN I DO ABOUT IT?

Aging doesn't mean giving up, sitting in a rocking chair, and letting life pass you by. Yes, our body systems DO slow down—in men AND women. But let's not confuse aging with menopause. They are separate issues. Some women, especially those whose identities have been tied to children and home and who didn't work outside the home, may find their forties a time of change. The "empty nest" syndrome is one reason, but there are many more reasons, other than just watching our children leave home. We have a husband edging toward retirement, and a wife, if she stayed at home, suddenly with "nothing to do." Often, a wife has a difficult time adjusting to having her husband "under foot" after retirement. There are many reasons for making transformative adjustments from ages 40 to 50, which just HAPPENS to coincide with women moving into menopause, but these adjustments are not the FAULT of, or because of, menopause!

I'VE HEARD THAT ESTROGEN IS REDUCED DURING MENOPAUSE, LEAVING ME OPEN TO BONE LOSS. IS THIS TRUE?

Yes, we do lose more bone as estrogen levels decrease naturally during and after menopause. However, estrogen continues to be released by the ovaries, as well as by the adrenal glands, *until the day we die*. All women lose 5–10 percent of their bone mass within 5 years after menopause. We must remember that the lowering of estrogen levels in our body is not a fatal blow that will lead us to osteoporosis. Osteoporosis is a disease that is NOT related to menopause.

Look at your mother and grandmother. Did they have osteoporosis because their estrogen levels get lower? No. In 75 percent of the population of women, there is no osteoporosis. Let's also be clear that this normal bone loss during menopause *NEVER* manifests into osteoporosis.

It's also true that if you take estrogen or HRT, this bone loss will slow, to a degree. However, in one study with post-menopausal women, bone loss was slowed for 3 to 9 months after starting treatment; then, the bone loss resumed—at an even higher than normal rate, despite the fact that they remained on ERT. Since HRT is so new to the drug scene, there are no studies to confirm one way or another that it, too, is following the same footsteps of ERT. HRT creates breast cancer in 30–70 percent of women who use it, depending upon age. This does not make HRT a good trade-off if you're worried about osteoporosis. Osteoporosis is NOT a part of menopause!

If you stop taking the hormones, bone loss accelerates and increases to levels that are abnormally higher than the average rate for women who were never on hormonal drugs. Ultimately, you could lose MORE bone mass if you start on HRT and then get off it.

Bone mass loss can be dealt with via natural means such as homeopathic treatment, nutrition, diet, and exercise, so why take a hormonal drug to slow down bone loss—and then have it accelerate way beyond normal levels of loss when there are natural ways to do it, instead?

WHAT ARE THE RISKS IF I TAKE HRT?

Many. To scare yourself into never taking HRT, just read up on them in the Physician's Desk Reference, the PDR—found in the reference section of your local library. I've already listed the risks in an abbreviated version in this section, but if you want to be convinced that these hormonal drugs are dangerous, check out the PDR.

I UNDERSTAND THAT BY GOING ON HRT, I WILL RETAIN OR RESTORE MY SEX DRIVE. IS THIS TRUE?

While we go through menopause, our libidos may fluctuate to some degree. Unfortunately, the HRT industry would like us to believe that the lowering of our estrogen levels means lowered sex drive or no interest in sex at all. This simply isn't true! Studies have found that women have discontinued sexual relationships or lost sexual interest—but this is because they lost their partner—not because of menopause!

As a matter of fact, it has been shown that only 4 percent of us actually have a lack of interest in sex through the 2–5 year menopausal time frame. I personally have experienced this. My husband understands and it has not been a source of stress or a problem. And in truth, my libido fluctuates so that it's a nice surprise when it resurfaces. And then, in a week or two, it goes away again ... only to resurface once more! However, the bulk of women do not have this particular symptom at all. That means 96 percent of us continue to be sexually interested AND active, providing we have a partner. Further, it means we don't need HRT to rev up our "motor," either. Our motors are just fine without such tinkering via the pharmaceutical companies and doctors.

A small percentage of us may not feel as sexually interested as we did in our earlier years. Others of us may feel heightened sexuality. Why? As the natural estrogen in our bodies slowly begins to lower, our natural level of testosterone maintains its level and doesn't fluctuate.

Testosterone is the male hormone that makes for a vital libido. Women with higher levels of testosterone in their bloodstream may find that their interest in lovemaking increases throughout menopause. Sex may be lots more appealing than it was before menopause! The nice benefit of this is that, because you can't get pregnant after menopause, you can truly enjoy your own sexuality and expression without worry. Isn't that nice?

Four percent of us may experience a lowering of our sex drive during menopause, but afterwards, we'll find our libidos restored. There may be a 2–5 year period where our libidos aren't as strong, but they'll be back! For more information, turn to the section titled "Our Reproductive System." There are several homeopathic remedies that can re-stimulate your libido to match its pre-menopause level.

ALL THESE ADS MAKE ME SO WORRIED ABOUT DYING FROM A HEART ATTACK OR GETTING OSTEOPOROSIS THAT I DON'T KNOW WHAT TO DO. IF I TAKE HRT, I'M LOOKING AT BREAST CANCER! IF I DON'T, I FACE A POTENTIAL HEART ATTACK. ARE THERE ANY DIETARY CONSIDERATIONS THAT MIGHT HELP ME TO NATURALLY LOWER MY CHANCES OF HEART ATTACK AND OSTEOPOROSIS?

Yes, there are. Remember, osteoporosis is a DISEASE and is NOT a menopause symptom. Only 25 percent of our population is inclined toward osteoporosis. See the section titled "Our Bones" for more information, as well as some dietary considerations.

There are many things we can do to keep our hearts healthy, too. See "Our Circulation and Heart" for valuable, life-saving information about diet and your heart.

We can sail through menopause without HRT, and be healthy going in, going through it, and coming out the other side of it—naturally. And homeopathic remedies will be there, supporting you, every step and with every symptom you experience along the way.

THE THOUGHT OF GETTING CANCER OF THE UTERUS OR BREAST IS ENOUGH TO SCARE ME INTO NOT EVEN THINKING ABOUT TAKING HORMONE DRUGS. CAN HOMEOPATHY MAKE ME LOOK YOUNGER?

If homeopathy could make people look younger or more youthful, we'd be making millions of dollars a year on the so-called Fountain of Youth. But, we aren't.

Taking a homeopathic remedy during menopause will make the transition far more comfortable, and it will enlist the natural help of your body in doing it, with no risk of contracting some horrible disease, such as cancer, as a consequence. There is much that homeopathy can do to make menopause smooth and uneventful. I would be lying if I said it could make you look younger—it can't. What it can do is give you an optimum quality of life at whatever your age.

I've treated many women on the Navajo reservation where I worked, both Indian and white, and it's amazing how after I get them off hormone drugs and put them on a constitutional homeopathic remedy instead, wonderful changes take place.

For example, they are more directly engaged with their lives, they become more focused on what their own needs are now, and they don't allow others to continue to overwhelm them with demands. There is more vitality and life in their eyes—they sparkle. Emotionally, they feel uplifted, happier, and more hopeful. Mentally, they begin to pursue goals that were important to them—but were put aside for various reasons. In other words, constitutional homeopathic treatment, especially during the menopause transition, gives a woman freedom from other people's demands, and puts her directly in touch with her own unique vitality, intelligence, hopes, and dreams. Isn't that exciting? I think so!

CHAPTER 4

OUR BREASTS: HOW THEY CHANGE AND HOW TO PROTECT THEM

I'VE READ RECENTLY THAT A LARGE STUDY WAS UNDERTAKEN THAT SHOWS CONCLUSIVELY THAT HRT CAUSES A HIGH INCIDENCE OF BREAST CANCER. IS THAT TRUE?

Yes! The *New England Journal of Medicine*, June 15, 1995, reported a study undertaken by Dr. Graham A. Colditz, MB, BS, and his team. With funding, they created the Nurses' Health Study from 1978 to 1992, with 121,700 female registered nurses between 30 and 55 years old, on ERT, estrogen, and HRT, with the addition of progestins.

They found that women who had taken HRT for 5 years or more had the greatest risk of breast cancer. Broken down into age groups, those 50 to 55 years old, if on HRT, had a 46 percent chance of contracting breast cancer. Those who were 55 to 59 years old had a 41 percent chance. And for 60 to 64 years old, a 42 percent chance. Those who are 65 to 69 years old had a 70 percent chance of contracting breast cancer. Interestingly, a woman's risk was reduced to only a 13 percent chance of breast cancer after getting off these drugs (a combination of estrogen and progestins).

This information should scare the living daylights out of any woman even minutely considering taking HRT! Who wants to trade breast cancer for easing some menopausal symptoms that can easily be taken care of with homeopathic remedies that will not cause any of the horrible problems or diseases that HRT does?

I HAVE A HISTORY OF LUMPS IN MY BREASTS. SHOULD I CONTEMPLATE USING HRT?

Absolutely not. First, get rid of wearing your bra. There's plenty of evidence that bras help create fibroids and cysts in our breasts—more on this topic below this question, so keep reading! Two types of lumps can occur in our breasts. The first is known as fibroids. These occur when long fibers grow and then create hard, scar-like lumps in our breasts. The second variety is when the body makes a pocket in our breast and fills it with either fluid or semi-solid material. This is known as a cyst.

Either condition enlarges and diminishes each month with our menses cycle because it is connected with the amount of estrogen in our body. The result is "lumpy" breasts. Sometimes a fibroid or cyst is very small, almost pea-like, or it can be the size of a grape, or larger. Whatever the size, they are usually quite painful just before menses and begin to wane as the period completes itself.

In some rare cases, fibroids may become malignant and cancerous. If you have fibroids and are thinking about going on HRT, which would be tinkering directly with your hormones, it would be best to think again and NOT take the drugs. Taking HRT makes these cysts and fibroids become even larger and more worrisome; further, women with fibroids in their breasts are advised NOT to be on HRT for fear of incurring cancer.

One of the great things about menopause is that for most women, cysts and fibroids cease to exist (in both the breast and uterine areas). They go away in most of us without doing anything.

I WOULD DO ANYTHING TO GET RID OF MY PAINFUL, LUMPY, CYST-FILLED BREASTS. WHAT CAN I DO THAT IS NATURAL AND SAFE?

One of the easiest answers to this dilemma is to get rid of wearing your bra! A Canadian study showed that women with fibrocystic breasts recovered from this disease in as little as 2–3 weeks after going bra-free! So, ladies, throw them things away! From a nutritional standpoint, you can take bioflavanoids, which are known to reduce cysts and make your breasts "unlumpy." They are part of the vitamin C family. You can get bioflavanoids directly from eating the white, inner flesh of any citrus fruit. That white layer is filled with natural bioflavanoids. So the next time you eat an orange, peel off that white layer and eat it too.

Another nutritional safeguard is to make sure you are getting enough iodine in your diet. You can do this by eating kelp (such as dulse, a great source!), using sea salt on your table instead of common table salt, and eating vegetables such as beets, mushrooms, and spinach. Fruits, such as apples, pears, oranges, and strawberries, contain iodine too. All are high sources of this mineral.

Vitamin E has been shown to reduce cysts, not only in size, but in number, with just 600 IUs taken daily, within 2 months.

At the end of this section is a listing of homeopathic remedies (called the Materia Medica). You can turn to the Materia Medica at any time to see if there is a remedy there that matches your symptoms.

I DRINK COFFEE, TEA, AND SODA POP. AND I LOVE CHOCOLATE! DOES THIS INFLUENCE THE CYSTS I HAVE IN MY BREASTS?

Several studies have shown that benign lumps in the breast disappear by simply removing caffeine products—coffee, tea, chocolate, and soda pop—from the diet. After 6 months of abstinence, the lumps should be gone. These products, while satisfying to the mouth, contain methylxanthines, which interfere with the enzyme actions in our body.

Elimination of such products from our diet can mean getting rid of the lumps. In one study by John P. Minton, MD, Ph.D., two-thirds of the women he tested who abstained from these products were lump free in 2 years.

If you take a homeopathic remedy, you have to get off coffee, anyway, because the oils in the coffee (decaf or otherwise) antidote the remedy, nullifying the effects of the remedy. That gives you a double reason to get away from coffee.

Selenium, a trace mineral, has been found to reduce breast cancer in mice; in one study, the incidence of breast cancer dropped from 82 percent to 10 percent. In the United States, selenium is largely missing from the soil because of overfarming the land, without replenishing this mineral, for the last 200 years. Where selenium levels in the soil are lowest, the cancer rates are the highest! In South Dakota, where the soil base has the highest amount of selenium, cancer is the lowest, whereas in Ohio, where the soil is most deficient in this trace mineral, there is the highest rate of cancer.

In another, more interesting study, the blood of 10,000 Americans was frozen. Then, as some of them contracted cancer, their blood was thawed and checked. It was discovered that those who got cancer had the lowest levels of selenium. The conclusion of this study was that low selenium levels in the blood doubled your chance of getting cancer.

Foods that are high in selenium (providing they come from selenium-rich soils) are corn, cabbage, whole wheat, beans or peas, vegetable oils, chicken, beets, barley, tomatoes, and soybeans. Nutritional doctors recommend no more than 200 micro milligrams of selenium a day, as an upper limit. Some people use the colloidal form. I would suggest that you change your diet instead of taking a supplement, but check with your health care provider, first.

Homeopathic remedies will also address the problem of cystic and fibroid breasts. However, for some women, just making a diet change can reduce cysts to a distant memory. It is a simple, straight-forward way to deal with the situation—without drugs!

AM I AT RISK FOR BREAST CANCER BECAUSE I HAVE CYSTS IN MY BREAST?

No, you aren't, although when a cyst forms in our breast, it can scare the living daylights out of us because it is a lump! Instantly, we think: Oh, no! I've got cancer!

The moment you detect any lump in your breast, you should have it checked. Usually, through palpation, X-rays, or sometimes biopsy, your doctor will tell you if it is a cyst or a fibroid (which can be benign or malignant) or if it is, indeed, a cancerous lump. They are also utilizing ultrasound, which is less invasive and far less painful!

Even if you are diagnosed with cancer, there is help from homeopathy. If I were diagnosed with cancer, I would see my allopathic doctors and then go see my homeopath. Cancer has been treated successfully with homeopathic remedies.

One study showed that women who had a hysterectomy, and who were not treated with HRT, had only a 10.2 percent chance of getting breast cancer.

Another interesting part of this study concerned longevity with or without HRT. The life span of women with no hormone treatment was 82.8 years compared with 83.9 years with HRT. That is IF you manage not to get cancer of the breast or uterus in the meantime! It is a very risky gauntlet you are running if you are on HRT, with a 70 PERCENT chance of getting cancer. Too risky for me!

MY BREASTS ARE BEGINNING TO SAG. IS THIS A SIGN OF MENOPAUSE?

No. It is a sign of aging. It is not caused by menopause. With age, our breasts will begin to "slide south" (as will everything else), because the muscles and ligaments that hold up and support the subcutaneous fatty tissue of our breasts begin to lose their tone. The glandular tissue also shrinks, because the need to breast feed an infant is no longer there. There is no homeopathic remedy to stop this from happening, although I would suggest some chest exercises or yoga to slow this process down.

As we age, we begin to lose the fat that was once part of our breast structure. What is left is the fiber. So, the fullness we once had, which was supplied by the fat, will slowly disappear. Then, our breasts begin to sag downward. Regardless of what our bra size was once, it will change as our breasts change.

I do not like bras and rarely wear them, but that is my personal bias. Many women will have to change their bra size to accommodate their heavier, larger breasts. My grandmother, Inez, wore a much larger bra size than she did in her forties because her breasts had sagged considerably—but at 99, she was allowed! Some women may end up wearing a smaller sized bra.

I JUST NOTICED THAT ONE OF MY BREASTS IS ABOUT ONE-HALF A BRA SIZE LARGER THAN THE OTHER. IS THIS SOMETHING TO WORRY ABOUT?

Not at all. As a matter of fact, because the heart pumps the fresh, arterial blood to the left side of our body first, and the red blood cells are carrying the most oxygen at that point, the left side of most people's bodies is slightly larger than the right side.

My left breast is about one bra size larger than my right one because of this physiological phenomenon. If you look in a mirror, most of you will see a difference in your breast size. Usually, the left foot is slightly larger (about half a shoe size) and your left hand is also larger than the right one. This is nothing to worry about and has nothing to do with menopause, cancer, or anything else. However, if you see a lump on one of your breasts, that is cause for concern and you should see your doctor.

MY NIPPLES ARE CHANGING. WHAT IS GOING ON?

As the fat begins to disappear from the breast tissue, our nipples may reduce in size, be less well shaped, and not be as firm. This has nothing to do with our enjoyment of our sexuality or feeling stimulation because that does not disappear.

If you are worried about this natural phenomenon, go see your doctor for confirmation, rather than worry that these changes might be related to cancer.

MY NIPPLES HAVE SOME DISCHARGE FROM TIME TO TIME. WHAT DOES THIS MEAN?

If there is a reddish discharge, there might be a duct papilloma tumor causing this symptom. You need to go to your doctor and have it diagnosed. Usually, only surgery can help this condition.

If there is a white or green colored discharge from one or both breasts—and you are not nursing a baby—this is known as galactorrhea. The body is producing small amounts of breast milk. There are many possible causes, including a pituitary dysfunction. It could be related to taking birth control pills or HRT, or being on tranquilizers or diuretics. It could be caused by a physical problem such as shingles, surgery, or nervous disorders. There are many other possible causes for this condition and it should be diagnosed by a physician before homeopathic treatment is attempted.

If you have cysts or boils around the nipple, they can be treated homeopathically. Sometimes, you can get eczema on the nipple area only. This condition is known as Bowen's disease. It may lead to cancer, so it should be checked by your doctor as soon as you note the condition.

Nipples that retract or are concave or indented may be very normal for you, but if you are breast feeding, it can be a problem. In some cases, it can be a sign of breast cancer, so go check it out with your physician to make sure.

I'VE HEARD FRIGHTENING STATISTICS ABOUT WOMEN GETTING BREAST CANCER. WHO IS AT RISK FOR THIS?

Women who go on either ERT or HRT are raising the stakes very high: They have a 50 to 70 percent chance of getting breast cancer if they stay on these drugs for more than 5 years.

Science has shown us that those most at risk are women whose bodies are producing a certain level of estrogen non-stop. This could include women who have never had a baby or women who had one after age 30, or late onset of menopause is also an indicator of possible risk.

There are other factors to consider: Has anyone in your family had breast cancer? Your grandmother, an aunt, a sister, or your mother? This could show a genetic predisposition toward it.

Women who have been on birth control pills should think about alternatives to taking "the pill." There are many other contraceptive methods that should be considered as an alternative to tinkering with our fragile endocrine system. How about condom use? Diaphragms? Spermicidal foam? The nice thing about menopause is that after menopause, we do not have to worry about getting pregnant.

I made a decision early in my life not to be on hormonal drugs—first, birth control pills and then, hormone replacement therapy for menopause. Our bodies are just too fragile to take this kind of bludgeoning from pharmaceutical drugs and the picture is quite clear at this point: Take hormonal drugs and cancer is the result. It may take a long time for cancer to show itself, but once a carcinogen is introduced, it is difficult to remove. Prevention is so much easier.

Another factor that contributes to your cancer risk is a high-fat diet. The breast has duct fluids. Higher levels of hormones and circulating blood fats or lipids are found in women who have a diet that is high in fat. Women who are overweight or obese run a higher risk of breast cancer because their breasts engorge with even more fatty tissue. Excessive fat also makes a woman very vulnerable to diabetes, heart disease, high blood pressure, and strokes. The argument to begin shedding those pounds becomes even more convincing when breast cancer is added to the obese woman's list. A low-fat diet may help alleviate the threat.

I'VE HEARD THAT NOT WEARING A BRA IS HEALTHIER FOR US. WHAT IS YOUR OPINION ABOUT THIS? AND WHY WOULD THAT BE?

Every woman should read *Dressed to Kill: The Link Between Breast Cancer and Bras* by Singer and Grismaijer (Avery Publishing). Five thousand women from the island of Fiji, at the end of World War II, inadvertently took part in a massive, ongoing study on whether or not wearing a bra helps create breast cancer. On Fiji, women do not wear bras. However, about half the female population, after the war, went to work in government offices, and therefore had to wear a bra and dress Western style. When the Singer and Grismaijer study concluded, HALF the women had breast cancer—and it was the ones wearing the bras! The other half did not. It is important to note that these women were from the same villages, ate the same food, and so forth, and the only major difference was wearing a bra!! So, throw 'em away!

I have noticed, and this is only anecdotal and not scientific, that women who DO NOT wear bras seem not to get breast cancer. If they have had a past history of cysts or fibroids in their breasts, not wearing a bra makes them go away. I have observed this in my 30 years of practice. Ninety-five percent of my clients are women and children, so I have had a large group to observe. As a result of this observation, I stopped wearing a bra at age 40. The reason is logical: bras, by their very nature, slow down the blood circulation into and out of breasts because we're wearing a tight, constricting appliance. We have lymph glands in our breasts and the chief reason for lymph glands is to remove dead cell debris and toxins from that region of our body. If we are wearing tight-fitting bras that impair circulation, then the lymph glands cannot "empty" out the garbage from our breast region. It makes sense to me that if blood flow is sluggish or backed up, poisons and toxins cannot get out of the breast region fast enough to prevent build-up. Life-giving and cleansing oxygen, which rides piggy back on red blood cells, is not getting to the breast tissue as much or as easily as Nature intended.

Another aspect of this is that I encourage my patients to not only throw away their bras, but also to massage each breast gently when they take their shower or bath. The reasoning behind this is that lymph glands do not have a pump to circulate anything they pick up in the way of garbage through the system to get rid of it. They are a circulatory system without a heart. So what "moves" the lymph? Muscle movement. That is WHY massage is so vital and important a preventative medicine to us. Our breasts do not have muscle. We do have muscle on the chest wall BEHIND them, but not IN them. As a result, if we do a daily or nightly massage on them, we are in essence moving the lymph garbage along and OUT of our breast region.

Further, if our breasts are free of bras, they hang and move, and that creates movement within the lymph glands, which moves the poisons and toxins out of our breasts. So both are important: allow your breasts to swing freely and gently massage them during your shower or bath once a day.

BUT I HAVE VERY LARGE BREASTS AND I CANNOT AFFORD NOT TO WEAR A BRA! WHAT SHOULD I DO?

Find a correct-fitting bra. I suggest, first of all, either cotton or washable silk for a bra because both "breathe" and your delicate tissue gets oxygen that way. Second, you do not have to have that bra so tight that it is making a red, wrinkled band out of your flesh—that is TOO TIGHT. Make the bra "loose fitting" around your torso as much as possible, to encourage lymph movement and draining. Every time you shower or bathe, then do your breast massage. That will help a great deal.

I HAVE FOUND THAT BY NOT WEARING MY BRA, I NO LONGER HAVE MID-BACK PAIN!

Exactly. Many women have noted this, among other symptoms from wearing a bra. Get rid of the bra; you also get rid of the middle-of-the-back ache.

Conversely, women with very large breasts will get a back ache if they do not wear a bra. Each woman must do what she needs to do to be as comfortable as possible under the circumstances. The main point here is massaging your breasts daily to increase the flow of lymph through them so that the materials can exit and not collect for years in your breasts.

IF I EAT A LOW-FAT DIET, ENGAGE IN A MILD FORM OF EXERCISE, AND STAY AWAY FROM HORMONAL DRUGS OF ANY KIND, AM I LOWERING MY CHANCES OF GETTING BREAST CANCER?

Without a doubt. Women in China get breast cancer at half the rate that we do. Why? Most likely, their diet. Intake of phytosterols and phyto-estrogens, such as yams and tofu, may discourage the body from producing too much estrogen, which nourishes hormone-dependent cancer. Tofu, a soybean derivative, is also high in vitamins and minerals.

A little tofu added to your diet certainly is not going to hurt and it is a great source of calcium, too. A yam a week won't hurt, either!

WHY IS BREAST CANCER SO HIGH AMONG WOMEN?

There are strong feelings among many concerned scientists that the ENVIRONMENT we live in is contributing to the alarming escalation of breast cancer. "Environment" refers to what we eat, smoke, drink (alcohol), and probably most important, the pesticides and herbicides used on the food we ingest. The breast is, in a sense, a fat storage area.

Poisons, no matter what kind they are, just love to nestle in fat. The result is that the fat becomes overloaded with poisons and voilà! Cancer. Our breasts are our greatest area of concentrated fat, unless of course, we're way overweight. Then we have lots of fat receptacles elsewhere, too. For most of us, our breasts store most of our fat cells.

We can eat organically grown produce or, better yet, raise our own! We can scrub the fruit and vegetables thoroughly, or allow them to sit in water for 30 minutes to allow the water-soluble insecticides to dissipate. A farmer who uses deadly chemicals on his produce once told me that the herbicides and pesticides were designed to break down in water after being submerged for half an hour. If that is what it takes to get them off the skin of a fruit or vegetable I'm going to eat, I'll submerge it for half an hour to make sure. There are also non-toxic "soaps" on the market designed specifically for washing toxic residues off fruits and vegetables. They can be found in many health food stores.

Of course, herbicides and pesticides are stored INSIDE the produce, too, and there's no way we can get around that. For myself, as a homeopath, I take Arsenicum Album 30C once every 3 months, to clean out my body of any of these deadly poisons. I do this as a routine for myself. Your homeopath should be consulted first before you try this regime for yourself.

ARE THERE HOMEOPATHIC REMEDIES TO HELP CURE BREAST CANCER?

Yes. This cannot be done by merely reading this book and taking a particular remedy, however. Cancer is one of our toughest opponents, homeopathically speaking, but I've seen it cured with constitutional treatment. Sometimes, homeopathy cannot help, and that is usually in cases where the cancer is very advanced and the person's vitality is low. Age, the person's energy level, how long they've had cancer, and how many allopathic drugs or treatments have beaten the body (and vital force) down so that it can no longer respond, also play a part in this determination.

I would say, based on my own experience, that if your cancer is not in its last stages, homeopathy can provide some KIND of help. Whether it is a cure, or not, depends upon many variables that cannot be addressed fully in this book. The best thing to do is go to your homeopath and find out. You have nothing to lose and everything to gain by doing this.

Homeopathic remedies are natural and gently stimulate the body's own systems to heal itself, so this kind of approach is the best, in my personal opinion.

HOMEOPATHIC REMEDIES FOR BREAST CANCER

From a homeopathic perspective, cancer is considered a major breakdown in the person's health, mentally, emotionally, and physically. There are no homeopathic 'magic bullets' to cure breast cancer. Instead, you must seek out your homeopathic practitioner and get your constitutional case taken. Only then can homeopathy begin to work its miracles for you. Do not try to take a remedy by yourself, if you have been diagnosed with breast cancer. This requires 1–2 years of continued homeopathic treatment, care, and prescribing. Turn to the appendix for directories to find a homeopath near you.

HOMEOPATHIC REMEDIES FOR BREAST CYSTS AND FIBROIDS

1. Conium Maculatum
2. Pulsatilla
3. Graphites
4. Belladonna

HOMEOPATHIC REMEDIES FOR GALACTORRHEA

1. Conium Maculatum
2. Bellis Perennis
3. Arnica Montana

HOMEOPATHIC REMEDIES FOR SWOLLEN OR PAINFUL BREASTS

1. Natrum Muriaticum
2. Carbo Vegetabilis
3. Conium Maculatum
4. Iodum
5. Calcarea Carbonica
6. Pulsatilla
7. Lac Humanum
8. Phytolacca

FLOWER ESSENCE TO PROMOTE LYMPH DRAINAGE

1. Chaparral

CHAPTER 5

OUR REPRODUCTIVE SYSTEM: KEEPING OUR UTERUS AND OVARIES HEALTHY

WHAT IS A FIBROID?

Fibroids can be found not only in our uterus, but in our breasts as well. It is a lump, primarily made up of muscle cells, that is surrounded or encapsulated by fibrous tissue. It then attaches itself to our uterine wall or our breast(s) where it remains, usually, harmless to us. There are many subtypes of fibroids, but your physician will know all about those.

Sometimes a fibroid is very small—the size of a button, let's say—or it can get as large as a peach or an apple. In a very few cases, they can be as large as a grapefruit or cantaloupe, but that is rare. About one in five women who are over the age of 35 have them. Women who have never had a baby are more prone to them than women who have had a child.

Fibroids are usually not cancerous—so that is the good news. Perhaps 1 percent of all fibroids turn cancerous.

WHAT ARE THE SYMPTOMS OF A FIBROID?

Generally speaking, they can produce an array of symptoms. If you think you have them, a trip to your gynecologist will confirm this one way or another. There can be "flooding" or a lot of clots in the menstrual blood. I might add that this flooding can be worse on the second or third day of a cycle; whereas usually, for many women, we all have a flood day, but not two or more of them. And it is usually the first or second day of our menses.

Other symptoms include more frequent urination, backaches, pressure sensation in the vaginal area (you may feel as if a weight or stone were inside you, pressing), and very painful cramping.

Fibroids can cause delay in bowel movements or the ability to urinate. Sometimes they can be indirectly responsible for cystitis because the bowel movement is not occurring and it is putting pressure on the urethra, the small tube that leads from the bladder to the outside world. If there is recurrent cystitis, get it checked out.

On a more serious level, fibroids have been known to cause miscarriage of a baby.

Over time, as the fibroid grows, fast or slow, there can be more flooding to the point of anemia. The cramping that may attend your menstrual cycle can be quite painful, and colicky in nature.

WHAT CAUSES A FIBROID TO GROW INSIDE ME?

Most medical people think it is because of estrogen levels in our bloodstream. It is well known that fibroids increase when a woman is on an oral contraceptive of any kind, and also, when she is pregnant.

DOES GOING THROUGH MENOPAUSE MAKE MY FIBROIDS WORSE?

Just the opposite! It has been found that if you have had fibroids in either the breast or the uterine area, they usually shrink up and disappear during menopause. Sometimes, if they are extra large, they will shrink, but not go away entirely.

IF I CONTINUE TO HAVE A FIBROID IN MY UTERUS AS I GO THROUGH MENOPAUSE, IS THERE HELP HOMEOPATHICALLY?

Yes. The homeopathic remedies are listed at the end of this section and you can go to the Materia Medica in the back of the book and check your symptoms against the remedy's symptoms. On something like this though, you should seek treatment from a homeopathic practitioner. This is not an acute ailment, but rather it is a chronic one and you need an experienced homeopath to help you get rid of those fibroids once and for all.

DOES HOMEOPATHY CURE FIBROIDS?

In many cases, yes. I had a call from a friend in Canada asking if I could treat her homeopathically to get rid of a fibroid that was as large as an orange in her uterus. I told her that I couldn't treat her long distance. Canada allows homeopathy to be practiced, and she found a very good homeopathic practitioner in Toronto, where she lived.

The homeopath put my friend on Aurum Metallicum (Aurum Met.), which is potentized gold. It is one of our premier homeopathic remedies for uterine fibroids. In one year's time, all her fibroid symptoms disappeared (she had heavy bleeding, clotting, and a lot of pain during her menstrual cycle). She went to her gynecologist every 3 months to have the fibroid size checked. The fibroid shrunk from the size of an orange to the size of a nickel in that time. Today, 10 years later (and she is in her forties now), she has no problems with it whatsoever since homeopathic treatment.

IF I WAS DIAGNOSED WITH A FIBROID IN MY UTERUS, SHOULD I CONSIDER HOMEOPATHIC TREATMENT?

The answer is a qualified yes. Homeopaths routinely work hand-in-hand with medical doctors on complex problems like this. After your gynecologist has diagnosed you, she should tell you if it is a fast or slow growing fibroid. If it is fast growing, that CAN be an indication that it MIGHT be cancerous. I'm sure she will have ordered the appropriate tests to find out.

When you have found out, and it is benign, then seek out the services of your homeopath. She will take your case and you'll be placed on a remedy. The homeopath will want you to schedule routine visits to your gynecologist to check the size of the fibroid under homeopathic treatment. Usually, it takes a year to get rid of a fibroid, so be patient.

On the other hand, if the fibroid is slow growing, this is where homeopathic treatment can interface medically. Other factors that may or may not indicate homeopathic treatment are how many symptoms of the fibroid do you have? Are the symptoms unbearable to the point to where all you want to do is have surgery to remove either the fibroid or the entire uterus? If the symptoms are still bearable, then you might consider homeopathic treatment—after informing your gynecologist of your decision, and continue getting those very necessary check-ups.

WHAT IF MY GYNECOLOGIST INSISTS THAT I HAVE SURGERY TO GET RID OF THE FIBROID IN MY UTERUS?

What every woman must do nowadays, in my opinion, is EDUCATE herself on anything that has to do medically with her body. It is impossible to cover all the what-ifs here in this book on every woman's condition. Read up on your condition, get a second, even a third opinion, and consult with your homeopath at the same time.

There are times when homeopathic treatment is not indicated with fibroids, usually in advanced cases where the flooding is at a hemorrhaging stage and the patient is anemic already, and surgery is the only viable alternative left. All these decisions must be made between you, your gynecologist, and your homeopath.

Homeopathy has its drawback from the standpoint that if a medical condition has advanced too far, that is, if it is verging upon surgical intervention, in these types of cases it is best not to use homeopathy. Again, your homeopath can help you determine this regarding your specific case.

WHEN MY MOTHER ENTERED MENOPAUSE, SHE HAD TERRIBLE HEMORRHAGING PROBLEMS AND HAD TO BE RUSHED TO THE EMERGENCY ROOM FOR A D&C. SHE HAD CONSTANT, NONSTOP BLEEDING. AFTER THE D&C, SHE HAD NO MORE PROBLEMS.

Abnormal bleeding during or in between our periods as we enter pre-menopause can be a problem for some of us. If you are hemorrhaging, obviously, get to an emergency room or to your doctor's office as soon as possible. If the bleeding is not too severe and you are not anemic yet, think about a homeopathic remedy that can halt this symptom. There are homeopathic remedies you can take on the way to see your doctor, and they are listed at the end of this section.

A FRIEND OF MINE HAS A CONDITION KNOWN AS A PROLAPSED UTERUS. IS THIS A PART OF MENOPAUSE?

For some women, yes. The biggest determiner of this is how many children you have had. The more you had, the more likely that this condition may occur. Also, genetics plays a big part in this, too. If your mother has this condition, the chances are higher that you might, too.

Our uterus is supported and held in place by muscles in the abdominal area and for some, they get weaker with age and time—and use (pregnancies). If these muscles allow the womb to sag downward, it can put pressure on the other organs in the area. Usually, this is the large intestine and bladder region.

Signs of a prolapsed uterus are urinary incontinence or having problems completely emptying your bladder. From a bowel movement standpoint, it might cause an incomplete stool. There are stages to a prolapsed uterus: (a) the uterus moving down into the vagina, (b) the cervix may protrude through the vaginal opening, and (c) complete prolapse where the uterus extends down the vagina to the outer opening.

If you are having problems with urinary or fecal incontinence, then go to the gynecologist and get a diagnosis. If this is not due to a uterine prolapse, homeopathic treatment may be beneficial and improve or cure the condition so long as there is not organic damage to the area already. Working with your gynecologist and homeopath simultaneously will help you determine which course of action is best for you.

I had one Navajo patient whose uterus was coming out of her vagina. I took her case and gave her the appropriate homeopathic remedy. Within a month, her uterus was no longer in her vaginal area.

MY UTERUS IS SO PAINFUL AND TENDER FEELING! WHAT CAN I DO ABOUT THIS?

First, go to your gynecologist and get a diagnosis. It is possible that you have adenomyosis, where cells from the endometrium lining grow in the uterine wall. Usually, this is found in the pre-menopause stage in women who have had a baby during this time frame. If that is so, there are homeopathic remedies that can help, but surgery may be in the offing, too. Again, consult with your gynecologist and homeopath simultaneously on this condition to determine the best course of action.

If your gynecologist gives you a clean bill of health and your uterus is fine, then homeopathic remedies may be very helpful during this time of change.

I'VE HEARD HORROR STORIES ABOUT THE LINING OF A WOMAN'S VAGINA THINNING OUT. IS THIS TRUE?

The vagina is, to me, a most amazing organ. It must adjust in size from sexual intercourse to widening enough to allow a baby to pass through. Many, many layers of epithelial tissue (40–50 layers!) are required to perform these functions.

As we enter menopause, these layers shrink—in some rare cases, to as few as four or five layers. Also, our clitoris shrinks and the glans is exposed, which is surrounded by the folds of our labia, which has thinned, too. Our labia is a nice, healthy pink color and with menopause, it becomes pale looking.

This is the thinning out process or atrophy that you're referring to. There is a natural decrease to the amount of mucus our vagina produces, too. In fact, our vagina walls shorten, thin, and lose some of their previous muscle tone as part of menopause. It is a natural occurrence and doesn't need to cause problems. However, for a FEW women, it does.

MY VAGINA IS ALWAYS DRY NOW AND IT NEVER USED TO BE. IT MAKES INTERCOURSE PAINFUL FOR ME. SHOULD I BE CONCERNED?

This condition is called dyspareunia, or painful intercourse, and it is due to the thinning of the layers of the tissue in the vaginal area, plus less mucus being available for lubrication purposes. It CAN make sexual intercourse painful. You may not lubricate as much or as fast as before and after a number of times, you may not want intercourse as a result of the pain.

I want to stress that this symptom of menopause doesn't happen to every woman—only 31 percent according to one study. Much depends upon many factors such as weight, body fat, or lack of it. Women who have extra fat tend to have extra amounts of estrogen stored so that this condition will not occur. Thin women may have a problem with this—but they may not, either.

Another possibility for painful intercourse is that your vagina contains a yeast overgrowth, known as candida, which is caused by an acid-alkaline imbalance in our vaginal area. Have it checked out by your gynecologist. There are many homeopathic remedies (some of which will be listed, but not all of them) to cure candida. It may require constitutional treatment to do so—but know that there is an alternative to going on a candida-free diet for the rest of your life. Get the diagnosis and if it is candida causing the pain in your vaginal area, see your homeopath for treatment.

Women who wear pantyhose (nylons) or tight synthetic fabrics do not have good circulation through their vaginal area, creating an incubator condition or environment for candida—it is hot and moist without proper air circulation. Women should wear cotton panties (not tight fitting, either) and stay away from pantyhose. Back in my mother's generation, they wore long skirts, no panties at all (!), and air circulation was plentiful! I had asked my grandmother, Inez, who lived to be 99 and was in good health, about this and she acknowledged that it was true—no panties were worn. Back in her day, no one had ever heard of candida—or the symptoms (burning and itching)—which were rare then, but are very common nowadays.

So, change what you are wearing from synthetic to natural fibers, and go for improved air circulation! Long skirts are great because they encourage good range of motion. Maybe some loose-fitting cotton panties are in order? Air circulation makes our vaginal area drier and discourages the growth of yeast or candida. I will go for air circulation any time!

Vitamin E has been suggested to help lubricate this region of our body. Generally, 100–600 IUs of vitamin E for 4 to 6 weeks can help this symptom.

A number of remedies for a dry vaginal tract due to menopause are listed below.

I GET THESE TERRIBLE PAINS IN MY VAGINA. IS THIS A MENOPAUSE SYMPTOM?

Yes, it is—for some women. Vaginismus is the involuntary spasm of the muscles that are located at the entrance to the vagina. Penetration can be extremely painful and perhaps, impossible. The good news is that there are homeopathic remedies for it! They are listed at the end of the chapter.

I'M EMBARRASSED TO EVEN ADMIT THIS, BUT I'VE BEEN HAVING THESE CRAZY SENSATIONS IN MY VAGINA. IS THAT NORMAL DURING MENOPAUSE?

Do not be embarrassed. This is a condition called formication. From a homeopathic perspective, the best way to characterize this symptom is that it's like an army of ants crawling over your skin—only, you feel this sensation in your vaginal area.

This itching may be caused by yeast overgrowth (known as thrush or candida), especially when menopause comes on fast and not slow (it takes 2–5 years to complete its cycle). The bacteria in your vaginal area, in a swift-moving menopause, labor mightily with these sudden changes, and for awhile there can be intense itching.

There are homeopathic remedies for formication and candida. Formication can occur during menopause, and not only in the vaginal region, but anywhere on our skin. Taking a homeopathic remedy will stop it—no matter where the symptoms of formication are located.

Another way to help the bacteria, the flora of the vaginal tract, and the acid-alkaline balance in that area to adjust to this swift-moving change, is to take acidophilis capsules (buy the kind that is refrigerated because that means those little critters are alive in there and that is what you want!) OR eat yogurt several times a week, which also contains acidophilis culture.

SINCE I'VE BEEN IN MY LATE FORTIES, MY VAGINA HAS BECOME TERRIBLY SENSITIVE TO ANY PENETRATION. IS MENOPAUSE CAUSING IT?

Yes. This is another symptom of what is known as vaginismus (it doesn't always have to be painful spasms). And, there's a drying out of the vaginal area, which does happen to some women as they go through menopause. A number of homeopathic remedies to take care of these conditions are listed at the end of this chapter.

I'M REALLY WORRIED ABOUT LOSING MY DESIRE FOR SEX. I'VE HEARD THAT MENOPAUSE WILL TURN ME INTO A CELIBATE BEING. HELP!!!

Nothing could be further from the truth! Sex is at its best, in my opinion, after menopause because we do not have to worry about getting pregnant! The horror stories you've heard about women drying up like old apples and no longer wanting sex is only that—unfounded gossip.

While it's true that our vaginal lining will thin over time, and we might not lubricate up as quickly, that doesn't dim the flame of our passion and ardor. Do not forget—men go through their version of menopause, too, so they might not be as responsive as before, either. If you have a loving, understanding partner, and there's communication between the two of you, your sexual life will be the same or improved—maybe a little slower—but so what? It's quality, not quantity, that counts.

And, while there are lubricants such as KY jelly or other products on the market, there are homeopathic remedies to stimulate your body to produce your own, natural lubrication. And, if all else fails, you still have these products.

For some women, our sexual needs may slow down—but they do not disappear! For another group, our sexual needs may increase because androgen is higher, which is a woman's parallel to male testosterone, and you may find yourself not only passionate, but rather assertive about enjoying those orgasms more often than before menopause!

I JUST DO NOT WANT MY SEX LIFE TO END!

Not to worry, those decisions are in our hands. There is a natural slowing down of certain organic functions of our reproductive system during and after menopause, but it doesn't mean it is the end to sexual expression and pleasure for us and our partner.

It is true, our sex life does change around age 50. Homeopathy offers a wonderful array of remedies to keep our reproductive organs in good, working order for as long as we want or desire sex.

Some women make a choice to not want sex as they go through menopause and it is a conscious choice on their part. For them, celibacy is the answer. That is okay, too. Nothing says we have to have sex until the day we die. Ultimately, women are in charge of their bodies and the decision-making process about being sexual. Remaining sexually active is an individual choice—menopause does not make that determination for you.

BUT, I'VE PUT ON 10 EXTRA POUNDS, AND I'M FEELING LESS SEXUALLY DESIRABLE. HELP!!!

I have always said that sex was in our heads, not our bodies. If you are feeling that menopause has made you feel less sexy or sexually desirable, I would recommend homeopathic constitutional treatment.

Being treated with the right homeopathic remedy can bring you back into harmony with yourself on all levels of your being: spirit, mind, emotions, and body. Although it's true that our hormones are changing and fluctuating to some degree during menopause, being treated constitutionally will make this whole cyclic transition smoother and less troublesome.

A remedy probably is not going to make you shed those 10 extra pounds you've gained, but it can help you with your psychological outlook about yourself and the world around you—which is vastly more important.

When I went into a peri-menopausal depression for 3 weeks, I lost interest in sex, too. I didn't feel like a sexual being in the slightest! Fortunately, I prescribed Sepia for myself, one of the great remedies for loss of sexual interest and depression, and voilà! Within 24 hours I was out of that awful depression and within 72 hours, I had my sex drive back and was feeling sexually desirable again.

IS IT TRUE THAT HRT MAY GIVE ME UTERINE CANCER?

There's no doubt about it. A 1992 study by L. Bernstein, R. K. Ross, and B. E. Henderson for the Southern California School of Medicine noted that estrogen replacement therapy was a major cause of endometrium cancer. Not only that, but combination therapy of estrogen with progestin enhanced your risk of breast cancer.

They remarked that in pre-menopausal and post-menopausal women, if we are on any kind of drug hormone therapy, our risk is "moderate." Of course, the most recent study, which was published in the *New England Journal of Medicine* in June, 1995, showed a 41–70 percent chance of getting breast cancer!

I HAVE A HORRIBLE TIME WITH MY PERIODS. SOMETIMES THEY'RE LATE, OR SHORTER THAN USUAL, AND WORST OF ALL, I FLOOD! I NEVER USED TO. WHAT IS GOING ON?

Off and on through our peri-menopause, usually between ages 40 and 50, our periods begin to change. Sometimes in small, almost unnoticeable ways, but in others, pretty dramatic. I have seen my menses go from 7 days, to 5 days, to 3 days, at the age of 48. I have seen the basic nature of my period change: usually, on the second day, I'd have a flood day, where my menses was heavier, and then it would lighten up for the rest of the cycle.

As we get to be 48 or so, our period may not show up for a month, and the next month it is there again! Sometimes it is only a shortened version. Over the next 2–5 years, you will see your periods come and go. For me, it was one month on and one month off for a year. Then, I began skipping periods for 2 months, and then I'd have one for a month, and then 2 more months would go by without one. I was really beginning to enjoy looking forward to having no period months!

As I have moved more and more into menopause, I have fewer and fewer periods. Right now, at age 53, I have not had a period for 8 months. It is luxurious! Over time, we have fewer periods—dry spells, so to speak. And then, one day, we will have none for a whole year and that is when we, by medical assessment, are in "menopause." That is the yardstick they use—one year without any periods. I don't know about you, but I sure have been enjoying not having one. No pads, no mess, no bloating or edema before the period, no emotional mood swings, or tender breasts, etc. I have thoroughly enjoyed this loss of periods.

One of the most disconcerting things about our cycle is the flooding, or heavy flow. My mother, Ruth, had one period like that when she was 51, and she bled heavily all day long and finally went to the emergency room of the nearest hospital, completely alarmed—thinking she was bleeding to death. They performed a D&C, and the bleeding stopped and she was fine. It never occurred again. She had four children, however. As her daughter, I have no children and have not had this experience of flooding during menopause and I doubt seriously if I will.

YOU MEAN I HAVE A D&C TO LOOK FORWARD TO?

Not at all. When this occurred, I was still in the U.S. Navy and hadn't even gotten into homeopathy at that point in my life. Let me tell you another true story:

When I was 29 years old, I began to have hemorrhaging with my periods—we're not talking about flooding here, which is an increase in menstrual blood flow, but rather going through one super pad every half hour for 12 hours at a time. THAT is hemorrhaging! I was also passing huge, black, tarry looking clots the size of nickels and quarters—which I'd never done before! I was frightened.

Alarmed, I went to the emergency room at the hospital in Akron, Ohio. They examined me and could find nothing wrong—no fibroids, no nothing. They wanted to give me a D&C, but I have a horror of surgery (which is probably why I became a homeopathic practitioner—I KNEW there had to be an alternative to surgery!). The physician's best advice was: "Well, gosh, I guess you'd better go home and sit in a tub of hot water."

In all fairness, this young man was a resident, learning his doctoring craft—but, I naively followed his advice—and turned an entire tub a bloody red color. I was still bleeding like a stuck hog, as my Kentucky father would have said, and by now, I was feeling very weak—because I'd lost more blood than I should have.

A week before, I'd been at a wonderful health food store in Akron, where we lived at that time, and had picked up a black, hardbound book with red edging. At first, when I saw this small book in the turnstile, I thought: "What on Earth is a Bible doing in a health food store?" Out of curiosity, I went over and picked it up—to find that it was *Boericke's Materia Medica with Repertory*—not a Bible. Intrigued, I bought the book and took it home.

I knew absolutely nothing about homeopathy at that time, but out of desperation, I picked it up and thumbed through the rear of the book under Repertory. I found Female Sexual System and in a panic, looked through the rubrics or symptoms for flooding at period time. I found what I was looking for under Menorrhagia, which means in our lingo, a profuse, premature flow of menstrual blood. I looked at a bunch of Latin names and began to read the materia medica portion of the book and read up on each remedy—trying to find the closest fit to my symptoms.

When I looked up Kali Muriaticum and read the symptoms described under "Female: excessive discharge; dark-clotted blood," I yelped for joy—that was ME! Excited, apprehensive, and hoping it would work, I drove back to the health food store. Luckily, they carried this homeopathic remedy—in a 6X potency. I bought it and took four tablets. On the way home, a half-hour drive, I could literally FEEL the hemorrhaging begin to slow down. When I got home, I took another four tablets and changed my soaked napkin. I noticed that my huge, black clots were smaller—about the size of a dime, now, and not a nickel.

Within an hour and a half of taking Kali Mur., my hemorrhaging stopped and my menses flow returned to normal! The clots also disappeared. I was flabbergasted. Amazed. Nothing the medical establishment had done had helped me. But this little black book with red edging that looked like a Bible had stopped me from hemorrhaging with the information contained within its pages.

This one incident is what led me into learning homeopathy and eventually becoming a practitioner. And of course, as Fate or Synchronicity would have it, I traveled everywhere with *Boericke's Materia Medica with Repertory*. I visited some friends in another part of the state, and a large, obese Greek woman named Helen, who was 49 years old, had the very same symptoms I had had earlier with my menses. She told me she'd never had this kind of flooding before and that she was going through menopause. Confidently, I told her to have someone run down to the health food store and purchase Kali Mur. 6X and take four tablets every half hour until her hemorrhaging stopped.

I received a phone call from Helen 2 hours later—she was so relieved and joyful—all her flooding symptoms had stopped, and there were no more ugly clots, either. She cried over the phone in thanks, saying that for the last year, each of her periods had been like this and nothing the doctor had done had helped—not even a D&C. I was elated. Homeopathy REALLY worked! Being a woman who has had her share (and who among us hasn't?) of menstrual symptoms, and finding that these little white pills could make the difference between continuing to enjoy my life through the days of my menses instead of dreading it—it was an incredible "a-ha!"

As I became more educated regarding the application of homeopathy, I found that it could do a lot more than just help women with their menstrual or menopausal symptoms. It could help, quite literally, in every condition known to humankind.

That was how I became a homeopath—because of my own experience with hemorrhaging at menstrual time. Homeopathy has saved a lot of women from the misery of their menstrual cycle and now, as I'm experiencing menopause, I am able to continue to do the same for women my own age—and to use something that is natural and nonsurgical, that will work with our bodies and not against us.

I'M GETTING HEAVIER FLOW ON MY MENSTRUAL CYCLE THAN EVER BEFORE. I DO NOT LIKE TO FLOOD LIKE THIS. IT'S SCARY AND UPSETTING TO ME. WHAT CAN I DO?

I am listing a number of homeopathic remedies that are the premier ones for flooding during our menstrual cycle (with or without menopause). If you are having flooding, make sure via your gynecologist that this is not due to a fibroid tumor, because they can cause serious hemorrhaging too. (If you are diagnosed with a fibroid tumor, there are homeopathic remedies to help shrink them.)

The remedies below are for what is known as nonspecific bleeding—in other words, the medical world doesn't know why we're bleeding like this and there's no reason for it, such as a fibroid, a cyst, or whatever—we're just bleeding more than normal and there is no explanation for it.

IF you match the symptoms of your flooding with a remedy below, take the information to your homeopath and discuss it with her or him. If they approve of the remedy, then try it. If it doesn't work and doesn't slow the flow down within 2 hours of taking it, then you need to go back to your homeopath and get your entire case taken from a constitutional standpoint to stop the flooding.

I JUST GOT MY PAP SMEAR BACK AND MY DOCTOR WANTS TO YANK OUT MY UTERUS! I'M ALARMED. I DON'T WANT SURGERY. CAN HOMEOPATHY HELP?

Yes, it can. Sometimes, very dramatically. Every woman should get a Pap smear test at least once a year. What I have seen, and this is not scientific, is that Pap smears begin to skew more as we enter menopause. Remember, a generation ago, we did not have Pap smears around, so no one really knows what our cervical cells go through during the changes of hormonal flux through menopause. I have treated many cases where Pap smears showed cell dysplasia to varying degrees up to and including pre-cancerous levels. Let me give you an example of this.

Karen called me up in a panic. She had severe dysplasia of her cervical cells and the doctors were telling her that they must operate immediately. The doctors could not tell her cervical cells from the cancerous cells. They said: hysterectomy or else! Karen did not want invasive surgery. She asked me if I could try homeopathy on her. I agreed, but with the understanding that IF, after the next Pap test, which would be 2 months from taking the homeopathic remedy, there was no marked improvement in the Pap test, she would think of surgery. Karen agreed.

I took her case and gave her the appropriate remedy based on her constitution. It was a 30C potency; very low as a matter of fact, given one time. Two months later she got the Pap test and it came back normal! Her doctors were open-mouthed. They said it was impossible. They re-tested her. The Pap came back normal again. It has been a year since Karen took the remedy and she is continuing to make positive changes for herself in all departments of her life because her constitutional homeopathic remedy is giving her back her health on all levels of herself. She is more confident, able to speak up for herself, able to say "no," and she is no longer allowing people to use her as a "doormat," in her words. And best of all, she was saved from surgery!

If you are getting Pap smears that are indicating a change in the cellular structure of your cervix, consult a homeopath in your area and be constitutionally cared for. There is NO acute remedy for cervical cell dysplasia. This must be treated on a deep constitutional level. But, in my mind, that is better than going to surgery!

HOMEOPATHIC REMEDIES FOR FLOODING DURING MENSES

1. China (Cinchona Bark)
2. Kali Muriaticum (Kali Mur.)
3. Lachesis Muta (Lachesis)
4. Natrum Muriaticum (Nat. Mur.)
5. Sabina
6. Secale Cornutum (Secale)
7. Sepia
8. Ustilago Maydis (Ustilago)

HOMEOPATHIC REMEDIES FOR FIBROIDS OF THE UTERUS

This is a condition that only a professional homeopath can prescribe for. There are more than 60 homeopathic remedies in our pharmacopoeia for fibroids of the uterus. Your case must be taken, as an individual, and then a single remedy found that corresponds to all your symptoms.

I'm going to list some of the more prominent ones, but this list by no means covers the only remedies available for uterine fibroids. If you think there's a match between you and the symptoms of a remedy listed below, please take this book and show the remedy to your homeopath so that he or she can make a final determination. You should not use self-treatment in fibroid cases—work with your gynecologist and homeopath simultaneously for best results.

HOMEOPATHIC REMEDIES FOR FIBROIDS

1. Aurum Muriaticum Natronatum (Aurum Mur. Nat.)
2. Aurum Muriaticum (Aurum Mur.)
3. Aurum Metallicum (Aurum Met.)
4. Thlaspi Bursa Pastoris (Thlaspi)

HOMEOPATHIC REMEDIES FOR VAGINISMUS (spasms in the vagina)

1. Belladonna
2. Cactus Grandiflorus (Cactus Grand.)
3. Coffea Cruda (Coffea)
4. Ignatia Amara (Ignatia)
5. Platina
6. Plumbum Metallicum (Plumbum)

HOMEOPATHIC REMEDIES FOR DRY VAGINA OR POOR LUBRICATION

1. Aconitum Napellus (Aconite)
2. Belladonna
3. Lycopodium
4. Natrum Muriaticum (Nat. Mur.)
5. Sepia
6. Staphysagria

HOMEOPATHIC REMEDIES FOR VAGINAL ITCHING

1. Caladium
2. Hydrocotyle
3. Natrum Muriaticum (Nat. Mur.)
4. Sepia
5. Sulphur
6. Tarentula Hispania (Tarentula)

CHAPTER 6

OUR BLADDER AND KIDNEYS: KEEPING THEM STRONG

WHAT CAUSES PROBLEMS FOR MY BLADDER AS I GO THROUGH MENOPAUSE?

Age, more than menopause, is the cause for a few of us. The epithelial cells, those that create our skin, begin to weaken. The urethra, the tube that leads from the neck of our bladder to the outside world, loses muscle tone over the years. Our bladder sits right behind our vagina, so if you have a sensation of pressure during intercourse or if you experience loss of bladder control during your partner's thrust into your vagina, incontinence can occur.

In an extreme and very *RARE* case, our muscles may relax too much, and the organs in our abdomen may collapse against one another. For instance, our uterus may "fall," which will force our cervix to rest on or enter our vaginal tract. If you have this sense of pressure or a feeling of protrusion, it might be a descending rectum, or uterus, or even your bladder and you should get it confirmed by your gynecologist.

For most of us, our urethra loses some of its muscle tone and it may not contract fully upon certain occasions, such as the act of laughing, sneezing, coughing, or lifting a heavy object, which may cause us to lose some urine. This is known as incontinence. In many cases, it can be controlled.

Also, our vaginal tract loses lactobacilli, which make lactic acid and help keep the pH low, which discourages the growth of what is known as uropathogens, which are responsible for causing cystitis infections. As we move into menopause, the pH increases in our vagina. The lactobacilli disappear from our "flora" and another flora called *Escherichia coli*, or *E. coli*, predominates instead. Scientists hypothesize that the multiplication of *E. coli* is responsible for many women's repeated cystitis infections or susceptibility to them. The good news is that homeopathy can stop cystitis infections in most instances.

HOW CAN I STOP MY INCONTINENCE?

Lack of exercise may induce some of these problems for us. There is an activity known as the Kegel exercises that may help. Some of you may already know about them because you have had children and you want to restore your vagina to its previous strength and tightness and promote bladder control.

All of you are familiar with sitting on a toilet seat and after urinating, you squeeze the muscles of the urethra. These are known as the pubococcygeus muscles, or the PC muscles. This contraction, if done daily, can bolster the weakened muscles of the urethra and make them strong to the point of halting urine leakage or incontinence. The recommended way to start flexing and strengthening our muscles in this part of our body is by doing two sets of 10 Kegels per day. You contract your muscles for 3 seconds, relax for 3 seconds, and then repeat. Slowly build up to 10 seconds. Over time, you should have a goal of being able to contract and relax those specific sets of muscles up to 10 sets daily.

You can also lie down on your back while doing this exercise. Doing it this way, you are also "massaging" not only your PC muscles, but those in your abdomen as well—which is a bonus! All you need to do is lie on your back with your knees bent and feet flat on the floor. You raise your pelvis until you feel a "pull" and then begin the squeezing exercise described above.

For many of us, this set of exercises will take care of our incontinence problem. However, incontinence can come from another area.

WHAT ELSE CAN CAUSE URINARY INCONTINENCE?

Those of us who have hardening of the arteries may experience a powerful urge to urinate—usually, during the evening or night hours. Your incontinence may result from a kidney or bladder infection. Give a urine sample to your doctor for testing to see if this is so. If you are diabetic, this may cause a frequent as well as an urgent sensation to urinate, too. Incontinence can occur because of a spinal cord injury, or during a mild or violent epileptic seizure. There are many types of incontinence.

Having had children via Cesarean section, having a hysterectomy or repeated pregnancies, drinking too much alcohol, having uterine fibroids, or having a history of constipation can also induce incontinence. Surgery of any kind that involves our pelvic floor region may be setting us up for weakened muscles in this region regardless of our age, but it can begin to be noticeable as we enter menopause and can gradually worsen much later.

If your labor was long (what one does not seem like that, right?) it could have stretched and weakened the bladder muscles and injured the nervous control mechanism. During labor, our urethra, which is short to begin with, suffers from being stretched or distended by the baby we carry.

I would strongly advise every woman to get a yearly check up, particularly during pre-menopause and menopause. Many of our problems can be traced to something specific. And knowing what THAT is, helps us in the long term. For instance, if your urinary incontinence is due to weakening muscles, all you need to do is begin the daily Kegel exercises.

I UNDERSTAND THAT THERE ARE A LOT OF DIFFERENT TYPES OF INCONTINENCE. IF SO, WHAT ARE THEY?

Urge incontinence is preceded by a desire to urinate. If this happens, the first thing for you to check for is a bladder infection. Other reasons for this type of incontinence are bladder stones, multiple sclerosis, or spina bifida occulta. Working with your gynecologist and homeopath, you can have the best of both worlds and cure this type once and for all.

Stress incontinence occurs when you sneeze, cough, laugh, or in some way strain your abdominal muscles—such as lifting a heavy object. The urinary sphincter does not contract enough to hold the urine in the bladder, and drainage or dribble occurs. This is the type of incontinence most post-menopausal women experience and homeopathic remedies are of great help in this type of situation. I had this particular symptom at age 52, and taking Lachesis cured it.

Overflow incontinence occurs when the bladder is overfilled with urine, and overcomes the urinary sphincter's resistance. Causes vary widely, but include prostate cancer for men, stricture of the urethral meatus (in children particularly), and spinal cord injuries. Common sense can prevail here, especially in the adult, and you go to the bathroom before you are ready to burst!

Ectopic incontinence is known as ectopic ureter in women. There is leaking, day and night, even though you may void urine normally. Surgical correction is necessary to solve this type of incontinence.

Psychogenic incontinence is usually seen in a child who otherwise displays the ability to void normally. They "fake" the incontinence to gain some form of emotional attention. If no pathology is uncovered in a careful work-up, then a therapist may be of value along with constitutional prescribing from a homeopath to correct this.

Functional incontinence occurs in elderly people who have no functional or organic problems with their urinary anatomy parts, but because of confusion, drug medications, or the inability to get to the toilet fast enough, there is leakage or dribbling. Homeopathic remedies can help this form of incontinence. Check the drugs you are on, too. Talk with your pharmacist to see if the drug(s) can cause incontinence as a side-effect.

Urinary fistula occur when there is a trauma to the body from an accident, a bullet wound, or a tumor. These usually occur in women. This may be helped with homeopathy, but if the organic damage is too great, then other measures will have to be taken instead.

Neurogenic bladder dysfunction is due to an injury to the nerves that serve the bladder. It can be caused by a disease in the brain, a spinal cord injury, or a congenital abnormality. Homeopathy may be able to help so long as there has been no major organic damage sustained.

There are other types of incontinence, but these are the categories MOST women fall into. Remember this: If you have involuntary loss of urine, go to your doctor and be examined and tested to rule out any of the other reasons for incontinence. Homeopathy can't fix a congenitally or organically damaged piece of our anatomy. It MIGHT be able to palliate or help in some way, but it can't cure it. If your doctor says "surgery," be sure to get at least two more opinions besides his before electing this option.

ARE THERE ANY COMMON-SENSE REMEDIES TO HELP STOP MY INCONTINENCE?

Yes. If you are going through menopause, I would strongly suggest that you do not drink a lot of liquids before going to bed—this will just invite incontinence because some of us will wake up in the middle of the night and go void, and some of us won't—and this strains our bladder muscles to the max and can weaken them until, finally, we begin to dribble, whether we are awake or asleep. Apple and orange juice, in particular, should not be consumed before bedtime as they seem to stimulate the bladder more than most other fruit drinks.

Drink plenty of liquids during the day to keep your kidneys flushed. My Grandmother Inez drank 4 ounces of cranberry juice daily and I never saw her get incontinence—and she was 99 years old before she left us.

Establish a normal pattern of urination. You can set the clock to get you up to urinate every 2 or 3 hours at night. The body is a sentient being and can be "retrained." So, if your incontinence always strikes at night, when you are asleep—it is time to retrain that body of yours.

ARE THERE PSYCHOLOGICAL REASONS FOR MY INCONTINENCE?

There can be. Some homeopaths, such as myself, look at the organs of our body as more than just a piece of equipment. We see them in a symbolic sense, too. Louise Hays has done a great deal of educating in this area—she sees our parts as first, connected to everything else, and second, in a symbolic sense, too.

I was taught by my Eastern Cherokee father that every organ in our body is more than just a working part of us. Our thoughts, emotions, experiences, traumas, grief, and anger can all influence different organs or systems of our body. As a homeopath, I see this all the time. Of late, the medical world has finally begun to catch up with us and they are just beginning to recognize the mind-body connection. Dr. Deepak Chopra has done a great deal to bring this concept not only to the public, but to medical people as well. Thank goodness!!

I see the bladder as a sac. And sacs 'hold' things. In this case, it holds poisons and toxins that, if not expelled by us, would eventually end up killing us. These 'things' reside in the form of water. Water, for me, is symbolic of our feelings and emotions. In my practice, I have seen a goodly number of people who have suffered with incontinence, bladder infections, or kidney infections and inevitably, a week or two, or even a month before the problem manifested, they had some kind of angry confrontation or experienced rage—but they were unable to express it or effectively "fight" for themselves or their truth in that situation.

I have seen some patients who are caught in a 'victim's mentality' and they are very angry, but they can't give voice to their anger. So it "simmers" silently somewhere else in the body. In their case, the bladder becomes a scalding hot, burning sac holding a lot of rage—which is probably justified—but they can't express it or act upon it—so it "blows up" in the body and the anger is turned inward on the individual, themselves. Then, the symptoms for incontinence, bladder trouble, or kidney infection appear.

Also, the adrenal glands produce our "fight or flight" hormones—adrenaline—and they sit atop each of our kidneys. Our kidneys are the organs responsible for cleaning up our blood and getting rid of the poisons and toxins. It makes sense to me that if one has been victimized in some way, mentally, emotionally, spiritually, or physically, that there's a lot of justified rage lurking SOMEWHERE in the body. It is just a question of WHERE.

My own mother, Ruth, who is 82, struggles to show her anger—she came from a generation of women who were taught not to display any anger toward anyone. Consequently, she's had bladder problems the last third of her life. She's been treated homeopathically from a constitutional standpoint by my good friend, Dr. Todd Rowe, MD (H), because I'm too close to her case to take it objectively. Todd has treated her constitutionally—not acutely for her bladder symptoms. This partly corrected the situation and I watched over the last 2 years as her bouts with urinary problems lessened by 50 percent. Later, I took over my mother's case to treat her acutely with a remedy that has corrected the condition completely.

What is even more interesting to watch is that my mother is now spouting off and learning how to give voice to her anger and display it—which is great! The constitutional homeopathic remedy helped her become healthy in many ways and on many levels—and one of those is the emotional level.

After Todd's help with Ruth's constitutional remedy, I saw another set of symptoms arise and treated her with Candida Albicans, a nosode remedy for those who have an over-proliferation of candida in their body. Many women get incontinence due to a loss of pH balance, and in her case, it was the final situation to be addressed. She has allowed herself to be in touch with all of her positive as well as negative emotional states and is able to voice them. With candida being given to her homeopathically, her voiding problems have abated dramatically.

YOU'RE SAYING THAT MY ANGER, IF NOT SHOWN OR GIVEN VOICE, CAN CONTRIBUTE TO MY INCONTINENCE?

Yes, it can. But before we all jump on this bandwagon, you still need to be cleared by your doctor to make sure there's no infection and nothing is organically wrong with your bladder or kidney parts.

If your incontinence is there—for no known medical reason (unknown etiology)—then I feel we should look at how we handle our anger. Do we? Do we display it? Are we in touch with our anger? Many women are not, because in our society, until very recently, women were not allowed to voice much of anything at any time—especially their anger.

In my experience, few women of my mother and grandmother's generation were ever allowed to show anger, among other feelings. In my generation, the 1940s group, we started to change that. I had to learn how to be in touch with my anger, too, and also, how to effectively and POSITIVELY express it. Women need to allow themselves the feelings of anger. After that, we need to learn how to effectively manage it.

By being on a homeopathic constitutional remedy, you will get healthy on all levels—that means being in touch with ALL of our emotions—the good ones and the bad ones, too. It makes us a whole, complete, and fully functioning human being. So, if your bladder is giving you trouble, ask yourself: "What am I really pissed off about?" Surprisingly, if you can get in touch with that answer (and you can), and if you can accordingly act upon it in a positive way, many times a woman's incontinence or infections will cease.

I'VE NOTICED THAT EVERY TIME I GET A BLADDER INFECTION, I DRIBBLE! THIS IS A KIND OF URINARY INCONTINENCE, TOO, ISN'T IT?

Most assuredly, it is. And, what is very surprising is that many times there is a low-grade bladder infection causing the incontinence in many of us and we do not even realize it! Did you know that 25 percent of post-menopausal women get a symptomless variety of bladder infection?

If you are having bladder incontinence, go to your gynecologist and get yourself checked to see if you have a low-grade bladder infection. If you do, this may be the potential cause of your incontinence problem. Homeopathically, there's much we can do to cure bladder infections with specific remedies, and they'll be listed below. Sometimes a homeopathic remedy won't cure a stubborn case of bladder infections, and then antibiotics do have to be used to clear it up. If this is the case, then get to your homeopath for constitutional treatment—which will end up treating this stubborn bladder infection problem down the line so that you won't have to keep going on antibiotics to clear up the next one.

JUST WHAT ARE THE SIGNS OF A BLADDER INFECTION?

There are many reasons for contracting a bladder infection and I'll list them. First, a true story to share with you: For a period of 2 years, I had cystitis every month, just before my menses. This was another of those times when the medical establishment failed me and drove me into looking for alternative medicine as an answer.

I would get burning, scalding pain before voiding, and during voiding. And then, it would only dribble out!! I would sit on the toilet seat crying because I was in so much pain. The doctor put me on a sulfa drug that turned my urine orange (and also stained my panties and other clothes and ruined them). I'd be on this sulfa drug for 10 days and then the very next month, here came the bladder infection once again. After 24 episodes of this, I got sick and tired of it, of the pain, and of the medical world not knowing how to help me and giving me drugs! I'm just not a pill popper!

One doctor told me not to use bubble baths, to be sure and wipe "front to back" with the toilet paper, to wear cotton panties, not nylon or other types of fabrics, and to stay away from tampons and go to external pads only during my menses. This is all sound advice—unfortunately, in my case, it didn't help at all. However, you should know that anything we put into the bath water is usually sucked up a little bit by our urethra as we sit in the tub. These chemicals or detergents can cause a bladder infection. If you wear non-cotton panties, the discharge from your vagina can be rubbed up into the urethra, causing an infection. If we wear cotton panties, for most of us, the discharge is absorbed by the fabric and halts potential infection.

Tampons also interfere with the urethra by squeezing it, and potentially stopping some drops of urine from flowing freely downward, and that can cause an infection. I made all these changes, which are predicated on common sense. My infection persisted.

At that point, I began to aggressively study my disease, cystitis. I found out it was caused by *E. coli* bacteria, which we all have in our bowels. Once it gains entrance to this region of our body, it multiplies rapidly and voilà, we get an infection.

At another point, another doctor suspected kidney-related infection, so I had an intravenous pyelogram—a fancy word for drinking some barium so they could take X-ray pictures of my kidneys as it flowed through to see if there was a problem. There was none.

In reading, I discovered that the ureters, those long thin tubes that emerge from our kidneys and connect into our bladder, have valves on them. Ideally, if everything is working great, these valves close up as we urinate. If there has been damage, or if they are genetically missing or weakened, then urine can "sneak" back up into the ureter and in doing so, cause pyleonephritis, or a kidney infection.

The X-rays found that my valves were there and in good working order, so the root cause of my problem was not organic. But I was still having monthly bladder infections! In desperation, I drank lots of cranberry juice to flush the kidneys and drank lots of extra water until I sloshed as I walked, but I still had the problem.

I finally discovered the culprit through educating myself in technical libraries and medical books: my husband, who had returned from Vietnam 2 years earlier, had contracted gonorrhea—and of course, had passed it on to me—only I got the symptom of chronic cystitis. I cured myself of the gonorrhea infection along with the cystitis with a homeopathic remedy. Since then, I have never had a recurrence of cystitis.

STDs—sexually transmitted diseases—can be a culprit, too. So be sure to get tested to find out—THAT was the cause of my problems!

I HAVE KIDNEY INFECTIONS THAT CAUSE MY BLADDER INFECTION. CAN ANYTHING BE DONE TO HELP MY INCONTINENCE?

Yes, it can—but this depends on many things. Homeopathy cannot cure an organic problem, such as no valve in your ureter tube—which will leave you wide open to continued and chronic kidney infections. However, it might in some instances strengthen a weak valve that does not close entirely. It can strengthen muscle tissue and help your valves and your urethra simultaneously. In cases where, like my own, there is no seeming reason for the incontinence or cystitis or kidney infections—and all avenues have been exhausted medically speaking—then I would step in with a homeopathic remedy through a homeopathic practitioner.

Symptoms of a kidney infection are many: pain in the region of the kidney that's infected (usually it is one or the other) in your back, shivering, a temperature between 101 and 103 degrees, a headache, and pain before, during, or after voiding. There can be blood in your urine, too, which is a very serious sign. If you have any of these symptoms, get to your doctor right away. After you've gotten treatment, then see a homeopathic practitioner for a long-term cure of this problem—if it is curable.

I'VE HEARD THAT SURGERY WILL CURE MY INCONTINENCE.

Before you consider surgery, which I consider the LAST resort, you should know that in a study on the use of surgery to halt urinary incontinence, 25 percent of the women experienced no improvement afterward, 25 percent improved only slightly, and 50 percent of the women couldn't empty their bladders after this surgery! That 50 percent had to learn how to catheterize themselves. Those aren't good odds to me. I would exhaust all other means and then if surgery was truly the only way to go—I would get at least three opinions before proceeding.

If surgery is the only recourse, then certain homeopathic remedies should be considered to help you heal up more quickly (see the appendix for remedies after surgery).

CAN HOMEOPATHY HELP MY INCONTINENCE?

Yes, it can. One of my Navajo patients, Darleen Whitney, who is revered because her husband, who recently died, was the last of the great traditional medicine men, came to me with this problem, plus her arthritis.

Darleen had urinary incontinence, and so did her daughter. I took their cases homeopathically, and different remedies were used to cure their problem, but the result was the same: they had no more incontinence. Those remedies are listed below.

HOMEOPATHIC REMEDIES FOR URINARY INCONTINENCE

1. Apis Mellifica (Apis)
2. Arsenicum Album (Arsenicum)
3. Cantharis
4. Causticum
5. Muriaticum Acidum (Mur. Ac.)
6. Natrum Muriaticum (Nat. Mur.)
7. Pulsatilla
8. Sepia
9. Squilla Martima (Squilla)

CHAPTER 7

OUR LEGS: INCREASING OUR CIRCULATION AND GETTING RID OF OUR CRAMPS

MY LEGS SEEM TO BE FALLING APART ON ME SINCE I'VE ENTERED MENOPAUSE. WHAT'S GOING ON?

Age slows us down in many ways—most of them not the fault of peri-menopause or menopause itself. It's just that time in our lives when the wearing and tearing we've done to ourselves catches up with us, usually beginning in our mid-forties.

We see varicose veins begin to appear, and we may start to get cramps in our calves, or experience pain in our legs, which is known as intermittent claudication. Our ankles or feet start getting puffy from time to time, or prickling, burning sensations known as chilblains may surface, which can be quite painful. Phlebitis may strike some of us, a condition where the blood clots in one of the superficial veins of the leg, or varicose ulcers. We'll discuss the less serious of these conditions in this chapter and how common sense and homeopathic remedies can work, hand-in-hand, to ease these discomforts of aging.

WHEN I TURNED 40, I SAW VARICOSE VEINS DEVELOPING IN MY LOWER LEGS. WHAT CAN BE DONE ABOUT THIS?

Varicosity is caused by too much pressure in our veins. If that occurs, the vein or veins begin to swell and distort themselves. They may not hurt at all—but just look ugly. Or, there can be pain or itching with them. Medically, they are called superficial thrombophlebitis. I call them "blow outs."

There are two types of varicose veins: primary and secondary. Primary varicosity is ugly to look at but not harmful to your health; it occurs in the "surface" veins of your legs. The other type, secondary, is far more serious because there's usually some kind of an obstruction or valve incompetence to the more deeply imbedded veins in our legs.

Usually those of us who stand for long periods of time or are lifting a lot of things are more prone to them. Because the circulation is slowed in these areas, a secondary symptom can pop up: itchy skin, which can be an unhealthy color, and if severe enough, can lead to eventual ulceration. If you have suffered an injury to your ankle or shin in your earlier years, this can make the situation worse, too.

Don't take varicose veins lightly—go to your doctor and discover the cause and reason for them appearing in the first place. It might involve osteoarthritis of the knee or hip area of your body, potential diabetes or alcoholic problems, arterial insufficiency, or lumbar nerve and root inflammation or irritation. All of these conditions have to be looked at and checked off by your medical doctor. If your varicose veins haven't been created by any of the above reasons, then there's a good chance that homeopathy can help you.

Our arteries send fresh blood, laden with oxygen, all around our body. It is the vein's job to take the blood back up to the heart. If the blood returning to the heart is slowed down, then a number of things can happen—among them, varicose veins, plus swelling of the ankles and feet.

Most women who get varicose veins don't need surgery—but some may in very serious circumstances. Again, check with your doctor first and find out.

IF MY VARICOSE VEINS ARE NOT CAUSED BY ANY OF THE ABOVE REASONS, WHAT CAN I DO TO GET RID OF THEM?

First, less standing or lifting of weighty objects will help. However, in reality, we may not be able to prevent these because we may have a job that demands a lot of standing, and we can't just quit our job! Try wearing support hose. You can also lift your legs up and rest them whenever possible.

The homeopathic remedies for varicose veins are listed below. Check with your local homeopath to administer the correct remedy for you.

I'M GETTING LEG CRAMPS AND I NEVER USED TO. WHAT IS GOING ON?

This is not menopause—this is aging catching up with us! Usually, leg cramps are due to our circulatory system becoming more sluggish with time and age. Or it can be that lactic acid, a waste by-product of our body, builds up in our calf muscles—particularly at night—and then as a result we wake up with cramps in the middle of the night. Other causes of leg cramping at night can be smoking, alcohol consumption, or fatigue (too much standing).

CAN HOMEOPATHY HELP MY NIGHTLY LEG CRAMPS?

In most instances, yes. But first, make sure that your so-called cramps aren't something more serious such as phlebitis, a blood clot in your leg. There could also be a magnesium, potassium, or calcium deficiency. Have your doctor examine you, check your diet, and if she gives you a clean bill of health, there are some homeopathic remedies that may help your particular situation.

WHEN I GET IN BED AT NIGHT, I JUST CAN'T KEEP MY LEGS FROM MOVING AROUND, TWITCHING, OR JERKING. WHAT IS GOING ON? IS MENOPAUSE AT WORK AGAIN?

We call this the "restless legs syndrome" and it is a condition that affects many people, men as well as women, in middle age. It has nothing to do with menopause. I started getting this condition about age 51, much to my consternation. It started shortly after my last menses. For the year that followed, I would, perhaps seven times a month, have restless legs. It is an interesting feeling. I would lie in bed, very tired and wanting to go to sleep. And then, I absolutely felt like I had to stretch first one leg, and then the other, outward. It felt good to really make those muscles stretch! As soon as I was done, I felt the need to do it again. And this would go on for half an hour or more. I would toss and turn; toss and turn. Sometimes I'd get up because I knew I was keeping my husband awake. As soon as I took Lachesis, this condition subsided considerably.

This condition can be due to insufficient minerals, such as calcium, magnesium, or potassium. Or possibly not enough vitamin D, which helps the body absorb calcium. The good news is that we have homeopathic remedies to help this condition and they are noted below.

HOMEOPATHIC REMEDIES FOR VARICOSE VEINS

1. Arnica Montana (Arnica)
2. Bellis Perennis (Bell. Per.)
3. Calcarea Carbonica (Calc. Carb.)
4. Causticum
5. Fluoricum Acidum (Fluor. Ac.)
6. Hamamelis Virginica (Hamamelis)
7. Lycopodium
8. Pulsatilla
9. Sulphur

HOMEOPATHIC REMEDIES FOR LEG CRAMPS AND LEG RESTLESSNESS

1. Arnica Montana (Arnica)
2. Calcarea Carbonica (Calc. Carb.)
3. Causticum
4. Cuprum Metallicum (Cuprum Met.)
5. Pulsatilla
6. Rhus Toxicodendron (Rhus Tox.)

CHAPTER 8

OUR SKIN AND HAIR: Getting Rid of Hot Flashes, Dealing With Itching, and Our Hair (too much in the wrong places or too little on our head!) And Why Do I Have Insomnia?

WHAT EXPERIENCE HAVE YOU HAD WITH HOT FLASHES?

When I turned 40, I thought of installing a fire alarm in my bedroom. In the middle of the night, I would bolt awake. Suddenly, I would feel as though a fire were coming up from my feet, sweeping upward and engulfing me. As these internal flames roared through me, I would break out into a heavy sweat that soaked the bedclothes. I never sweat very much, so to drench my nightclothes and sheets was unsettling—to put it mildly.

Well, I was right on target. This was peri-menopause—a transitional time from about 40 to 48, when women begin to experience menopause symptoms. Hot flashes are one of the clearest indicators.

I experienced several minor changes—but they were small potatoes compared to my hot flashes! From time to time, I would get day sweats, too—which were just as sudden, drenching, and uncomfortable. At age 51, my night sweats would wake me up in the middle of the night. This was an interesting turn of events compared to my earlier years of moving through menopause. Now, for the last 8 months, when I am going to have a night hot flash, I wake up instantly, and a minute later my flush and sweat occur. I might be awake 5 or 10 minutes, and then I drop right back to sleep. This occurs three to five times a night for me.

At first I thought: "Uh oh, sleep deprivation!" And I was right. Speaking from first-hand experience, I can say that night sweats are the MOST debilitating of all the menopausal symptoms. Why? Because over time, the woman becomes extremely sleep deprived. This will affect her work, her ability to think, her energy level, and her emotions. It is not unusual to see depression or the "blahs" creep in after a month or two of this kind of cycle. It is highly interesting as a scientific observer to see this going on! I also noticed another trend to this new cycle. The only time I got night sweats that woke me up was after my last menses. From a homeopathic standpoint, my body, my vital force, saw the ending of my menses as a form of suppression. And that is literally when all hell broke loose for me and I nose-dived into a viscious cycle that nearly broke me emotionally and physically speaking.

What was really occurring was that my pituitary gland was sending out the hormonal signal to the estrogen to 'switch on.' Well, my ovaries did not want to switch on, so they ignored the signal from the master gland, the pituitary. As a result, the pituitary incessantly continued to send the signal. Added to this endocrine recipe from Hell was the fact that my adrenal glands (they sit perched atop our kidneys) were being stimulated and were part and parcel of this "dance," which helped create hot flashes.

I have noted that when I do have a period, I do not get hot flashes or night sweats and am not awakened during the night. This may be different for other women, but it is important to note it here as an experience so that we have a baseline to work from and compare our own unique responses to. I have a 48-year-old friend who wakes up in horrific night sweats and she sweats through her nightgown and dampens the sheets, too!

To say I was miserable was an understatement. Finally, the professional homeopath in me took over and said: "Enough is enough!" I went to a friend, a professional homeopath, who took my case and prescribed Lachesis 30C for me. Just one dose gave me relief from my own peronsal hell of 9 months worth of sleep deprivation. From that point on, I began to remain asleep at night, I had fewer night sweats, and in general I had a life once again because I could get 8 hours of relatively uninterrupted sleep.

Folliculinum, another popular homeopathic remedy for all menopause symptoms, is often used in these cases. It was originally derived from a synthetic substance by Dr. Donald Foubister of England. It was created to closely approximate estrogen, the hormone produced by a woman's ovary glands. I have seen women whose symptoms paralleled this particular remedy—one dose, and they have not experienced a night sweat or hot flash since. Just imagine, we can cure ourselves of bothersome menopausal symptoms—with no help from hormone replacement therapy (HRT), either!

SO THERE ARE HOMEOPATHIC REMEDIES TO HELP ME WITH MY HOT FLASHES AND NIGHT SWEATS?

Yes, there are. In fact, homeopathy works by matching your specific symptoms to a remedy that produces similar symptoms. It is a case of like curing like. Low doses are often all that is needed. And how long you remain on a remedy simply depends on the persistence of your symptoms. Your homeopath will take your past medical history and review all of your current symptoms—mental, emotional, and physical. Then she will compile this information and select one remedy. And like me, hot flashes and night sweats will be a thing of the past for you too!

WHAT IS A HOT FLASH?

A hot flash is known as a "vasomotor instability," which means changing activity in the veins. In medical terminology, it is known as a "flush." In brief, your veins are constricting or dilating more than they used to. This is the "old" definition and explanation, which science is finding out is not true at all. Recent research and testing by the University Medical Center has determined that there is no constriction! Instead, what they found was that adrenal gland involvement is the seat—and the reason—for out hot flashes! The level of norephinephrine, one of our "flight or fight" hormones, made and distributed by the adrenals, rises significantly in our bloodstream during the time of the hot flash occurrence. Core body temperature does rise—but it is due to the release of this particular hormone and is not driven by peripheral vasoconstriction. This is a natural sign of your transition into menopause. Women are all different and so is the pattern of our hot flashes. If you have ever blushed, then you will get a real quick read on what a hot flash feels like!

During a hot flash, a woman may feel heat and may perspire, sometimes profusely. Her skin color can change from slightly pink to fire-engine red. For some women, redness will appear in streaks, spots, or blotches. For others, it will be an overall flush. This heat and high color may affect all, or only a part of the body. Some hot flashes may be followed by chills.

My hot flashes made me perspire enough to wipe my upper lip off with my fingers or dab my forehead. In my forties, my face would turn a dull red when I was having one. In my fifties, there is no change of color in my skin. In my forties, mine tended to start mid-torso and move upward; my whole body was not involved. However, now, at age 53, my night sweats and hot flashes sweep from my toes up to my head in seconds. Not only that, I get a warning sign of a biting, almost nerve-like pain or crawling sensation about 30 seconds before the flash or night sweat actually occurs. This is known as an "aura" and some women get this and some do not.

Hot flashes may come and go with varying length and frequency. They can last a few seconds, more commonly for a few minutes, or even up to an hour. Women may experience only one, or up to 50 hot flashes a day. Two years is the length of time most of us experience hot flashes, but they can span just a few months to 5 years. I have been experiencing hot flashes on and off since my early forties. They tend to show up if I do not have a monthly period. Since my period has ceased for 8 months, I get 20 or so hot flashes a day, which is more than what I had in my late forties. Plus those nasty night sweats have increased my sleep deprivation. Because hot flashes are so varied, the only way to arrive at a successful homeopathic treatment is to use the remedy that responds to your specific experience.

WHAT CAUSES HOT FLASHES?

The medical jury is still out on the question of what causes hot flashes. Although there is no test currently available that can precisely pinpoint their onset, there are two prevailing theories. One implies a connection with estrogen levels, the other does not.

A good deal of evidence points to the hypothalamus gland as the instigator of the hot flash phenomenon. The hypothalamus is the temperature regulator inside the pituitary gland, deep in the center of the brain. Before menopause, the hypothalamus kicks off an amazing monthly cycle featuring a hormonal chain reaction.

The cycle begins when the hypothalamus secretes the hormone gonadotrophin (GnRH) into the bloodstream. The release of GnRH tells the ovaries to 'switch on' estrogen. Then, in the presence of estrogen, the pituitary gland releases FSH (follicle-stimulating hormone). And at this signal, the ovaries release an egg.

As each month's egg develops in the ovary, the pituitary gland secretes another hormone. This hormone stimulates the ovary to release the egg into the Fallopian tube for its downward journey into the uterus. If the egg is fertilized, a pregnancy results; if it is not fertilized, the egg washes out of the body with the menstrual blood.

Each woman has a certain number of eggs that may be fertilized during her lifetime. As menopause approaches, there are fewer eggs left to expel each month from the ovaries. Estrogen and progesterone levels begin to decline. But GnRH doesn't give up easily. Even if there are no eggs left for the GnRH to stimulate, the hormone still persists for a time—sending signal after signal to the ovaries. The resulting symptom is hot flashes and night sweats!

One theory is that these GnRH signals are partly responsible for triggering hot flashes. Eventually, with no response from the egg, the body stops sending the GnRH messages. Then, hot flashes cease. If GnRH is really responsible, then a direct correlation between decreasing estrogen levels and hot flashes exists.

Another, less popular theory is that during menopause the adrenal glands secrete sporadic bursts of adrenaline into the bloodstream. This causes hot flashes. And there is finally proof that this theory is correct. Adrenaline is our hormonal "fight or flight" response to perceived threats. When adrenaline pours in, we experience many of the effects of hot flashes—a pounding heart, sweating, and shakiness or trembling. If adrenaline is indeed the trigger, then hot flashes may NOT be correlated with decreasing estrogen levels.

In my own experimentation with this last theory, I drink coffee (when not on a homeopathic remedy). Caffeine is well known to trigger the adrenal glands. One of the no-no's during menopause is drinking coffee because it stimulates hot flashes. I can drink a few sips of coffee and I can guarantee myself a hot flash right after that. Caffeine DOES stimulate the adrenal glands, so I'm of the opinion that the adrenals are locked into this "dance" on hot flashes and night sweats to some degree or another. It was nice to see that a recent study corroborates my own observations and findings. We can thank the adrenal glands for this—which is why some women get allergies during menopause. The adrenals, once again, are part and parcel of the immune system balance and strength. If they are being triggered constantly, then our immune system is going to be slightly weaker or lowered. Hence, we may get allergies to things we never had trouble with before (I certainly have!). The good news is that once the adrenal glands stop getting triggered, the allergies—and the hot flashes—subside and finally go away. Hooray!

WHO GETS HOT FLASHES?

There is no typical profile of a woman who gets hot flashes, but there are some factors that can influence them. For example, women who have had both their ovaries removed during a hysterectomy tend to suffer the longest-lasting and most severe hot flashes. This is because the ovaries are normally partners in a vital hormonal dance. If they are removed, an important component of a woman's constitution is gone, and this may create a permanent imbalance in her already sensitive system. She may thus experience severe menopausal symptoms, including very intense hot flashes. In natural, non-surgical menopause, however, there is a much more gradual decline in ovarian function.

Women who are thin also tend to experience more intense hot flashes than those with a little more fat cell padding. One reason may be that hormones are stored in body fat, so that heavier women may not deplete their supply as readily.

There are also racial and cultural factors—some known and some unknown—affecting the occurrence of hot flashes. Estimates are that 50–60 percent of Caucasian women will get hot flashes. Worldwide statistics, however, indicate that in some countries, only 25 percent of women have them; in others up to 85 percent experience this uncomfortable but natural phenomenon. And in another study, 69 percent of all Canadian women had hot flashes. In a U.S. study, only 40 percent of women got hot flashes.

Interestingly, only 20 percent of Japanese women experience hot flashes. Some studies suggest a connection with their consumption of foods, like tofu, that contain natural phytoestrogens (plant estrogens). And the Mayan Indian women of Mexico report no menopausal symptoms at all, including hot flashes! My theory as to why Mayan menopause goes so gently is that Mayan women are respected and honored throughout every stage of their lives. Their bodies' functions are considered sacred from puberty through motherhood and 'cronehood'—and at menopause, they are considered to be at the peak of their experience and wisdom. Therefore, I believe, they enter the transition with much less psychological stress, and experience only negligible symptoms.

A number of other cultures around the world—largely Africa and the Far East—also have a very low incidence of hot flashes. Very possibly, both diet and a culture's philosophy about women—and their stress levels—influence how women experience menopause. Although research hasn't proven why some cultures have such a low incidence, I suspect that matriarchal societies, and those with spiritual values characterized by gentleness and compassion, contribute to a less stressful menopause.

HOW CAN I RELIEVE MY HOT FLASHES?

Hot flashes are not life-threatening, just uncomfortable, at times embarrassing, and always poorly timed. Here are some common-sense tips that seem to help during this period of instability:

* Wear clothes in layers, so you can add or subtract as you need to. I suggest wearing cotton or silk versus your unnatural types of fabric because they "breathe" and believe me, you will want to rip these clothes off during an intense hot flash. Anything that breathes does give you some relief—you might be someplace where you cannot divest yourself of your clothes in a hurry!
* Drink a lot of liquids, especially water and natural fruit juices—without sugar, of course. Sugar is rich in oxalic acid, which can prevent absorption of the calcium you need to keep your bones strong and healthy.
* Stay away from alcohol, coffee, and tea. Coffee and alcohol are particularly intense stimulants for the adrenal glands. I have a glass of wine every night for medicinal purposes, and I can take one sip of it and voilà! Within a minute, I have a hot flash. Same holds true for the coffee I drink. I've not noticed it with tea, however.
* Avoid spicy foods, which trigger hot flashes in some women. "Bland is in" for some of us, at least for awhile! If I eat some chili I will get a hot flash. I personally am not going to give up my spicy food just because of a hot flash. That is your decision, however.

CAN I PREDICT WHEN THEY'LL STRIKE?

Most hot flashes seem to occur between 6:00 a.m. and 8:00 a.m., or between 6:00 p.m. and 10:00 p.m. Some women report a hazy, confused, or somewhat 'spacey' feeling 5–10 minutes before the actual hot flash. This is nothing to be concerned about, as these are natural sensations. This is the "aura" sensation that I spoke of earlier. Mine resembles an almost nerve-like pain or prickling sensation on the surface of my skin and it sweeps from my toes up to my head in a millisecond! And within 15–60 seconds after that, here comes the hot flash or the night sweat.

Melissa Assilem, a homeopath in London, England, has a unique way to help women track the cycle of their hot flashes. She uses a 28-day lunar calendar, which shows the phase of the moon for each day. Melissa has her patients write down when a hot flash occurs. After recording their hot flashes for 2 or 3 months, these women can predict when they'll strike. Then, forewarned is forearmed!

WHY SHOULDN'T I TAKE HORMONES FOR A HOT FLASH?

Although hormonal drugs may stop hot flashes, I do not advocate their use until other complementary forms of medicine are tried without success. Besides, it is the adrenal glands that are knee-jerking, not the ovaries. Why would someone want to take estrogen when that is not what really needs to be addressed? It is our adrenal glands. I'm not an advocate of using an adrenal-hormone pill to "fix" it, either. Homeopathy can certainly respond to it, instead. You may want to look at your diet, nutrition (vitamins and minerals), herbs, acupuncture, or homeopathy. Personally, I wouldn't want ANY unnecessary drug in my body—particularly one that increases my risk of uterine or breast cancer markedly. See Chapter 3 for more on hormone replacement therapy.

WHAT HOMEOPATHIC REMEDIES CAN I USE FOR MY HOT FLASHES?

Remedies are listed at the end of this section. Go back to the Materia Medica and look them up. These remedies are each keyed to a particular set of symptoms. Remember, homeopathy is based upon 'like cures like," and respects the fact that you are an individual, with individual symptoms that may not be exactly like anyone else's symptoms.

A homeopath will match your unique set of hot flash symptoms to one of 1,400 homeopathic remedies that are FDA approved here in the United States. Therefore, there is a very good chance that one of these is just right for you. The remedies mentioned at the end of this section are used most often. About 75 percent of women will find that one of them will be a fit. If you do not find your particular set of symptoms among these, an experienced homeopath can find the correct remedy for your hot flashes. Check in the appendix at the back of this book to locate the homeopath nearest you.

CAN I TAKE MORE THAN ONE HOMEOPATHIC REMEDY?

The classically trained homeopath, such as myself, believes in this saying: One remedy, one dose, one time, and then wait. The reason that classical homeopaths work with only one remedy at a time is to let your body reveal how, and in what order, your symptoms change after you take a remedy.

If you take two or more remedies (also known as polypharmacy or combination remedies), we do not know *which* remedy helped you. Only one of those remedies is really working at curing you, and usually at very low potency. When you need a higher potency (to be evaluated by your homeopath), the homeopath will not know which remedy to increase! So, to best help yourself and your homeopath, take only one remedy, one time, and then wait.

CAN I CHOOSE MY OWN HOMEOPATHIC REMEDY FROM THIS LIST OR MUST I CONSULT A PROFESSIONAL HOMEOPATH?

Generally speaking, if you do not fit the symptom picture of the remedies below, or if you are unsure which is most appropriate, you should consult a professional homeopath.

First, look at the remedies presented below. Read up on them in the Materia Medica at the back of this book. If you recognize yourself in the symptom picture of one of them, you should take the information from this book to your professional homeopath, discuss it, and receive the appropriate remedy. It is absolutely essential to work with a professional homeopath because you can ask a skilled practitioner questions about your homeopathic treatment.

CAN NUTRITION HELP EASE HOT FLASHES?

Absolutely! A good alternative approach to menopause symptoms is through high-quality nutrition. Vitamin, mineral, and herbal supplements can help, too. Because there is adrenal gland involvement, two "foods" that support this gland are vitamin C and pantothenic acid. Ask your physician for specific amounts, or go to the back of this book to the section on vitamins and minerals and read up on them.

One option is orange juice fortified with calcium citrate. Just taking 4 to 8 ounces daily, along with 400 IUs (International Units) of vitamin D in fish liver oil, can stop hot flashes and night sweats in some women. However, avoid using calcium supplements made from bone meal (dolomite) because of a possible high lead content. Women with a history of kidney stones need to talk to their urologist about this, as they tend to form stones out of calcium intake and this is not what you want to do. Clear it with your physician first.

Why is calcium so important? This mineral makes up more than half of the total mineral component of our bodies, so it's vital to every function. It keeps our hearts beating, gives strength to our bones and teeth, and supports metabolism and the healthy function of our muscles and nerves. Without enough calcium, our blood would not clot, our gums would bleed, and our bones would weaken.

Interestingly, some calcium deficiency symptoms parallel the symptoms of menopause, such as heart palpitations, softening of the bones (osteoporosis, which is a disease), bleeding gums, slow blood clotting, insomnia, depression, forgetfulness, mood swings, headaches, tension, and weight gain. This is why adequate calcium is one of the nutritional pillars of menopause. But so is taking care of our adrenal glands with vitamin C and pantothenic acid.

Women also sing the praises of vitamins E and C to cool off hot flashes. When taking vitamin E, be sure to choose the superior D-alpha tocopherol form, not the less effective Dl-alpha. A safe dose is 100 IUs daily. And add 2,000–3,000 mg of vitamin C to your daily regimen (from natural sources such as rose hips or acerola cherries). If your stomach cannot tolerate natural vitamin C, try the synthetic version—ascorbic acid.

In a study by N. R. Kavinosky, MD, 10–25 IUs of vitamin E were given to 92 menopausal patients. Thirty-seven women stopped having hot flashes. When Dr. Kavinosky increased the dosage to 50–100 IUs daily, 75 percent of the women in the group stopped having hot flashes. Half also reported improved sleep patterns, less fatigue and nervous strain, fewer heart palpitations, and less shortness of breath. Vitamin E supplements often bring positive changes in as quickly as 1 or 2 weeks.

In addition to vitamins and minerals, hot flash symptoms may be helped by a particular herb. In my opinion, vitamins, minerals, and herbs are secondary (but sometimes, necessary) supports that prop up an out-of-balance body. But if, like many busy women, your diet skimps on important nutrients such as calcium, supplements can be an important safeguard. When you stop taking them, however, their protective benefits vanish.

Fortunately, that isn't true of homeopathy. Homeopathic remedies coax the body into bringing itself back into balance by stimulating its own organs and systems, to place itself back into harmony once again. So, if your regular diet is healthy and varied, you can certainly consider using homeopathy instead of supplements. And you do not have to take homeopathic remedies daily, as you do vitamins and most herbal formulas. Most women need only take a homeopathic remedy once or twice. The hot flashes disappear, the body rebalances itself naturally, and there is no need to spend a lot of money on supplements.

If your hot flashes do reoccur, it means that, in your case, they cannot be treated as an acute problem, and you need to see a homeopath for a constitutional remedy. This remedy will treat *all* your menopausal symptoms once and for all, together.

CAN I MIX HERBS AND HOMEOPATHIC REMEDIES TO CURE MY HOT FLASHES?

This is not recommended. Vitamins, minerals, and herbs change the balance of your body chemistry, which makes it impossible to determine the appropriate remedy for your particular case. In other cases, the woman has to supplement with particular vitamins and minerals.

Generally speaking, there is a homeopathic remedy that will stop your hot flashes permanently. However, about 10 percent of the female population cannot benefit from homeopathy, because they are so sensitive to the remedies that they cannot take them without creating a "proving." A proving occurs when the symptoms that are supposed to be cured by a remedy are actually intensified by it. In these cases, your hot flash symptoms can probably be helped by herbs or vitamins or by flower and gem essences (see Chapter 20).

But for most of us, homeopathy alone is a powerful, effective form of complementary medicine that encourages and stimulates the body to cure itself. For women who do not have the luxury of having a homeopathic practitioner nearby, then flower and gem essences are a wonderful place to find help.

WHY IS IT SO HARD TO COPE WITH HOT FLASHES?

It is probably because we feel as if we are out of control, and that is very unsettling. Hot flashes come on suddenly, and usually at the most embarrassing times. We cannot predict or control how many times flashes will occur each day, either.

But then, when we were going from childhood into puberty and our hormones started engaging, we could not control that either—we just felt intensely sexual for the first time in our lives. For that matter, during our menstrual years, we often felt out of control of the changes going on in our bodies (swollen breasts, abdomen, etc.) and our emotions (hypersensitive, moodiness) either shortly before or during our menses. The signs then were just as obvious, sometimes, as hot flashes are now, as we enter menopause—the third cycle of our lives.

It would certainly be to our advantage if we could change our feelings about menopause. Why not a gracious surrendering to the signs of menopause, hot flashes included, instead of hitting the panic button and thinking something is wrong with us? That kind of thinking is old-fashioned and prevents us from keeping our self-image strong. Remember, all menopause changes are signs of *maturing*, not symptoms of illness. And they are ushering us into a brave new world of exciting changes and opportunities.

I'M GETTING A LOT OF UNWANTED HAIR ON MY FACE. WHAT'S GOING ON?

As we move through menopause we can have hair popping out in places we'd never seen it before—or, at least not in that quantity! I noticed at about age 42 that hair was growing out of the two moles on my face. At age 46, I began to have hair pop out on my chin—much to my amazement and consternation! Now, at age 53, it's settled into a routine of sorts. I do have more hair than "before" menopause.

Androgens, produced from the male hormones we have always had, made by our adrenal glands, are revealing themselves more and more as our estrogen begins to gradually decline (but never disappear). The androgens aren't suddenly becoming higher—nor are we becoming more masculine—they're at a fairly fixed level. Some women never experience this because they've got such high levels of estrogen to begin with. As their estrogen declines, they will not get any excessive hair growth like I did.

Estrogen is no longer as dominant as it was before menopause and the hair growth on our body will begin to imitate the male pattern of growth and distribution as a result of hormonal shifts.

If you end up with a "beard"—and this is a *very* rare occurrence—then you need to see an endocrinologist first to verify it. Then go see your homeopath for constitutional treatment to rebalance your endocrine system naturally—and without drug interference—and the hair will go away. The remedies at the end of this section may not necessarily include the one you need, so go see the professional homeopath for help.

I'VE SUDDENLY GOT HAIR GROWING AROUND MY NIPPLES, HAIR GROWING FROM MY BELLY BUTTON TO MY PUBES. IS THIS NORMAL?

Some of us may experience more hair around our nipples as we go through menopause. Even some hair sprouting between our breasts. Others of us may see a hairy line of demarcation right down the center of our abdomen between our belly button and pubes. This is nothing to be alarmed about it—it's a natural part of our menopausal trek.

EVER SINCE I ENTERED MENOPAUSE THE HAIR ON MY HEAD IS FALLING OUT FASTER THAN IT SEEMS TO BE REPLACING ITSELF. HELP!

Yes, I have lost about half of my once thick, abundant head of hair, too. For some women, who have thin, fine hair, this can be worrisome—they do not have that MUCH to lose! Baldness is extremely RARE during menopause. We will all lose some of our head hair—and I'm sure it may seem like we are putting this misplaced hair everywhere else on our body! Our face, our belly, the insides of our thighs (where hair never really grew at all, before this).

Our hair will not grow as fast, will not be as long as before, and will dry out sooner, and split ends will be a nuisance for some of us. The shiny quality of our hair may dull to some degree. I would recommend a scalp massage at least two or three times a week. Place a little almond oil (your choice of what kind of oil is up to you, but I love almond oil!) on your fingertips and gently knead your scalp for 10 minutes. It stimulates circulation, and adds a little oil to replace what is lost by our aging scalp.

Ideally, washing your hair once a week is best—doing it every day or several times a week will take away the natural oils on your scalp. If you need a permanent, try to have it as infrequently as possible because this truly dries out your hair. Choose a pH balanced or natural shampoo (preferably not animal tested) that is specific for your type of hair and doesn't cause needless irritation or inflammation of your tender and sensitive scalp.

I have found in my own experience that I lost a significant amount in my early forties. Alarmed, I repertorized my symptoms and took a remedy, Calcarea Carbonica, which is my constitutional state, and my hair stopped falling out and started growing back—and I have gotten back about half of what I lost. Although I suffered about a 25 percent loss even with homeopathic intervention, I'm happy that homeopathy is helping me retain most of my hair.

CAN HOMEOPATHY HELP ME WITH THESE PROBLEMS?

Yes, and the remedies are listed below. If your condition is severe, though—let's say you are truly going bald or truly growing a beard on your face—you need to seek constitutional homeopathic treatment.

One of my patients, I'll call her Joyce, came to me because she was 50 years old and going through menopause. She had problems with depression and excessive hair growth on her face—to the point of having to shave every day. My heart went out to her as I saw the pain she carried over that secret admission. I had to treat her at a constitutional level with Sepia, and within 3 months, her hair problem disappeared. No more shaving!

Sepia was able to readjust Joyce's endocrine system so that it encouraged her body to create more estrogen—naturally via her ovaries and adrenal glands—to be more equal with the level of androgens or male hormones in her body. When this adjustment was made, excessive hair could be addressed positively. Joyce was cured of her depression, too.

MY SKIN IS BECOMING MORE AND MORE WRINKLED. WHY IS THIS HAPPENING? WHAT CAN I DO TO PREVENT IT?

Our skin is an incredible organ. There are three main layers and several sublayers that create a dynamic team that works for us. Skin cells are constantly being created, and roughly every 30 days, we literally are wearing a new, outer skin called the epidermis layer!

Our skin plays many roles: it helps regulate our temperature, gets rid of deadly toxins and waste products via sweating or perspiring, and acts as a barrier to keep bacteria or environmental pollutants from entering our more vulnerable organs or systems. So, it's not a small player in our health—it is a major one.

Women who possess darker, thicker, and more oily skin will not have as many wrinkles. The outer layers are more heavily pigmented and as a result, these skin cells can protect the inner cells in the sublayers from the brutal effects of sunlight, which in overdose, can be harmful, and creates lots more wrinkles! On the other hand, women who are fair-skinned with light hair tend toward more wrinkles because there is a smaller layer of fat beneath their skin.

Collagen, which is a protein in our body, has a wonderful chemical relationship with estrogen. As our estrogen declines a smaller amount of collagen is produced, so our skin begins to wrinkle and sag accordingly. Collagen is a powerful support protein in our body that gives everything, from our skin to our connective tissue and our ligaments, the power to hold things in proper position.

Wrinkles occur because our skin, which had a layer of fat beneath it, declines with age, and the result is more wrinkles. Our sweat glands do not "sweat" as much for us, which adds to the equation. Smoking, taking recreational drugs, or drinking too much alcohol just worsens the wrinkles—they appear more quickly, they are deeper, and there are more of them. So if you want to stop wrinkling to a degree, give up the culprits helping to create them. And you can take a look at your mother's face and know that you will inherit her tendency toward wrinkling—which may be a lot or very little. Some of it is genetics and there's no getting around that.

IS THERE ANY WAY TO STOP WRINKLING FROM HAPPENING?

There is NOTHING to stop it completely—if there was—someone would be a billionaire by now! There are all kinds of ways to deal with wrinkles, but frankly, I like my face—wrinkles and all. I figure I earned them by living Life and to me, they are an open testament to me, as an individual.

Some women will opt for cosmetic surgery or Retin-A treatment to make them "disappear." Others will take care of their faces the best they can—and there are many ways to do that, too. I wash with soap and water every night and because I live in a desert, I put a homemade concoction I make myself on my face just before I go to bed at night—but that is all.

CAN HOMEOPATHY STOP WRINKLING?

No—or I would be a billionaire! What it CAN do is rebalance the estrogen in your body more in your favor so that the wrinkling is LESS instead of more. Of course, your eating habits have a lot to do with this, and other living habits, too. If you insist upon smoking cigarettes, a homeopathic remedy will not be of much use in stopping wrinkles from forming whether there is a more balanced estrogen environment in your body or not.

The only way to soften the impact of wrinkles is to seek out homeopathic constitutional treatment. I've treated women for other menopausal symptoms and their skin also gets the advantage of it, too, and becomes softer, less dry, and less wrinkled.

Wrinkling is a fact of life and nothing will stop it entirely—so, let us approach our wrinkles with a more positive mindset. Let us view them as badges of courage we've earned by surviving thus far—and medals that are worn for all to see and admire. I do not see wrinkles as something bad or disastrous. I see them as a statement of selfhood.

THERE ARE TIMES, LATELY, THAT MY SKIN CRAWLS! IT FEELS LIKE HUNDREDS OF ANTS RUNNING AROUND ON ME. I NEVER HAD THIS BEFORE I WAS 49—AND NOW, I HAVE IT. HELP!

Some women, during menopause, report "formication" or a tingling sensation in their extremities—especially in their fingers and toes. It feels like little bugs crawling across your skin. Many women have reported this sensation in their legs and arms, as well. We really do not know how menopause and these sensations are connected—yet. But, they do occur. Luckily, homeopathic remedies can address these concerns directly, and usually quite easily. Those remedies are listed at the end of this section.

MY SKIN ITCHES UNTIL I WANT TO SCREAM. I NEVER HAD THIS PROBLEM BEFORE MENOPAUSE. CAN HOMEOPATHY HELP ME KEEP SANE?

Yes, there are remedies to deal directly with acute skin conditions such as this. However, if you have had a past history of skin ailments such as eczema, psoriasis, or other chronic conditions, you shouldn't use the remedies below. See a homeopath for constitutional treatment, instead. There IS help for any and all skin conditions.

I treated a young Navajo boy, age 6, who was, quite literally, covered with thick, red, oozing, cracking skin from head to toe. He'd been born with this dermatitis condition and it was getting worse with age. After taking his case, I gave him the homeopathic version of potentized Petroleum, one of our great skin remedies, and within 6 months, his skin had healed over and had stopped oozing and cracking. His skin was leathery (whose wouldn't be after 5 years of these types of symptoms) but was slowly continuing to heal and form new, healthy skin beneath it. His mother was more than grateful. Her boy would scratch himself until he cried and she was unable to do much of anything with him due to the deteriorating skin condition. (The medical doctors had him on all kinds of cortisone treatment, which was simply worsening his condition over the years.)

This gives you an idea of how deeply homeopathy can work on skin ailments—even something this severe—and still have the body's vital force respond valiantly to the stimulation of taking the remedy. So, do not despair if you have a menopausal skin condition—homeopathy CAN help!

HOMEOPATHIC REMEDIES FOR HOT FLASH SYMPTOMS

WARNING: Any acute or persistent symptoms—such as pain in the chest or pelvic region—should be immediately evaluated by a physician. After serious problems are ruled out, you can safely proceed with your non-hormone, non-drug homeopathic treatment.

1. Amyl Nitrate
2. Crotalus Horridus (Crotalus)
3. Folliculinum

4. Graphites
5. Kali Carbonicum (Kali Carb.)
6. Kreosotum
7. Lachesis Muta (Lachesis)
8. Pulsatilla
9. Sanguinaria
10. Sepia
11. Sulphur
12. Sulphuricum Acidum (Sulph. Ac.)
13. Xanthoxylum

HOMEOPATHIC REMEDIES FOR ITCHING SKIN

1. Calcarea Carbonica (Calc. Carb.)
2. Lycopodium
3. Phosphoricum Acidum (Phos. Ac.)
4. Rhus Toxicodendron (Rhus Tox.)
5. Sepia
6. Sulphur

HOMEOPATHIC REMEDIES FOR HAIR LOSS

1. Natrum Muriaticum (Nat. Mur.)
2. Oleum Jecoris Asselli (Oleum)
3. Sepia
4. Thuja Occidentalis (Thuja)

CHAPTER 9

OUR CIRCULATION AND HEART: REDUCING BLOOD PRESSURE, CHOLESTEROL, AND PALPITATIONS

I'M 48 YEARS OLD, AND I GET HEART PALPITATIONS FROM TIME TO TIME AND IT SCARES ME TO DEATH! WHAT ON EARTH IS GOING ON? IS THIS MENOPAUSE?

Scientists are unsure whether heart palpitations and shortness of breath are related to some extent to menopause or not—or to the hormonal shifts that are going on in our bodies at that particular age. It could be nothing more than an age-related phenomenon, not a menopause-related one. It just isn't known. And, in the United States, 75 percent of us get these nagging, scary palpitations off and on through menopause.

Many of us experience our heart racing or jumping around, plus shortness of breath DURING our hot flashes—and some do not. For those who do experience them with their hot flashes, go to Chapter 8 and check out the hot flash remedies to address these particular symptoms. And for those who get palpitations or shortness of breath, look below for potential remedies that match your set of symptoms.

In my forties, I took Folliculinum, one of the major homeopathic remedies for menopause symptoms, and my palpitations stopped and have never returned. However, what came along at 51 was vastly different and new to me.

I have experienced palpitations without my hot flashes—just heat and a lot of discomfort. But, off and on during my forties, for no reason, palpitations would occur, usually during the day, and my heart would race wildly for a few seconds as if it were suddenly experiencing a shot of adrenaline into it—and then it would resume normal beats. Folliculinum took care of that.

When I was 51, I got an interesting new symptom, however. At night, as I laid down to sleep, I would get "cannonballs" of huge pulsings up both sides of my neck in my carotid arteries. I could literally place my fingertips gently against this region of my neck and feel these huge, galloping pulses. This symptom would last 15 or so minutes. I noticed that if I laid on my back, they would come on. If I laid on my left side, there would be less of them!

I knew there was nothing wrong with my heart and I figured out that they were just part of the hormonal changes taking place in my body because of the shifts and fluctuations due to menopause. I am sure, to a woman who is not as medical-minded, this kind of symptom would scare her out of her wits! It would certainly send her running to her doctor, and it should. Anyone with this kind of throbbing pulsations should be checked by their physician first. If nothing is found to be wrong, then perhaps homeopathy or flower essences may be of benefit for such a symptom.

Here is what I did. I found this particular symptom highly bothersome. Because of my Eastern Cherokee blood and the fact that my father raised us in a Native American way, I was very close to

Mother Earth. I had many experiences early in life with Her sending healing energy into me or into my animals to help them or save their lives. One night, as I lay in bed with this galloping carotid pulse, I remembered a vision quest I'd taken up on Bear Butte in South Dakota one year. On that particular vision quest, just at sunset, a thunderstorm came along and drenched me. I was cold and shivering as nightfall came on. I remember lying down on the wet, grassy slope asking for help from Mother Earth. Within seconds, I felt a shift of energy and I literally felt myself being absorbed INTO the earth. I felt like a child being pulled to her mother's breast not only for protection, but for warmth and love as well.

I remember waking up about 4 hours later and as I sat up on that damp, windy, and cold slope of the mountain, I realized to my utter astonishment that I was completely DRY except for a small spot on the tip of one of my boots. It was impossible that I, who was soaked to her skin through three layers of clothing, would be dry in 4 hour's time! I realized that Mother Earth had absorbed me, dried me off, and cared for me when I asked for Her help.

Recalling that vision quest, I visualized myself sinking down into the Earth once more. As I did, all my heart palpitations stopped! Amazed (I know I should not have been, but I was), I visualized myself up on top of Mother Earth. My heart palpitations began once again. I concentrated and visualized myself sinking back down into Mother Earth. The heart palpitations ceased. So, I did this every night as I lay down to sleep. Inevitably, as I lay prone, the pulsing would begin. As soon as I visualized my entire body sinking into Mother Earth, they stopped. I did this for about 3 weeks. Now, they no longer occur, except very sporadically, and as soon as I do the visualization, they cease. So, give it a try! You have nothing to lose and everything to gain from this. Science is now confirming that visualization is a powerful healing tool.

MY MOTHER DIED OF HEART DISEASE. WHEN I EXPERIENCE THESE HEART PALPITATIONS WITH MENOPAUSE, I GET REALLY SCARED. WHAT SHOULD I DO?

Common sense should guide us, first, to our family doctor to have our heart checked out—regardless of whether we have heart disease in our family lineage or not—just to be on the SAFE side. If you come back with a clean bill of health—no heart problems—then any number of homeopathic remedies or flower essences may help ease heart palpitations during our transition phase through menopause.

Women who have heart problems, on either their mother or father's side, should be checked out by their physician FIRST before taking a homeopathic remedy.

I go for a general physical every year and I feel this is a good way to stop anything before it can get started—and so should you! Many health-related symptoms can be dealt with homeopathically—and some cannot—but at least forewarned is forearmed—and then you can make an informed decision about what kind of "tool" you want to work with to heal your symptoms—mainstream medicine or a complementary form, such as homeopathy.

IF MY PHYSICIAN TELLS ME THERE'S NOTHING WRONG WITH MY HEART, AND I HAVE THESE DARNED HEART PALPITATIONS DURING MENOPAUSE, WILL HOMEOPATHY HELP ME?

Absolutely. Remedies are listed at the end of this chapter. And remember, if your particular set of symptoms do not match the symptoms of the remedies below, seek out your nearest homeopath and have your case taken—I am sure she will find just the right remedy for you and your particular set of symptoms!

I'M VERY WORRIED ABOUT MY CHOLESTEROL RISING AS I GO THROUGH MENOPAUSE. IS THIS A NORMAL OCCURRENCE?

It is true that the cholesterol and lipid structure in our body changes as we go through menopause. Past generations of women didn't live as long as we will, and as a group, we are expected to live past 80. What this means is that one-third of our lives is spent post-menopausal.

It is an understatement to say that science or medicine does not yet understand female aging. This is the longest-lived generation to come about, so we're going to have a period with a lot of "I don't knows" insofar as our health as women is concerned. Science is discovering a lot about our bodies that no one knew previously. Among those discoveries is that our cholesterol does rise after age 50 and the reduction of female hormones has a role in this—but it is still not understood HOW or to what degree.

That said, we should take our cholesterol rising with great seriousness after menopause. However, I am not an advocate of climbing on the HRT bandwagon to lower it, either, should it rise. Who wants to trade cancer for a cholesterol rise? No thank you. I will look to homeopathy, my diet, and an exercise regime for answers, first.

Because medicine and science have never dealt with an aging group like us before, there is bound to be confusion, misunderstanding, the throwing out of old concepts about women and health, and some revelations that will come only with TIME—perhaps 30 years or more down the road. Perhaps then we'll have an accurate assessment about what can be learned from the Baby Boomer generation in relation to women's aging versus menopause—what is tied to these things and what is not.

I believe that it is irresponsible to hand out HRT for cholesterol problems. Why not choose drug-free steps first, such as diet? Or a drugless therapy such as vitamins or minerals? Homeopathy has certainly not been included—but it should be.

CAN HOMEOPATHIC REMEDIES REDUCE MY CHOLESTEROL LEVEL?

Yes, your cholesterol levels can be maintained in the normal range with homeopathic constitutional treatment. There is no single remedy, or group of remedies, that are specific for reduction of cholesterol, so this means that you must go to a homeopath and have your case taken in its totality.

Over the years I've treated patients who had high cholesterol, high triglycerides, or high blood pressure, but they were treated at the constitutional level, and these levels would return to normal ranges provided there was no "obstacle to cure."

"Obstacle to cure" means that, as an example, if you have a diet high in fats, and you do not stop ingesting them after the constitutional remedy is given, then your cholesterol level will not be lowered because you're not changing your diet to reflect and help the body maintain that level of normality.

DOES DIET PLAY A BIG PART IN MY BEING ABLE TO MAINTAIN A HEALTHY CHOLESTEROL LEVEL DURING MENOPAUSE?

There is no question that it does. And homeopathy, by itself, if you insist upon old eating habits, won't keep these levels lowered, either. It is a combination of factors: a change of diet along with the correct remedy for you.

WHAT IS THE BEST DIET FOR A WOMAN GOING THROUGH MENOPAUSE?

I am a big fan of raw fruits and vegetables—but there is a glitch to this. Nowadays there is so much pesticide usage—our foods absorb these poisons—that I suggest seeking out an ORGANIC source. Here at "la Casa de Madre Tierra" (the House of Mother Earth), we have 50 fruit and nut trees, as well as a huge garden where we raise everything—without any pesticides or chemicals. My horse, Cinnamon, contributes to our compost pile, too! Plus, we have a greenhouse. I grow any number of vegetables indoors during the winter, and in our garden outdoors, during the summer months. We put all of them into the freezer and use them year around.

If you live in a city, there are usually farm markets or co-ops that carry organic foods. If you live out in the country, it is even easier to get products from local farmers—or if you have time, create your own garden and plant a few fruit trees!

Our intake of fat should be less rather than more as we move into menopause (the ideal diet is 30% fat, 30% carbohydrates, and 40% protein). I use olive oil (cold-pressed) as it is a marvelous unsaturated fat, whole grains, small amounts of starches (because these turn into sugar and sugar is then stored in fat cells and voilà! our weight goes up), beans, peas, and lentils (a major part of my diet), and some lean meat such as turkey, chicken, or fish. Keep in mind that I buy only organically raised meat—there are far too many hormones, antibiotics, and other chemicals in meat nowadays. And for a woman going through menopause, hormone-laden meat jars her sensitive, changing endocrine system even more.

I'm not a health fanatic, but I do know that my body responds to good food as opposed to bad food—junk foods, chocolate, and dairy products such as cheese and milk (which are loaded with hormones and antibiotics!). And in the same breath, I will tell you that I simply adore Godiva chocolates and will eat one every day! I consume a glass of wine a day for medicinal purposes, as well.

I don't feel that you have to turn into a health fanatic regarding diet. I deny myself nothing that I want—but I also try to tune into what my body is really asking me to eat. For instance, I noticed that when I had a period, I didn't want heavy foods such as meat. I ate only vegetables instead, and rice as a source of protein. When I was finished with my cycle, then I wanted more meat in my diet.

Calories for us, at middle age, should not go below 1800 to 2000 daily. To keep our cholesterol normalized, severely reduce the dairy products in your diet (milk, cheese, ice cream, and butter). In the meat department, switch from beef and pork to lighter meats such as turkey, chicken, game hens, or fish. Stay away from the mayonnaise, nuts, and junk food, and go easy on desserts.

I've never seen a woman stay on a diet when she suddenly stopped eating her favorite food—so, experience has taught me that you need to cut back on the AMOUNT you're consuming—whether it be chocolate or a bowl of ice cream—rather than denying it all together. If you stop it completely, then you'll more than likely return to your old habit!

Fortunately for those who are overweight (and I was—at age 40 to 48, I put on 25 unwanted pounds!), Dr. Barry Sears wrote *Mastering the Zone* and *Enter the Zone*. It is not a diet so much as a sensible way to eat. I encourage every woman who is overweight to read these books and just TRY his way of eating. If you do, you will lose the excess weight, just as I did. My friend lost 55 pounds in a year on the Zone way of eating. So, try it!

I'M WORRIED ABOUT A HEART ATTACK AFTER MENOPAUSE. IT'S BEEN IN THE NEWS SO MUCH LATELY THAT WOMEN ARE PRONE TO THEM. IS THIS TRUE?

Did you know that IF you have no heart disease in your family history, the median age to die of a heart attack is 74 years old? And that a 50-year-old woman has a 46 percent chance of developing heart disease, and there's only a 31 percent probability of dying from a heart attack in the first place? That is good news!! So don't let the ads by pharmaceutical companies throw you into such a dither!!

There have been a number of studies on this. And you should know that women who smoke have a MUCH GREATER risk of heart attack than those who do not—so stop smoking! And birth control pills also increase the chance for having a heart attack. There is a direct correlation and indictment of too much estrogen (again) from a drug hormone source. And at the other end is HRT where contracting cancer could be the end result of taking it!

Birth control pills clot the blood faster and raise blood pressure—two things that can contribute directly to heart attacks. Also, cholesterol and triglyceride levels are higher in women who take contraceptive pills.

If a woman is taking birth control pills AND smoking—she's really asking for heart-related problems. There is a rise in our LDLs (low-density lipoproteins) after menopause, and this is directly connected with our heart and its function. The Japanese have also learned that triglycerides, another type of fat, are found in higher levels in a woman's bloodstream after menopause.

But there is hope! Dr. Emil Ginter, Ph.D., has noted a drop in the number of heart attack deaths in our country—he believes it's because we now take vitamin C. Also, vitamin E interacts with the platelets in our bloodstream to help prevent clots that could clog an artery in the brain or heart.

Lack of folic acid, one of the B vitamins, may be directly linked to the potential for heart attack. Heart attacks do not all occur just from a high level of cholesterol or triglycerides—there is more and more proof that an amino acid known as homocysteine is implicated in them, too. This amino acid, if there's too much of it, can cause atherosclerosis, which leads to heart attacks and strokes.

Dr. Irwin Rosenberg, Tufts University School of Medicine, stated that high homocysteine levels are easier to treat than high cholesterol levels. He noted that in some people with high cholesterol and triglycerides, diet may not budge these levels. However, ingesting folic acid always lowers the homocysteine levels—which lowers the risk of heart attack or strokes. This B vitamin will not protect a woman against all forms of heart attack, but if she is found to have high levels of this amino acid, then there is something she can do cheaply and easily to avoid the heart attack possibility: Use a daily folic acid supplement or get it via dark green, leafy vegetables.

HOMEOPATHIC REMEDIES FOR HEART PALPITATIONS AND SHORTNESS OF BREATH

1. Aconitum Napellus (Aconite)
2. Cactus Grandiflorus (Cactus Grand.)
3. Lachesis Muta (Lachesis)
4. Nux Vomica
5. Pulsatilla
6. Sepia

CHAPTER 10

OUR BONES—KEEPING THEM STRONG AND SAYING GOODBYE TO ARTHRITIS!

WHAT IS OSTEOPOROSIS?

A strict medical definition is "porous bones, softening of the bones, or absorption by the bones of calcium, which causes them to become porous or soft." This can occur during menopause, but the medical establishment is not sure of the linkage. Vitamin D deficiency may be involved, leading to a breakdown in calcium absorption.

Further, every woman should know this: Bone is like other living tissue. Its cells die and are sloughed off by the body, just as occurs with the skin. As new cells replace those that have been sloughed off, a majority of us will continue to have strong bones. Homeopathy can ensure that the body will maintain healthy levels of calcium—and thus avoid osteoporosis.

WHO IS A CANDIDATE FOR OSTEOPOROSIS?

Only women with a genetic history of osteoporosis should even be mildly concerned. However, if your mother or grandmother has or had osteoporosis and you fit the profile below, then you should be concerned, *not* panicked, about the possibility of osteoporosis. The condition can be halted homeopathically as well as through sensible eating habits and exercise. It is not necessary for you to think of HRT as your only choice.

You may be at risk if you:

- Had a hysterectomy before age 35.
- Are of northern European heritage.
- Are skinny, wiry, and chilly.
- Are small-boned and petite.
- Are a cigarette smoker or an alcoholic.
- Have maintained a low-calcium or high-protein (meat) diet.
- Have a family history of osteoporosis.
- Have a history of bone fractures.
- Have a history of chronic diarrhea or have had gastrointestinal surgery.
- Have kidney disease and are presently on dialysis.
- Use cortisone daily in some form.
- Are on daily thyroid medication.
- Take antacids containing aluminum daily.
- Ingest large amounts of caffeine (soft drinks, coffee, and tea).

For once, women who are medium and big-boned and slightly overweight to plump are winners. Women of African-American or southern European heritage (among whom medium and large bones are the norm) need not worry, because they usually have sufficient bone mass to take them through menopause.

HOW CAN I TELL IF I HAVE BONE PROBLEMS?

Your body sends out clear warnings when significant bone loss occurs. Your "long bones," the arms and legs, will ache at either end. Your fingernails will develop transverse (horizontal) ridges. Your gums will recede rapidly. (Your dentist will alert you to this problem.) Broken capillaries may develop under your skin, and from time to time, your hands, legs, or feet may tingle.

These are all red flags for potential bone mass deterioration. Don't forget that homeopathy can halt this problem and restabilize your system. A balanced diet and an exercise program will also support your road back to wellness.

WHAT KIND OF FOODS SHOULD I EAT AS I ENTER MENOPAUSE?

First, women have to know what causes loss of massive amounts of calcium from their bodies. Here is a list of things to avoid, or at least, to moderate:

* Soft drinks are very high in phosphorus, which leaches calcium out of the body at a horrific rate.
* Diuretics aren't good for us at all. Look to homeopathic remedies instead.
* Eating too much table salt will cause the kidneys to excrete large amounts of calcium.
* Solanum family vegetables, such as tomatoes, potatoes, eggplant, and bell peppers, contain inhibitors that stop the absorption of other calcium-bearing foods into the body. Eat these vegetables sparingly, please.
* Too little exercise causes us to lose calcium—as does too much. Don't be a couch potato, but don't be a marathon runner, either, as you enter menopause. A one-mile "power walk" which gets your heart rate up and moving, will do just fine—providing you do not have knee or hip problems. Consult with your doctor first, about this.

Some phytoestrogen foods naturally contain small amounts of estrogen. You should include these foods in your diet: whole grains, seeds, carrots, ripe bananas, apples, royal jelly, and bee pollen.

If you want foods that are very rich in calcium, I suggest sea vegetables. The Japanese regularly include seaweed in their diet and, though small bones are the norm, very few Japanese women suffer from osteoporosis. Hijiki seaweed contains 1400 mg of calcium per cup, wakame 1300 mg, nori 1000 mg, and dulse 214 mg. For those of you who live in areas where such foods are easily obtained, this could be a very good way to supply your body with calcium!

I am not a big supporter of dairy products for menopausal women. All dairy products cause an incredible accumulation of mucus, which isn't good for us. Further, they are adding so many hormones and antibiotics to the milk that this will definitely throw off a woman's endocrine system and cause problems down the road. You should consume very little milk (use it for cereal, cooking, and for your coffee or tea only) and go very light on ice cream and cheese. Further, at this age, most adults lose the enzyme to break down milk products. This is the body's way of telling us that dairy products (healthy ones, that is, without hormones and antibiotics in them) are best for babies and children, not adults. Many high-calcium foods are dairy products; personally, I stay away from them. I get my calcium from sources that are more friendly to my body (see the following list). Eating one cup of spinach, collards, turnip greens, or kale is as good as drinking a glass of milk. So, think Green!

Calcium (in milligrams) per 100 grams of food

Agar-agar 400	Egg yolk 131	Salmon (with bones) 190
Almonds 245	Egg (whole) 56	Salmon (without bones) 79
Beef 10	Halibut 13	Sardines (with bones) 290
Bluefish 23	Haricot beans 1146	Sesame seeds 1160
Brazil nuts 180	Hazel nuts 290	Silverbeet 105
Broccoli 123	Kale 200	Spirulina 131
Brown rice 56	Lima beans 110	Sunflower seeds 174
Carob powder 325	Mackerel 5	Tofu 120
Chicken 111	Okra 82	Tuna (with bones) 290
Chinese cabbage 1106	Parsley 203	Turnip greens 191
Collard greens 117	Pinto beans 1135	Walnuts 99
Cottage cheese 60	Pistachios 135	Watercress 1511
Dried figs 240	Rhubarb 100	Yogurt 147

WHAT'S THE CHANCE OF ME GETTING OSTEOPOROSIS? THERE MUST BE STUDIES OUT ON THIS?

Yes, there are. A risk assessment done by Dr. Deborah Grady, MD, and published in the *Annals of Internal medicine*, December 15, 1992, reviewed all of the critical research published since 1970 on the risks and benefits of hormone therapy for healthy post-menopausal women.

Keep in mind that this is post-menopausal women, meaning AFTER menopause, which can be age 52–55 (assuming menopause starts at age 49). Here's what they found out about hip fractures.

If a woman never takes estrogen in any form, HRT or otherwise, at age 79 she is at the median age for the first hip fracture! AGE 79!!! And our life expectancy is 82.8 years old! Further, a 50-year-old white woman has a 15 percent chance of having a hip fracture, and only a 1.5 percent chance of DYING from it!

Given the fact that 70 percent of women will get breast or uterine cancer by being on HRT for more than 5 years, it is not a good bet for those who do contract osteoporosis (and it has nothing to do with menopause!) to take estrogen in any drug-related form, such as HRT, to prevent hip fractures. The statistics speak for themselves.

CAN HOMEOPATHY HELP OSTEOPOROSIS?

The answer is a qualified yes. There are no "magic bullets" or acute remedies that one can take to stop this disease. You must locate a homeopath near you and go to her and receive CONSTITUTIONAL treatment. This will mean 1–2 years, usually, of treatment via a homeopathic remedy, to help stabilize your condition.

AREN'T THERE ANY "QUICK FIXES" FOR OSTEOPOROSIS?

No, not homeopathically speaking, there aren't. Just think how many years it took your bones to get into this condition—and really, 2 years of homeopathic treatment is a short duration, comparatively speaking. Plus, you are dealing with a disease in a natural, gentle fashion—and it will not give you breast or uterine cancer in trade, either!

I'VE GOT ARTHRITIS. AND I DIDN'T HAVE IT BEFORE AGE 50. IS MENOPAUSE DOING IT?

No, menopause is not responsible for arthritis. Age is! However, there is good news on this ailment. Homeopathically, we can do a great deal to cure arthritis.

One of my Navajo patients in her late sixties, Peggy Wheeler, had suddenly been brought to her knees, quite literally, within a year, with rheumatoid arthritis. When I met Peggy at her hogan, she could barely get out of bed. She had not washed dishes or cleaned her house for days because it was just too painful to move around.

Her knuckles were large, swollen, and hot to touch. With the aid of an interpreter, I took her case homeopathically. After an hour, I decided on a remedy to help this beautiful woman who was at one time so tall and regal looking. Now, she was stooped over and could barely move.

I gave her Rhus Toxicodendron (Rhus Tox.) 30C, one dose, which is a small potency, but powerful. We went back the following day to check up on her. When I walked into her hogan it was spotless! The dishes had been washed. The floor had been swept. The curtains, which had been so tightly closed, lending a gloom to the hogan, were now thrown open and light suffused the interior.

Peggy was no longer in bed, but was on her sofa. She rose with the remarkable grace of a 20-year-old ballerina on center stage! I was amazed at the change in just 12 hours from taking that homeopathic remedy!

Peggy spoke in soft, lilting Navajo to us, and through the translator, she told us that after taking the "spirit medicine" she went to sleep. When she awoke several hours later, she could move without pain. She felt so good and had so much energy that she cleaned up her hogan!

I stood there with tears in my eyes at this beautiful and proud-bearing woman who stood nearly five foot, nine inches tall. That was nearly 3 years ago, and Peggy continues to be strong and well—with no return of the arthritis symptoms!

CAN HOMEOPATHY CURE OSTEOARTHRITIS AS WELL AS RHEUMATOID ARTHRITIS?

Absolutely! You need to find a homeopath near you and have her take your case constitutionally. It will mean saying goodbye to arthritis. In Peggy's case, her symptoms disappeared dramatically and swiftly—and for some people, it happens that way. It just depends on your vital force, your constitution, your age, and your state of health when you take a homeopathic remedy.

MAY I USE HOMEOPATHIC REMEDIES FOR ARTHRITIS?

I would prefer that you go to your local homeopath—and not treat yourself "acutely" for such a serious, deep-seated problem. However, I do list some of the major arthritis remedies that your homeopathy MIGHT entertain utilizing for you. If you find a match with one of them, take the information to your homeopath so that constitutional treatment can be undertaken.

WHAT ABOUT TAKING CALCIUM TO STRENGTHEN MY BONES?

Dr. Alan Gaby has written an excellent book, *Preventing and Reversing Osteoporosis*. He suggests that a woman should not take calcium alone as a supplement to strengthen her bones. Instead, magnesium also needs to be considered. He noted that in one study, women who took calcium plus all the micronutrients that were known to increase bone density, did just that, versus women in a study taking just calcium by itself. The two studies proved that taking calcium by itself, or with estrogen, couldn't hold a candle to calcium taken with appropriate micronutrients.

He has found that magnesium should be taken along with the calcium to derive the best benefits of bone strengthening. Traditionally, calcium is taken in higher amounts, and magnesium less. Many nutritional supplements contain 800–1,000 milligrams of calcium and 400–500 milligrams of magnesium. However, he also notes that some doctors are reversing this, more magnesium and less calcium, and are seeing benefits in their patients.

I invite you to go to Chapter 19 and read up on vitamins and minerals. I urge you to talk to your nutritionist about a cohesive plan if you are going to take supplements. I take them myself, and I make sure I also take, besides calcium and magnesium, boron, vitamin D, and lecithin (which contains phosphorous) every day. For me, it fills my bill of making sure I'm getting a BALANCED program of supplementation. Taking calcium by itself is well known to upset the "magical trinity" of magnesium, calcium, and phosphorous in our bodies. All three of these minerals are needed in their particular ratio to one another, within us, to work in concern to keep our bones strong.

SO, THESE ACUTE ARTHRITIS REMEDIES ARE TO BE USED AS A GUIDE AND NOT TO BE TAKEN? WE'RE TO SEE OUR NEAREST HOMEOPATH FOR TREATMENT?

That's right. So, here are a few of the best of our homeopathic remedies for symptoms of arthritis.

HOMEOPATHIC REMEDIES FOR ARTHRITIS SYMPTOMS

1. Arsenicum Album (Arsenicum)
2. Aurum Metallicum (Aurum Met.)
3. Bryonia
4. Calcarea Carbonica (Calc. Carb.)
5. Causticum
6. Kali Bichromicum (Kali Bich.)
7. Kali Carbonicum (Kali Carb.)
8. Pulsatilla
9. Rhododendron
10. Rhus Toxicodendron (Rhus Tox.)

CHAPTER 11

OUR EYES: SHARPENING OUR VISION

DOES MENOPAUSE HAVE AN EFFECT ON MY EYES?

No, not directly. However, aging does! Our eyes may be a little more sensitive to light. If you must wear sunglasses every time you go out into daylight, then there's a good chance you have photophobia

Another problem is night blindness. As we get older, the oncoming brightness of headlights at night blinds us temporarily and our eyes do not adjust as quickly or easily as they used to.

I HAVE SOME NIGHT BLINDNESS ALREADY AND I'M 52. WHAT'S THE CAUSE? OLD AGE? MENOPAUSE?

Yes to aging and no to menopause. This ailment was thought to be a symptom of a lack of vitamin A, and it is—up to a point. In a study done on rats, however, inadequate consumption of protein was found to be the other culprit. So, if you're taking vitamin A and you still have night blindness, then look at your diet more closely. Are you getting enough protein?

MY EYES ARE ALWAYS DRY! I'M 56 AND HAVE JUST FINISHED MENOPAUSE. WHAT CAN I DO ABOUT THIS?

Vitamin A is the culprit here, not menopause. A loss of the fluid that bathes your eyes can cause a thickening across the entire eye and can lead to a condition called xerophthalamia, and the cornea dries out. You should try getting more vitamin A—10,000 IUs once a week for 4 weeks. If this corrects your condition, that is fine. Sometimes, acute homeopathic remedies will cure the condition, and they are listed below. However, if the remedy of choice does not help within several days, then seek homeopathic constitutional treatment.

MY EYES ARE ALWAYS ITCHY, BURNING, AND CRYING. I'M 43 AND MENOPAUSE IS HERE. HELP!

Then you are experiencing a B-2 deficiency symptom, not a menopausal symptom. Try 100 mg every third day for 2 weeks and see if this clears up the condition. If it does, great. But if it does not, then you need to look at your diet and add more B-2 foods to it. Some acute homeopathic remedies are listed below, but if they don't correct the condition within 2 weeks, seek out constitutional help, instead.

CAN HOMEOPATHY HELP THESE EYE CONDITIONS?

Yes, to an extent. First, though, check your diet. Frequently, I will use diet considerations along with a certain vitamin or mineral supplement for a client. I never allow the person to go more than 30 days on a supplement because you can imbalance a lot of other vitamin and mineral functions in the body if you do—or, you urinate them out—which is a waste of your money. Fat-soluble vitamins such as A, E, F, and K are stored in the liver, for example, and unless you've experienced liver damage, such as hepatitis, you can store adequate amounts so that you don't need to take them every day for the rest of your life.

Vitamin and mineral supplements do not cure a condition—they only stop the system or organ from declining more rapidly. But to "fix" such a condition permanently, constitutional homeopathic treatment must be undertaken.

I will list some acute homeopathic remedies, but go see your homeopath for treatment of this condition—and talk to her about your diet, and a possible supplement for a short period of time.

MY UPPER EYELIDS ARE STARTING TO DROOP! THIS HAS TO BE MENOPAUSE! WHAT'S GOING ON?

Nope, you can't blame menopause for this symptom. As we age, the upper eyelid begins to go "south" and sag. This is known as ptosis. Sometimes it can be an indicator of something far more serious, and it should be checked by your physician. The nerve that holds the eyelid in a certain position may have been damaged in an injury or accident. Or, it could be a sign of diabetes, myasthenia gravis, or an aneurysm.

Sometimes, women want to correct this condition with cosmetic surgery. At times, homeopathic constitutional treatment may correct the condition. I list one remedy, which can be used acutely, below. Please seek the services of a homeopath for deeper, more comprehensive homeopathic help with this condition.

LATELY, I'VE NOTICED BLACK THINGS FLOATING IN FRONT OF MY EYES. ALARMED, I WENT TO MY OPHTHALMOLOGIST, AND HE SAID THEY WERE FLOATERS. CAN YOU TELL ME ABOUT THEM? DO I HAVE TO LIVE WITH THEM FOR THE REST OF MY LIFE, OR JUST DURING MENOPAUSE?

You were correct in going to your opthalmologist to get this condition checked out. It could have been a detached retina in your eye or bleeding occurring in your eye—and both conditions require medical help with homeopathic backup. If your eye doctor said it was floaters, it means that your eyes are aging along with degeneration of the vitreous humor within the eyeball. This is not the fault of menopause.

If the above serious conditions have been dismissed by your ophthalmologist, another consideration is that your liver is sluggish and there are excessive toxins in your body. Seek the services of a naturopathic doctor if this is the case.

CAN FLOATERS BE HELPED WITH HOMEOPATHIC TREATMENT?

Yes, in the short term. Several remedies can be tried on an acute basis, with the understanding that you have seen your eye doctor FIRST. If one of these remedies fits your condition, then seek homeopathic treatment.

HOMEOPATHIC REMEDIES FOR EYE FLOATERS

1. Arnica Montana (Arnica)
2. Hamamelis
3. Phosphorus

HOMEOPATHIC REMEDIES FOR DRY, BURNING, OR ITCHING EYES

1. Aconitum Napellus (Aconite)
2. Belladonna
3. Euphrasia
4. Natrum Muriaticum (Nat. Mur.)
5. Rhus Toxicodendron (Rhus Tox.)
6. Ruta Gravolens (Ruta Grav.)

HOMEOPATHIC REMEDIES FOR EYE STRAIN

1. Gelsemium
2. Natrum Muriaticum (Nat. Mur.)
3. Ruta Gravolens (Ruta Grav.)

FLOWER AND GEM ESSENCES FOR EYES

1. Yellow Iris for pterygiums. This incredible essence is helping 100 percent on these fleshy tumors that will eventually cover the person's eyeball and render them blind for the rest of their life. It is also good, in general, taken for a few days every month, for eyestrain or as needed when the eyes are feeling weary.

CHAPTER 12

OUR EARS: SHARPENING OUR HEARING

WHEN I TURNED 40, I NOTICED A REDUCTION IN MY HEARING. IS THIS CAUSED BY MENOPAUSE?

No, it's not. This is part of aging, unfortunately. However, statistics show us that loss of hearing has increased two-fold in the last 40 years! Part of the reason is the increase of noise in our industrial world. Second, a junk food diet robs us of needed nutrients to keep our hearing wolf-sharp! Or it can be due to ear infections as a youngster, or something as simple as too much earwax.

Worse, listening to loud heavy metal or hard rock music will also damage our delicate inner ear parts. At 120 decibels, we can incur deafness. Studies show that young people living at home and blasting the music throughout the house will lose hearing—but so will the other people living there.

HOW DID I LOSE SOME OF MY HEARING?

It depends on many variables. Within our ears is a small, snail-shaped oddity known as the cochlea. Within it are tiny little hairs. These hairs are like radio antennae of a sort, picking up sound vibrations and then transforming them into electrical impulses that the brain identifies as sound of some kind.

Research has shown that listening to loud music will destroy those hairs in our cochlea and we'll no longer be able to hear the high-pitched sounds we used to hear. Job-produced sound can be just as damaging.

Noise pollution comes in many and varied forms, and depending upon you and your vital force, certain sounds may cause you more damage than another person. City folks encounter far more of it daily, whereas if you live out in the country, you're not as subjected to such nonstop bludgeoning from pollution noises.

I PROBABLY EAT MORE JUNK FOOD THAN I SHOULD. YOU MENTIONED EARLIER THAT IT MIGHT HAVE SOMETHING TO DO WITH LOSS OF HEARING?

Yes, a high-fat diet has been shown in several studies to incur hearing loss. For instance, the people of Finland have a very high fat diet and the Mabaan tribe in Africa eats only fruits, some nuts, and vegetables. The Finnish people in a hospital went on a low-fat diet and then discovered that they had developed better hearing than people 10 years younger!! The African people have a very low incidence of deafness at ANY AGE. So a diet with more fruits and vegetables should be considered, too.

A low-fat diet is good for everything and everyone. It helps to lower cholesterol and high blood pressure. Any time we omit something we love, like junk food, we inevitably return to it. I recommend two books that make for sensible loss of weight, as well as a rational way of having fat, carbohydrates, and proteins in a reasonable amount to one another: *Mastering the Zone* and *Entering the Zone* by Dr. Barry Sears. These books can help you with the fat dilemma, and he also discusses how you can have desserts and gain no weight!

DOES NUTRITION HAVE TO DO WITH HEARING LOSS?

There's no question that it does. Pregnant women often incur a low iodine level and can transmit the deafness problem to their baby. Iodine is for our thyroid gland, located in the center of our neck. One of the symptoms of hypothyroidism is loss of hearing.

Other nutrient deficiencies that can cause partial loss of hearing are vitamins A, D, and C, plus the B-complex.

I'M A VEGETARIAN AND IN MENOPAUSE. I'VE EXPERIENCED SOME HEARING LOSS. ANY CONNECTION?

Not to menopause, no. If you are not getting enough vitamin D, that can directly affect your hearing. Most of us get vitamin D via fish, liver, eggs, milk, or cheese. If you do not use dairy products at all, then you may have a vitamin D–induced hearing deficit. Check with your nutritionist and find out.

I GET A LOT OF RINGING NOISES IN MY EARS SINCE I TURNED 45. ANY EXPLANATION AND HELP FOR THIS PROBLEM?

Many things can create noises in the ears. And yes, there are many homeopathic remedies to address these situations. Tinnitis is any noise in the ear or ears. Sometimes aspirin can cause this problem, so check this out. Are you taking too many aspirin? Is the ringing in your ears happening after you take aspirin? Many other drugs create this problem too. If you fly a lot, the air pressure changes in the cabin can help create this condition, too. Or, something as simple as earwax buildup, or possibly a foreign body lodged in your ear, like an insect. Another possibility is high blood pressure.

These potential symptoms need to be checked out by your physician. If no cause can be found for your noisy ears (defined as "unknown etiology"), then homeopathy may be of help.

HOMEOPATHIC REMEDIES FOR HEARING LOSS DURING MENOPAUSE

1. Aconitum Napellus (Aconite)
2. Arnica Montana (Arnica)
3. Cinchona Bark (China)
4. Gelsemium
5. Graphites
6. Phosphorus
7. Silicea

CHAPTER 13

OUR NOSE: CONTROLLING OUR ALLERGIES

IS MENOPAUSE GIVING ME MY ALLERGIES? I HAD NONE UNTIL I REACHED MY MID-FORTIES. WHAT GIVES?

No, menopause is not responsible for your allergies. However, there are many homeopathic remedies that can take care of allergies for you.

As we age, our stomach secretes less hydrochloric acid, which helps break down foods after we eat them. Digestive enzymes may also have become insufficient for the same reason. Usually, after about age 40 our digestive system isn't as keen as it used to be.

Development of poor digestion can mean that large protein molecules aren't as easily broken down as before. The result is that these larger protein molecules escape back into our bloodstream via our intestines. Then, they can cause an allergy reaction. Dr. James Braly, MD, who created the Optimum Health Laboratory in Encino, California, calls this the "leaky gut syndrome." He is an allergy specialist.

SO MY SUDDEN ALLERGY MAY BE DUE TO INDIGESTION AND NOT MENOPAUSE?

That's right. There are many other reasons for allergies besides weak digestion—things such as water and air pollution, herbicides or pesticides being ingested from the food we eat, growth hormones and antibiotics in our dairy products—things that trample our immune system until it leaves us open for allergens to attack us. It could be something as simple as an odor in your home or office, or a particular food.

I don't want to get into lists of causes, but would rather come up with an answer to help eradicate our allergies—no matter what our age is.

CAN I USE A HOMEOPATHIC REMEDY TO CURE MY ALLERGIES?

Yes, you can. Again, allergies are a red flag for a deeper problem within your body and the only way these symptoms are going to be cured is through constitutional homeopathic treatment—which means contacting your nearest homeopath and getting an appointment to have your case taken and a remedy administered.

CAN'T I TAKE A HOMEOPATHIC REMEDY ON MY OWN?

You can, but in the long run, it will be self-defeating. I will list some acute homeopathic remedies for allergies, but please realize that you need constitutional treatment to truly cure it for the long term.

And, if your symptoms fit one of the remedies listed below, take it and this information to your homeopath for consideration, and show it to her. At that point, you should have your case taken for complete cure.

MY ALLERGIES BRING ON MY ASTHMA. CAN I USE THESE ACUTE HOMEOPATHIC REMEDIES IF THAT HAPPENS?

No, you cannot. Asthma is a life-threatening disease and you should NEVER take ANY homeopathic remedy on your own without first consulting your homeopath. Asthma can be cured through constitutional treatment, so I would advise you to see your local homeopath, instead.

MY ALLERGIES CAUSE ME TO HAVE AN ANAPHYLACTIC REACTION AND MY THROAT STARTS TO CLOSE UP. MAY I USE THESE ACUTE HOMEOPATHIC REMEDIES FOR MY NEXT ALLERGY ATTACK?

No. If you will seek out homeopathic constitutional treatment, there is a good chance that your condition can be cured. You cannot take a homeopathic remedy acutely for your life-threatening condition.

HOMEOPATHIC REMEDIES FOR ALLERGY SYMPTOMS

1. Arsenicum Album (Arsenicum)
2. Dulcamara
3. Euphrasia
4. Natrum Muriaticum (Nat. Mur.)
5. Sanguinaria
6. Sabadilla

FLOWER ESSENCES FOR ALLERGY SYMPTOMS

1. Chaparral
2. Echinacea—purple cone flower.

CHAPTER 14

OUR STOMACH: STRENGTHENING OUR DIGESTIVE SYSTEM AND AVOIDING DIARRHEA AND CONSTIPATION

EVER SINCE I REACHED MY FORTIES, MY DIGESTION SEEMS TO BE SLOWING DOWN. I DON'T SEEM TO DIGEST MY FOOD AS WELL. IS MENOPAUSE THE CULPRIT?

Typically, when we are in our forties, our digestive processes slow down. We might not have as high a level of hydrochloric acid, a natural component of the stomach, to break down the foods. Low levels of this acid allows undigested food to go on through the intestinal tract. And it can also cause a calcium deficiency, because hydrochloric acid is needed to help assimilate calcium. This can mean weaker bones as we move into our aging process.

Some feel that yes, menopause is implicated, but there is sparse research available to say this for sure. Due to the hormonal changes in our body, the liver becomes overworked and cannot deal with all the demands, so our digestion is less important to the body's way of thinking, and enzyme functions that are necessary for completely breaking down food suffer as a result.

One way to tell if you might have low levels of hydrochloric acid is BAD BREATH. If the food remains unbroken by the acid, then it putrefies and the result is bad breath—so this is a general red flag for this condition. Bad breath can also be caused by constipation.

SINCE TURNING 40, I GET A LOT OF STOMACH PAINS. WHAT'S GOING ON?

Roughly one out of three people suffer from heartburn once a month in our country. One out of four suffer indigestion in a 2-week period. And, about 5 million of us have peptic ulcers. All three may cause a similar type of pain: peptic ulcers, heartburn, and indigestion.

If you have stomach pains, go to the doctor and be examined to find out the cause. If she says you have peptic ulcers, seriously consider antibiotic treatment for them. Until very recently, doctors treated ulcers with a lot of different drugs—which didn't work. Now, thanks to an Australian doctor, they've found that ulcers are caused, in many cases, by a bacteria!

The new treatment is to give you antibiotics. However, homeopathy may have a valuable part to play in this, too, so I would seek out constitutional treatment and try it before using antibiotics or other drugs—but the choice is up to you.

Stomach pain can be caused by aspirin! How much are you ingesting weekly? Do you notice the pain occurring after taking aspirin? It's another stealth culprit for stomach pains.

WHEN I ENTERED MENOPAUSE, I STARTED HAVING INDIGESTION, SO I TAKE OVER-THE-COUNTER ANTACID TABLETS. I HEAR THEY AREN'T GOOD FOR ME. WHAT SHOULD I DO?

Fortunately, homeopathy can cure most cases of indigestion, heartburn, and stomach problems, but constitutional treatment is required.

I am not a big advocate of using antacids primarily because they come from an aluminum base and high levels of aluminum have been found in the brains of Alzheimer's patients. So, needless to say, I wouldn't want to trade off stomach distress for Alzheimer's!

Get to your homeopath to get rid of this uncomfortable set of symptoms.

HOW ABOUT IF I TAKE A HYDROCHLORIC TABLET OR SOME ENZYME TABLETS FROM A HEALTH FOOD STORE?

Over the years I have come to realize that vitamins, minerals, and enzyme tablets often hide a deteriorating condition in a system or organ of our body. For instance, low hydrochloride may be present in your stomach, and so long as you take those tablets with each meal, everything is fine. But when you stop taking them, you once again become low in hydrochloric acid and your digestion becomes impaired. This is not a cure of a condition—just a palliation of it.

I would go for cure on this problem. By taking your constitutional homeopathic remedy, you can restabilize the natural acid and enzyme levels in your digestion—once and for all. You do not have to waste a lot of money buying bottles of the above, month after month. It's not only a savings in the long run monetarily, but homeopathy gently stimulates your body to return to balanced functioning as well.

MY INDIGESTION SEEMS TO HAVE GOTTEN WORSE AS I REACHED AGE 40! I'VE HAD HEART BURN, BELCHING, AND BLOATING AFTER EATING. IS MENOPAUSE DOING IT? HELP!

No, we cannot point a guilty finger at menopause. As we age, the "juices" in our stomach are not as strong as they were when we were younger. "Indigestion" is a common term associated with heartburn, belching, passing of gas, bloating after eating, experiencing discomfort at some point after eating, hiccups, or pain in the stomach region.

In the stomach and duodenum (the first 11 inches of the small intestine below the stomach) is a mixture of hormones and other digestive fluids, including hydrochloric acid, that all blend together to break down the food we eat.

IF your "indigestion" is of short duration and you have not had it for years, please look at the homeopathic remedies below and match your symptoms to the remedies. However, if you have had long-standing indigestion, you need to see your doctor and then your homeopath and get a constitutional treatment to cure this problem.

WHAT CAUSES HEARTBURN? MY MOTHER HAS GASTROESOPHAGEAL REFLUX DISEASE. IS THAT ONE AND THE SAME THING?

Heartburn is a symptom of GERD. If you think about our esophagus, which is a straight tube that goes from the mouth down to the stomach, you will find that it has strong, circular muscles that act as a valve. After we eat, the muscles tighten and protect the esophagus from contact with the stomach contents, which includes the acids.

If the muscle relaxes and opens at the wrong time, then whatever is in the stomach at the time this happens can splash upward into the higher reaches of our esophagus. This results in gastroesophageal reflux disease (GERD). So, a burning sensation or pain rising up from our stomach through our esophagus, or an acid taste in the back of the throat or mouth, are common symptoms of GERD.

The good news is that in most cases, except about 10 percent that require surgery, this condition can be "fixed" by use of homeopathic intervention. If your heartburn is temporary and only happens occasionally, take a look at the homeopathic remedies below. However, if you've had a reflux problem for many years, only homeopathic constitutional treatment may help—after you have seen your doctor and made sure that surgery is not the best course of action.

LATELY, I'VE BEEN GETTING A LOT OF ABNORMAL GUT PAINS AND I'M LOSING WEIGHT—AND I'M NOT DIETING! WHAT'S GOING ON?

If you are suffering these kinds of symptoms the very FIRST thing you should do is go see a physician and get a diagnosis! This can be serious and should be checked out immediately. This is not menopause related.

I'VE EXPERIENCED A LOT OF ABDOMINAL BLOATING AND HAVE HAD VOMITING ALONG WITH IT—AND I DON'T HAVE THE FLU. SHOULD I SEE A PHYSICIAN ABOUT THIS?

Yes! These are not symptoms of menopause at all and you should see your physician immediately about this problem.

I USED TO HAVE GREAT BOWEL MOVEMENTS—BUT LATELY, THEY'VE GONE TO DIARRHEA, AND THEN BACK TO MY 'NORMAL' BOWEL MOVEMENT. IS MENOPAUSE DOING THIS?

No, it is not. Again, this is a red flag and you need go to your physician and get it diagnosed. After being given a clean bill of health, you might then look at some of the homeopathic diarrhea remedies at the end of this chapter.

I'M JUST THE OPPOSITE! I HAD GREAT BOWEL MOVEMENTS, TWICE A DAY, NO PROBLEM. AND THEN, ALL OF A SUDDEN, I WOULD GET CONSTIPATED! I SEE-SAW BETWEEN GOOD BOWEL MOVEMENTS AND CONSTIPATION. IS MENOPAUSE AT THE ROOT OF ALL THIS?

No, it is not. This is an indication for you to go to your physician and get checked out. IF she finds nothing wrong with you, then consider the homeopathic remedies discussed below.

I HAVE GOTTEN TERRIBLE CONSTIPATION DURING MY FORTIES! I WENT TO MY DOCTOR AND HE SAID I HAVE A PROLAPSED UTERUS, WHICH IS CAUSING THE PROBLEM. WHAT IS GOING ON? IS MENOPAUSE TO BLAME FOR THIS?

The uterus can "slip" downward because the muscles in our abdomen are relaxing with AGE. Menopause may be partly to blame. And yes, constipation and incontinence can be the result.

HAVE YOU EVER HAD A CASE OF CONSTIPATION AND UTERINE PROLAPSE AND HELPED IT WITH A HOMEOPATHIC REMEDY?

Yes, I have. This was a client in her sixties whose uterus was literally bulging into her vagina. I took her case on a constitutional level, not acutely, and gave her a remedy that addressed the most important symptoms of her, as a person, including this problem. She was having not only constipation, but also urinary incontinence.

One month after taking the remedy, the prolapsed uterus was not bulging from her vagina and was "resettling" back up into her body where it should have been. Her constipation and urinary difficulties were also ebbing.

A homeopathic remedy addresses every part of the body—including the muscles. It can re-strengthen them so that the organs no longer droop and put weight or pressure on the surrounding organs in the abdomen.

DO YOU THINK A HOMEOPATHIC REMEDY WILL STOP MY UTERINE PROLAPSE AND I'LL GET RID OF THIS AWFUL CONSTIPATION?

So long as your physician knows you are going to a homeopath for help on this condition, I'd say go for it. Sometimes, homeopathy CANNOT help an organic condition—and the only way to find out is to have constitutional treatment to correct this condition. Much has to do with the extent of the organic problem, your age, and the strength of your vital force. Still, I would rather seek homeopathic help than surgical help, if I had the choice. Sometimes, however, only surgery will correct this condition and you need to be in communication with your gynecologist on this point before seeking homeopathic help.

I HAVE HORRIBLE CONSTIPATION, BUT I'M ON IRON PILLS. BEFORE I WENT ON THE IRON SUPPLEMENT, MY BOWEL MOVEMENTS WERE FINE, TWO TO THREE A DAY!

Most women who are pregnant automatically get placed on iron supplements by their gynecologist (folic acid ought to be thought of, too, in my opinion). That is when you realize that iron causes constipation—a lot of it!

Anemic women get put on iron supplements sometimes, too, and this also causes constipation.

Frankly, homeopathy can overlap into all these areas so you will not have to take iron supplements, which are well known to cause constipation. Go see your homeopath for help.

I'VE GOT MY CONSTIPATION PROBLEM SOLVED! I TAKE A DAILY ENEMA.

Taking an enema daily to fix your constipation is asking for trouble down the road. I am not an advocate of enemas—only when they are truly necessary and nothing else has worked—or if your doctor has prescribed it.

The colon, the last foot or so of our large intestine, is a highly intelligent organ. If you decide to take enema after enema to get your bowel to "move" so you won't be constipated, it will become LAZY and let you do the manual routine of enemas. It is not that your intestine is weak, and constipation can occur for many reasons. To resort to enemas is not the way to go about it.

Homeopathy can do a great deal to alleviate both constipation and diarrhea. And it's far less messy than an enema!

I SOLVED MY CONSTIPATION BY TAKING DAILY HERBAL LAXATIVES. WHAT DO YOU THINK OF THIS?

I respect the medicinal qualities of herbs. I am not an advocate of using herbal laxatives DAILY because, again, it makes the bowel LAZY. Further, there are some herbs such as cascara sagrada, senna, or capsicum that can, over a long period of time, cause intestinal inflammation, addiction, and dependence by the body upon them. And I have seen capsicum cause an allergy condition in one patient. These herbs, if not used judiciously (and over a very short period of time—a week or two at the most), can destroy the natural peristaltic action of the bowel. Peristalsis is the contraction and relaxation of our entire digestive system from the esophagus down to our intestines—which moves the digested food along—now a stool in the large bowel, that creates a bowel movement.

OKAY, WHAT DO YOU SUGGEST TO GET RID OF CONSTIPATION, THEN?

There are many gentler ways to stimulate your body to help solve the constipation problem. Here are some ways to solve it:

* Are you drinking enough fluids (water) every day? As the food passes through the bowel, a certain amount of water is taken out of the food that's been digested and is passed through the intestines. If you are a "thirstless" person and drink only one to three cups of fluid a day, then you fit into this category.

  The body needs a certain amount of water to operate. If you are thirstless, then as the food passes through your bowel, the water is taken out (what little there is) and the stool becomes dry and hard and constipation can result.

  Drink at least four to six glasses of water a day, and give your body enough fluid, and there will be enough fluid left over to keep your stool soft and "moveable" and constipation will cease.

* Fruit is a good "mover and shaker." Not everyone is a fruit eater and not everyone eats from all the major food groups. Some women are big on salads and greens, but not fruits—or vice versa. Eating from all food groups daily is often the cure of constipation.

  I know, you've already heard of the prune juice routine—and it's true, in some instances of constipation, fruit loosens up a person's stools. You can drink prune juice or eat this tasty fruit for breakfast or snack on dried prunes during the day. It doesn't take many, so try it. Another fruit to consider is figs—have 'em for breakfast or as a dried fruit snack during the day.

* Exercise, or really, the lack of it, will give us constipation, too. Do you sit in an office chair 8 hours a day? Well, that's a good inducement for constipation! Get up frequently and move around. On your breaks and lunch hour, go for a walk—outdoors, preferably, if the weather cooperates. Or, if you have a job where exercise is going to be held to a minimum, do some mild form of exercise before and after work.

  Walking half a mile or a mile a day is one of the BEST forms of exercise for anyone—at any age. Besides, you get fresh air in your lungs after inhaling all that "dead air" in an office building!

BUT I'VE TRIED ALL THE THINGS ABOVE AND THEY DON'T WORK!

Then it's time to get checked by your doctor. If she says there is no reason for the constipation, you are a candidate for homeopathic treatment.

In a case of chronic constipation (where it has gone on longer than 3 months) I strongly advocate constitutional homeopathic treatment—not acute treatment for this serious condition.

However, if it is acute and happens off and on, then look at the remedies presented below. See if your symptoms match one of them. If they do, seek out a homeopath who can deal with a much larger holistic view of you via constitutional treatment.

I'M 52. SOMETIMES I'M ON ANTIBIOTICS. EVERY TIME I TAKE THEM, I JAM UP! WHAT CAN I DO TO AVOID THIS?

Any time you take antibiotics, and many other types of drugs, they can constipate you. The reason is this: There is a colony of friendly bacteria living in your intestines. It is their job to keep the "bad" bacteria controlled. However, antibiotics and drugs are well known to destroy these friendly flora and when they are killed off, constipation, candida, and a host of other problems can occur in their wake.

I would suggest the following: IF you have to be on antibiotics, eat a cup of yogurt (fruit or plain) every day. The yogurt contains live culture that will reinstate the flora that got killed off by the drug. You will end up with less constipation or none, as a result. This is a very simple, inexpensive way to correct acute constipation due to drugs. On the last day you take the antibiotic, eat one last cup of yogurt the following day and you should be in good shape—without constipation!

I'VE HEARD THAT DRINKING LOTS OF LIQUIDS DURING A MEAL WILL CAUSE CONSTIPATION. CAN YOU EXPLAIN WHY?

The stomach has only so many enzymes and hydrochloric acid available for the food you ingest. If you drink a lot of liquids DURING your meal, you are diluting the level of hydrochloric acid in your stomach, which is there to break down the foods properly so that vitamins, minerals, and other enzymes can be absorbed later on, in the intestinal tract.

It's best to keep fluids DURING a meal to a bare minimum. Use some to swallow your food with, but that is all. I suggest lots of fluids BETWEEN meals, and this will often rectify a stubborn case of constipation.

I'M JUST THE OPPOSITE: I GET DIARRHEA OFF AND ON—FOR NO REASON. IS THIS MENOPAUSE?

No, it's not. This can be a red flag of something deeper that is going on, so first things first: go to your doctor and get a diagnosis. If there is no apparent reason for it, then consider homeopathic treatment.

WHAT CAUSES DIARRHEA IN THE FIRST PLACE IF MENOPAUSE ISN'T THE CULPRIT OF MY PROBLEMS SINCE ENTERING MY FIFTIES?

Diarrhea can occur for many reasons, and I will list some of them:

* Food poisoning. Nowadays, our food supply is getting worse and worse and food is becoming poisoned with toxic bacteria. Diarrhea is a symptom of this.

* Sorbitol, which is found in many foods and drinks, is an artificial sweetener. Read the labels on your food containers. Sorbitol is found in soda pop, ice cream, bakery goods, jelly, and many processed food products. Interestingly, NATURAL sorbitol is found in prunes—which can relieve constipation in some cases. Sorbitol is a natural laxative and eating too many foods that contain this substance may be the reason for your diarrhea.

* Stress is one of the major reasons for diarrhea. Excessive emotional strain and tension—whether at work or home—can cause diarrhea. People who contract irritable bowel syndrome (IBS), diverticulitis, or Crohn's disease are being overwhelmed with stress from some direction and they are not able to cope with it, so the "blow out" for the stress occurs in the intestinal tract and chronic diarrhea is the result.

* Excessive vitamin C will also cause diarrhea. Generally speaking, a person would have to take a very high dose, such as 6,000 mg or more a day, for many days, before this would happen. Because vitamin C is a water-soluble vitamin that is gotten daily from the food we eat, the unneeded C is then "washed out" in the urine. However, if the body is bombarded with too much vitamin C, it will cause diarrhea.

* Allergies to food are well known to cause diarrhea. Are you allergic to a certain food or food group? Often, gluten, a protein found in wheat, oats, rye, and barley, will cause it. If the body knows that it is allergic to a certain food, it will try to get rid of it just as fast as it can—sometimes within an hour of eating it—via diarrhea. Celiac disease, which occurs due to the lack of being able to absorb gluten, is the end result.

I HAVE 'IRRITABLE BOWEL SYNDROME' AND MY SISTER HAS DIVERTICULITIS. CAN HOMEOPATHY HELP THESE PROBLEMS?

In many cases, yes, it can. BUT, it requires constitutional homeopathic treatment. Do NOT use any of the homeopathic remedies below for either of your conditions because these serious ailments need the judicious eye of a professional homeopath to help you get well.

HOMEOPATHIC REMEDIES FOR ACUTE CONSTIPATION

1. Alumina
2. Arnica Montana (Arnica)
3. Lycopodium
4. Nux Vomica
5. Silicea

HOMEOPATHIC REMEDIES FOR ACUTE DIARRHEA

1. Arsenicum Album (Arsenicum)
2. Gelsemium
3. Pulsatilla
4. Vertatrum Album (Veratrum)

HOMEOPATHIC REMEDIES FOR INDIGESTION

1. Arsencium Album (Arsenicum)
2. Carbo Vegetabilis (Carbo Veg.)
3. Lycopodium
4. Nux Vomica
5. Pulsatilla

CHAPTER 15

OUR HEAD: CURING MENOPAUSAL HEADACHES, MIGRAINES, AND VERTIGO

I CONTINUALLY GET MENOPAUSAL HEADACHES. WHY?

According to one study, 21 percent of us will get "sick" or "congestive" type headaches as we go through menopause. Because your endocrine system is undergoing major changes in a relatively short period of time, headaches may come on suddenly, and without any discernible reason.

And menopause may also bring on allergies that disappear when it's over. In the meantime, you may experience headaches when you eat certain foods.

Headaches can be caused by your surroundings and environment, such as STRESS on the job, or at home—or both. Some foods cause allergic reactions in some women, and a headache is a symptom of that. How is your diet? Sometimes a specific food group, such as wheat products, may be responsible. Or, the Solanum family of foods, such as potatoes, tomatoes, and eggplant. Look at your diet. If you suspect a certain food or food group, eliminate it from your diet for 7 days and see if your headache goes away. If it does, this confirms that a food allergy is responsible. And if that's the case, seek constitutional homeopathic treatment, which will address not only your headache, but the root cause, your food allergy.

Sometimes there is an "obstacle to cure" which means that a person, a situation, or a spouse is helping to create your headache condition. So long as this situation is allowed to exist as is, your headaches will continue to come back regardless of what homeopathic remedy you take. Changing the situation or person is really the "cure" to this sort of problem—if it will change. If not, then you have the choice to make changes on your part—which is the healthy way to go in this circumstance.

I WAS IN AN AUTO ACCIDENT A YEAR AGO. EVERYTHING WAS FINE UNTIL ABOUT 6 MONTHS LATER, AND I STARTED GETTING THESE HORRENDOUS HEADACHES. I'M 44 YEARS OLD. IS MENOPAUSE BRINGING THEM ON?

Some women do suffer congestive or sick types of headaches—migraines—during menopause. In your case, I would suggest that you see a Doctor of Osteopathy or a chiropractor to look at your spinal alignment, first, before pointing the finger at menopause.

It is not unusual to slip, to fall, or to be in an accident that might push a vertebra out a little, and it starts putting pressure on one of the nerves running off the spinal cord. The result can be headaches.

In your case, I would eliminate the possibility that you need a spinal adjustment first, before thinking of homeopathic intervention. Homeopathy, unfortunately, cannot "adjust" your spinal column. That has to be done by a licensed health practitioner. If, after the adjustment, your headaches persist, then yes, it may be due to menopause.

EVER SINCE I WENT ON HORMONE REPLACEMENT THERAPY, I'VE HAD HORRIBLE MIGRAINE HEADACHES. WHAT CAN I DO ABOUT THEM?

It is well known that HRT has many side-effects. One of them is a congestive or migraine type of headache. And if you want to get rid of it, then you have to get rid of the drugs that are causing it. No homeopathic remedy will be able to cure this condition so long as you elect to stay on HRT.

I WAS ON BIRTH CONTROL PILLS AND I GOT MIGRAINES. SO, I GOT OFF THEM AND VOILÀ! NO MORE MIGRAINES! AND THEN I WENT ON HRT, AND THEY'RE BACK! HELP!

If one looks carefully at the list of side-effects that birth control pills can cause, headaches are certainly one of many. If you are presently on the pill and have headaches, check with your doctor and see if the two might be related. And HRT is well known to cause migraine headaches. Who needs them?

I WAS ON A DIURETIC AND IT GAVE ME AWFUL HEADACHES DURING MENOPAUSE! I GOT OFF THE DRUG AND THEY WENT AWAY.

Any woman on ANY drug who is currently having headaches should check with her pharmacist to see if any one of these drugs has the side-effect of headaches.

WHEN I'M UNDER A LOT OF PRESSURE, MY NECK TIGHTENS UP AND I GET REALLY TENSE. THEN I GET A HEADACHE. CAN HOMEOPATHY HELP?

This is what I call a stress headache and these are common—whether you are going through menopause or not! You have a number of choices: First, seek out constitutional homeopathic treatment. It will restore your vital force, helping you cope with stress.

Second, you may want to take a regular time out and do something that allows you to "come down" from the stress highs of life. That may be swimming, walking, or puttering in your flower garden—any pursuit that allows you to relax.

I myself get a weekly full body massage by a woman in my area, and there is nothing better for stress—not to mention the lymph gland system in general—than a massage. It also gives me an hour to relax, to just "be."

Frequently, when women are under stress, they become shallow breathers or forget to breathe fully or completely. As less oxygen is inhaled and less old air leaves the lungs, our cells are clamoring for fresh, clean oxygen molecules. Headaches result from not breathing in and exhaling fully, and deeply. You can tell if you are not getting enough oxygen because you may start doing some deep sighing from time to time, or yawning a great deal—which is the body's way of forcing you to get extra, needed oxygen into your body.

EVER SINCE I TOOK UP YOGA IN MY FORTIES, MY HEADACHES STOPPED, EVEN THOUGH I'M IN THE MIDDLE OF MENOPAUSE.

Yes, yoga is a wonderful way to keep in shape, from breathing properly, to keeping flexible and shedding those "extra" pounds. If this appeals to you, by all means, incorporate yoga into your life!

Sometimes headaches occur due to sluggish circulation, and a little exercise (even a quick walk around the block) can increase circulation. Sluggishness can be the root cause of headaches.

EVER SINCE I TURNED 40, I'VE GOTTEN MIGRAINES.

Migraines occur for many reason. They usually begin around 6 a.m. and last through noontime. A dilation of the blood vessels allows too much flow of blood into the brain.

Tyramine, a nutrient known to cause migraines, can be found in the following foods: bananas, beer, champagne, some types of red wine, pickled herring, soy sauce, hot dogs, ham, bacon, chocolate, egg plant, sour cream, chicken liver, aged cheese, and beef. And another culprit, MSG (monosodium glutamate), is a preservative found in cured meats such as ham, bacon, sausage, hot dogs, and salami. Also, if you are going to a Chinese restaurant, inquire as to whether or not they use MSG. If they do—and you get migraines from it—do not eat the food.

Often, acute homeopathic intervention can cure food migraines during menopause. However, if you have had migraines before menopause, you need constitutional treatment, instead, to CURE this painful problem once and for all.

EVERY TIME I DRINK A CUP OF COFFEE, I GET A NAGGING HEADACHE. AM I ALLERGIC TO IT?

Caffeine is a well-known allergen. It is found in many, many products, not just coffee—soda pop and tea are prime examples.

Interestingly, if you take a homeopathic remedy, you must not drink coffee (decaf included) because the oils will antidote the remedy. Fortunately, there is a wonderful homeopathic remedy for those who get headaches from caffeine and it is mentioned below.

IF I TEND TO USE MY EYES TOO MUCH, I'LL GET A HEADACHE. I'M 42, AND I READ A LOT OF BOOKS. IS MENOPAUSE THE CULPRIT?

No, but aging might be. As we get older, our eyes weaken, too. Eyestrain can cause headaches, from sitting in front of a computer monitor too long, or reading too long. There are some excellent remedies for strained eyes—either looking at something for too long, reading books, or just plain over-use of your eyes. They are noted below.

I HAVE HYPOGLYCEMIA AND EVERY TIME I MISS A MEAL, I GET A HEADACHE.

Hypoglycemia, low blood sugar, can certainly cause headaches. In this case, if you eat your meals on time (which can sometimes be hard to do), there will be no headache. This is one of those "obstacle to cure" situations, and I would advise constitutional treatment, instead of looking for an acute headache remedy.

EVER SINCE I ENTERED MENOPAUSE, I GET HEADACHES WITH MY PREMENSTRUAL TENSION.

PMS often appears with a headache in tow. Look at the remedies below for help.

I HAVE HAD HIGH BLOOD PRESSURE FOR 20 YEARS (I'M 50 NOW), AND RECENTLY, I'VE BEEN GETTING HEADACHES. ANY CONNECTION OR JUST MENOPAUSE?

For anyone with high blood pressure, regardless of whether it is accompanied by a headache, constitutional homeopathic treatment is the only course of treatment I advise. If you have high blood pressure, do NOT take an acute homeopathic remedy for your headache. See your homeopath, instead.

EVERY TIME I HAVE AN ATTACK OF SHINGLES, I GET A HEADACHE! BOTH ARE WORSE SINCE ENTERING MENOPAUSE.

I would suggest constitutional homeopathic treatment for both your shingles and the headaches that occur in conjunction with them. Don't take any of the homeopathic remedies listed below for your condition.

I'VE NEVER BEEN MUCH OF A WATER DRINKER. IN FACT, MY FRIENDS THINK I'M DEHYDRATED MOST OF THE TIME. I GET THESE HEADACHES OFF AND ON, FOR NO REASON SINCE ENTERING MENOPAUSE. COULD THIS BE THE CAUSE OF MY HEADACHES?

You are what is known in homeopathy as a "thirstless" person. I am too—I tend not to drink enough water or liquids throughout the day. Sometimes, headaches can occur due to dehydration—so your friends may be right.

Ideally, five or six glasses of water a day are good. If I drank eight glasses of water a day, I'd slosh like a bathtub as I walked! So, I try to drink at least four—which is doing good for me, because I could subsist on two or three quite easily. So, increase the amount of fluids you're intaking for a week and see if your headaches clear up. It is worth a try.

Women who drink too much alcohol are prone to dehydration more than others—so check your level of consumption in this area, too. Consuming a lot of alcohol can dehydrate!

CAN'T A HEADACHE BE A WARNING SIGN OF SOMETHING SERIOUS?

Yes, it can. A yearly checkup can detect this possibility. In rare cases, headaches can be a symptom of damage to the blood vessels in and around the brain. Or perhaps an infection in the brain tissue that surrounds the brain matter itself, or the spinal cord. In cases like this, quick medical intervention is a must, followed up with homeopathic treatment secondarily.

I SUFFERED A CONCUSSION BACK IN MY TWENTIES. I'M 49 NOW AND I'VE NOTICED THAT MENOPAUSE HAS BROUGHT BACK HEADACHES THAT SEEM TO CENTER IN THAT AREA.

A person who has suffered a concussion or brain injury may later go on to have painful, nonstop headaches—at any age. And, they may come and go—for no apparent reason. I've seen people with old head injuries get headaches if they were under too much stress—and they always occurred in the area of the original injury, so this is not unusual.

I would advise constitutional homeopathic treatment of this situation. If you've had an old head injury, don't treat this acutely with any of the remedies below—go straight to your homeopath, instead.

IF I KNOW SOMEONE WHO HAS HIT THEIR HEAD, SHOULD I GIVE THEM ONE OF THE REMEDIES BELOW?

No, absolutely not. If someone has struck their head, be on the lookout for drowsiness, nausea, or vomiting. Further, their eye pupils may be unequal in size, and there may be varying levels of consciousness. These are all signs of bleeding taking place in the brain, and that individual should be rushed to the emergency room immediately. Give them no homeopathic remedy until after a diagnosis from a doctor—if then. Always consult with a homeopath after the person has been to the doctor. Do not attempt to use any of the remedies mentioned in this section.

CAN FLUORESCENT LIGHTS CAUSE HEADACHES? IF SO, CAN THEY BE HELPED WITH HOMEOPATHY?

Fluorescent lights affect many people adversely and are a big reason for what I call "office headaches."

Constitutional homeopathic care can end this problem, so go see your homeopath. Getting rid of the fluorescent lights is a must for long-term cure.

I'VE HAD A NONSTOP HEADACHE FOR 72 HOURS. WHAT SHOULD I DO?

First, if ANY headache lasts more than 48 hours, it may be an indication of something more serious than you first thought. The nature of headaches is not to last that long. If yours does, then see your doctor immediately so that he or she can rule out other possibilities. Do NOT take a homeopathic remedy. Get to your physician, instead.

WHAT IS VERTIGO?

Vertigo, from a strict medical definition, is the sensation of moving around in space or having an object(s) move around the person. The person may also pitch either forward, backward, to the left, or to the right.

Vertigo can be caused from an inner ear infection, drugs that you're presently taking, high blood pressure pills, aspirin (salicylates), alcohol consumption, low blood pressure, toxic food, infections, or sunstroke.

IS VERTIGO A MENOPAUSE SYMPTOM?

No, it's not. That's why if you have vertigo you should see your doctor to get a diagnosis. Many times, homeopathic remedies can be selected AFTERWARD to clear it up.

I once had a patient with vertigo so severe that she couldn't walk without help. It turned out to be caused by a head cold. After taking her case, I gave her the appropriate remedy and within hours, the vertigo cleared up.

HOMEOPATHIC MENOPAUSE HEADACHE REMEDIES

1. Aconitum Napellus (Aconite)
2. Arnica Montana (Arnica)
3. Belladonna
4. Bryonia
5. Cactus Grandiflorus (Cactus Grand.)
6. Coffea Cruda (Coffea)
7. Gelsemium Sempervirens (Gelsemium)
8. Ignatia Amara (Ignatia)
9. Melilotus
10. Pulsatilla

CHAPTER 16

OUR MEMORY: SAYING GOODBYE TO FORGETFULNESS

WHEN I TURNED 40, MY MEMORY STARTED TO SLIP. BY AGE 45, I WAS HAVING TO RELY ON LISTS TO REMEMBER THINGS. IS MENOPAUSE DOING THIS TO ME?

No, it is not menopause—it's the aging process. Our memory abilities begin to change in our thirties (whether we realize it or not)! As we reach our forties and then fifties, we REALLY notice the difference! The good news is that this "curve" of forgetting things is slow and gradual, giving us time to adjust to the circumstances. Lists are a good idea, regardless of our age!

Recently, scientists tried an experiment where 32 faces from a notebook were shown to two groups of subjects, one old and one young. These photos were flashed at 4-second intervals. The test subjects were asked to recognize them later. As this was done, the blood flow to the brain and to the hippocampus (an area of our brain that is important for collection and organization of our memories) was different.

The scientists likened the memory to film in a camera. In the young, less "exposure" time was needed to remember something. In older people, more exposure time was needed to remember something. The good news is that on another test, they found that the perception needed to match up two pictures was the same for both age groups. This indicates that we have to find creative ways to continue to recall, and also that we should take more time to focus our attention to remember what we choose to put in our memory bank.

The swiftness of our memory recall is usually the first thing to start to erode—we are not as fast as we'd like to be and that causes us frustration, impatience, and embarrassment.

I HAVE ONE HECK OF A TIME REMEMBERING NAMES ANY MORE! IT'S VERY FRUSTRATING, NOT TO MENTION EMBARRASSING!!

According to a research report, 83 percent of us are going to forget names we once knew—or people we were introduced to.

Dr. Barry Gordon, who wrote a book called *Memory: Remembering and Forgetting in Everyday Life*, is a brain researcher who contends that no one's memory is "glitch-proof." That is good news, so we can all relax and not feel so unsettled about our memory power fading here and there!

SOME DAYS I FEEL LIKE I'M LOSING MY MIND: I CAN'T RECALL A NAME, A WORD, WHICH DIRECTION I'M IN, OR WHERE I PLACED SOMETHING IN THE HOUSE! AM I GOING CRAZY?

A Johns Hopkins researcher, Karen Bolla, reported in *Memory* that we forget names 83 percent of the time; where something is placed, 60 percent; telephone numbers that were just checked (again), 57 percent; words, 53 percent; repeating a story to the same person, 49 percent;

what was said, 49 percent; faces, 42 percent; directions, 41 percent; what they were doing or saying, 41 percent each; and whether they have just done something, such as lock the door, 39 percent of the time.

I HEARD THAT AS WE AGE, WE LOSE 10,000 BRAIN CELLS A DAY AND THAT'S WHY I'M FORGETTING SO DARNED MUCH!

That is one of the myths about memory. It is possible to lose a few brain cells here and there, but certainly, nowhere near that many!! More important—it's not the number of brain cells we have left, but HOW we use them.

I have found for myself that in my forties, I began to rely on lists (and I never had before, so it was highly disconcerting!!). Then, as I entered my fifties, I saw how I was unconsciously beginning to make unique reconnections in my brain to remember things, but it works for me. I put facts together differently, but I now have better recall than before—plus, a homeopathic constitutional remedy didn't hurt this process at all, either—and it boosted my lagging memory tremendously.

FRANKLY, AT 48, I DON'T REMEMBER NAMES LIKE I USED TO, BUT YOU KNOW WHAT? I FIND MYSELF REALIZING THAT A PARTICULAR NAME ISN'T AS IMPORTANT TO ME AS BEFORE.

Experts suggest that you make a conscious choice to remember a name, to put something in a particular place. They say do not waste your energy on trying to remember everything anymore. Instead, concentrate on what YOU feel is important.

When this started happening to me, I was embarrassed if a name slipped my mind, or if I forgot a word that was on the tip of my tongue, and I kept floundering around for it—and then would end up describing around this frustratingly elusive word instead. Finally, the other person would have to speak up and say, "Oh, yes, you mean ..." and naturally, that was the word I couldn't get unstuck from my tongue!!

Anymore, if I can't remember a name, I tell the person that I've forgotten and not to take it personally and with that explanation, all things are set right again. Humor usually makes forgiveness golden and I will also say, "I'm having a senior moment ..." and all is well with the world once again.

MY FRIEND, WHO IS THE SAME AGE I AM, 46, DOESN'T HAVE HALF THE PROBLEMS I DO REMEMBERING THINGS.

The old myth that we are all born with the same brain and the same memory abilities, but lose them as we grow older, is just that: a myth. Scientists are finding that the culture we are born in, our gender, and parental environment all have an impact on our memory and how we utilize this (and all the rest) of our brain capacity. They aren't able to sort out environment or culture from what is learned, yet.

Don't compare yourself to your friends, because they are different, and that is perfectly fine.

MY HUSBAND IS MY AGE, 50, AND HE DOESN'T SEEM TO BE FORGETTING AS MUCH AS I DO!

I feel that most women have noticed the differences between male and female memory systems. We women tend to remember things based on visual points of reference, such as a gas station, a bush at the corner of two streets, or the color of a building, whereas men seem to have a compass stored in their memory. A man will say, "Go east on Perkins, …" and our way of getting to Perkins is, "Turn right at the gas station and you will be on Perkins."

Both genders lose some of their capacity to remember like they used to, but both are able to compensate by using other ways to remember the same things, faces, names, or places.

I DON'T KNOW. SOMETIMES I THINK WORRYING ABOUT MY DISAPPEARING MEMORY MAKES IT WORSE!

That's another old wives' tale—that if we gnaw away at our eroding memory, it will make the situation worse. Not true!

ISN'T THIS FORGETTING A SIGN THAT THERE'S SOMETHING WRONG IN MY BRAIN?

There is no denying that when we begin to forget names, places, or events, it's highly disturbing. And it's normal to think: Am I losing my mind? Do I have early Alzheimer's? No, you don't. If you are truly concerned about Alzheimer's (especially if it runs in your family), you can seek out your physician and find out. So, if you're worrying that much about it, find out—do not sit back and worry yourself endlessly about it.

SINCE I REACHED MY FIFTIES, I GET EASILY PREOCCUPIED AND THEN I FORGET WHERE I'M GOING OR WHAT I WAS SUPPOSED TO DO NEXT!! I THOUGHT IT WAS MENOPAUSE!

No, it is not menopause. In this case, what has happened is that the memory of where you were going was strong enough in the first place, but these other details in the moment took priority. I do it all the time—I will think, aha, I've got to do this! I jump up from my office chair, go out to the other room and sure enough, by the time I get there, I've forgotten what I was going to do! It's highly frustrating.

If I analyze what happens, I find that between point A, my office, and point B, the other room, my mind has been "rat-trapping" on at least four or five other "things" in the meantime. So that by the time I get to point B, I have completely lost the reason why I was going there in the first place.

Now, as I get up to go from point A to point B, I repeat my reason for going there in the first place, focus in on it more strongly and try NOT to think of five other things simultaneously! And, it works! It will work for you, too. It's a matter of focus and concentration and making it your TOP priority, not down the list somewhere.

WHEN I STARTED FORGETTING THINGS AROUND AGE 45, I GOT MEMORY AIDS SO THAT I WASN'T CAUGHT FLAT FOOTED OR EMBARRASSED ANY MORE!

Yes, we all need to have ways to help us remember better. For instance, I have a note pad, my list of things to do on a given day. Or, I rely heavily on Post 'ems that I can stick on my desk, my kitchen table, my phone, or my refrigerator with reminders on them.

Some women I know use a miniature pocket tape recorder that has a tiny 15-minute cassette tape in it, and they routinely carry it on their person and if there's something they need to do or want a reminder of, they just press a button, speak into it, and they are on their way.

Another client, every night before her bedtime, writes down on an index card things for the coming day that she doesn't want to forget. For many people, just WRITING it down locks it into the memory and automatically prioritizes it so that it is easier to recall.

Whatever memory aid you choose, be SURE to use it consistently, and in doing that, we are retraining our neurons and memory brain cells. After a while, you may not have to write so many things down—at least, that's what I have discovered for myself.

I'VE NOTICED THAT SINCE MY MOTHER WENT ON SEVERAL DRUGS, HER MEMORY HAS COMPLETELY FLOWN THE COOP! WHAT CAN I DO?

It is very important to ask ourselves: Are we on any medical drugs? If we are, many, many of them have nasty side-effects, and one of them is memory loss. So, if you're on any drug, and you are experiencing forgetfulness, then you had best call your pharmacist and ask if the drug can cause this problem.

If your pharmacist says yes, then you need to call your doctor and discuss this situation with her and either get the drug changed or at least, educate yourself.

I HAD A BIZARRE EXPERIENCE. I WAS USING ASPARTAME AS A SUGAR SUBSTITUTE AND WITHIN 3 MONTHS, HALF MY MEMORY WAS GONE! I GOT OFF IT AND WENT BACK TO PLAIN OLD SUGAR, AND IN THE SAME AMOUNT OF TIME, MY MEMORY SLOWLY CAME BACK!!

Yes, I had a similar experience to yours. I wanted to cut back my sugar intake, so decided to test out Aspartame, a sugar substitute, and in about 6 months, I noticed that I was forgetting more and more. At first, I chalked it up to the fact that I was so busy and overwhelmed—but between the third and sixth month, it was OBVIOUS.

I went over all the possible reasons for memory loss: I was not on any medical drugs, I was overworked, but not that bad, I had not had an accident where I injured my head, nor had I suffered a debilitating acute illness. Finally, I settled on the sugar substitute and got off it. I, too, went back to white sugar. Within 3 months, my memory came back fully. I was just astounded by this revelation and experience!!

My advice to all women (and men): Do NOT use any sugar substitute—especially Aspartame, which is found in many foods now. So, read the labels, and do not buy those products if you want your memory to stay intact!

AT 47, I NOTICE THAT WHEN I HAVE TWO GLASSES OF WINE, MY MEMORY REALLY GETS SLUGGISH. IF I DON'T DRINK, OR ONLY HAVE ONE GLASS OF WINE, IT'S OKAY. WHAT OTHER THINGS CAN MAKE ME FORGETFUL?

Drinking too much alcohol can impair one's memory. As we age, our liver doesn't work as fast as it used to, and it doesn't break down the alcohol entering our bloodstream as fast. Less alcohol may be the answer for some of us.

Suffering from a high fever can make us forgetful afterward, too, but this should be only a temporary condition. Epileptic seizures, a blow to the head, an accident of any kind, or a fall can affect one's memory. Hysterical amnesia may create partial or complete loss of memory, caused by some painful and traumatic feeling. Strokes and presenile and senile dementia all involve loss of short-term memory.

HOMEOPATHIC REMEDIES FOR MENOPAUSAL MEMORY LAPSES

1. Anacardium
2. Baryta Carbonica (Baryta Carb.)
3. Calcarea Carbonica (Calc. Carb.)
4. Carboneum Sulphuratum (Carb. Sulph.)
5. Conium Maculatum (Conium)
6. Crotalus Horridus (Crot. H.)
7. Kali Bromatum (Kali Brom.)
8. Kali Phosphoricum (Kali Phos.)
9. Lac Caninum
10. Lachesis Muta (Lachesis)
11. Lycopodium
12. Plumbum
13. Rhododendron
14. Rhus Toxicodendron (Rhus Tox.)
15. Sulphur
16. Zincum Metallicum (Zincum)

CHAPTER 17

HEALING OUR EMOTIONS: UNDERSTANDING, COPING WITH, AND CURING DEPRESSION

I'M ABOUT TO ENTER MENOPAUSE AND I'M TERRIFIED OF BECOMING DEPRESSED. WILL IT HAPPEN TO ME, TOO?

Unfortunately, the medical establishment is to blame for the old wives' tale that as a woman enters menopause, she will automatically get depressed. Rubbish! Statistics bear out that this simply is not true. Only 10 percent get depression during menopause, according to studies. It was assumed by the medical establishment that if you had a hysterectomy at any time (menopause or not), you were far more susceptible to depression, anxiety, or other psychiatric symptoms—and again, statistics bear out that this is simply not true.

Did you know that women in their mid-thirties are far more likely to get depression than any other age group!?! And in a New Zealand study, women from ages 35 to 60 had such symptoms as feeling tense, depression, not being able to make decisions, crying, worrying, panic attacks, or clumsiness, so it cannot be blamed on menopause (which lasts only 2–5 years). Instead, it could be argued that equal education, employment, availability of child care, and shared home-making responsibilities might lead to improved psychological health.

In another study of 2,500 women over a period of several years, it was discovered that women with low self-esteem were more likely to have psychological symptoms than those who had high self-esteem. It also blew another hole in the theory that menopause creates low self-esteem, and it does not.

In the United States, 40 percent of all women have been victimized (rape, incest, beatings, or mental and emotional abuse). This instills rage and humiliation, to name just a couple of feelings evoked by such a tragic experience. The biggest feeling is ANGER. And women have been taught in this country to not show their anger. So where does it go? Deep inside them and it transforms into depression. Grief, similarly, will camouflage itself as depression. With nearly half of all women in our country being victims, there are a lot of us sitting around with a lot of righteous rage, which may be parading around in the guise of depression.

And, nearly two-thirds of all women in the United States are below the poverty level—and believe me, this is enough to make anyone depressed! So, there are many reasons why women are displaying the symptom of depression—but 90 percent of it is NOT due to menopause—it is due to outrageous conditions that should not exist, but do.

Don't set yourself up to have depression as you enter menopause. Nothing could be further from the real truth! In one study with 7,500 women, there was a slightly higher rate of depression, but they attributed this to the fact that they were having discomfort of OTHER menopausal symptoms, such as hot flashes, night sweats, or insomnia; if you are deprived of enough sleep over a period of time, you can bet that depression will manifest.

Further, those women who are already depressed before entering menopause, according to this study, are more likely to report menopausal symptoms in general! So, becoming menopausal is NOT a predictor of automatically becoming depressed.

More to the point, this study concluded that OTHER experiences, such as stress from interpersonal relationships, decline in one's physical health (non-menopausal related), getting a divorce, or being widowed, are far more likely to depress you than menopause ever will.

This study also noted that women who experience the most distress during menopause are those who relied on their childbearing and child-rearing roles and status for self-esteem. We need to realize that women with less than a high school education, the lower socioeconomic strata, those with a boring, poorly paid job, are more prone to depression—and why not? Finances, or lack of them, and being unhappy at your job, are certainly causes for this particular feeling.

Further, studies have found that women feel RELIEF when their children leave home, not grief or depression! And, in another study, single women who never married, but were educated and happy with their employment, were in the "least depressed" category. Small wonder why.

I DON'T KNOW ABOUT OTHER WOMEN, BUT I CAN TELL YOU, I WAS HAPPY TO SEE MENOPAUSE COMING. I'M FREE NOW!

The studies bear out that we are feeling RELIEF more than any other feeling as we go through menopause. Why? Because of a number of events. First, we don't have to worry about getting pregnant any more—after menopause. We can truly enjoy sex as the "spirit moves us" and we don't have to worry about what time of the month it is, when we can or can't do it—not to mention worrying about the foam spermicide and if it's too old, or if there's enough in the can—little things like that. So, no more pregnancy worries!

And, the children are gone, leaving you more time to pursue hobbies, dreams, or goals that you wanted to accomplish, but could not, before this time in your life. In essence, it is a newfound freedom.

I NEVER HAD PMS TROUBLE DURING MY MENSTRUAL YEARS, BUT WHEN I TURNED 48, I GOT ALL THESE EMOTIONAL HIGHS AND LOWS THAT I'D NEVER HAD BEFORE! WHAT ON EARTH IS GOING ON? IS MENOPAUSE DOING IT?

An Oxford study showed that some women get PMS-like symptoms (irritability, depression, and other mental or emotional symptoms) just before menopause. Dr. John Studd has put forth a potentially viable theory that we should think about these unexpected PMS symptoms as part of a continuation of PMS; even if we didn't have them during our menstrual years, we can get them in the peri-menopause phase (roughly age 47–49, with menopause usually beginning at age 49–54). This is hypothetical.

Doctors don't know exactly WHAT does cause PMS symptoms. There are four hormone possibilities currently being considered: estrogen excess, progesterone deficiency, the estrogen/progesterone ratio, or falling estrogen or progesterone. Before, doctors always pointed a guilty finger at estrogen for all the so-called menopausal symptoms, but there is also progesterone to look at and study, too.

Dr. Malcom Whitehead points out that because women get these PMS-like symptoms just before menopause, they confuse the two and then end up blaming menopause (as their physician does, also), when really they could be part and parcel of the ending of our menstrual cycle years, instead—and may have nothing to do directly with the menopause years.

Because we don't have the answers as to exactly what causes these symptoms yet, women should NOT be blaming menopause, or themselves. Nor should their physician be trying to do it, either.

I'M 42 AND I WAS FINE. AND THEN, ONE DAY, I BECAME DEPRESSED! FOR NO REASON! IS THIS MENOPAUSE AT WORK?

Not always. We need to look at what ELSE is going on in your life right now, too. Are you under stress? Are you going through a relationship change, such as a separation or a divorce, or were you recently widowed? Do you have job-related stress? Recently have you or your spouse lost a job? Financial stress and worry? Are you having to take care of an aging parent? Are you currently on any other drug medication? Is your husband in early retirement and home all the time now? Are you getting enough rest and sleep? Is there a child you are worrying about?

All of these factors can be the cause of your depression. There are also organic reasons, for example diabetes. It is wise to seek out a physician and find out if your depression is caused by one or many of these other reasons. If it is not, then it can potentially be due to the menopausal shift taking place.

I'M SICK AND TIRED OF MY DOCTOR SAYING EITHER IT'S "IN MY HEAD" OR IT'S BECAUSE OF PMS OR MENOPAUSE. WHEN ARE THEY GOING TO STOP DAMAGING US WOMEN BY SAYING THESE THINGS?

The medical model, made up mostly of men, and run by men, has not done any of us women any favors by saying these damaging things that harm our natural self-esteem and wound our womanhood. I have often wondered how a man would like it if he went to his doctor and the doctor insisted it was HIS hormones making him the way he was feeling! The shoe would quickly come off that foot!

Every woman is going to have to embrace the knowledge that her body is sacred, and yes, we go through a number of hormonal phases in our lives, but these are NATURAL and they should be celebrated—not cursed. We should not be made to feel as if it is our fault, or that there is something intrinsically wrong with us (or our body) when really, there isn't!!

In part, this is why this book is being written—to not only give you the freedom of choice through a natural means of medicine, but also to educate you that you're fine just the way you are—hormones and all!

The joke is (and no one is laughing) that most women sail through menopause with hardly a ruffle on the surface of their lives. Most see it as freedom, and shift gears and go for dreams or goals they wanted to pursue in their twenties, but couldn't due to family responsibilities. Let us keep control over our identities, and who we are. Let's not listen to someone else trying to define them for us.

Let us use menopause as a way to reassess how we've lived our lives up to this point—and what lies ahead of us—and how we want to live it. To me, that is a very exciting opportunity—certainly not one that I want to spend on drugs that rob me of my quality of life. I don't need HRT, Valium, Prozac, or any other medical drug to tell me how I should live my life according to someone else. We need to have the courage to stand up, be ourselves, and most important, accept ourselves and our bodies, hormones and all, without apology. Because, if we don't, who will?

Now that I am 53, looking back on the last 5 years I find that I am far more assertive, bolder, and able to speak out about how I feel, and I've been injected with an incredible sense of hope, excitement, and wonder about myself and what I will do with the rest of my life! I am now undertaking projects that I had wanted to do all my life, but never had the time. I wake up each morning filled with excitement, and wondering what this day will bring. I have such enthusiasm, and more important since entering menopause, a palpable PASSION for living my life the way I want to live it—not the way I'm supposed to live it according to the social context of how a menopausal woman is supposed to be. Nope, I am thrilled with the deeper, inner discoveries that I am now able to access. I feel like a wonderful treasure chest, full of gems, gold, and other precious gifts. Now, as never before, I am determined to find out in this wondrous inner journey who I really am—without the trappings of spouse, mother, and housewife.

Menopause is a time when we can leave behind the labels we have carried and the roles we have played for the first 48 years of our lives, and what is left is the REAL you! What an incredible adventure of discovery each of us is on!

HAVE YOU EVER BEEN DEPRESSED?

Yes, it happened to me at age 47. Most depression is a pervasive thing, many times subtle and sneaking up on a person. But mine wasn't. I woke up one morning feeling like I had fallen into the blackest, deepest hole I had ever been in. As I struggled through my busy day, my mind kept turning back to what had happened. Why was I in this incredible morose, black state? There had been no crisis in my life; indeed, I was very happy and things were going well for me professionally as well as personally. There was nothing I could point at and say that it was causing my terrible sense of despair.

I slugged my way through each day for 2 weeks and each day, I got a little deeper and a little darker about how I saw life—which wasn't like me at all. I am an upbeat, optimistic person with a hefty dose of reality thrown in, but I am certainly not a negative or pessimistic person. Finally, after 2 weeks, I said "Enough is enough."' Here I was, a practicing homeopath, and I was moping around in this state and not doing anything about it! That was how far down I had gone, I realized—I despaired of any recovery.

The old saying, "physician heal thyself," was on my plate, staring back at me. So, as clearly as possible, I took my own homeopathic case and chose four solid symptoms and repertorized them. The remedy that came up was Sepia, which is the ink of the cuttlefish or squid. When I saw that Sepia came up, a light went on in my mind—this was a premier menopausal remedy that was used quite often for menopause-related depression. But, first things first. I took Sepia and within an hour of taking it, my depression began to lift. I know how miraculous homeopathy can be, and have seen it work beautifully for 28 years, but the results were so dramatic in my case—and I was so grateful—that I was in awe of the healing process.

The happy ending to my story with depression was that within 24 hours all traces of the symptoms were gone and to this day, it has never resurfaced. I do not want to leave you with the mistaken impression that ALL women who go through menopause get depression. Most do not—I happened to be one of those lucky 26 percent who did!

I'm glad I had this brush with severe, sudden depression. Oh, I've had momentary sadness, usually due to bad news or some personal loss, I would experience sadness, usually, for a couple of days, maybe even a week or two, but inevitably, I would bounce back from it, and it would dissolve on its own without homeopathic intervention. Many times, in cases like this, I would take a natural essence, which I'll discuss at the end of this section, and that would get me over the hump with the sadness.

All of us have experienced sadness, grief, disappointment, failure, or loss, but this is not depression, although, if the trauma, shock, or emotional devastation isn't worked through, depression can set in as a result. Most people have a spouse, a friend, a family, or a support group to help them through these difficult times.

I BELIEVE THAT IF I DON'T PROCESS MY FEELINGS, AND OWN THEM, EVENTUALLY THEY CAN CAUSE ME TROUBLE. HOW DO YOU FEEL ABOUT THIS IDEA?

Unfortunately, some of Life's broadside hits can strike us at a time when we cannot work through the emotional or mental processes linked with it, so we suppress or repress it. If either of these situations exists, then the trauma can sit in our subconscious—out of sight, out of mind, so to speak—and it can ferment or rot, creating a psychic infection, if you will, in our subconscious. That infection can lie there for years, even decades. When it does break through the seal of our subconscious, and stains us consciously, it manifests as depression. Every emotional trauma MUST be worked through, or it creates one of these infected pools in our subconscious and if not addressed through therapy or some other means, it will throw our vital force out of balance. When that happens, it can affect us spiritually, mentally, emotionally, or physically. Or, it can hit us on several levels—all at once.

WHAT CAN YOU TELL ME ABOUT DEPRESSION?

Depression is ALWAYS a mask, a symptom of something else. It is a red flag waving in our face that we need to examine the contents of ourselves, usually emotionally, and find out what the ROOT CAUSE of the depression really is. In a review of 4,000 psychiatric patients in 40 years, approximately HALF of them had a major illness (of which depression was a part), but the illness went undiagnosed!

So, anyone diagnosed with depression should seek a second or even a third opinion to make sure there is not some physical reason for the depression appearing in the first place.

WHAT DISEASES CAN HAVE SYMPTOMS OF DEPRESSION ALONG WITH IT?

I want to list some of the major diseases or conditions that can create depression. If you suspect that any of these are the reason for your depression, seek the appropriate physician to test for it:

- Sleeplessness, insomnia, or sleep apnea. If a person loses enough sleep over an amount of time, symptoms such as fatigue and tiredness (a symptom of depression) set in. If it goes on long enough, sleep deprivation can look like depression. It also produces irritability, another depression symptom. Apnea makes a person drowsy, slows the mind functions, and increases forgetfulness, yet another symptom of depression.
- Hypothyroidism is something that strikes more women than men. Especially women who have had children. Their thyroid gland never returns to its normal function, but remains "borderline hypo" or slow functioning. Over time, hypothyroidism can be easily mistaken for depression and the depression is treated, but the real culprit is still the malfunctioning thyroid. Some of the symptoms of hypothyroidism are hair falling out (it may also become sparse, coarse, or dry), dry skin (it may thicken over time), a feeling of continual exhaustion and tiredness, never waking up refreshed even if you sleep 8, 10, or 12 hours, low blood pressure, weight gain for no discernible reason, forgetfulness (and it continues to get worse over time), and edema (swelling of the hands and feet, but also anywhere else in the body).

  Other endocrine-related diseases that may be misdiagnosed as depression are Cushing's and Addison's disease (involving the adrenal glands).

* Infections such as flu, viral hepatitis, mononucleosis, tertiary (late) syphilis, and tuberculosis can have mask-like symptoms such as depression.
* Any number of pharmacological drugs create adverse side-effects such as depression. Check with your pharmacist if you are on medication to make sure that the pills you're taking aren't the cause of your depression.
* Neurological diseases such as multiple sclerosis, Parkinson's disease, brain tumors, and early dementia may be misdiagnosed as depression.
* Tumors, benign or cancerous, in the brain or pancreas, or malignancies in general have been misdiagnosed as depression.
* Lupus and rheumatoid arthritis may have depression symptoms.
* Bipolar disorder, which is a mood disorder that commonly begins with depression but is characterized by at least one period of elation, or periods of manic depression.

WHAT ARE THE SYMPTOMS OF DEPRESSION?

There are a number of red flags that warn us that we might be in a state of genuine depression, not caused by some other major disease. There is a loss of interest in our normal, everyday activities, our pleasures or hobbies. There is depression, a sense of pervasive sadness or hopelessness, and there may also be irritability. Along with this symptom, there must be at least four of the following present nearly every day for at least 2 weeks:

* Weight loss or gain; increased or decreased appetite.
* Sleeplessness or insomnia.
* Loss of sexual interest or desire; loss of interest in normal activities or things that give you pleasure.
* Tiredness, loss of energy, fatigue.
* Feeling worthless, guilt-ridden, or self-reproachful.
* Unable to concentrate, thinking is slowed down, decreased ability to think, and loss of subjective ability or indecisiveness.
* Suicide attempt(s), thoughts of suicide, repetitive thoughts of death or of dying or wanting to die.

Now that we know the symptoms of depression, as opposed to misdiagnosis due to another disease, let's discuss the root cause of depression. The best news is that depression, regardless of its root cause, can be CURED, many times without the use of pharmacological drug intervention, although therapy or other alternative healing methods may be involved in the path to wellness.

MY BEST GIRLFRIEND HAD DEPRESSION AND TOOK A FLOWER ESSENCE AND IT WENT AWAY! IS DEPRESSION CURABLE IF YOU USE A FLOWER OR GEM ESSENCE? IT'S CERTAINLY BETTER THAN THE ALTERNATIVE: MEDICAL DRUGS!

Depression can be helped tremendously with homeopathic treatment. There are many "roads" and "tools" from our alternative medicine tool box to get help, but not all these tools cure. In some instances, I've found that essences (herbal tinctures made from flower blossoms, a bush, tree bark, or gemstones), generally speaking, do not cure, but rather, can take the "edge" off the depression or lighten it to a considerable degree—and it IS better than taking drugs.

I have seen cure of depression via natural essences, so it's not out of the question. In part, I've seen new cases of depression, when they aren't chronic or too "deep," be potentially cured by a flower or gem essence. On the other hand, someone with depression that's been established for more than a year can be helped by natural essences, but thus far, at least in my practice, I've not seen cure. Homeopathy must be used instead, because of its deeper and broader range of power to cure depression.

Another time to use a flower or gem essence instead of a homeopathic remedy is when you are too sensitive to use the more powerful homeopathic route. Remember, 10 percent of the population is too sensitive to use homeopathic treatment. This is where flower and gem essences, which are far gentler and yet just as powerful, can work on your behalf. All you need to do is match your symptoms to the flower or gem essence symptoms. The one that is the closest match to your symptoms is the one that you would take. Like cures like.

DO YOU USE FLOWER AND GEM ESSENCES IN YOUR PRACTICE AGAINST DEPRESSION?

Yes, I do. Flower and gem essences are strong tools in my arsenal of strategies and tactics of case management for a client. If I prescribe a homeopathic remedy, I will often back it up with the use of an essence, which gently supports the work of the homeopathic remedy. Often, an essence will help a person come through old, painful emotions (Hering's Law of Cure) much more easily and with less discomfort than without it. The essence will mute the aggravation, or sometimes keep the uncomfortable mental or emotional symptoms down to a dull roar until it is worked out of a woman's vital force.

Flower and gem essences used for depression can be found in the appendix. And flower and gem essences specifically used for depression can be found at the end of this chapter.

CAN YOU GIVE ME AN EXAMPLE OF A WOMAN 'RETRACING' AFTER SHE TAKES A HOMEOPATHIC REMEDY?

As an example of a homeopathic "retracing," let's say that our client once experienced depression when she was in her mid-twenties; she is presently 45. By giving her the correct homeopathic remedy, her vital force will eventually peel off and expose the layer of the depression that she hasn't yet worked through—it was medicated with drugs, instead—which means that the root cause was not addressed, and the drugs only suppressed these emotions. As this layer comes to the surface to be cured, the woman will re-experience all of the symptoms of depression, but usually not to the intensity or length of the first time.

During this retracing period, natural essences become primary adjuncts and support tools in supporting the woman through this painful period in her life. Flower and gem essences do NOT interfere with the curative ability of a homeopathic remedy. This is why they should be used to help alleviate the discomfort of the client during this "healing crisis." If we have suppressed something through drug therapy, or have used sheer willpower or desire to jam down our grief, our anger, or whatever, during constitutional homeopathic treatment, it will be uncovered and we will have to work through it one last and final time.

YOU MEAN I HAVE TO RE-EXPERIENCE ALL THOSE AWFUL FEELINGS OF SO LONG AGO?

That is the bad news. The good news is that by working through it or retracing it with a homeopathic remedy, we get rid of it once and for all. It is cheap therapy compared to years spent at a psychiatrist's office, let me tell you! There is more good news: flower and gem essences take the edge off of the pain while moving through the depression phase and that is why I want to list these valuable allies, with the understanding that in most cases, they probably won't cure depression, but will help us get through this phase with less pain. I do not believe we have to suffer unnecessarily; and there ARE natural, safe, and effective tools out there if we know where to look.

I'm listing not only homeopathic remedies that will aid acute depression and cure it, but also natural essences that can aid and support the action of a homeopathic remedy as well.

HOW DO I USE THE INFORMATION BELOW REGARDING DEPRESSION AND HOMEOPATHY?

If you are experiencing acute or short-term depression, and if one of the remedies below fits your symptoms, please take this book with you to your homeopathic practitioner and talk it over with her or him before taking the remedy. Depression, even the acute type, can be the tip of the iceberg regarding your condition, and a homeopath will know whether this acute depression is a new "layer" that is forming within your vital force, or if it is a hint of deeper problems that should be addressed constitutionally rather than through an acute homeopathic remedy.

HOMEOPATHIC REMEDIES FOR DEPRESSION, ANXIETY, IRRITABILITY, AND INSOMNIA

1. Aurum Metallicum (Aurum Met.)
2. Ignatia Amara (Ignatia)
3. Natrum Muriaticum (Nat. Mur.)
4. Pulsatilla
5. Sepia

FLOWER AND GEM ESSENCES TO SUPPORT HOMEOPATHIC TREATMENT DURING DEPRESSION

1. Century Plant
2. Black Tourmaline
3. Gower Ramsey Butterfly Orchid
4. Prickly Pear Cactus
5. Sea Pink
6. Menopause Orchid
7. Almond Blossom
8. Goldenrod
9. Crested Prickle Poppy
10. Peruvian Blue Opal

CHAPTER 18

SAYING GOODBYE TO ANXIETY

HOW MANY WOMEN GOING THROUGH MENOPAUSE GET SYMPTOMS OF ANXIETY?

Only 26 percent of all women have anxiety-related symptoms, off and on, during peri-menopause and menopause. One study found that anxiety reached a peak during peri-menopause, (around age 49), and then continued to decline rather sharply as we enter post-menopause, around age 53 to 55. The good news is that we are not going to be burdened with anxiety for the rest of our lives—only for a finite period, if at all.

I DIDN'T HAVE ANXIETY SYMPTOMS UNTIL I ENTERED MY FORTIES. WHAT HAPPENED?

As we enter menopause, the adrenal glands, triangular shaped glands that sit atop the kidneys, have to bear extra responsibility. Why? Because they help create estrogen and estrone to help support our changing hormones, besides creating our "fight or flight" hormones; they are doing double duty. This can potentially exhaust the adrenals, and many of the symptoms I talk about below can be attributed to adrenal exhaustion, not menopause.

Stress is another major factor that creates anxiety. When you turn 40, which is considered pre-menopause, the children have usually left the home, and chances are, you have been not only Mom, but also a wife and an income provider outside the home, too. You have been balancing your job pressures against other demands and expectations for how many years? Twenty? Thirty?

Is it any WONDER that by the time you reach 40, your system may be a little stressed out? As we grow older, our bodies and especially the adrenal glands are pretty tired out from all the distress from our lives and the demands upon us.

There are two types of stress: positive and negative. EUSTRESS is considered positive AND productive, whereas DISTRESS tears down the adrenal gland function with its "fight or flight" hormones. Eventually stress will impair the immune system, opening us up to possible illness.

EUSTRESS gives you a "high" from doing whatever brings you a sense of satisfaction, and productivity. For instance, I may have 20 to 30 Navajo patients waiting for me when we open the clinic doors, but I'm pumped up by it, not distressed, because I know I can handle whatever is presented to me, and I know that homeopathic remedies WILL often make miraculous changes in these people's lives and they are going to feel better very soon, as a result.

Here's a typical example of DISTRESS: You have been at your job for 8 hours, and you come home to find that your husband's got a cold coming on, you have to fix dinner, the animals have to be fed, you have to do a load of washing ... I think you see the picture. This is not positive stress, it's the type that tears us down. Until this changes, and you get some well-deserved help, this is DIStress, which can build up toward ANXIETY symptoms.

WHAT ARE THE SYMPTOMS OF ANXIETY?

Ready? There are a lot of them! Nervousness, nail biting, insomnia, trembling or shaking, clenching your teeth (in sleep or unconsciously during the day), sweaty palms, fidgeting, inability to relax, PMS menstrual symptoms (before, during, or after menses), heart palpitations, narrowing of eyes or lips, compulsive behavior (overeating, binge eating), high blood pressure, dry mouth or throat, premature aging (yep, stress will definitely help create those wrinkles!), exhaustion (going to bed tired and waking up tired), headaches, indigestion (including diarrhea or constipation), and weakening of the immune system, leaving us wide open to arthritis, colds, flu, and worse.

From a strict medical definition, stress is a neurotic disorder characterized by apprehension, uncertainty, and fear directly out of proportion to any known cause, and often elevated to attacks of intense panic.

What happens when unusual stress makes us feel anxious? Our autonomic nervous system goes into a "fight or flight" response to fearful inner impulses and emotions. The result can be anxiety or a panic attack.

When I was a volunteer firefighter at the West Point, Ohio VFD for 3 years in my mid-thirties, I contracted adrenal exhaustion due to the DIStress of my job. We'd have 600 fire calls annually, and I'd run on 400 or more of them because I worked at home and was on call 24 hours a day. The first 3 months, I was in such a heightened state of stress that I quickly got most of the above symptoms.

When I realized what was going on, I did three things for myself. First, I knew that my adrenal glands were exhausted and could no longer manufacture enough "fight or flight" hormones to protect me from stress. Second, I knew that the "food" for this endocrine gland is pantothenic acid and vitamin C, so I bought both vitamins. I took 2,000 mg of pantothenic acid a day (no time released, please—it doesn't digest well in our systems) and 7,000 mg of vitamin C a day. I did this for one month and within that time, nearly all my symptoms had disappeared. I was giving the adrenal glands the nutrients they needed to heal themselves and to start making the necessary quantities of their hormones once again. After that, I stopped taking the vitamins.

Third, I took my case homeopathically, and chose the remedy I needed, which was Gelsemium, 30C potency, taken one time. Between these three steps, I cured myself of negative stress symptoms. I never had them again because when I caught myself deteriorating, I would take another month's supply of these vitamins and another dose of Gelsemium 30C. In 2 days I'd be fine, with no symptoms. The reason the symptoms came back was that I was continuing to put myself under severe mental, emotional, and physical stress with my firefighting duties. In homeopathic terms, this is known as an "obstacle to cure."

If I would have stopped, then the anxiety symptoms would have stopped too. However, how many of us can stop being a mother, wife, homemaker, and career woman? Not many. So, we have to do something in between to help ourselves. I've listed a number of homeopathic remedies for anxiety at the end of this chapter to safely help you get de-stressed.

I'VE BEEN DIAGNOSED WITH ANXIETY AT 45, BUT I CAN FIND NO REASON FOR IT!

Some of the known causes of anxiety are loss of a job, a divorce, a move (usually from one country to another, or one state to another), a change of jobs, or financial losses or ruin. The unknown causes are many and endless. The subconscious is our great treasure chest of inner drives, woundings, and fears. Drives such as neediness, sexuality, and aggression, suppressing our anger, humility, or shame, and low self-esteem can contribute to anxiety. Women who were sexually molested as infants or children may bury the trauma for years, but will later have panic attacks. Usually these feelings will surface with an abortion, a miscarriage, the birth of a baby, or something involving the reproductive system, which then triggers the sexuality trauma. All of this creates deep anxiety and panic.

I'VE HAD ACUTE ANXIETY FOR THE LAST 2 WEEKS AND I'M IN MENOPAUSE. MY DOCTOR SAID ITS DIFFERENT FROM CHRONIC ANXIETY. HOW?

The signs and symptoms of ACUTE anxiety are many and are different from CHRONIC anxiety. Both are covered here. No one person will have all the symptoms listed below. Here are the acute symptoms: Usually, panic attacks or acute anxiety occur episodically over a period of time. They are self-limiting, lasting a couple of minutes to a couple of hours. Sometimes the anxiety will leave as soon as the person leaves the circumstance (a room, a crowd, an elevator, or a shopping center, for example).

Sometimes, it will not. The person will experience alarm or terror for no obvious reason. They may have a terrible sense of dread that an unknown and nameless catastrophe will occur.

One of my patients told me that she always has a low-level fear that she is in potential danger. It turns up in volume when she experiences a panic attack, and then subsides to a duller level until the next attack occurs.

Heart palpitations, pain around the heart, or occasional escape beats can be felt. A cold sweat or general perspiration may occur. There may be fine tremors of the hands that are not physically visible, but are felt by the individual. There can be dizziness, muscle weakness in the legs or the entire body, butterflies in the stomach, nausea, or diarrhea. Hyperventilation is possible, with a desperate need for air intake. If the hyperventilation is bad enough, the person will get a sensation of pins and needles in the fingers, toes, and around the mouth, as well as muscle stiffness in the arms and legs. If the hyperventilation continues, the person may feel as if she will lose consciousness or die.

Very often, the person may experience a floating sensation, or they tell me they feel like they are having an out-of-body experience. Sometimes they will say they are in the corner of the room, floating near the ceiling, watching and hearing everything below them. The sense of disconnection can be severe, as can the surreal quality of the attack as it unfolds and deepens.

CHRONIC anxiety symptoms may be similar to acute episodes, but they last longer, perhaps for days, weeks, or even months. These symptoms may be less severe or debilitating than during the ACUTE stage. The person may feel undefined tension, apprehension, dread, or fear—and will be unable to explain WHAT they are afraid of or why.

There is a tendency to startle easily, experiencing uneasiness in normal situations, such as grocery shopping. There can also be a vague, persistent fear of the future. Insomnia and general fatigue can be pronounced. Weight loss or gain is possible. Headaches and other symptoms related to the chronic anxiety may also be a part of this picture. Although the person can continue to function on basic levels, a person with chronic anxiety will experience dysfunction in personal relationships, at work, and in daily activities.

Fatigue can also affect the ability to work, with an inability to maintain concentration for more than short periods of time. Hypoglycemia, low blood sugar from a pancreatic origin, also invokes anxiety reaction, which is worse at night and is accompanied by insomnia. Liver-origin hypoglycemia will invoke a sense of anxiety all day long.

I'VE HAD ANXIETY SINCE I WAS IN MY MIDDLE THIRTIES. AND I'M 52 NOW. WILL I HAVE IT THE REST OF MY LIFE?

The course and prognosis of anxiety from the medical establishment say that it tends to be long-term, emphasized by acute panic attacks of various intensities and frequencies. About a third of the people will recover, with men having a better prognosis than women! As the person reaches middle age, the anxiety has a tendency to become less severe and troublesome, which is good news for you.

WHAT ELSE CAN CAUSE MY ANXIETY BESIDES GOING THROUGH MENOPAUSE?

If you think you have acute anxiety, there are other diagnoses that a physician may consider: myocardial infarction, Grave's disease (thyroid dysfunction), or pheochromocytoma (tumor in the adrenal system). If the anxiety is acute, other possibilities are a chronic viral fatigue syndrome (CFS), post-traumatic stress syndrome (PTSD), or vitamin or mineral deficiency.

All of these will be considered if you see a physician. It is doubtful that a traditional doctor will consider a nutritional deficiency. A deficiency in the B vitamins niacin, B-6, or B-1 (thiamin) can cause anxiety reactions. Mineral deficiencies may result from too little magnesium or calcium. L-tryptophane has also been implicated, along with B-12 deficiency.

CAN HOMEOPATHY HELP WITH PANIC AND ANXIETY ATTACKS?

Homeopathy offers a wonderful array of remedies for this condition, either acute or chronic. The good news is that anxiety and panic attacks can be cured. This means going for treatment to a professional homeopath. Contact the National Center for Homeopathy (see appendix) to purchase a directory of homeopaths practicing in this country.

HOMEOPATHIC REMEDIES FOR 'ACUTE' ANXIETY–PANIC ATTACKS

Below are some potential remedies for acute anxiety, but I urge you to seek out a professional homeopath for treatment. You can always bring this book along with you to discuss remedy possibilities.

1. Aconitum Napellus (Aconite)
2. Argentum Nitricum (Arg. Nit.)
3. Arsenicum Album (Arsenicum)
4. Aurum Metallicum (Aurum Met.)
5. Bryonia
6. Calcarea Carbonica (Calc. Carb.)
7. Camphora
8. Carbo Vegetabilis (Carbo Veg.)
9. Chamomilla
10. Kali Carbonicum (Kali Carb.)
11. Lycopodium
12. Phosphorus
13. Pulsatilla
14. Rhus Toxicodendron (Rhus Tox.)

FLOWER AND GEM ESSENCES TO SUPPORT HOMEOPATHIC TREATMENT DURING ANXIETY OR PANIC ATTACKS

1. Aquamarine
2. Blanket Flower
3. Colville's Yellow Columbine
4. Broom Snakeweed
5. Monkshood
6. Petrified Sequoia
7. Tiger Lily

CHAPTER 19

VITAMINS AND MINERALS AND MENOPAUSE: CHOOSING NATURAL HELPERS FOR MID-LIFE HEALTH

Generally speaking, women who are on constitutional homeopathic treatment do not need other adjunct or supportive treatment. This can change if the woman is not on a healthy diet to begin with, and short-term application of vitamins or minerals may be indicated. With our food supply so depleted because our soil now relies on fertilizers instead of natural compost, we are NOT getting the necessary nutrients we usually would receive from our food. Even the U.S. government is now advocating the use of vitamins and minerals to supplement the foods we eat on a routine basis! This is an area that you and your homeopath need to seriously discuss. If you live in the country or on a farm and have access to home-grown food, or if you live in a city and can afford organically grown produce, then you're getting more, rather than less, of the necessary nutrients. If not, you may need occasional supplements.

After any possible nutritional deficiencies are addressed, and within 30 days they usually are, then the woman can stop taking the vitamin or mineral that was needed. One supplement that I feel needs special attention is vitamin E. This one should probably be taken on an ongoing basis because it is intimately tied in with the endocrine system and our ovary functions. As always, check with your physician first.

THE LONG-TERM HEALTH OF OUR OVARIES AND REPRODUCTIVE SYSTEM

VITAMIN E

Synthetic Form: D-alpha tocopherol is the one I recommend, although there are other synthetic forms available.

Sources:

Vegetables: Alfalfa, broccoli, outer cabbage leaves, carrots, cauliflower, dandelion leaves, nasturtium leaves, soybeans, spinach, sprouts, and watercress.

Fruits and Nuts: Whole raw seeds in general, sunflower seeds in particular, almonds, filberts (hazelnuts), nuts in general, and avocados.

Fish and Meat: Haddock, kidney, ham, and chicken.

Grains: Wheat germ and wheat germ oil (must be kept in the refrigerator); one tablespoon provides 30 IUs of vitamin E, the RDA for women.

Dairy Products: Unknown.

Herbs: Avena sativa (oat), bladderwrack, and nettle leaves.

Natural Supplements: Dulse, kelp, cold-pressed safflower oil, peanut oil, cottonseed oil, bran oil, wheat oil, soybean oil, tocopherols, and d-alpha tocopherol.

Dosage: The recommended daily allowance (RDA) is 30 IUs.
Therapeutic Dose: 100 to 600 IUs daily are recommended, but women with high blood pressure or chronic rheumatic heart ailments cannot tolerate large dosages of vitamin E; they should consult a physician before taking any vitamin E. And anyone taking the vitamin should start with very small amounts, building up to a therapeutic range under the guidance of a doctor.
Megadose: Under a physician's guidance, from 600 to 2,000 or more IUs daily are recommended.

Toxicity: Vitamin E is essentially nontoxic; however, some people taking 4,000–30,000 IUs for long periods may experience some side-effects, such as heart palpitations, shortness of breath, and dizziness. Only when taken in large doses by a person with high blood pressure or a rheumatic heart condition can vitamin E become deadly.

Deficiency Symptoms: Very rarely is there a deficiency of vitamin E. Deficiencies related to vitamin E actually develop because the vitamin is not available in sufficient quantities to synthesize properly with other substances, such as polyunsaturated fatty acids (PUFA), nonspecific antioxidants, selenium, or sulfur-containing amino acids. For example, if vitamin E is insufficient to halt the oxidation of fatty acids, hemolytic anemia may occur because the hemoglobin is not kept within the cells.

When a deficiency in vitamin E does occur, however, there may be degeneration of the cardiopulmonary region, the formation of clots, decreased circulation, and strokes. Problems with sterility related to cell regeneration and other reproductive disorders in women, such as miscarriages, resorption of the fetus, and menopausal ailments, can also be brought on by lack of vitamin E.

Severe deficiencies of vitamin E can damage the kidneys, liver, and pancreas. A lack of the vitamin is implicated in nephritis (kidney tubules blocked by dead cells, halting the flow of urine out of the body), pancreatic inflammation, and gastrointestinal upsets from faulty absorption of fats and fat-soluble vitamins.

Allies: Vitamin E is most effective when taken with vitamin A, the vitamin B complex, vitamin C, fatty acids, and manganese. It works in concert with the microtrace element selenium: together vitamin E and selenium seem to destroy toxic peroxides that form within capillary cells; they also help produce antibodies.

Antagonists: Iron supplements interfere directly with assimilation of vitamin E. Doctors suggest that the two antagonists be taken 12 hours apart. Mineral oil, usually ingested for constipation, will also interfere with vitamin E by dissolving it. Only *cold-pressed* vegetable oils will release their inherent vitamin E.

Other antagonists to vitamin E are estrogens found in birth control pills and HRT, long known to be destroyers of vitamin E. Thyroid supplements, such as that derived from crushed sheep's thyroid, high amounts of chlorine in water (swimming in or drinking chlorinated city water), cod liver oil, and rancid fats and oils, all destroy vitamin E.

Recent Clinical Developments:

1. With vitamin E patrolling the body capillaries, veins and arteries also remain elastic and smooth so that no plaque or fiber can build up on the walls and produce atherosclerosis.

2. Women with varicose veins and phlebitis have been helped with supplements of vitamin E.

3. Women who suffer from menstrual pain, irregular cycles, spotting, or hemorrhaging have been helped when vitamin E was added to their diets. During menopause it helps hot flashes.

VITAMIN C

Synthetic Forms: Cevitamin acid, ascorbic acid, and sodium ascorbate.
Natural Supplements: Acerola and rose hips.
Sources:
Vegetables: Alfalfa tablets, asparagus, brussel sprouts, cabbage, carrots, celery, chard, collards, tomatoes, turnip greens, and water cress.
Fish and Meat: Chicken liver, rabbit heart, and liver.
Fruits and Nuts: Oranges, orange juice, lemon juice, tangerines, strawberries, almonds, bananas, blueberries, currants, cranberries, grapefruit, pineapple, cantaloupe, and apple juice.
Grains: Unknown.
Dairy Products: Skim milk.
Herbs: Buffalo berries, burdock seed, capsicum, coltsfoot, elderberries, marigold, oregano, paprika, parsley, and rose hips.
Dosage: The RDA for women is 60 mg.
Therapeutic Dose: 100 to 10,000 mg daily.
Megadose: On average, anything more than 115 grams (115,000 mg) constitutes a megadose for some individuals.

Toxicity: The level of toxicity is unknown. Because vitamin C is excreted on a daily basis, there is no fear of build-up or excessive storage in the body; however, when some people take 10,000 to 15,000 milligrams in one dose, symptoms such as a burning sensation during urination, diarrhea, or skin rash may occur. A skin rash reaction is probably caused by the filler holding the vitamin together. Diarrhea or a burning sensation during urination is an indication that the body has ample amounts of vitamin C, and the excess is being sloughed off through the urine or intestinal tract.

Deficiency Symptoms: Many of the symptoms of scurvy that Americans have in common are spongy gums, bleeding gums (especially during brushing), pyorrhea (a disorder of the gums), and loose teeth. More advanced signs of scurvy include capillary hemorrhaging, easy bruising with the bruises disappearing only after many days or weeks, swollen joints, and continual susceptibility to infections. In later stages of the disease there can be fractured bones, anemia, and respiratory and intestinal infections.

Other signals of vitamin C deficiency are wounds or broken bones that take an inordinate amount of time to heal, nosebleeds, peptic and duodenal ulcers, a reduction of hemoglobin which causes secondary anemia, and impaired adrenal function, which brings about fatigue, irritability, and exhaustion.

Allies: Vitamin C is most effective when taken with the vitamin B complex, bioflavonoids, calcium, and magnesium.

Antagonists: Many substances and circumstances can either diminish vitamin C's full effects or stop it from helping other vitamins and minerals in their particular synthesization processes. Following is a brief discussion of some of the worst antagonists.

Deoxycorticosterone depresses the action of vitamin C, consequently affecting the growth of the skeletal tissue. Aspirin, barbiturates, adrenaline, silbestrol, estrogen, sulfonamides, ammonium chloride, antihistamines, thiouracil, thyroid medications, and indomethacin either destroy vitamin C or inhibit uptake.

Recent Clinical Developments:

1. Vitamin C prevents adrenal exhaustion from stress. Adrenal exhaustion symptoms often parallel PMS symptoms. Vitamin C accelerates the natural production of cortisone and helps

improve the usage of cortisone within the body. (Pantothenic acid, a B vitamin, can also be used if adrenal exhaustion is present.)

2. Wrinkles and aging are accelerated without vitamins E and C present as anti-aging agents. Sagging skin is created by too little collagen in the cells, and vitamin C is very important to healthy collagen.

3. Vitamin C helps iron to be assimilated, and therefore helps with menstrual problems that create anemia because too much iron is being lost.

STRENGTHENING OUR BONES

If you suspect that you have osteoporosis, the first thing to do is see your physician and get a diagnosis. If you want to deal with it homeopathically and nutritionally, then the following information will help educate you. Take it to your nutritionist and talk it over and see what is best for you to take.

It's important NOT to take just one mineral, such as calcium, and nothing else when strengthening our bones. For instance, one study showed that if you took vitamin D alone, you would lose cortical bone. If you took calcium gluconate WITH vitamin D, then there were no bone changes. If you take only calcium, it will leach the magnesium, one of our great bone-builders, out of the body, thereby sabotaging our efforts to strengthen our bones.

There is a lovely chemical and metabolic dance going on inside our bodies to keep our bones strong. We need adequate amounts of vitamin C, for instance. And there is a "magic triangle" between calcium, magnesium, and phosphorus that must be taken into consideration or again, our bones won't be strong; they'll grow weaker. It has been found that the trace mineral boron plays an active role in bone strength, too. According to Dr. Mark Hegsted, professor of nutrition at Harvard University, osteoporosis is more than just a calcium problem. Boron, phosphorus, silicon, and magnesium are involved, too.

BORON

In 1993, the *British Journal of Nutrition* published a study where the intake of boron was increased from 0.25 to 3.25 mg per day. They found an increase in estradiol and testosterone in the blood and a decrease in the amount of calcium and magnesium lost via urination. This suggested that a higher intake of boron could reduce the bone loss associated with menopause and cessation of ovarian function.

In another study in the United States, boron was increased from 0.25 mg to 3.0 mg per day, producing the same results. They also found an increase in estrogen and testosterone levels in the blood.

Sources:

Vegetables: Legumes, cabbage, broccoli, or any leafy vegetables in general.
Fruits and Nuts: Almonds, apples, dates, honey, peanuts, hazel nuts, pears, prunes, and raisins.
Fish and Meat: Unknown.
Grains: Soy meal.
Dairy Products: Unknown.

Dosage:

Therapeutic Dose: 3 mg or less daily.

Toxicity: Boron is toxic if you take too much. Before taking any boron supplement, you should check with your physician or nutritionist.

Deficiency Symptoms: Because of boron's intimate chemical relationships with calcium, magnesium, estrogen, and testosterone, there can be a potential loss of bone, more than normal.

Recent Clinical Developments: In another study where participants consumed 3.0 mg of boron per day, after only 8 days the post-menopausal group of women had lost 40 percent less calcium, 30 percent less phosphorus, and 33 percent less magnesium. They in fact had retained 52 mg of calcium per day from the intake of this trace mineral.

VITAMIN D

Synthetic Forms: Irradiated ergosterol and calciferol D-2.

Natural Sources: Yeast, fish oils (cholecalciferol), cod liver oil, D-3, and viosterol, a solution of irradiated ergosterol in vegetable oil. (Unlike cod liver oil, viosterol does not contain vitamin A.)

Sources:

Vegetables Watercress.

Fruits and Nuts: Sunflower seeds.

Fish and Meat: Chicken liver and salmon.

Grains: Wheat germ.

Dairy Products: Yogurt, egg yolks, and butter.

Herbs: Annotto seed.

Dosage: The RDA is 400 IUs.

Therapeutic Dose: This should be under a physician's guidance.

Toxicity: Vitamin D-2 can be toxic if taken in excessive doses, especially for infants. The toxicity of vitamin D-3, the natural form found in fish liver oils, however, has not been proven. For this reason it is best to take the natural form. And anyone who is receiving megadoses of vitamin D under a doctor's guidance should have frequent serum calcium blood tests to keep a check on the levels of calcium in the blood. At the first suggestion of hypercalcemia, the dosage should be reduced.

The symptoms of acute overdose of vitamin D are frequent urination, loss of appetite, vomiting, diarrhea, dizziness, muscular weakness, nausea, weariness, and calcification of the soft tissue of the lungs, heart, and blood vessels. General malaise or depression may also appear. And calcium deposits in the liver, lungs, kidneys, and stomach may occur. Sunstroke is thought to sometimes be a toxic effect from too much vitamin D as well.

To halt hypervitaminosis, an individual should stop taking the vitamin D supplement. If the poisoning is severe, he or she should avoid all foods that tend to increase the blood calcium for a length of time decided upon by the physician—that is, until the toxicity has subsided and calcium has returned to normal levels.

Deficiency Symptoms: Each winter vitamin D shortages appear in people who live in the higher northern latitudes, because their main, natural supply is cut off: the ultraviolet rays of the sun cannot penetrate clothes. Too little vitamin D in the intestinal tract leads to inadequate absorption of calcium, which in turn creates a retention of phosphorus in the kidneys, triggering faulty mineralization of bone structures.

One of the most severe diseases caused by insufficient vitamin D is rickets, which affects children all over the world, especially in the Third World. This disease, resulting from a lack of calcium, unassailable without vitamin D, produces soft bones.

In adults this ailment is referred to as osteomalacia; in older adults it is called osteoporosis and is marked by mineral depletion of the bones. The bones become pitted with holes and look like sponges. They become weak and brittle. A small bump can cause a broken hip or pelvic bone; an elderly person can be up to 6 months in the hospital or in a cast because the bones knit so slowly from the deficiency of vitamin D.

The endocrine system suffers badly with insufficient vitamin D. The parathyroid gland may be particularly affected. This gland, which sends out hormones to regulate the transport of calcium to parts of the body, may begin to place too little calcium in the system, thereby accelerating tetany: the symptoms include muscular numbness of the limbs, tingling, and spasm. The thyroid may also be affected by too little vitamin D, resulting in flabbiness, poor metabolism of ingested food, and diabetic distress.

As I've indicated, calcium cannot be properly absorbed without vitamin D. And if the level of calcium becomes dangerously low, the heart can be adversely affected. Thus heart racing, flutters, or fibrillation (twitching) suddenly and without warning can result from lack of vitamin D.

Eye problems may occur. For example, myopia (nearsightedness) is known to manifest from an imbalance of calcium. Other ailments that can result from insufficient vitamin D are faulty tooth development, constipation, potbelly (especially in children), pyorrhea, faulty jaw development, and perspiration on the back of the head when one sleeps.

Allies: Vitamin D's primary allies are calcium, vitamin A (ten parts vitamin A to one part vitamin D) and vitamin C. It is also more effective when taken with cholin, fatty acids, and phosphorus.

Antagonists: Vitamin D stored in the intestinal walls can be destroyed by the use of mineral oil.

Recent Clinical Developments: Side-effects from corticosteroid therapy to relieve arthritic and rheumatoid symptoms may cause urinary losses of calcium and phosphorus, in turn leading to bone demineralization.

Cigarette smoking affects the bones, which are made mostly of calcium and phosphorus. These minerals are responsible for the hardness of bones, and they become more soluble in acidic solutions: smoking is known to increase the acidity of bone tissue. Moreover, bone minerals dissolve and are absorbed into the blood much more quickly when a woman smokes. Smoking makes calcium leave the bones to move into the blood. Thus the bones become brittle, and the woman can develop symptoms of hypercalcemia.

In addition, women going through menopause may benefit from increased amounts of vitamin D, perhaps received through a mixture of powdered calcium bone meal, cod liver oil, and raw vegetable juice. As the ovaries cease production of eggs, estrogen declines. Vitamin D acts as an expediter of calcium into the bones, and the pituitary and adrenal glands use vitamin D as an energizer. The vitamin helps to metabolize the calcium through the hormones to strengthen the bone-building cells—a function previously performed by the estrogen hormone.

CALCIUM

Synthetic Form: Microcrystalline hydroxapatite (Metagenics—I recommend this variety), calcium carbonate, calcium pantothenate, (used in the treatment of deficiencies of pantothenic acid and not a good source of calcium per se), and calcium sulfate anhydrons.

Natural Sources: Kelp, bone meal calcium (not recommended because it is unreasonably high in phosphorus), calcium lactate (a lactic acid salt derived from milk that is easily absorbed by the body and that works mainly on muscle-related ailments; it contains twice as much calcium as the gluconate variety, but people who have allergies to milk may react adversely to it), calcium gluconate (a gluconic acid salt derived from glucose that is easily absorbed by the body and works mainly on the nerves and blood calcium levels; since it is not as high in calcium as lactate or bone meal varieties, more supplementation is needed), eggshell calcium (derived from crushed chicken egg shells), oyster shell calcium (derived from crushed oyster shells, containing a minimal amount of phosphorus with natural trace minerals), di-cal (di-calcium) phosphate (natural or synthetic with 22% phosphorus added), liquid calcium (used when a person has problems absorbing calcium; it should be taken with vitamin D), and dolomite (a source of bone meal calcium and magnesium in proper proportions; it may or may not have vitamin A or vitamin D with it—so check the label).

Sources:

Vegetables: Chard, watercress, cauliflower, broccoli, endive, kohlrabi, rutabaga, spinach, turnips, parsnips, carrots, rhubarb, green beans, lettuce, onions, soybeans, alfalfa sprouts, beet greens, celery, chick peas (garbanzos), collards, flax seed, kidney beans, lentils, okra, and tomatoes.

Fruits and Nuts: Almonds, avocados, dried apricots, bananas, cranberries, coconuts, currants, dates, figs, grapefruit, lemons, limes, plums, peaches, prunes, pineapple, raisins, raspberries, and black walnuts.

Meat and Fish: Oysters, shrimp, lobster, liver, and broiled chicken.

Grains: Soy flour.

Dairy Products: Buttermilk, most cheeses, evaporated milk, and skim milk.

Herbs: Arrow root, carrageen (Irish moss), chamomile, chives, cleavers, coltsfoot, dandelion root, flaxseed, horsetail grass (equisetum), meadow sweet, nettle, pimpernel, plantain, rest harrow, shepherd's purse, silverweed, sorrel, and toadflax.

Dosage: The RDA for women 18 and over is 1800 mg.

Therapeutic Dose: Continued immoderate doses of calcium, along with vitamin D, can cause hypercalcemia (the calcification of organs or bones), so anyone believing that her level of calcium is low should consult a physician, undergo the appropriate testing, and adhere to a program set up by their doctor.

Toxicity: The level of toxicity for calcium has not been established, but symptoms of toxicity include calcium deposits within the kidneys or other organs, as well as sluggishness of those organs.

Deficiency Symptoms: At the onset of a deficiency of calcium there may be restlessness, nervousness, and even tremors of the hands. In addition, muscles may cramp and there may be numbness and tingling in the extremities. The heart may race or palpitate erratically. Stunted growth and bone problems, such as rickets in children, osteoporosis (the softening of the bone or the bones becoming porous and brittle), and teeth problems, as well as slow blood-clotting, may also occur.

Insomnia seems to be the most common symptom of insufficient calcium. Other symptoms of a deficiency are lack of courage, will power, or the will to live. There may be difficulty in thinking or completing thoughts, forgetfulness, brooding, depression, afternoon headaches, sighing, excess saliva in the mouth, or cramping toes at night. The inability to relax or stay put, puffiness in parts of the body, or an increase in weight can also manifest.

Allies: Calcium works as a team with phosphorus. Calcium also acts in cooperation with vitamins A, D, and C and magnesium. Other nutrients that aid its effectiveness are fatty acids (vitamin F), manganese, and hydrochloric acid, usually given in the form of glutamic acid hydrochloride.

Antagonists: Any time one or both of the other members of the "trinity"—vitamin D and magnesium—are missing, calcium is not absorbed. On the other hand, if magnesium is taken in large doses alone, a deficiency of calcium can occur.

In addition, a high intake of phosphorus will cause a loss of calcium. A lack of hydrochloric acid in the digestive juices will further retard calcium's assimilation.

During times of negative stress for a menopausal woman, the adrenal glands release cortisone, which pulls minerals, including calcium, from the bones. And cortisone medication or shots, as well as supplements of aspirin or thyroxine to aid the thyroid, also lower the levels of calcium in our bodies.

Other drugs that stop absorption of calcium are penicillin, chlormycetin, neomycin, and the steroids prednisone and dexmethasone.

Phytic acid, found in wheat, is known to block absorption of calcium, too. Moreover, foods such as spinach, rhubarb, and chocolate contain oxalic acid, which will bind with free calcium to form a non-nutritious compound called calcium oxalate: this oxalate can build up crystal formations in the kidneys or bladder, creating stones.

Recent Clinical Developments: Menopausal or PMS symptoms may be nothing more than a calcium deficiency. Symptoms such as nervousness, irritability, crying, tremors or trembling, restlessness, and lower back aches indicate that the blood calcium levels are low as the monthly cycle approaches. Then, if the calcium is still low as the cycle begins, further problems with spotting, cramping, and irregularity may occur.

Women also suffer the symptoms of a deficiency of calcium during menopause. Some women during that time feel like they are going crazy. Calcium will help women get through this period of changing hormones without tranquilizers.

Victims of osteoporosis are usually deficient in magnesium, vitamin D, and phosphorus, as well as calcium, an indication of how closely these vitamins and minerals work as a team. Magnesium is especially important: it calms the pituitary gland, the master controller for the entire endocrine system. With too little magnesium the pituitary sends out a hormonal signal for the bones to give up their calcium and send it to the blood, part of the probable cause of osteoporosis.

The parathyroid gland (composed of four pea-like glands located on either side of the thyroid at the base of the throat) is responsible for how much or how little calcium enters the bloodstream. It is postulated that the hormone released by the parathyroid and the hormone thyrocalcitinon, which prevents the loss of calcium, are out of kilter with one another, causing the bones to lose too much calcium and become porous, brittle, and easily broken.

Doctors can successfully keep thyrocalcitonin in check so that the other hormone does not rob the bones of needed calcium. A little known herb called springtime horsetail (equisetum), rich in silica, is being used on osteoporosis patients in California with tremendous success: the patients' bones are beginning to knit and mend within 2 weeks of taking the tablet-form herb under a physician's guidance.

Women who wake up screaming in the middle of the night because of spasm and cramping in their muscles are also lacking sufficient calcium. Lower back pains may be related to a deficiency in calcium as well. Furthermore, the discs that act as shock absorbers and cushions for the bone vertebrae also rely on a continued supply of calcium so that they do not harden, become brittle, or deteriorate.

Bruxism (the grinding of one's teeth during sleep) was once thought to be an emotional disorder. Instead, it is caused by a deficiency of calcium and pantothenic acid and is easily corrected.

In many cases, women whose bones are slow to knit have low levels of hydrochloric acid (found in the stomach), which is necessary to help assimilate calcium: without adequate calcium bone healing takes much longer.

Calcium is barely absorbed anytime sugars are eaten because sugars trigger alkaline digestive juices instead; however, in experiments using milk sugar or lactose, absorption of calcium was increased tremendously so that within 30 minutes the mineral was being whisked to the bones.

MAGNESIUM

Synthetic Form: Magnesium citrate (a laxative), magnesium sulfate (a laxative), magnesium hydroxide (milk of magnesia), magnesium gluconate (felt to work best on nerve-related problems, including fear, nerve and muscle twitching, restlessness, bed-wetting, and apprehension), magnesium phosphate (considered best for dealing with cramping muscles), magnesium oxide (best for muscle aches and pains or stiffness in the muscles), and magnesium sulfate (used to treat delirium tremens in association with alcoholism).

Sources:

Vegetables: Asparagus, beet greens, beets, corn, cabbage, cauliflower, cucumbers, dandelion greens, kale, kohlrabi, lettuce, radishes, spinach, savoy cabbage, soybeans, okra, watercress and most leafy, green vegetables.

Fruits and Nuts: Apples, cherries, figs, gooseberries, grapes, lemons, limes, persimmons, plums, pomegranates, peaches, pears, most nuts and seeds, and carob.

Meat and Fish: Kidneys.

Grains: Oats, buckwheat, and raw wheat germ.

Diary Products: Unknown.

Herbs: Bladderwrack, black willow bark, broom tops, carrot leaves, devil's bit, dandelion herb, meadow sweet, mullein leaves, parsley, peppermint, walnut leaves, and wintergreen.

Dosage: The RDA is 300 mg.

Therapeutic Dose: Adelle Davis reported that between 600 and 900 mg seem to be required to maintain our health in our present-day environment.

Toxicity: Large amounts of magnesium can be harmful, especially if a person is evidencing low calcium and high phosphorus intake. Because excess magnesium is excreted via the kidneys, anyone with weak or diseased kidneys will not be able to get rid of the mineral as quickly as the body might wish, and toxicity can build up. If large amounts of magnesium upset the calcium ratio, what seem to be symptoms of a deficiency of calcium will develop: nervousness, muscle spasms, tics, trembling, tremors, and so forth.

Deficiency Symptoms: One of the most common symptoms, and many of these plague a certain percentage of pre-menopausal and menopausal women (and it's blamed on PMS), is a sensitivity to noise. A continual state of grief or depression, coupled with apprehension, may also manifest.

Muscles may spasm and jerk, and eyes will have a tendency to "wander." There may be a yellowish cast to the white area of the eyeballs, and women will sleep with their eyes HALF OPEN.

Teeth may prove to be extraordinarily sensitive to moderately cool water, or may ache for no reason. There can be twitches or tremors in any part of the body. And the heart may suddenly race and then settle back to its normal rhythm.

Other less obvious signs of magnesium deficiency may be an aching neck and shoulder muscles, an allergy to woolen products, bloating of the intestines, gas, bed-wetting, and a common menopausally blamed symptom, a BURNING sensation in the mouth.

Allies: Magnesium's primary ally is calcium. It is also more effective when taken with vitamins B-6, C, and D, phosphorus, and protein.

Antagonists: Heavy milk drinkers who are adults can have severe deficiencies of magnesium. Other foods that inhibit absorption of magnesium are those high in phytic acid, such as brown and whole-wheat bread and oatmeal.

Several drugs are antagonists of magnesium. Diuretics as a whole are dangerous enemies of magnesium: most doctors will advise a patient on diuretics to eat sufficient amounts of food containing potassium and neglect to say that the person should also increase the amount of magnesium.

Patients who suffer from congestive heart failure and are treated with ammonium chloride and mercurial diuretics will also have deficiencies of magnesium.

In addition, calciferol, a synthetic variety of vitamin D, and fluorine will bind with magnesium and carry it out of the body before it can be absorbed and used. Anyone who ingests large amounts of calcium carbonate (an antacid preparation) will also suffer a severe magnesium deficiency, which, if continued, can create kidney stones.

The worst enemy of magnesium is X-rays. The deadly rays can decrease the amounts of magnesium in the body.

Recent Clinical Developments: A certain type of insomnia responds to magnesium. The insomnia associated with nervousness that leads to tossing and turning all night can be aided by this mineral.

High cholesterol can sometimes be attributed to a lack of magnesium as well. Even though vitamin B-6 may be adequate, too little magnesium available will prevent lecithin from being formed so that it can use the fats and cholesterols that have collected within the body. In one test, patients with heart ailments who were given 500 mg of magnesium daily had their blood cholesterol levels fall dramatically within 30 days of beginning the supplementation.

High blood pressure is known to drop dramatically when ample amounts of magnesium are given to heart patients. The temperature of the human body is regulated in part by the amount of magnesium available. People who have depleted magnesium stores often get chilled easily.

PHOSPHORUS

Synthetic Form: Calcium phosphate.

Natural Supplement: Bone meal.

Sources:

Vegetables: Lima beans, brussel sprouts, chick peas (garbanzos), corn, dandelion greens, lentils, okra, parsnips, peas, soybeans, spinach, and watercress.

Fruits and Nuts: Grapes, apples, avocados, cherries, grapefruit, lemons, limes, pumpkin, passion fruit, plums, raisins, almonds, pecans, and walnuts.

Meat and Fish: Veal chops, beef liver, lean beef, salmon, halibut, and oysters.

Grains: Oatmeal.

Dairy Products: Cheese, egg yolks, and milk.

Herbs: Calamus, caraway seeds, chickweed, garlic, licorice root, marigold flowers, meadow sweet flowers, sesame, and sorrel.

Dosage: The RDA is 1800 mg.

Therapeutic Dose: Anyone wishing to take higher doses of phosphorus should exercise caution. Any megadoses should be administered under a physician's care, and a proportionate amount of calcium should be ingested to insure that the metabolism will not become imbalanced.

Toxicity: There is no known toxicity with this mineral, but a person taking an excessive amount of phosphorus without a proportionate amount of calcium may begin to exhibit a deficiency of calcium.

Deficiency Symptoms: Without adequate phosphorus, vitamin D, and calcium, stunted growth, poor tooth development, and bone deformation will develop. And if the calcium-phosphorus metabolism is unbalanced, ailments such as arthritis, rickets, cavities of the teeth, and pyorrhea of the gums may manifest.

Some of the less obvious symptoms of a moderate deficiency of phosphorus are loss of appetite, irregular weight gain or loss for no reason, irregular breath, and mental or physical fatigue. Vague nervous disorders may also occur, such as being frightened of the next day, dislike of the opposite sex or of a job, and fear of the unknown. Moreover, there may be a loss of muscle tone or a numbness of the arms and legs. And a deficiency of phosphorus may also induce repeated attacks of bronchitis or jaundice.

Allies: Phosphorus's primary allies are calcium and vitamin D. Vitamin C is also indispensable to phosphorus: without enough vitamin C, the mineral is depleted from the body. And phosphorus is more effective when taken with vitamins A and F, iron, manganese, and protein.

Antagonists: Excess white sugar is probably the biggest threat to the phosphorus balance in the body. One doctor believes that ailments such as arthritis, pyorrhea, and tooth decay are brought about by a calcium-phosphorus imbalance from high sugar intake.

Other substances that deplete phosphorus are excessive amounts of iron, aluminum, and magnesium. Antacid tablets containing aluminum or magnesium hydroxide will interfere greatly with the phosphorus balance: anyone buying such over-the-counter products for digestive upset or ulcer conditions should check the labels carefully.

Aspirin, thyroid or cortisone medication, and many other drugs will also leave the body deficient in both calcium and phosphorus.

Recent Clinical Developments: Phosphorus is also beneficial in preventing osteomalacia (an adult form of rickets) and osteoporosis. In addition, because phosphorus helps calcium in the ossification to create strong bones, phosphorus speeds up healing of fractures and reduces losses of calcium.

Emotional situations, such as menopausal stress, illness, or surgery may cause the adrenal glands to release large amounts of cortisone to protect the body. The cortisone then draws minerals from the bones, precipitating the urinary loss of both calcium and phosphorus—a vicious cycle that continues until the stress is relieved or until proper supplementation takes place.

CHAPTER 20

FLOWER AND GEM ESSENCES FOR MENOPAUSE

Another tool in our box of natural healing options is known as natural essences. Many of us are familiar with Dr. Edward Bach's flower remedies. He was a very famous British homeopathic doctor in the early 1900s through the 1930s who pioneered new concepts in homeopathy, including bowel nosodes, a discovery also shared with Dr. Paterson.

Bach was always looking for something from nature that would not cause the aggravations or "retracing" (Hering's Law of Cure) that homeopathy could bring on. It should be noted that only 20 percent of all people suffer from an aggravation (an intensification of the symptoms they had at the time they took the homeopathic remedy) and it would last a few seconds to weeks, depending on the strength of the potency given and the problems the client had at the time.

Hering's Law of Cure states that when someone takes a homeopathic remedy, the Vital Force, in its infinite wisdom, begins the cure from the most important organs (the brain and heart) to the least important organs (the skin). It starts at the head and works downward to the feet. It works from the inside to the outside. I call this law "retracing" because the vital force will make the body release whatever is still held in the cells, tissue, bone, cartilage, and so forth, that has not yet run its full course. That could range from shock and trauma due to an emotional experience to a car accident and anything in between. The body does hold a memory of all the damage ever done to us—whether it is on a spiritual, mental, emotional, or physical level.

Our body is like a sponge that retains all the injuries experienced by us—unless we totally work through those events, completely. If we don't, then what is left is retained and remembered by our body. That, in part, is what helps to create dis-ease, or being out of balance or harmony—because we have not been able to release that shock or trauma from our system. Homeopathy is an energy medicine that connects with our physical body and stimulates our central nervous system or parasympathetic nervous system.

Bach was always striving to find a gentle cure that would help a client return to a state of harmony or wellness. He finally left the field of homeopathy and moved into one that I call "natural essences." For more than a decade, he worked with buds from trees, flowers, and even water to try to find a safe, natural healing process. Eventually he chose 38 natural essences, and the name Bach Flower Remedies was coined. Today, they are known and used around the world. More important, they have opened a huge door to an area that has been little explored until just recently. It is not only safe, but is even more gentle than homeopathy.

As a homeopathic practitioner, I started using Bach flower remedies decades ago right along with the remedy I dispensed to my client, because I wanted to spare my patients the discomfort of aggravations or retracing as much as I could. The Bach flower remedies were reputed to help mental and emotional areas of discomfort. I have found that they also resonate not only spiritually, but physically, as well. I've talked with many other users of these natural essences over the years, and they have had similar experiences with them. From a legal standpoint, at least in the United States, by FDA law, there can be no claims of what they are used for—at all. Thank goodness a number of books are available on these natural essences so that interested people can find out how, when, and why to use them.

As the years went by in my practice, I saw my clients experience discomfort on the spiritual, mental, emotional, or physical levels that the Bach natural essences did not address. Having been raised by a mother who was an herbalist and a father who was an Eastern Cherokee shaman, I was no stranger to understanding my connection with the plant people—be they flowers, trees, weeds, or any organic substance. I had been trained by an Apache medicine woman, Oh Shinnah Fast Wolf, on how to work with herbs and gemstones as energy medicine; these applications parallel Dr. Bach's discovery.

I have found, as Bach did, that each and every plant, tree, rock, grass, or any other natural material, has a unique and specialized area of skill and expertise that can immediately translate to a particular human condition. Native Americans have known for thousands of years that wherever they lived, the Great Spirit provided medicines that could heal them. They learned of herbs, flowers, grasses, and trees that could help them come back into harmony or balance, and therefore get healthy once again.

Natural essences are created with Dr. Bach's method by setting the flower blossoms into a bowl of water outside into direct sunlight for 1–3 hours. The natural essence would then be strained off and mixed with a certain amount of brandy and the energy imprint was held in it forever.

One of the greatest benefits of using a natural essence is that they are safe, non-addictive, and free of adverse side-effects and aggravation. They "dance" in concert with homeopathic remedies and do not antidote them—a big plus because many items can antidote a homeopathic substance. For every human ill or ailment, I'm sure that there's an equivalent out there in Nature to help them.

The field of natural essences is small, indeed. When you consider that Dr. Bach settled upon 38 essences for use with his patients, and there are literally millions of flowers and other plants out there to be researched to find out what each can be used for, we have a long, scientific road ahead of us! But what an exciting prospect! My natural essence pharmacopoeia currently has about a hundred essences that I have used on patients over the years.

Natural essences can help all human conditions, whether in the spiritual, mental, emotional, or physical fields of manifestation. Generally speaking, when a natural essence does affect the physical body, it is much more gentle in its movement than a homeopathic remedy. Roughly 10 percent of the population cannot use homeopathic treatment because they are too sensitive to it; they "prove" every remedy they take, which is a miserable experience for them.

Natural essences can help this 10 percent become well without the rigors or suffering brought on by homeopathic treatment. The more sensitive you are, the more I encourage you to use natural essences as a tool in your wellness kit to stay healthy. They can be used acutely (for short-duration problems when the illness has a natural end to it—usually 7 days or less, such as cold or flu) or for chronic conditions, such as major disease patterns.

Often, when a client has been through the medical mill and has come out the other end worse for wear and financially destitute, natural essences can be like a miracle—not only in gently stimulating the vital force to begin to heal them, but also in being a cheap resource compared to pharmacy drugs. Natural essences are especially useful when a client has been drugged too long and too often; a typical case in point is too many rounds of antibiotics. The elderly, who fall into a special category because they are on a fixed income and their vital force may not be strong enough to respond sufficiently to a homeopathic remedy, will respond to a natural essence, which can make all the difference in the world; sometimes miraculously so.

SEXUALITY

BLANKET FLOWER is well known to gently stir the 'fires' of our body and make us feel more sexual, more feminine and womanly. It can put us back in touch with those deep, sensual, and sexual feelings we had before menopause and help us to reconnect to them in a very earthy way, but creatively, also. It stimulates orgasm.

OCOTILLO has given provers a warm, wonderful rushing sensation from deep in their tailbone region, right up their spine. This is known as the seat of the Kundalini where the "fire" of our sexuality resides. This essence will stimulate that area. It gives you a sense of freedom, of having your feet planted solidly in the earth and your hands stretching into and reaching the sky. It's a every exhilarating, yet earthy essence.

TIGER LILY should be considered if your libido is dragging or nonexistent. This essence gives a heightened sense of one's own sensuality and sexuality. If you had a healthy sex drive before menopause and now find it gone, then this essence may be of assistance in urging it to return.

DEPRESSION

Please note that these natural essences are a SUPPORT to prescribed homeopathic treatment. They will not, in a majority of cases, cure your depression, but rather will alleviate it to a certain extent. Do not take a natural essence in lieu of homeopathic treatment—rather, use them in conjunction with one another.

Where a natural essence can be used is IF the depression is less than a month in duration, and is considered acute. Then, one or more of these remedies may aid in symptoms known as depression.

BLACK TOURMALINE GEMSTONE is an essence that brings trapped or hidden (repressed or suppressed) issues to the surface. This is for menopausal women who have held onto their emotional hurts, memories, and traumas (usually unconsciously, although it can be conscious too) and are ready to release them—once and for all. This is a very gentle-working essence that brings these issues up, one at a time, and does not overwhelm the person with too many feelings or memories at one time. It will definitely raise suppressed or repressed issues, and you might want to start out with only one drop under your tongue three to four times daily.

Our provers have found this to be a powerful essence to bring up old, unresolved issues and feelings. The key here is that you can control how much or how little, depending upon how many drops you take a day; so a little goes a long way until you find your comfort zone. When an issue does arise, STOP taking the gem essence and work on the issue or emotion until you've completed it. Then take another dose when you're ready for another issue to come up to be addressed.

CENTURY PLANT is known as the cocoon to butterfly essence. It helps a woman who is stuck in a particular pattern in her life, to break it and punch a hole through it, or dissolve the barrier, and move on. This is a catalyst type of essence that acts quickly and decisively anytime a woman feels trapped or unable to get out of a situation. It helps the woman make choices and become actively motivated to change her direction or lifestyle.If you want to change—then use this essence. It's gentle and helps you to look at your life in a more macrocosmic way. You will see the forest for the trees.

GOWER RAMSEY BUTTERFLY ORCHID is good for its name. The orchid's flowers are literally shaped like small, bright yellow with red spotted butterflies! Known as the transformation essence, this helps a woman who is mired deeply in her negative feelings, where such feelings thrive, unabated or unchallenged. This essence helps turn the tables on negativeness toward a positive outlook that begins with a deep knowing within the woman. As the essence takes hold, this inner positiveness expresses and manifests itself outward in positive directions, decisions, and choices for the woman.

MEADOW GOLDENROD is an incredibly euphoric and uplifting essence that can lift menopausal depression of the darkest type. It is for heart-wounding issues (divorce, rape, incest, separation, loss of a loved one, etc.), healing them and replacing them with a constant state of joy about living life. This essence has the ability to make a woman feel as if every minute of her day is felt and experienced to the fullest in a positive sense. Even bad news and problems are ameliorated to a degree with this essence so that you don't get "hooked in" personally by whatever issues you have to deal with. It bestows compassion instead of judgment on others.

OWLS CLOVER is for a menopausal woman who is depressed, but really, there's a lot of festering anger boiling just beneath the surface of her subconscious. Depression is anger turned against ourselves because we feel helpless or unworthy. Owls Clover essence directly confronts these issues and makes you feel as if you are worth caring about, worth loving from an inner standpoint. This is a major "victim's essence," and I use it when dealing with codependent issues in a woman. This essence puts you in direct and positive touch with the fact that you are worthy on every level of not only being helped, but being healed. It breaks the victim's response in you and puts you in touch with far healthier aspects of yourself.

PEAR BLOSSOM is a wonderful menopausal depression remedy. It addresses issues of the ability to nurture the self and deal with mothering and nurturing issues with mother or with women, in general. This is for anyone who has had a bad relationship with their mother and wants to repair this wound with her. If our mother has wounded us, we struggle on several levels with this. First of all, if the mother is still alive, we must interact with her. Second, the female energy within ourselves (the left side of our body) has been wounded, too. If we continue to avoid mother on the outside, external world, we are also suppressing our feminine-female-mothering energy within ourselves simultaneously. The net result is that we aren't operating fully or completely as a human being—we're in denial, rage, humiliation, or some other emotionally "stuck" position, so the energy cannot be released, transformed or utilized in a more positive direction or way.

This fruit tree remedy allows us the conscious choice to begin to remember and to bring up whatever mother issues we have, and to begin to heal it. Although you may never be able to fully resolve the mother issue with the human who bore you, you CAN change yourself and your attitudes toward her—which is where this remedy will create the healing. It does not mean you're necessarily going to "fix" mother and make all things right with her. The real target of this remedy is getting you to see mother differently, in a more compassionate, understanding, and forgiving light. And when you can do that, you are also being compassionate, understanding, and forgiving of yourself and your inner woman. Then, true healing takes place.

This remedy is of special use for those who were adopted or put in an orphanage, or who were put through a series of foster homes and really never were able to be mother-nurtured in the positive sense. If you came out of a family where mother was never there (Super Mom of the 80s and 90s, particularly where she is juggling job, children, spouse, and house), or if you came out of a family where mother was physically there, but was never there for you emotionally to nurture you as you needed, then this is the remedy for you.

PERUVIAN BLUE OPAL is what I call a little slice of Heaven. This semi-precious gemstone is the color of the blue sky above and has definite uplifting qualities. This is an excellent essence for acute depression. On days when you get up and feel "blah," just take a couple of drops and watch the storm clouds within you melt away. It also bestows a sense of joy about being alive that is hard to match with another essence.

PINK EVENING PRIMROSE deals with menopausal depression issues regarding our family, our guilt that maybe we weren't a good enough parent, or just weren't up to the job of being a mother in the first place. This essence is about cleaning up the toxicity found in our family that stunts our growth, creates guilt, brings on depression, or in some way stops us from growing—which is our right in the first place. It helps to cleanse the past slate of ourselves in relation to our family. If we have a child who has "gone wrong" and we've taken on the burden of guilt that it was our fault, then this is the remedy to consider. This is also a good essence to consider for women who get into the "empty nest" syndrome.

PRICKLY PEAR CACTUS is for a menopausal woman who feels trapped—and there is no place to go—at least as she perceives it in her state. This essence dissolves the walls of imprisonment, whatever form they take, and allows her to see what the bars are, and to make the choice not to be trapped any longer. It imbues the woman with a personal sense of freedom within herself, and later this will reflect in the environment around her and she'll respond or react differently to the situations.

SEA PINK is a beautiful dry, desert flower of the Southwest that gives a woman a sense of light-heartedness, and enables her to tap into the menopausal woman's inner child. This is a very playful and uplifting essence that can aid in pulling a woman out of the depths of her own personal darkness. It aids in helping the woman to re-integrate her own, damaged child and own her and love her, and herself. There is an incredible child-like joy that suffuses the woman when taking this essence.

YARROW is one of the most powerful essences for menopausal women who have problems setting up boundaries to protect themselves from Life, from the demands of others (be it on a personal level or a business level). This essence instills a sense of what is right and not right for you to do in your daily life. It gives you the ability to say no and stick to it and mean it. I use this essence a great deal because most women, whether depressed or not, have not learned to say no often enough and this essence starts to break the cycle of codependent habits of serving others all the time, but forgetting to serve yourself. Yarrow instills a healthy sense of what is right or wrong for you to focus your energy, time, and care into. Most important, from a healing standpoint, women need this to learn to give themselves permission to heal.

MENOPAUSE ANXIETY OR PANIC ATTACKS

AQUAMARINE essence is one I have used over decades. I call it "Mother Nature's natural tranquilizer" and have often used it in lieu of anti-depressants for my clients. Anyone who has seen this translucent green-blue gemstone can attest to its inherent beauty. It reminds us of the ocean—a calm, lovely ocean, not a raging one. When taken as an essence for menopausal anxiety and panic attacks, it calms us within minutes and allows us to operate in our daily world with coherence and focus.

BLANKET FLOWER essence helps calm a person who is hyperactive, nervous, high strung, or unable to simply relax. This is excellent for women who are Super Women or who have been balancing job and family issues and they are stressed out to the max.

COLVILLE'S YELLOW COLUMBINE is an essence of inestimable value in menopausal depression, anxiety, and panic attacks. This remedy has the capability of reconnecting a woman with her head AND heart. Too often, in depression, we're mired in the depths of our emotions, and we struggle to think coherently. This essence bridges that gap and helps us think clearly, with focus, and helps us to make decisions, instead of waffling on them or being unsure. A powerful essence for any woman who is too much into her "head," that is, the mental realm, where she's escaped to find solace from her emotional pain—or, just the opposite—she's mired in the refuse of many negative emotions such as anger, depression, guilt, insomnia, and anxiety, to name a few, and she cannot find a way to balance her feelings with her mental attributes.

BROOM SNAKEWEED is used for menopausal depression, anxiety, and panic attacks almost exclusively because it has the ability to help a woman deal directly with her fears—whether they are known fears or unknown doesn't matter. Any time fear stops you from acting appropriately under the circumstance, this essence will free you and allow you to speak up for yourself—or others, as the case may be. A premier anxiety and panic attack essence if fear is fueling your symptoms.

MONKSHOOD has been shown to stop a panic or anxiety attack in its tracks. This is an excellent essence for any kind of shock or trauma that sends you out of balance. It will quickly restore you, and the shock symptoms will go away within minutes. The same holds true if you begin to feel anxious (and you may or may not know why you are feeling this way) or full of panic (identified or not as to the reason for it occurring); this essence will grapple with it quickly and successfully.

This is one of our most influential essences. If your heart is beating hard, you're sweaty and shaking, and you feel like you're in "flight or fight" mode, this essence will unplug the adrenaline rush you're experiencing and help stop the anxiety or panic reaction. It is an essence that can be used for post-traumatic stress disorder symptoms, as well.

PETRIFIED SEQUOIA is a powerful essence to bring calm to the inner storm of menopausal anxiety or panic that a woman is experiencing. It allows her to know that she's in that state, but it stops her from connecting into it so that she reacts to it. I call this the "Zen" gem essence because it bestows a benign, compassionate outlook regarding yourself and whatever emotional state you are feeling at the time; it is not disconnection. Instead, it brings in your mind to look upon all your chaotic feelings and you are able to decide, via your own free-will choice, to either get totally immersed in that emotion, or not. This essence bestows a very calming sense around a woman; it engages her own inner sense of peace and harmony (even though she may not feel as if she has any, she does, and this essence will connect her directly with that core of herself).

TIGER LILY is for the woman who is anxious. She fears she's going to contract some kind of virus, bacteria, or disease, and die from it. Her fears are extreme and without basis, but in her mind, the fear is very real and alive. When in this state, she can curse like a sailor, and strike out and hit others. She fears insanity. Sometimes, she thinks she's going insane (she's not), but that is the fear. And most important, she has wild, crazy feelings that make her feel almost berserk and out-of-control.

GENERAL MENOPAUSE SYMPTOMS

RED BROMELIAD is about us, as women, using menopause as a time to connect deeply and powerfully with our inner spirit; to touch areas of ourselves we haven't known before because we were so distracted by outer worldly demands made upon us. Red Bromeliad is a gentle, deep-acting essence that uplifts us in a spiritual sense and enables us to connect with our inner core as a woman. Too often, a woman's spiritual life is trampled in everyday existence, but with this essence, we can tune in to our own, unique essence. This is of great help for those who want to meditate and "hold" that altered state with ease.

MAGNOLIA BLOSSOM is an essence that I generally suggest to clients who are going through menopause. This remedy has the ability to address the wound of a woman, whatever it is, and to facilitate healing of that issue. If a woman wants to get in direct touch with her true femininity (and often, it has been shunted aside due to the demands placed upon her), then this essence will gently but firmly bring her back to her own center.

PHALEANOPSIS 920030, the "menopause orchid," is an incredible gift to womankind. I have included the latest proving information on this amazing orchid and how it can help you through menopause. It is at the end of this chapter.

TIGER LILY women get profound depression. They may cry all the time, or it will seem like they are crying a lot. If someone tries to console them when they are in this mood, they will hate it and get angry and curse or strike at the person who is trying to comfort them. Their feelings and moods alternate rapidly and without rhyme or reason. They feels like they're on an out-of-control roller-coaster ride and can't get off.

This is also for the woman who is experiencing "PMS" symptoms. There can be strong sexual desire, excitement, and apprehension felt simultaneously. Sex is good for you, and you like it. You can see-saw between jealousy toward others, weeping, being angry, and feeling dissatisfied. Nothing pleases you. Everything irritates you. It is as if you're no longer in control of your emotions—your hormones are, instead! On bad days, you'll throw things at the other person, or at the wall, in utter frustration. There is a wild, insane feeling inside you; you know you're going crazy and you can do nothing to prevent it and it's all driving you (and your family) to distraction. It's all hormones. This essence can help take off the edginess you're feeling and give you a calm harbor during a stormy period.

YELLOW BEARDED IRIS is an essence that helps us to release old conditional tapes and behavior patterns. By doing that, we can set ourselves free from the past. It enables us to unfurl our wings and fly toward our newfound freedom in the final third of our lives. Any negative emotions that have stunted us as human beings are addressed by this remedy. It is proving to be a cure for an eye-related problem known as pterygium, as well.

MENOPAUSAL IRRITATION AND ANGER

AFRICAN DAISY is for the menopausal woman who cycles in and out of irritation, usually before or during her menses. This is for those angry, uncontrolled outbursts that just seem to pop out of us—and we're equally surprised at the vehemence and rage behind our explosive outburst. This essence allows us to continue to feel our anger, but helps us manage the anger in a far more positive sense for ourselves and others. It can stop you from projecting anger onto others who don't deserve it—but just happen to be at the right place at the wrong time. It helps us own our anger, and look more deeply at the real issue that is creating this anger.

SCORPIONWEED is the "abusive essence" that helps us get in touch with our abuse of others—whether it is our children, friends, spouse, or coworkers—it stops this attacking on our part and makes us realize what we're doing. At that point, we have control and choices in our hands, where it should be, putting a stop to abusive behavior on our part toward anyone or anything else. I frequently use this remedy for male abusers, but some women going through menopause, in particular, may unleash this side to themselves, also. Many times victims (usually women) begin to act out the aggression that has been heaped on them by turning around and becoming abusive to others—usually those less able to defend themselves, such as children, the elderly, or animals. This essence stops that and helps us grapple with this issue far more positively without making anyone a victim of our abuse.

SPANISH BAYONET YUCCA is for the menopausal woman who gets irritated, but is not aware that she is in that state. As a consequence, she snipes, picks, hurls innuendoes and has the ability to see everyone's Achilles' heel—and deliberately goes after it—and them! The passive-aggressive qualities that we can all get into, especially women, are halted by this essence, which is very positive for ourselves and others, who become unwitting and sometimes undeserved targets of our unconscious (or conscious) aggression. This essence stops that, brings the matter of our feelings fully back to us in a far more positive sense, and allows us to control our behavior more rationally and less emotionally.

TIGER LILY is for the woman who is rushing around; she feels hurried, she walks fast, and doesn't know why. She's snappish. She's tormented about many things. If someone tries to console her, she can blow up into angry retorts or get highly irritated. Little, non-essential things bother her greatly. Everything irritates her and on top of that she feels horribly depressed. There is a constant desire to just break down and cry—and she will, quite often—crying out of frustration more than anything else.

You don't know when to stop, so your central nervous system takes the brunt of your pressure. Weeping is your major outlet, but after a stormy outburst you may feel numb and indifferent to whatever the situation is that triggered you. This essence can help.

MENOPAUSE AND OUR CREATIVE EXPRESSION

DESERT PAINTBRUSH is a great help to a woman who has always wanted to be creative in some sense, but has always used the excuse that she had her family, her children, her spouse, or her job that took priority. There is a bit of crutch-like behavior going on in this woman ... she admires the creativity in others, but says continually that she really has none herself—when she really does. This essence pushes this woman out of that mind-set and gets her motivated to become fully artistic and creative in her own right. If she's dreamed of taking an art class for years, but feels she just doesn't have the right stuff to do it, or is afraid she's going to be laughed out of the class or humiliated because of her creative abilities, then this essence will stop those feelings from stopping her—and she'll sign up for that art class or writing course, or wherever her creative juices and interests take her.

ECHO BLUE (Lithansus) is for the menopausal woman who always dreamed of being a poet, or writing a book, or working in some kind of creative mental field, but felt she didn't have the ideas to bring it together. This essence is of inestimable value to the writer. It brings up so many creative ideas and directions that at times, it is like opening up Pandora's Box! This is an extremely high creativity essence and especially for any kind of mental idea type of work. So, if you've always wanted to write, use this essence to spur and tap into the creativity you've had all along, and have fun! You may write the next great American Novel. Who knows? It's worth a try.

OCOTILLO is a wonderful menopausal essence because it infuses us with a spirit of creativity so vast, so exciting, and so swift that it can leave us a little breathless in the wake of taking it! For the menopausal woman who wants to rapidly and eagerly explore all of her unique talents and skills, this essence will act promptly to put her in touch with them. This is also a remedy to be used during meditation, particularly a Kundalini type, to put us in touch with our own vast powers of creation in a more cosmic and spiritual sense.

MENOPAUSE AND THERAPY

CRESTED PRICKLE POPPY is of inestimable value if a woman is seeking therapy during menopause. This essence is so powerful that I recommend it only if the woman is under the present care and guidance of a therapist and wants to dig deep into issues that are stopping her from breaking past conditional patterns. Those who are familiar with Carl Jung, the great Swiss psychotherapist, know about the Shadow—our dark side that we project out onto others and of which we have no inner, conscious awareness. This essence will bring Shadow issues via dreams to the person taking it. Because of the depth and power of this essence, it should NOT be used by a woman who is bi-polar or on tranquilizers or anti-depressants.

This essence may be used if you are in a good space with yourself and you want to grow and get in touch with what is left within you on deep, subconscious levels, to confront it, own it, and work through it. Be sure to keep a pad and paper handy next to your bed, as this essence brings profound, healing dreams into your nightly sleep. Hopefully, you have a Jungian therapist nearby to help you unravel the goldmine of dreams that will come because of this wonderful, deeply healing essence.

MARIPOSA LILY (WHITE) is an excellent essence to use during therapy and menopause when we have never valued ourselves fully as human beings. Too often, women get stuck and stereotyped and made to feel as if what they think, feel, or know is not as good as what a man thinks or knows. This essence is about triggering our own integrity, honoring it, recognizing it, and most important, embracing it and ourselves as a result. By doing that, we awaken our morals, values, and self-esteem even more and this helps guide us ever more clearly, like a compass, through our menopause. It bestows a clear sense of direction of who and what we are—and are not—and the graciousness to accept the "all" of us and be content with ourselves as a result.

SKIN CONDITIONS

TIGER LILY has been found to be beneficial for women who suffer from "formication"—a sensation that feels like bugs are crawling on top of or just beneath the skin. Sometimes it's a prickling feeling; other times it's just a fleeting annoyance and we scratch at it. This essence can stop tingling, burning, crawling sensations no matter where they occur on your body.

THE MENOPAUSE ORCHID: Phaleanopsis 920030. This flower essence, from an orchid, deserves some special attention. The information below has been gleaned from a 2-week proving and a number of the women provers suffered menopause symptoms to a remarkable degree. I am putting this information in so that women may consider the use of this incredible flower essence if they desire. This is a beautiful lavender moth orchid. It can be seen with its beauty and information on the Internet at the following address: www.medicinegarden.com.

Here is the proving information:

Woman Prover #1 experienced needle-like, hot sensations around the nipples of her breasts and this lasted 5 minutes. She got hot feet at night. Her feet became sore and achy. Her bowel movements became better (she usually had hard stools, but this essence softened them considerably).

Her breasts were sore off and on throughout the 2-week proving. She also had a pressing-down sensation in her uterus. She found that by being on this essence, her PMS symptoms or irritability, anger, and nerves decreased remarkably to the point where she felt nothing more than "calmness." She also reported that she had two huge migraine headaches with this essence.

Woman Prover #2 also experienced hot flashes with this essence. There was sweating with the hot flash. It was better when outdoors, in the breeze. And she had cravings for salty or fatty things (like potato chips and pretzels).

And, she had a headache—a bursting, dull sensation at the top (vertex) of her head—and another type of headache that started at the back of the head and moved up to the top of it and then to the back, once again.

Her skin itched off and on for hours. And of course, in menopause, some women get "formication," which feels like insects crawling under or on top of their skin.

Woman Prover #3 had prickly itching on her legs, which was intermittent. She said that it "itches on legs like insects" and was reminiscent of formication, which menopausal women may encounter. Her vagina was itchy with a slight discharge. She felt clammy and flushed from time to time—but no perspiration was associated with it.

Woman Prover #4 experienced migraine headaches: from the base of her skull to the temples. Dull ache. Nothing she did helped stop it (like resting or sleeping). She experienced hot flashes of nervousness, perspiring, a sense of hurry, and an inability to do things fast enough. She had chocolate cravings. Many times, when she took the essence, she would immediately feel "nervous and perspiring." Both can be associated with hot flashes.

This is just a peek at the natural essences that can support our journey and adventure through menopause. There are many others for specific issues that cannot be covered here, but are available. I invite you to look in the appendix for a catalog that will give you that information.

CHAPTER 21

MENOPAUSE MATERIA MEDICA

HOW TO USE THIS MATERIA MEDICA

A materia medica is a compilation of symptoms for specific FDA-approved homeopathic remedies. There are many ways to create a materia medica, but to make it simple and straightforward for this book, each homeopathic remedy is alphabetized by its Latin name. The "shorthand" name that we homeopaths prefer to use is in parentheses. If there is no shortening of the name, then we use the original, full name.

Information about each homeopathic remedy is divided into sections. What it is made from is first. Then the Comments section provides information that I feel you should know about the remedy, such as what it is (plant, animal, etc.), its history, if any, and any relevant items or experiences that are directly related to menopause. This does not mean that this is the only information concerning this remedy; just items specific to menopause are presented.

Some of the constitutional or polycrest homeopathic remedies may have a Typology section that describes a likely body type, kin complexion, eye color, or hair color. it's important to note, however, that modern-day homeopaths don't place much emphasis on typology. Any woman, regardless of the color of her hair or eyes or her skin type, can use Sepia—or any other remedy—if her symptoms match it. Symptoms are the most important key to choosing the menopause remedy that's right for you.

The remedy may have a Physical Symptoms section. These are sensation-related symptoms that a woman can experience. She will not get ALL of them—perhaps two or three of them. If you "match" two or three of the symptoms in each of these categories, this may be the remedy to consider.

The Mentals section is a combination of mental attitudes and emotional symptoms that may be experienced during menopause; so don't be confused—in this case the word "mental" includes our emotions, too.

The Modalities section details things that make our symptoms (physical, emotional, or mental) better or worse. These can include the time of day or night, the temperature, the weather, or other items.

Some homeopathic remedies will not list all these categories because they are considered to be "small" remedies; they do not have the scope, breadth, or depth of the larger, more inclusive, "constitutional" or polycrest remedies.

Sometimes these categories will appear within a specific ailment, such as headache, for example. When you see this, don't be confused. Many of the remedies used here are polycrests or constitutionals. I've noted the physical symptoms, mentals, and modalities that are general for that remedy type because it's easier to identify or see yourself in it. Find your specific symptom, such as headaches or hot flashes, and you may well find the physical symptoms, and possibly mentals and modalities listed for each individual remedy. Both sets of symptoms apply to you. If you fit these symptoms, then consider this remedy for your menopausal ailment.

WHAT IF I FIND A MATCH OF MY SYMPTOMS WITH A PARTICULAR HOMEOPATHIC REMEDY IN THIS MATERIA MEDICA?

Make an appointment with your homeopath, take the book and this information to her, and discuss it. The homeopath may want to take your entire case, as a result, to ensure that this is, indeed, the correct remedy. If she finds a remedy that more closely matches (because she will have a larger materia medica than what is presented here, in this book), then she will prescribe that remedy to you, instead. And then just follow her prescription and directions and you will be on your way to cure from menopause-related symptoms!

❀ACONITUM NAPELLUS❀

(ACONITE)

Origin: Derived from the plant, monkshood.
Comments: This remedy is used in cases where shock or trauma has made an indelible mark on the individual. Sometimes, if menopause comes on too quickly (such as in the case of a hysterectomy), it is a different kind of "shock" to the body, but is still a shock, nevertheless.
Mentals: This woman is vital, robust, enjoys being outdoors, and loves fresh air and exercise. She's compassionate and is usually an extrovert.

ACUTE ANXIETY OR PANIC ATTACKS

Comments: This remedy should be considered if you have experienced some kind of trauma or accident BEFORE the anxiety or panic attacks began to appear in the first place. Don't trivialize the trauma in your life. It could arise from a move, a change of jobs, or a divorce, for example. Trauma should be defined as whatever is DISTRESS to you, not what someone else may consider it to be. Aconite is one of the premier remedies to cure anxiety. For those of you who have experienced earthquakes, this is THE remedy of choice if you have been traumatized by such a shattering event.
Mentals: If you have a fear of death, this is the remedy to consider.
Modalities: WORSE – there is anxiety in the company of others, with known or unknown fears, and no one can console you or make your anxiety lessen. BETTER – if you drink cold water, or if you break out into a cold, chilling sweat.

EYES DRY, ITCHING, OR BURNING

Physical Symptoms: Aconite is for eyes that feel dry and hot, as if there's sand in them. Your eyes will appear red and inflamed. The lids may be swollen, hard, and red.
Modalities: WORSE – there is aversion to light, especially to direct sunlight. Profuse watering can occur, especially if in a cool, dry wind, or during cold weather or looking at snow in bright sunlight.

MENOPAUSAL HEADACHES

Comments: This is for weather-related headaches. The headache is caused by getting damp or chilled, or even from something as innocuous as experiencing a gust of cold wind. Or walking into an air-conditioned room.
Mentals: If you are nervous or upset about a coming confrontation, or have a stressful day or event ahead, and you are getting a headache because of this anticipated event or feel pressure, Aconite can bring relief.

Physical Symptoms: A weather (or air conditioning) induced headache will appear shortly AFTER exposure to a cold temperature or experiencing a chilling draft. Dizziness may strike you upon arising. The headache may resemble a tight band around your head, or you may feel as if your brain is going to be forced out of your skull. You may feel anxious or apprehensive. There can be left-sided, nerve-like pain, along with restlessness, tingling, and numbness. Pain in the jaw region or a heavy feeling in the face may occur. Other headache sensations are fullness, pulsating, hot, bursting, or burning pain with an undulation or wave-like feeling to it.
Modalities: WORSE – if you experienced fright or violent emotions (of any kind); if you lie down in bed, or experience excessive noise or light, your pain deepens. Headaches get worse during your menses, at night, sleeping in the sun, lying on the affected side, when music is being played, when having to inhale second-hand tobacco smoke, or being in an over-warm room. BETTER – when you are outdoors, resting, or having worked up a warm sweat.

HEARING DIFFICULTY

Physical Symptoms: Music is unbearable to you. There may be a sensation of a drop of water heard in your left ear. If you notice that your hearing deteriorates after being exposed to a drop in temperature or windy, cooler conditions, entering an air-conditioned office, or from a draft in a room, this remedy will help.

HEART PALPITATIONS AND SHORTNESS OF BREATH

Mentals: Fear or anxiousness is the root cause of your heart beating so hard.
Physical Symptoms: High anxiety or stressful states trigger heart palpitations. There may be pain in the left shoulder along with the palpitations. A feeling of faintness with a tingling sensation occurs in your fingertips. Palpitations are strong, hard, bounding, and sometimes intermittent.

VAGINA DRY OR POOR LUBRICATION

Physical Symptoms: Your vagina is hot, dry, and sensitive. There may be stitching or burning pains.

❋ALUMINA❋

Origin: Made from the metal, aluminum.
Comments: It is derived from bauxite, which is found in Europe, Africa, the United States, and the Caribbean. The remedy is made from oxide of aluminum.

Aluminum is found not only in our kitchen utensils, but in antacids as well. Alzheimer's patients have been found to have high levels of aluminum in their brains. Ingesting antacids or using aluminum pots and pans in cooking exacerbates the problem. From a homeopathic standpoint, Alumina, when potentized, can cure senile dementia—which is what Alzheimer's was called long before this modern-day label was given to it. Like cures like.

CONSTIPATION

Comments: Anyone who has thrown clay on a wheel knows the thick, gooey consistency of clay. If your stools are clay-like, this may be the remedy to consider. When too much water is taken out of the stool during its transit through your intestines, Alumina can address this problem. A diet low in fiber may help create this lack of movement, which means you need a change in diet. On an acute basis, Alumina may help, but don't use this remedy as a replacement for adding fiber to your daily diet!!

Alumina is frequently used by homeopaths in "worst-case scenario" types of constipation. When nothing else works, Alumina usually does. Keep in mind that there is a dryness throughout the woman's body—dry stools, dry nasal passages, and a dried-up feeling inside of her—and that means on the emotional level too—her feelings have "dried up" and she's no longer able to access them.

Physical Symptoms: The stools look hard and are dry and knotty. There is NO desire to go to the bathroom—at all. The rectal area is very sore, tender, and dry feeling, and you may bleed if you strain. Straining (a lot of it) can barely move this stool.

Pains will pass from the rectal area all the way down to your ankles. And sometimes, the only way a stool can be passed is to stand up and do it. There may be a sensation that the stools are lodged in the upper left part of your abdomen.

Modalities: WORSE – in the morning, from cold, chilling temperature, and from consuming starchy foods (pasta, flour products), vinegar, spices such as salt or pepper, and wine. All of these items will "stop up the works." BETTER – when consuming warm food or liquids. And there's a better chance of a bowel movement if you are warm, not cold or chilled.

❁AMYL NITROSUM❁
(AMYL NITRITE)

Origin: This remedy is made from nitrite of amyl.

Comments: You've heard of it, all right. Back in the sixties when the psychedelic crowd was using LSD and similar drugs, amyl nitrite was a weak sister to the hallucinogens. But remember, homeopathically speaking, you do not have to worry about this! That is because the dilution and potentization process ensures that none of the actual substance remains in the remedy you take. You are using only the "energy signature" of the amyl nitrite, not the drug form.

HOT FLASHES

WARNING: Any acute or persistent symptoms such as pain in the chest or pelvic region should be immediately evaluated by a physician. After serious problems are ruled out, you can safely proceed with your non-hormone, non-drug homeopathic treatment.

Comments: This is the premier hot flash remedy to consider when no other remedy seems to help get rid of them.

Physical Symptoms: It acts specifically on the capillaries, which are the source of hot flashes in the first place. This is especially good for women who have red-hot flushing in the face or head, and for hot flashes that have a sudden, powerful onset.

❁ANACARDIUM ORIENTALE❁
(ANACARDIUM)

Origin: Made from the marking-nut tree.

Comments: This tree grows in Asia and the East Indies. Hindus have used the nuts from this tree for centuries. The thick hull is peeled off and the black juice was used to get rid of warts and leg ulcers. Later, this acrid, oil-based juice was mixed with chalk to mark linens. Arabian physicians used marking-nut juice to treat spasms and memory loss as well as mental illness.

MEMORY LOSS

Comments: If your memory is worse in the morning, improves during the day, and then takes a dive in the evening hours until midnight, consider Anacardium.

Physical Symptoms: You cannot remember names to save your soul! Many will accuse you of being absent-minded. Thoughts, quite literally, vanish as you read, write, or talk. You are frustrated because you cannot remember the right word. Sometimes, it is just too much work or energy to try and remember something—so you do not! You can even forget the names of those around you, which is highly embarrassing. You are quite easily offended by this happenstance—more than you should be.

One of the keynotes for this remedy is that you may feel as if two people are living in your head at the same time and you are carrying on a conversation with both of them. There is a general weakness of the mind and loss of memory. This is an excellent remedy to consider when there is a slow, progressive weakness of the mind.

Modalities: WORSE – from experiencing excessive emotions (anger, fright, being humiliated or shamed), caring too much for another person (we call it codependent behavior), getting caught in a draft, being out in open air, or getting chilled. BETTER – from eating, remaining warm, being in warm temperatures, taking a hot bath, or being out in sunlight.

❀APIS MELLIFICA❀
(APIS)

Origin: This remedy is made from crushed honeybees.

Mentals: The mental and emotional state of this woman is that of a "queen bee"—she is a leader, in charge and confident, and her behavior may be extreme, just like an imperious queen in her realm. She is often found in corporate America, or is a woman who owns her own business (big or small).

Modalities: WORSE – always worse from any kind of heat, particularly warm to hot water, and at night. BETTER – always improved if a cool or cold cloth is placed against the area or if a cool shower or bath is taken.

URINARY INCONTINENCE

Physical Symptoms: There can be soreness along with dribbling from the urethra. When stooping or leaning down, this soreness and pressure increases. There is a frequent desire to urinate accompanied by a scalding, smarting, or burning sensation, but only a few drops will occur.

This woman is thirstless, so she will not be drinking as much fluid as she should, which can exacerbate her problem. Her abdomen is highly sensitive to touch. After taking this remedy, do not be alarmed if you void a lot more urine than normal—this is a good sign. And, drink more fluids!!

❀ARGENTUM NITRICUM❀
(ARG. NIT.)

Origin: This remedy is made from silver nitrate.

Comments: The source of this remedy is acathite, which is the main ore of silver. The silver nitrate is extracted from this valuable mineral, which is found in North and South America, as well as Norway. Its common names are hellstone, devil's stone, or lunar caustic. Silver nitrate is used by the traditional medical establishment to cauterize wounds, treat eye infections in newborns, get rid of warts, and control epilepsy.

It is a highly poisonous toxin if ingested and wreaks havoc not only on the skin, but in the major organs of the body, such as the liver and kidneys. In its homeopathic potentized form, it is harmless and is used for women who are highly nervous individuals with digestive problems.

ACUTE ANXIETY OR PANIC ATTACKS

Mentals: Anxiety is brought on by anticipating an engagement where you have to perform in some way, especially giving a speech or taking part in a play, for example. An attack may occur while you are walking, out in open air, or after eating. You may suffer frequent attacks with accompanying weakness in your legs. The attacks are usually worse around 11 a.m. You may be tormented with anxiety or with thoughts about some serious disease that you think you may have.

Feelings of intense anxiety, apprehension, and fear (of airplanes, heights, crowds) could be accompanied by an impulse to leap out a window.

Physical Symptoms: There can be a loss of coordination, a feeling of imbalance, and trembling with the attack. Heart palpitations are common, and there may be a feeling that your heart will leap out of your chest because it is pounding so hard.

Modalities: WORSE – if you are left alone or if you lie down on your right side. BETTER – if someone remains with you.

❋ARNICA MONTANA❋

(ARNICA)

Origin: This remedy is made from an herb known as leopard's bane, mountain tobacco, or sneezewort.

Comments: Growing in the mountains of Europe and Siberia, the whole, flowering plant is used. Arnica has been in use since the sixteenth century. People who lived in the mountains ate the plant because it was well known for getting rid of bruises, aching muscles, and sprains. Nowadays, it is considered one of the most all-purpose remedies in homeopathy because it not only addresses muscle and tissue-related injuries, but can also easily handle shock or any type of bleeding, even hemophilia.

Modalities: WORSE – from being touched by another person, any kind of continuous motion, rest, drinking wine, or experiencing damp, cold conditions. BETTER – lying down or with your head slightly lower than the rest of your body, and upon rising.

CONSTIPATION

Comments: This remedy should be considered if you have suffered an injury (auto accident, surgical operation, hysterectomy, a fall, etc.) and since then, have suffered from constipation. This is categorized and known as a "mechanical injury." Arnica is one of the great remedies to correct this type of problem.

If there has been spinal cord injury, this must be treated constitutionally, but remedies such as Hypericum and Magnesia Phosphorica may help repair injured nerves and hopefully, stimulate the body so that the constipation is a condition of the past.

EYE "FLOATERS"

Physical Symptoms: For floaters that occur after any kind of head trauma injury.

EYE STRAIN

Physical Symptoms: If you have been looking at a distance for a long time and your eyes feel strained, this is the remedy to use.

GALACTORRHEA

Comments: If, after receiving an injury to your breast, whether in an accident or having it struck by something, there is expression of milk from your nipple(s), then this remedy should be considered.

Other: Stop wearing a bra for 2 weeks. There is plenty of evidence that wearing a bra stops lymph gland drainage, and cysts and fibroids may result, as well as breast cancer. Take it off and see what happens!

MENOPAUSAL HEADACHES

Comments: A keynote to use this remedy for a headache is that your head is hot, but your body feels cold.

Physical Symptoms: A bruised feeling or aching pain is felt in the head. Sometimes it will become a sharp or pinching pain. And if you stoop down or lean over, the headache pain increases markedly. Mentally, you may feel tired, and your scalp feels tight across your skull. The headache may feel as if someone has driven a nail into your head. There can be a cold spot on the brow and a hot spot(s) on the top of your skull.

Modalities: WORSE – from touch, motion, drinking wine, experiencing damp cold, after sleep, experiencing any kind of jarring or jolting (even walking), and over-exertion. BETTER – when lying with your head lower than the rest of your body or stretching out.

HEARING DIFFICULTY

Physical Symptoms: If your hearing has been worse since any kind of accident, a car wreck, a fall, a concussion, severe jarring, something jammed into your ear canal, noise from an explosion, and so forth, this remedy may be of assistance. With a rush of blood to your head, there are noises that begin in your ears. Your hearing is dulled by any kind of loud noise.

LEG CRAMPS

Comments: This is a particularly useful remedy if you have been standing too long, or have had too much exercise for the day. Your legs begin to cramp due to overuse, such as too much aerobic exercise, walking, standing, or hiking.

Physical Symptoms: You don't want anyone to touch you or the area that is cramping, which is a major keynote of this remedy. There can be a soreness to the area, as if your muscles were bruised or badly beaten. Another unique keynote is that the upper part of your body is hot, but the lower half of you is cold!! There is also a sprained sensation to the cramped muscles.

Modalities: WORSE – during cold, damp, rainy, or foggy weather. Getting jarred makes your cramps worse. You cannot walk erect and anything you lie upon seems too hard to you—no position is comfortable.

VARICOSE VEINS

Comments: Consider this remedy if you have varicose veins that appear after you have suffered some kind of trauma or injury to that site (which might have been decades before). You might have had an auto accident 10 years before, but now, where your leg was struck, varicose veins are starting to appear.

Physical Symptoms: There is a bruised and sore feeling in the region of the varicosity—the same sensation as if you bruised yourself. The veins tend to become inflamed-looking with time.

❀ARSENICUM ALBUM❀
(ARSENICUM)

Origin: Made from arsenic oxide.
Comments: Obtained from arsenopyrite, a mineral found in the Scandinavian countries, as well as England and Canada, this infamous poison cannot be destroyed—even by fire! The crystals have a metallic gleam to them and if heated or struck by another stone, give off a garlic-like odor. At one time, in the nineteenth century, it was used by the traditional medical establishment (unsuccessfully) to treat syphilis. Interestingly, earlier in this century it was used as white arsenic oxide on humans and livestock, particularly race horses, to improve their muscle tone and increase their endurance—not to mention giving their coats a beautiful shine.

It is completely safe as a homeopathic remedy because no molecules of the poison are left—only the energy signature. It is one of the most powerful and deep-acting constitutional remedies in our pharmacopoeia. Arsenicum is often used in cases of asthma, digestive tract ailments, and cancer.
Modalities: WORSE – at midnight, from cold temperature, bathing, drafts, food or drink, and rainy weather. BETTER – from heat, when your head is slightly elevated, and from warm drinks of any kind.

ALLERGIES

Comments: This is a good remedy to think of for an allergy condition usually referred to as "hay fever."
Mentals: When you get these symptoms, you become anxious, irritable, and very restless. There may be a sense of hopelessness that nothing will ever help get rid of these symptoms. Your irritability soars, and often you can make mountains out of molehills.
Physical Symptoms: There is a thin, watery mucus that has a BURNING sensation to it. You can sneeze repeatedly: 5, 10, or 15 times in a row, nonstop. The congestion coming from your nose is always watery in consistency. You may develop cold sores inside your nostrils and be unable to bear the odor of food, much less the sight of it.

Your throat may be swollen and constricted feeling with that BURNING sensation present. Your eyes are burning, with heat (a fiery sensation) in the eyeballs along with profuse tears. Your eyelids will be red and swollen and will often have granulation in the corners of them. With your symptoms, you become supersensitive to sunlight or any bright light (time for the sunglasses!). There is always a burning pain present in your eyes with the allergies.
Modalities: WORSE – allergies worsen in open air (outdoors). BETTER – symptoms improve and become tolerable indoors.

ACUTE ANXIETY OR PANIC ATTACKS

Comments: This is another top anxiety remedy. Attacks may occur in bed around midnight. You are alone when it happens. Anxiety may arise from a twinge of conscience, events involving other people, over some trifle, or upon waking. The anxiety comes on with constriction of the chest, nausea, extreme nervousness, restlessness, and an inability to sit or lie still; you *must* move around.
Mentals: With this anxiety comes great discontent, irritability, snappishness, and criticism of others. Lack of control makes you crave perfectionism, and if one little item is out of place, you will put it back exactly where it came from. There may be a fear of dying and getting a disease, particularly cancer. Other fears that may trigger your anxiety reaction are about poverty, starvation,

financial loss, being robbed, or your house being broken into. Any of these errant thoughts may set off an anxiety reaction in you.

The deeper the anxiety, the more controlling you will become. It may be evidenced by your spotless home, containers labeled and numbered, frequent dusting, or keeping your desk cleared of any loose papers or other items. This compulsiveness and perfectionism are signs that the more you control your outer environment, the less control you feel inside yourself.

Modalities: WORSE – in wet, cold, or damp weather, after consuming iced drinks or cold food, or being at the seashore. BETTER – if you have company around you—not necessarily in the same room, but in your house or place of employment. You feel better being warmed up by either hot drinks or food. The more you can move around, the better you feel. You improve lying with your head elevated, or being out in open air.

ARTHRITIS

Comments: There is either a nightly cycle or a 14-day cycle to this pain. Or it will have an established rhythm of showing up and then disappearing—a keynote of this remedy. Those who need Arsenicum are "cold babies"—they cannot stand the cold in any way, shape, or form! Insomnia can dog your heels because of the pain, and usually you will wake up at midnight or 1 a.m. Your sleep is highly restless and very light.

Mentals: When the pain comes on, you can plummet into an anxious state of mind and emotions. The more pain there is, the deeper the depth of your anxiety, despair, and worry. You do not want to be left alone, and need company for reassurance.

Physical Symptoms: The pains wander all over your body. There is tension involved with it, as well as worry. Extreme restlessness is a keynote. If you try to remain in control of this pain, you will sometimes exhibit compulsive-like behavior. Always cold, you cannot get warm enough. Thirsty most of the time, you will SIP liquids. The arthritis will be worse on the right side of your body than on the left side, but pains can wander. The pain has a hot, BURNING quality to it. Trembling, twitching, spasms, weakness, and heaviness in the affected limb or area are common.

There is always coldness of the arms, legs, hands, and feet, no matter how burning the pain is. The affected parts that are painful also ITCH, but scratching makes the pain worse. The itching can continue without the skin erupting.

Modalities: WORSE – the arthritis always flares up at night—particularly around or right after midnight. BETTER – if you take a hot shower or bath, or place a warm cloth over the area that is painful.

DIARRHEA

Comments: Think of this remedy if diarrhea appears shortly after eating (within an hour). This is due to food poisoning of a mild nature. If the food poisoning is severe, get to the hospital immediately and take this remedy on the way there.

Physical Symptoms: Diarrhea that comes on due to consuming melons, watery fruits, being on a vegetable diet, or when hot weather appears, will respond well to this remedy. Consuming too much alcohol, which causes diarrhea as an after-effect, will be helped with Arsenicum.

This remedy's keynote is a BURNING sensation in the rectal area. The stools are small, dark (black or dark brown), very frequent, involuntary, watery, and thin. There is complete exhaustion after a bowel movement. The stools may also appear green or yellow, and may have mucus or appear slimy or look like "rice water" (colorless, odorless diarrhea).

At its worst, you may see some of the lining of your intestine mixed with the stool—shredded, stringy, membranous-like scrapings of tissue. The stools may be dark and bloody and have an intense, offensive odor to them. The odor is reminiscent of a rotting carcass. There can be great thirst and you will drink a lot of fluids—only in small, constant sips.

There can be gnawing, burning pains likened to coals in a fire, and this may be somewhat relieved by a warm cloth or heating pad across this region. The abdomen may be swollen and painful and pain will be felt in that region if you cough. The upper right side of your body, just beneath your ribcage where the liver resides, will be swollen and sore.

Modalities: WORSE – at night, usually around midnight or 1 a.m., and after drinking or eating. BETTER – from heat application, having your head elevated, and sipping warm drinks.

INDIGESTION

Comments: This remedy is used for heartburn that occurs around midnight or 1 a.m.

Physical Symptoms: Your stomach may feel as if there is a weight or a boulder lodged in it. There is an anxious feeling in the pit of the stomach, accompanied by a BURNING sensation or pain. If ice water is consumed, you will immediately vomit. There is a feeling of rawness to the stomach, or possibly a tearing sensation. Pain in the stomach will occur even if the smallest amount of liquid or food is consumed.

You may experience heartburn in the throat region. Food that is swallowed lodges in the esophagus. The stomach is touchy and irritable. Foods such as ice cream, vinegar (also found in salad dressings), water, vegetables, or any watery fruit (melons, oranges, grapefruit, etc.) will bring on a rolling, nauseating feeling to your stomach region. You may not be able to stand the sight or odor of food.

Modalities: BETTER – from walking around, remaining in motion, sitting erect, lying down with your head elevated, sweating, or being in open air.

URINARY INCONTINENCE

Physical Symptoms: If you are driven out of bed with a strong desire to urinate, around midnight, this could be your remedy of choice. You can experience involuntary discharge of urine with a burning sensation in the urethra. The urine can escape—any time day or night—but this is an especially good remedy for those night-time attacks of incontinence.

The woman who can use this remedy is always a chilly sort of person—adding on layers of clothes even if no one else is—and she becomes highly anxious when the incontinence is about to occur, or shortly afterward. You are a thirsty person (good news!) and you like to take small sips of cold water frequently. When you experience these burning pains, a warm cloth, shower, or bath always soothes that region of your body.

VARICOSE VEINS

Comments: If your varicose veins worsen at night, and have an intense, burning, scalding sensation to them, as if on fire, especially around midnight, this is the remedy to consider. There's a unique keynote to Arsenicum: your body may feel hot as an oven, but your head feels chilled—as if in a freezer.

Physical Symptoms: The varicose veins can be inflamed and tend to ulcerate, and there is always a stitching pain as you walk and put weight on that extremity. There is a fiery sensation to the pain.

❁AURUM METALLICUM❁

(AURUM MET.)

Origin: Made from gold.

Comments: Potentized from the metal, gold, this remedy has many diverse applications from the homeopathic standpoint. Mined in Africa, Australia, the United States, and Canada, this is considered a constitutional homeopathic remedy. Arabian physicians used gold to cure heart conditions in the twelfth century. In traditional medicine, it has been tried for curing arthritis by actually ingesting the metal in small amounts.

Homeopathically, the potentized energy of this marvelous remedy helps in areas such as manic depression, bipolar symptoms, rheumatism, and suicidal urges. When one stops to think that the metal gold is expensive and looks, literally, like sparkling sunlight, one can appreciate its healing qualities for those who suffer from acute or chronic depression. Gold, quite literally, becomes the light that can heal your darkness.

ACUTE ANXIETY OR PANIC ATTACKS

Mentals: This type of anxiety comes on due to grief, being frightened, being disappointed in love (divorce, separation, a death of a spouse, etc.), carrying heavier than normal responsibilities, experiencing the loss of your job, loss of property, or a shift in your financial fortunes. Your entire demeanor is built upon your success in the business world or in the home as a homemaker extraodinaire. If you are suddenly without those icons of success (or if you are downgraded and are made to feel less important by others) than previously, then anxiety can set in. Your greatest fear is of being or becoming a failure.

Your anxiety comes with a sense of absolute hopelessness; it's depression without end. Many times, you worry that you have heart disease or that you'll die of a heart attack. There is fear of death, fear from the smallest of noises. Your anxiety heightens if someone contradicts you and you can become hateful, quarrelsome, and grumbling. Many times, in this state, you will refuse to talk to anyone. If this anxiety is prolonged, you may seriously think about suicide and see it as a way out of this unrelieved anguish that you are suffering with 24 hours a day and feel trapped within.

Modalities: WORSE – with mental exertion, cold weather, cloudy weather, or during the winter. Your worst anxiety surfaces from sunset to sunrise, with the night being a particularly bad time for you. Alcoholic beverages can trigger an anxiety reaction in you. BETTER – with cool, open air, being able to bathe or shower in cooling water. Music helps, as does taking a walk, or being bathed in luminescent moonlight.

ARTHRITIS

Comments: This remedy is useful if your symptoms begin to get worse after the sun goes down. The pains are worse during the night and usually disappear during the day—with a sense of well being restored—only to come back to haunt you at sunset the next evening.

Mentals: Depression is common because you feel an absolute sense of hopelessness because nothing you do makes the horrible pain go away. If you experience these symptoms for a long time, you may feel as if you are going out of your mind with the pain. Suicide may be contemplated.

Physical Symptoms: Deep pains are felt in the bones, and they wander. The glands in your body (in the groin, under the arms, and in the neck region) may swell up when an attack occurs. There is also great swelling to the feet, ankles, and knees. It may feel as if all the blood has rushed from your upper body to your lower body.

The pain you experience has a TEARING, wrenching quality to it, and is located in the joint regions. Your knees feel weak. There can be an unusual sensation of "blood boiling" in the body from time to time.

Modalities: WORSE – the pain begins at sunset and in the early morning hours, when it is most intense. BETTER – music helps relieve some of your pain.

DEPRESSION

WARNING: If you or someone you know is depressed AND suicidal, call 911 or the appropriate resource where you are living, give the person Aurum Muriaticum, and stay with them until help arrives. Always take the threat of suicide seriously. Get professional help. Therapy and homeopathy work beautifully hand-in-hand, and often cut much time out of therapy as a result, and the person is able to work through their mental or emotional angst more quickly and less painfully—which is good news.

Warning: If your depression is more than 3 months old, you are considered a chronic case. Do NOT take the homeopathic remedy indicated below. Instead, seek out constitutional homeopathic treatment from your nearest homeopath. See the appendix for the phone number of the National Center for Homeopathy (NCH) for that information.

Comments: The symptoms of depression, and indeed seasonal affected disorder (SAD), can be helped tremendously by this remedy because the symptoms are always worse in the winter.

Over the years, I have treated a number of people who had depression linked with suicidal tendencies. The one remedy that has saved lives, quite literally, is Aurum Met., potentized gold. When one thinks about it, gold is the color of sunlight, of self-worth and value, and it makes sense that this remedy would stand out—depression is about feelings of worthlessness, low self-esteem, utter hopelessness, and being buried in a dark hole that prevents the possibility of light shining in.

Aurum Met. should be in every emergency homeopathic kit in America in my personal opinion. Even if the suicidal urge is not present, Aurum Met. is one of the premier depression remedies. It literally brings light into the darkness of the person's soul and wounded spirit. And with light comes realization, and positive changes have to occur when that happens!

Mentals: Aurum Met.'s symptoms include a sense of absolute worthlessness. You feel as if you can no longer contribute to anything or anyone at all—on any level. Women who respond well to Aurum Mur. when depressed are very hard working people who have played by the rules and run into a brick wall, have lost their job, are given a lateral transfer, have had their business go bankrupt, or have suffered some severe blow in a business or financial way, which translates directly to their own innate value as a human being.

Aurum types value themselves through their success in the business and corporate world. Many of these women own their own businesses, whether it be a cottage industry at home, or a multimillion dollar corporation. Their entire self-esteem, their self-worth, is tied to how they do or do not perform on a job. They take it as humiliation if they are less than perfect on the job and rate their success by dollars and cents or sales figures—the bottom line.

Aurum types are highly idealistic, and set big goals for themselves. So, it's no surprise that if an Aurum type gets fired, laid off, transferred, or in some way demoted, depression can set in quickly and deeply. And regardless of whether thoughts of suicide are present, this remedy can alleviate the deepening, dark spiral of depression.

You may resort to drinking alcohol or taking recreational drugs as an escape from your pain, fall from importance, or humiliation. Other Aurum types suffer depression because of a shock and loss of a loved one—be it through divorce, death, or a disappointment in a love relationship. This

literally puts you into a tailspin of depression. You can become anorexic as a result, or manic-depressive where you are high and happy one moment, and then are plunged into the darkest of pits of maudlin sadness, the next.
Modalities: WORSE – in the winter, when the depression deepens markedly. Night brings out your worst depression, from sunset to sunrise. BETTER – from moving about, walking, and getting warmed up.

ANXIETY

Mentals: Your anxiety takes the form of hypochondria (the fear that you have a dreaded disease) or makes you feel that you are lost hopelessly forever. Heart palpitations arise with these feelings and thoughts. There is an apprehensiveness and the mere noise of a door or some small sound can set you off into a spate of anxiety reactions.
Physical Symptoms: There is anxiety that you are going to have a heart attack, which is a keynote of this remedy. Heart palpitations are part of this symptom picture. Your anxiety alternates with black despair. When the anxiety strikes, it will literally drive you from place to place and you feel tormented. And after the anxiety reaction leaves, you are weary and exhausted. Sometimes the anxiety is so overwhelming that you begin to think in terms of taking your life because, in this state, you feel that death would be a great release, a freedom from all this pain and fear that is relentlessly pounding against your sensitive and vulnerable psyche.

IRRITABILITY

Comments: As the depression deepens, Aurum Met. women become disconnected. Irritability is a hallmark symptom of this remedy and the word "irascible" fits well. Along with this razor-sharp irritability you may harbor violent thoughts toward others—even of injuring the offending party who brings out this irritability in you.
Mentals: There can be constant complaining followed by a hysterical mood; laughing one moment, crying the next. You can howl and scream at others, drive yourself furiously into a state of hurrying, and only you—and no one else—can do things fast enough to suit you; hence your irritability arises. The irritability can rise and fall like a roller coaster, a feeling of joy can be followed by profound mental anxiety. Lowliness of spirits can be felt and your anger manifests in reaction and takes the form of grumbling, and becoming quarrelsome. You can be peevish and moody, flying into a passion, and you are easily excited into that irritable state.

SLEEP

Physical Symptoms: Symptoms that can accompany your depression are heart palpitations and wandering bone pains at night. You may moan or cry out during sleep, and often awaken 3–4 hours after going to sleep. You may have insomnia along with very disturbing nightmares. Or, you are extremely tired and want to sleep, but you lie in bed, unable to do so. Your chest may feel as if it's encased, quite literally, in armor or a binding of some type, and it is hard to take a deep breath.

Or, it feels as if a great, invisible weight is on your chest making it impossible to breathe properly. A keynote for this remedy is that just as you begin to fall asleep, some little sound or activity will frighten you wide awake once again, heart pounding with over-reaction and dread.

UTERINE FIBROIDS

Mentals: You have an enormous oversensitive reaction to noise, excitement, or any chaotic situation. Low self-esteem is one of your earmarks, and you may hide this feeling from others by being spectacularly successful in a business mode. Behind closed doors, you have many nagging problems. Inside you is a feeling of detachment from life, as if the obstacles are too many for you to surmount. There can be a sense of hopelessness, along with grumbling, irritability, and becoming quarrelsome. There are highs and lows emotionally; one moment you are happy (or as close to it as you think you will ever get—Aurum Met. women will often tell me that they do not know what joy or happiness is) and the next, you are cast down into the depths of a hellish black hole called despair.

Physical Symptoms: A burning heat and cutting pain on the right side of your abdomen may be present, combined with the feeling and need to have a bowel movement (but you don't). There is aching in the abdomen, with a sense of fullness. There can be a lot of flatulence, especially at night, along with a lot of grumbling or rumbling sounds in the abdomen as the gas moves through.

There is a sensation in your abdomen as if your menses was going to come on (but it doesn't), but the colicky type of pain is still present. The right side of your abdomen (you swear it's the right ovary acting up) is tender and sore to the touch. There can be jolting pains in the right ovary region. Discharge from your vagina is profuse, yellow, or white, and very thick, but not offensive smelling. There is a corrosive, burning quality to the discharge.

Modalities: WORSE – in cold weather or from getting a chill, from cold, whether it be air conditioning or during winter weather, or from walking. Your symptoms are always worse from sunset to sunrise, which makes nights miserable for you. BETTER – when you are at rest. Your symptoms subside as soon as dawn comes, and improve dramatically throughout the daylight hours.

AURUM MURIATICUM
(AURUM MUR.)

Origin: Made from chloride of gold, this remedy is one of several from the Aurum family of potentized gold homeopathic remedies.

UTERINE FIBROIDS

Comments: This remedy is considered for severe hemorrhaging due to a diagnosed fibroid(s) in the uterus.

Mentals: You are very restless and change position frequently (crossing legs, uncrossing them, etc.). Your central nervous system is involved, and you can become highly irritable and nothing can be done to please you. Fretting constantly, you are depressed by your deteriorating health condition. Even thinking about your symptoms causes your heart to beat fast or palpitate, which is a keynote for this remedy. At night, insomnia may nag at you because every little noise will make you start or jump and you will awaken. You may hate your job, and hate life in general at this point, and you can find no good reason to keep on living.

Physical Symptoms: Heat and itching in the vagina; constant leucorrhea (discharge) from the vagina that is light yellow in color. It is most prevalent in the morning, and there may be an acrid state to it, making you feel as if it were burning your inner thighs and simultaneously creating itching in your genital region. Your uterus may feel very full and be painful, plus there may be vaginal spasms.

Modalities: WORSE – you hate to go inside a house because it is usually warmer, and therefore aggravates all of your symptoms. Worse in a warm room, in a bed (you throw off the covers), or in warm or hot weather. Walking quickly, having to climb stairs, 'suffocating' from wearing clothes (the warm factor again), and being spoken to in a sharp tone, causes your heart to palpitate. BETTER – in cold temperatures (be it air conditioning or weather conditions) and walking slowly outdoors in fresh air.

❀AURUM MURIATICUM NATRONATUM❀
(AURUM MUR. NAT.)

Origin: Made from sodium chloroaurate, or double chloride of gold and sodium (salt).
Comments: This is a double salt of Natrum and chloride of gold. Dr. Burnett, one of our old, great nineteenth-century homeopaths, felt that this remedy, in particular, was the most powerful to cure uterine fibroid tumors.

UTERINE FIBROIDS

Comments: A history of spontaneous abortions is a keynote for this remedy. Other physical symptoms may include warts on the tongue, a white-colored tongue, a history of delayed menses, low sexual desire, and other ovarian-related problems. High blood pressure may be present with this picture due to your nervous nature.
Physical Symptoms: There may be pressure on the right side of the abdomen. There may be an acid-like mucus from the vagina, with an almost corrosive, burning sensation to it. There may also be attending edema within the abdominal region, with swelling.
Modalities: WORSE – in cold, wet weather, from October to springtime, and being at rest.

❀BARYTA CARBONICA❀
(BARYTA CARB.)

Origin: Made from barium carbonate, also known as witherite.
Comments: Found in the Earth's crust as barite and witherite, this mineral was discovered by William Withering in 1783. The mineral has white crystals that appear in a lattice-type arrangement on the rocks containing this substance. Uses for this compound have been many: it was used for swollen glands and tuberculosis, in radiology, and in manufacturing glassware as well as creating optical glass.

MEMORY LOSS

Comments: This remedy is especially useful for the very young and the elderly. Typologically, these women are normally plump to obese. Its value is in areas where there are true signs of early senility and then it should be carefully considered. An excellent remedy for the mentally impaired or mentally retarded.
Physical Symptoms: You are unable to retain or remember what you have read, and confusion or clouding of the mental faculties is common. And if you forget something, the emotion most sharply felt is grief—and too much of it. There is a slowness to mentally grasping something and you cannot retain knowledge or what was said.
Modalities: WORSE – if you think about your forgetfulness, from having too much company, from cold exposure to your feet or head, or from direct sunlight and becoming over-heated. BETTER – from walking in open air, being in cold temperatures, eating cold food, and being in a warm wrap.

❀BELLADONNA❀

Origin: Made from a plant known as deadly nightshade.
Comments: Grown in Europe, the leaves and flowers are used to make this remedy. Belladonna has a profound effect on a person. It has been used since ancient times; the drops were placed in the eyes of women to make them look larger because it dilates the pupils! To have large, dark-appearing eyes was thought to be beautiful. During the springtime, the plant is known to grow a

foot a day! Such is its active, aggressive nature. Hahnemann proved Belladonna in 1799 and successfully used it to treat the symptoms of scarlet fever.

Mentals: You are hypersensitive in nature to almost everything: being jarred, being physically touched, being in a draft of wind (include air conditioning), getting too much light (including sunlight), or getting wet. An interesting keynote to this remedy is that after getting your hair cut, your menopausal symptoms may worsen! You are highly excitable and are supersensitive to your environment and to visual impressions around you, and yet, when disturbed, you can turn into a furious rage, much like a thunderstorm suddenly popping up. The world around you must be protective so that you aren't bombarded by all of these things. Your central nervous system is highly strung, and normal everyday occurrences that would not bother the rest of us truly bother and irritate you.

BREAST CYSTS AND FIBROIDS

Physical Symptoms: A keynote for this remedy is that your breasts have heat radiating from them (much like a wood stove throws off heat). They throb, feel heavy, and may have a flushed or blushing red color to them.

Modalities: WORSE – with movement, jarring, lying down, or touching them (even fabric lying across your breasts will bother you).

Other: Stop wearing a bra for 2 weeks. There is plenty of evidence that wearing a bra stops lymph gland drainage, and cysts and fibroids may result, as well as breast cancer. Take it off and see what happens!

EYES DRY, BURNING, OR ITCHING

Physical Symptoms: Your eyes will have a throbbing sensation in them; they will feel dry and burn, and you may experience photophobia (aversion to light). Your pupils are dilated, a keynote of this remedy. A shooting pain may be present in your eyes. They will feel swollen—as if they are protruding from their sockets. There is a staring, brilliant, or shining look to your eyes.

MENOPAUSAL HEADACHES

Comments: This kind of headache includes "cluster" headaches and migraines that come on with a swift, sudden vengeance. Women who have long hair and tie it up or anchor it to their skull can get this type of nasty headache—and when they let down their hair and allow their scalp to relax, their headache goes away! Other women find that the headache comes on AFTER getting their hair cut or washed.

Physical Symptoms: Your headache occurs in the temples. Sometime it will strike you in the rear of the skull or your forehead. The main sign of this type of headache is FAST onset. There is such throbbing pain that you feel as if hammers are striking inside your skull with an outward motion. Your breathing may become labored or forced as a result. There can be wave-like, pulsating pain that feels as if it were literally rising and falling in your head like an ocean tide. Your face will become flushed and very red looking. The pupils of your eyes will dilate. Belladonna is an excellent migraine remedy, especially for headaches with a swift, sudden onset.

Modalities: WORSE – if you are in hot, direct sunlight, are jarred, hear any noise (even talking), are getting a nasty cold, if people are around you, from pressure applied to the head, on lying down, from looking at shining objects (the glare from windshields, chrome from an automobile, mirrors, for instance), from hearing running water, or from hanging your head downward (such as from stooping or bending down). The headache is always worse in the afternoon, between 3 p.m.

and around 11 p.m. to midnight—and there is no sign of a headache during the rest of the day or during the morning hours. BETTER – from placing a light cover across you, bending backwards, sitting semi-erect in a chair or bed, resting in bed, standing, or leaning your head against something. Bending or turning the head from side to side also helps.

VAGINA DRY AND POOR LUBRICATION

Physical Symptoms: There is great dryness in your vagina along with shooting, violent pains that move upward into the abdomen. Cramp-like pains begin and end abruptly. A keynote for this remedy is that these symptoms come on suddenly and violently, and end just as quickly—a hit and run type of action.

SPASMS IN THE VAGINA (VAGINISMUS)

Physical Symptoms: There is dryness as well as heat radiating from your vagina. The vagina feels very heavy; a major keynote for this remedy is the extraordinary feeling of WEIGHT in that region of your body. The spasms have a weighty sensation to them, a burning heat, and a throbbing and pulsation in the vagina that is always made worse by the slightest movement or being jarred. There is almost a feverish sensation in the vagina, along with the painful, spasmodic throbbing. You can be extremely restless, but movement countermands it. The vaginismus may come on suddenly, without any warning, and there is a marked violence to the symptoms.

❀BELLIS PERENNIS❀

(BELL. PER.)

Origin: Made from a plant known as the European daisy.
Comments: This remedy is a cousin, in some respects, to Arnica Montana, because it, too, is used after suffering from an injury. The entire plant is used, when it is in flower. Although this is a very small, delicate looking plant with a white daisy and a yellow center, the leaves contain a powerful, acrid juice that makes it second only to Arnica Montana. Historically, it was called wound-wort or bruise-wort, and it was used during the Middle Ages to treat injuries. Often, homeopaths will use Bell. Per. on an accident victim following treatment with Arnica Montana. This plant can 'clean up' any swelling or trauma to tissue that Arnica did not originally address shortly after the accident or surgery.
Modalities: WORSE – on the left side, taking a hot bath or lying in the warmth of bed, before a storm, after a cold bath, or being caught out in a cold wind.

GALACTORRHEA

Comments: If your breast(s) remains swollen or hard after experiencing an injury, and liquid is expressing itself from your nipples, and you have tried Arnica Montana and it did not work, then consider Bellis Perennis as the remedy to cure this condition.
Other: Stop wearing a bra for 2 weeks. There is plenty of evidence that wearing a bra stops lymph gland drainage, and cysts and fibroids may result, as well as breast cancer. Take it off and see what happens!

VARICOSE VEINS

Comments: In the sphere of varicose veins, this remedy is good at getting rid of venous stasis, or sluggish circulation to our venous system. There is an interesting keynote to this remedy: You will wake up promptly at 3 a.m. and be unable to go back to sleep. Another unique keynote for this

remedy is that if you are hot and sweaty from working out (aerobics or any other form of cardiovascular exercise) and you drink ice cold water, you suffer badly from the effects of it.
Physical Symptoms: The varicose veins are intensely sore and feel better with cool (not cold) bathing. The varicosity is usually on the left side of the body, but it can be on the right, too. The soreness in the leg can be so bad that you cannot walk or put much weight on that extremity as a result.

❀BRYONIA❀

Origin: Made from the plant, white bryony.
Comments: This plant's root has been used since the time of Hippocrates. Later, the Romans used it. Bryonia is extremely poisonous and can cause death within hours in its crude, non-homeopathic form. It was used by the ancients to cure epilepsy, hysteria, gout, and many other ailments. Bryonia grows in central and southern Europe. The bulb looks like yellowish nodules—gout-like, from a Doctrine of Signatures standpoint.

ACUTE ANXIETY OR PANIC ATTACKS

Comments: Anxiety may center around your business, be it corporate or a cottage industry in your home. Fear of poverty, financial loss, and excessive or nonstop worry about money will trigger your anxiety.
Mentals: When anxiety hits you, there is despair of ever recovering from it, along with a fear of dying. In that state, you want to be left alone, in a dark, quiet room, undisturbed. Pity the person who comes in to check on you to see if you are alright: in that state, you are more than likely to become angry and snap irritably at them. Sympathy only makes you grumpier.
Physical Symptoms: The anxiety centers in the sternum or center of your chest, over the heart region. There may be pressing or painful sensations accompanying it. The attack usually occurs around 9 p.m. or while you are in bed, before midnight. Anxiety is felt through your entire body and you are driven to do something constantly.
Modalities: WORSE – from being exposed to dry cold, becoming too hot in an overly stuffy room, in hot weather, eating vegetables or acids (such as orange juice or vinegar products), or being touched by another person. BETTER – on cloudy and damp days, in hot weather, if you rest, in cool, open air, in a cool room, or remaining quiet.

ARTHRITIS

Comments: This remedy should be thought of when rheumatoid arthritis comes on very slowly, over a long period of time. It develops first in one joint, and slowly moves to the next, and so on.
Physical Symptoms: It is not unusual to have gout along with these other symptoms. Your joints are red, swollen, and hot, with a stitching, tearing type of pain. There can be swelling of your feet. There is usually an aggravation around 9 p.m. Lying on the painful side or part of your body can provide relief from the pain. Generally, there is a worsening of your symptoms upon rising in the morning. These symptoms are more RIGHT-sided than left-sided.
Modalities: WORSE – after eating, with motion, in damp weather, or when the affected part is uncovered. The pain worsens if you are jarred or accidentally bumped or you bump into something. BETTER – with pressure on the painful region—such as massage or having it tightly bandaged (such as an Ace wrap). Your pain is always better with heat of any kind—a heating pad, a warm cloth, or taking a hot shower or bath.

MENOPAUSAL HEADACHES

Comments: This is a preeminent migraine remedy.
Physical Symptoms: Your head has a very bruised feeling to it. Usually the pain begins in the left eye and moves up and over your head to the rear of your skull. Then it becomes seated in this region. It can be frontal, too, with the sinus cavities involved. Your scalp is terribly sensitive and you cannot bear to have anyone touch your head. To brush your hair or try to arrange it would be excruciating. If you have to stoop, the headache becomes bursting or splitting.

Many describe the feeling as hammers being banged inside their brain. The pain is sharp and stabbing and is made worse by any kind of eye or body movement. Pain is less if your eyes remain closed. A bruised, sore feeling can be felt in your eyeballs. There is nausea.

When you get this type of headache, you want to be left completely ALONE. You do not want to be touched or have people around you. You desperately need to have the room darkened, to have complete quiet, and you will not move an inch because every movement increases the pain in your head or the nausea you are experiencing.
Modalities: WORSE – with dry cold or heat, by becoming too warm, stooping, coughing, deep breathing, eating vegetables, acids (citrus fruit, vinegar, tomatoes, etc.), early in the morning, or becoming upset and irritable. BETTER – from lying on your painful side, applying pressure to the affected region, rest, or a cold cloth. Wrapping the head tightly helps. Improvement occurs with cool, open air, on cloudy days, or when damp weather is present. Pulling the knees upward, sitting up, or drinking cold liquids also helps.

❀CACTUS GRANDIFLORUS❀
(CACTUS GRAND.)

Origin: This is night-blooming cereus, a beautiful member of the cactus family.
Comments: This remedy was proved by Dr. Rubins in 1862 and was used primarily for heart problems, and in particular, angina. The flower is a beautiful multi-petaled white blossom with lemon yellow stamens. The stem and blossoms are used to make this marvelous remedy.

MENOPAUSAL HEADACHES

Comments: This remedy is considered one of the best "congestive" or migraine headache remedies in our pharmacopoeia. A major keynote for this remedy is that the headache always has a cycle where it will return daily or weekly—at the same hour as previously.
Physical Symptoms: The violence and onset of this headache is startling and powerful. It can make you feel tearful and sad, and you will cry for no reason. There is a sensation as if the blood vessels within the brain feel distended (swollen), or as if your head is being smashed in a vice. The pains are pulsating, compressive, and periodic. It is so bad that you may want to scream.

There may be vertigo present, with a heavy, weighted sensation of pressure felt on the top of your head that is made better from pressure being applied to that area with your hand. This type of headache usually attacks the right side of your head and temple. It can have a violent, nerve-like pain associated with it. Your eyesight may dim when it becomes a migraine.
Modalities: WORSE – after eating, missing a meal, fasting, walking, talking, climbing up stairs, from noise, light, sunlight, or dampness (weather-related). The headache worsens at 11 a.m. or 11 p.m. It is at its worst at night. BETTER – from being in open air and from pressure applied to the painful region.

HEART PALPITATIONS AND SHORTNESS OF BREATH

Physical Symptoms: For those who experience not only palpitations, but shortness of breath and dizziness along with bloating or gas. This remedy should be thought of if these symptoms appear just before your menstrual cycle begins. Palpitations may also be accompanied with vertigo. If palpitations ensue and you hold your breath to stop them, they become worse.
Modalities: WORSE – if you lie on your left side. The heart may feel as if a steel band was wrapped around it, and it feels gripped and released, gripped and released. BETTER – if you lie on your right side, with your head slightly elevated.

SPASMS IN THE VAGINA (VAGINISMUS)

Comments: This remedy acts profoundly on female problems such as vaginismus. If you have a past medical history of heart problems AND vaginismus simultaneously, this remedy should be considered. Your past menses history is one of coming on too early, and when it does appear, it is scanty. When you lie down, the blood stops flowing. If you rise, the blood begins to flow again—a keynote for this remedy. The flow always consists of dark-colored blood.
Mentals: Your nature is to be taciturn and you may cry for no known reason. There is a sadness that pervades your daily life and you feel more miserable if someone tries to console you.
Physical Symptoms: Your symptoms of vaginismus are severe and make you cry out: There is a painful, spasmodic contraction of your vagina that does not allow for any penetration. There is a twitching of the muscles that can be set off by physical touch alone. The pain and spasm may be left-sided.

There may be a feeling of a hot steel band wrapped around your vagina, squeezing it and constricting it closed. This is a very violent and powerful sensation. It can be so severe that your breathing becomes oppressed and if you move, the pain, which is sharp, intensifies.
Modalities: WORSE – if you try to walk, lie on your left side, or lie down. There is a marked time when your symptoms are WORSE – 11 a.m. and 11 p.m.

❀CALADIUM❀

Origin: Made from American arum (also known as dumb cane in South America).
Comments: This remedy is a specific for the genital organs. It has a special sphere for those who smoke cigarettes, pipes, or cigars. This remedy is also used to help wean smokers from the habit if they want to quit. There is an interesting keynote that the affected parts may feel COLD. If you have severe itching during your pregnancy, then this is the remedy for you.
Modalities: WORSE – when the temperature is warm, or during motion. BETTER – after sweating, or taking a nap during the day. If there is a burning sensation, the area feels better if cold water is placed against the affected part of the body.

VAGINAL ITCHING

Comments: One of the villains that can cause this itching is candida. Check with your gynecologist to rule out this possibility, before taking a remedy. Other villains can be spermicidal creams, vaginal deodorants, soap used to clean the vaginal area, soap residue on your panties, tampon use, napkin rubbing and irritating the skin, or use of any powder, to name a few. You may be allergic to one of these products and this could be the source of the itching. After you have made sure that none of these are the culprit for the itching, then match your symptoms against the remedies presented below.

If you have been diagnosed with candida, it can be dealt with homeopathically. So can the other conditions listed above, but the use of the remedy below is not recommended, if this is the case. Work with your homeopath because the vaginal itching is only a minor symptom to an overall larger picture that needs to be addressed on a constitutional level and not an acute level.

For minor relief from itching, you can use NON-ALCOHOLIC tincture, such as calendula. Wash three times a day with it. Or, try urtica ointment, and apply lightly to the area where the itching is located. Both products are used only topically and not internally. If there is no relief after 2 days, then stop using it and see your homeopath.

Physical Symptoms: This type of itching reduces a woman to a world of ongoing torment where nothing else exists except the maddening burning and itching in her vulva region. There is marked perspiration to the genital region, with an itching and burning sensation to the vulva. The labia region is greatly swollen and you may be able to visually confirm the distention of the veins in that region. There can be a mucus discharge along with itching and pimples around the vagina or vulva. Your sexual organs feel larger than normal (although they may not be, but this is the sensation you experience).

Modalities: WORSE – upon falling asleep, or when using or inhaling secondary tobacco smoke. There is an aversion to cold water, although cold water on the affected parts makes the itching better, from engaging in sexual activity, and from motion (which creates warmth and that induces the itching). BETTER – after sweating, from sleeping during the day (a nap), being out in cold air, and from a cold cloth placed on the itchy area.

❁CALCAREA CARBONICA❁

(CALC. CARB.)

Origin: This remedy is made from calcium carbonate taken from the inner lining of oyster shells.

Comments: Those who are familiar with the mother-of-pearl luminescent inner part of the oyster will appreciate where this remedy comes from. As one of our major constitutional remedies, Calc. Carb. addresses areas having to do with bones, calcium distribution in the body, slow growth in children, and dental problems such as soft teeth. Like the oyster, from the constitutional standpoint, Calc. Carb. women are shy and introverted, yet each has a pearl hidden within her. Typologically, this is an especially good remedy for plump or obese women or for women with medium or large bones. They are fleshy and out of shape.

Modalities: WORSE – from exertion (mental or physical), climbing or ascending stairs or a hill, experiencing cold in any form—temperature, weather, being caught in a chilling draft (air conditioning included), or bathing. Moist, damp, or humid conditions aggravate you greatly, and you are always much worse 5 days before and during a full moon, which creates insomnia during that time frame. BETTER – in a dry climate (deserts are perfect for you!!) and dry weather, or lying on the painful side.

ACUTE ANXIETY OR PANIC ATTACKS

Comments: Your anxiety surfaces because you have worked yourself into a corner by taking on too much responsibility. There is a Type-A work-a-holic tendency brought into play here because the underlying, driving need is for you to keep a roof over your family's head. Calc. Carb. women are hard working, trustworthy workers who end up collapsing under the Atlas-like loads they take on and carry—and this is when their anxiety will manifest. Your strong sense of duty to your family and your employer are the driving forces behind your exhausted state.

Mentals: Attacks usually occur in the evening and in bed, but not always. You may suffer an attack after hearing about or seeing cruelty done to another person or an animal. When the anxiety hits, your greatest fear is that you are going to go insane. You have many, many fears about the future in general, and about health (am I going to die and leave my family without a roof over their heads?) The attack may occur just as you are dropping off to sleep.
Physical Symptoms: You may suffer an anxiety attack after a bowel movement. There may be nausea, restlessness, heart palpitations, and sweating on the back of your skull along with the anxiety reaction.
Modalities: WORSE – in cold, damp weather (rain, snow, or fog), walking in cold air, from too much mental or physical exertion, or from getting wet. BETTER – in a warm, dry climate, from a massage, after breakfast, or inhaling fresh air.

ARTHRITIS

Comments: Oftentimes, this remedy follows Rhus Tox. well.
Physical Symptoms: The pains are sharp and sticking—as if that part of your body has been strained. Your feet are always cold and you may even wear socks to bed—but sometime during the night, you get rid of them.

The soles of your feet may feel raw or burning. There can be arthritic nodosities present. Your joints swell, particularly your knees. There may be sweating only on your hands. Your knees may be cold and you can experience cramps in your lower legs. The muscles will feel as if they are tearing apart. And there can be weakness in your arms and legs, too. Your fingernails will be distorted, brittle, easily broken, or peeling. Fibrositis is possible. Your legs may feel weak and trembling, especially climbing anything, such as stairs or a small hill.
Modalities: WORSE – after exposure to cold or damp weather, rain, or fog conditions.

BREASTS SWOLLEN OR PAINFUL

Physical Symptoms: Breasts are tender and swollen, with heat felt in them. The nipples may be cracked, tender feeling, or ulcerated. There is severe stitching pain in the breasts if you are breast feeding.
Modalities: WORSE – movement of any kind, pressure of a too-tight bra or tight-fitting clothes against your breasts, allowing the breasts to hang down without support, and before menses. BETTER – after gently massaging the breasts and after menses.
Other: Stop wearing a bra for 2 weeks. There is plenty of evidence that wearing a bra stops lymph gland drainage, and cysts and fibroids may result, as well as breast cancer. Take it off and see what happens!

LEG CRAMPS

Comments: For those of us who have a calcium-related deficiency that is causing leg muscle cramps, this is the remedy to consider.
Physical Symptoms: Cramping occurs when you are easily chilled, with the keynote that the feet may get so cold that you will wear socks to bed at night. Midway through the night, you take them off because your feet have warmed up sufficiently—and it is a technique to stop them from cramping. The cold in your feet or legs may set off the cramping. You may have cold knees with cramps in your calves. There can be a burning sensation in the soles of your feet, or they may feel raw. There is a tearing pain associated with this type of cramping that may become more pronounced in cold or wet weather.

Your leg cramps may be due to over-exertion during the day, and you do not have to over-do in the exercise department hardly at all for the cramps pop up. There is a sharp, sticking sensation to the cramps, or a feeling that your muscles were wrenched or sprained.
Modalities: BETTER – a warm cloth applied to the area, a bath or shower, or a heating pad always makes these cramps subside.

MEMORY LOSS

Comments: One of the greatest reasons to use this remedy is if you are the type of woman who has been overwhelmed with work and you have TOO MUCH to remember. Your memory bin is so full that it cannot handle one more piece of information! As a result, forgetfulness sets in.
Mentals: Women who worry about having a roof over their head, or being able to pay the mortgage, and who are very attached to family and family matters, find forgetfulness occurring all the time—and this is the remedy that can help resolve it.
Physical Symptoms: Worrying about trifles, about your responsibilities and duties both at home and at work, will soon drive your brain cells into a frazzle and your memory begins to slip—sometimes, quite dramatically, depending on how much is on your mental "plate" already. The more overworked you are, the more your memory fails you.

You become forgetful or confused, or you misplace words or express yourself with the wrong word. The word may be on the tip of your tongue, but it will not connect with your brain so you can verbalize it. After awhile, you honestly begin to wonder if you have early Alzheimer's (you don't) or if you are slowly losing your mind (you aren't). You may even think that you are going insane and will end up in the mental ward of some hospital—permanently! (Not a chance, so stop fretting about it.)

Your memory becomes weak and you cannot remember places you have been, or when you were there. Undertaking any kind of mental processing can become extremely tiring to you if you are in this quandary and it takes the greatest of Herculean efforts for you to think of something.
Modalities: WORSE – when the weather turns damp, humid, cold, or rainy, during the full moon phase, from eyestrain, or from exertion on a physical, mental, or emotional level. BETTER – if the weather is dry or warm, after eating breakfast, and from getting a whiff of fresh air.

SKIN ITCHING

Comments: Calcarea women, in general, usually have very pale-looking skin, and frequently have a flushed-looking face or bright red cheeks. I call this a "fair English complexion."
Physical Symptoms: This remedy is considered when the skin cracks after washing, or during the winter time. The skin is dry and the itching is relieved by scratching the area.

VARICOSE VEINS

Comments: Remedies in the Calcarea family are considered sources of calcium, so they can be of special help if the vein walls or the valves within them become weak due to lack of this mineral being available in our bodies to keep them strong. If calcium is in short supply, varicose veins will begin to appear. By strengthening the walls or valves with this remedy, many times the varicosity will disappear—or at least new ones will stop forming.
Physical Symptoms: The varicose veins look like a spider-like network over your skin. There is a burning sensation to these veins. They may appear distended, and may have a smarting sensation to them—especially in your lower legs—yet, you will have cold feet (and may even go to bed at night with socks on).

❁CAMPHORA❁

Origin: Camphor is made from the gum of Laurus camphora.
Comments: This remedy was made by Samuel Hahnemann in 1831 when there was an outbreak of cholera in Europe. In 1854, Dr. Quinn, who founded the London Homeopathic Hospital, was able to use this remedy again when a cholera epidemic struck England. Interestingly, Quinn contracted cholera himself and cured it with a dose of Camphora. There were 30 percent less deaths from cholera when this homeopathic remedy was used over traditional medicine in that country at that time.

Historically, from a traditional medical standpoint, it was used as spirits of camphor and in tincture form and the patient would repeatedly inhale the odor of it.

ACUTE ANXIETY OR PANIC ATTACKS

Comments: This remedy is for a state of collapse.
Mentals: During the attack, you are afraid of your own thoughts, and you desire any kind of diversion in order NOT to think about them. You fear being alone during an attack, and you need to have company. There is such a sense that you are going to die during the attack, that after you survive it, you are relieved to find yourself still alive; such is the intensity of your anxiety. These attacks always occur at night, and there is torturous anguish accompanying it. In the extreme, you may bite, scratch, or tear at your clothes during such an episode.
Physical Symptoms: Chills are a leading keynote for this remedy. A bone-chilling cold is accompanied by shivering, but you do not want to be covered. Fainting is possible. Restless tossing in bed and tearfulness may occur. There is anxiety in your heart region, with palpitations after eating. You can break out in a cold sweat during the attack.
Modalities: WORSE – with motion, being exposed to cold air, experiencing a cold draft, when half asleep, during mental exertion, or when experiencing a shock of some kind (usually emotional in nature). BETTER – from sweating, drinking cold water, being warm, having company, and receiving attention.

❁CANTHARIS❁

Origin: Made from an insect known as the Spanish fly.
Comments: This bright green, metallic-looking beetle lives in southern France and Spain. It has a very long and interesting history. The beetle excretes cantharidin, and in ancient times it was used to remove warts. Then it was found to help rheumatism, and most of all, it was used as an aphrodisiac! Cantharidin is highly toxic if taken in large, crude doses (who wants to eat beetles?). It attacks the urinary tract, which gives sexual stimulus to that region—but you'd better be prepared to do a lot of vomiting to get this sexual stimulation—not my cup of tea!!

Homeopathically, the remedy is rendered harmless and is widely used for bladder infections, cystitis, and serious burns to the skin.

URINARY INCONTINENCE

Mentals: You can be temperamental during your bouts of incontinence, restless and almost hysterical with the pain in your urethral region. Your incontinence comes on suddenly and with a violent intensity.
Physical Symptoms: There is pain in the lower abdominal region where your bladder resides; there is a cutting, knife-like, burning pain that accompanies your incontinence. The pain associated

with it is enough to send most women screaming. If incontinence takes place AFTER voiding or takes place during menses, then you should consider this your remedy of choice.
Modalities: WORSE – with movement of any kind, consuming coffee, or being exposed to cold water. BETTER – with warmth of any kind, from gently massaging the area, and at night.

❀CARBO VEGETABILIS❀
(CARBO VEG.)

Origin: Made from beech, silver birch, or poplar trees.
Comments: The wood is heated (without air being present) and turned into charcoal, before becoming known as Carbo Vegetabilis. The main property of this process is the carbon, an element found in all living things. Hahnemann, upon seeing that doctors of his day used charcoal as a mouthwash for ulcers, decided to make this into a homeopathic remedy. In traditional medicine, to this day, charcoal is used in tablet form for gas in the intestinal tract.

ACUTE ANXIETY OR PANIC ATTACKS

Comments: Attacks can be brought on by drinking alcohol, drinking ice water, eating too rich a food (with too much butter), experiencing any kind of shock, or after surgery. You are driven toward fresh air, and will do anything to get out of a stuffy car, apartment, home, or office. A keynote is that you will often fan yourself just to have air movement around you. This remedy helps those who suffer their attacks in the evening hours, from being in bed and upon closing their eyes, or during or after eating.
Mentals: When anxious, you are truly irritable and nasty—usually only to family members. You cannot concentrate, your memory is gone, and there is a great fear of the darkness, and of ghosts haunting you. Consuming ice-cold drinks also worsens your state.
Physical Symptoms: During an anxiety attack, you may feel "air hunger" and may gasp repeatedly to draw in deeper breaths of air to compensate for this sensation. Or, you will place yourself in front of a fan or an air conditioner to seek relief. Many times your anxiety comes on with indigestion (you will be bloated after a meal, anyway). You will consume carbonated drinks in order to belch and relieve the pressure in your stomach.

Your legs and feet will grow cold and you will feel weak. Anxiety in the heart region is common, along with palpitations and a feeling that you will die from a heart attack. Often, you will grab a newspaper or magazine and frantically fan yourself. There is trembling anxiety upon waking in the morning. You have cold breath and experience cold perspiration with an attack.
Modalities: WORSE – from extremes of weather and temperature, warm, damp weather (humidity), pressure of clothes, cooling off, night air, or frosty conditions. BETTER – from belching, being fanned, and elevating your feet.

BREASTS SWOLLEN OR PAINFUL

Comments: If you have had a past history of breast abscesses, consider this remedy.
Other: Stop wearing a bra for 2 weeks. There is plenty of evidence that wearing a bra stops lymph gland drainage, and cysts and fibroids may result, as well as breast cancer. Take it off and see what happens!
Physical Symptoms: Your breasts may resemble a lumpy old couch. They feel hard and swollen.
Modalities: WORSE – from walking, or from pressure of clothes against your breasts. BETTER – from elevating your feet.

INDIGESTION

Comments: This is for the woman who gets bloated shortly after eating. Belching does help to reduce the pressure in your stomach region.

Physical Symptoms: Your digestion is slow. A keynote symptom (a highly unusual one) is that there is a slight burning sensation felt in your stomach all the way through your body to your spinal column. There is a driving need for fresh air. Frequently, you will fan yourself with anything you can find (your hand, a magazine). If you are given a choice, you will throw open a window or a door or escape into fresh air, which will make you feel better. You suffer from what is known as "air hunger."

The source of indigestion comes from consuming too many rich foods, including chicken, milk, wine (particularly brandy), butter, fast foods, or coffee. You have a desire for sweet, salty foods or sour liquids (such as lemons). Your stomach and abdomen can become huge and bloated after a meal, and you absolutely cannot bear anything tight around your waist or abdominal region. You will continually belch and pass gas to relieve this highly uncomfortable state.

The reason your digestion is slow is that it lacks enough oxygen to properly break down the food you have eaten, so bloating is the result. Even eating simple foods may bring on this condition. It becomes far worse on high-living or rich foods. There is always relief when you belch or pass gas—but this is only a temporary band-aid for your symptoms.

There is a sense of heaviness and fullness to your body, and you may yawn (air craving) or get sleepy right after eating a meal. If you try to lie down, the food moves upward and you can taste it in the back of your throat and mouth. This is known as "waterbrash" or "acid reflux." There may be nausea the next morning. Stomach cramps may force you to bend double.

Indigestion usually hits a half hour after eating. The stomach region feels tender and highly sensitive to the touch. Some women experience vertigo that originates out of the stomach region and causes them to faint.

Modalities: WORSE – in a warm, stuffy room, from being too hot, when overlifting, or from the pressure of your clothes. It will become worse with extremes of temperature, cold air, warm, damp weather, humidity, wind or draftiness felt on the head (this includes air conditioning), and when consuming iced drinks. BETTER – from fanning yourself, being in cool, fresh air (an open window), elevating your feet, and belching.

❁CARBONEUM SULPHURATUM❁
(CARB. SULPH.)

Origin: This remedy is made from bisulphide of carbon.

Comments: Historically, this was made into an alcohol-based tincture that was used locally on sciatica nerve inflammation and facial neuralgia. Men who worked in rubber factories inhaled this substance all the time. Intoxication of the workers with Carb. Sulph. caused many different ailments and symptoms, which was why it was potentized homeopathically—to get rid of the various ailments experienced by workers who were exposed daily to these noxious odors.

MEMORY LOSS

Physical Symptoms: Your memory is defective and you struggle to find the right word. You are a great talker but frequently are at a loss for just the right word. Sometimes you cannot find something that is sitting right in front of your eyes! Often you forget where you have placed something. Eventually, your thoughts come with excruciating slowness.

Modalities: WORSE – after breakfast or bathing. Being in damp weather doesn't help, either. BETTER – if you are in the open air.

❁CAUSTICUM❁

Origin: Made from distilling burned lime and potassium bisulfate and adding water. It is then known as potassium hydrate.
Comments: Prepared by Hahnemann in the early part of the nineteenth century. It is used for elderly people who are in a general weakened state of being, for weakness or paralysis of any kind, and for rheumatism, with excellent results.
Modalities: WORSE – in a dry, cold wind, cold air, or clear, fine weather, and from motion or walking. BETTER – with the heat of bed, rest, in damp, wet weather, and from any kind of warmth.

ARTHRITIS

Comments: This remedy is of great use where a progressive loss of strength along with joint deformity occurs. The tendons will contract, especially in the hands and toes.
Physical Symptoms: The pain is a tearing, drawing type in the muscles and fibrous tissues of the body. There can be a fainting sensation. Weakness can progress until there is partial paralysis. There can also be local paralysis such as a hand or an arm. When burning, rawness, and soreness occur, this is the remedy to think of.

Numbness may occur in your hands, and there may be unsteadiness of the muscles in your forearms and the hands. The ankles are weak and you cannot walk without suffering. Popping, crackling sounds in the joints are a keynote of this remedy—especially when you rise or begin to move about. Your gait is unsteady and you can easily take a spill. There may be severe itching on the heel of the foot. You might drag one or both feet as the arthritis progresses. The tendons in your arms and legs may not only become taut and tense, but may be hard to the touch, as well. Carpal tunnel is helped by this remedy.
Modalities: WORSE – from cold, from overuse of the part that is affected, from bathing, or in dry weather. And you feel worse when having to rise from a sitting position. BETTER – if it is raining!—a keynote. You feel better with any kind of warmth, particularly being wrapped in an afghan or blanket.

LEG CRAMPS

Comments: This is not only an excellent cramping remedy, but is a "restless legs" remedy, too.
Physical Symptoms: There is a tearing pain with these cramps, and your legs are restless at night; you can't keep them from moving around. With this type of cramping, the feet and toes may actually curve or curl inward; the pain is excruciating, and the cramps make you scream.

If this condition has gone on long enough, there can be a numbing sensation to the region, or a paralysis-like situation arises with the cramping. The pain can be knife-like, as if someone were cutting repeatedly into your leg. One of the keynotes of this remedy is that your limbs can jerk, twitch, and jump convulsively, and if you try to stop it, it will not help.
Modalities: WORSE – the cramps will appear because of a draft or from experiencing cold air on the affected part. BETTER – your cramps will disappear in warmth or the heat of your bed. A unique keynote is that this condition improves during rainy or damp weather.

URINARY INCONTINENCE

Physical Symptoms: Urine is lost involuntarily when you sneeze, laugh, cough, or lift a heavy item. It is the remedy of choice for stress-related incontinence, regardless of age or gender. Urine will also spurt out when you walk or move about.

You are highly sensitive to colder temperatures or weather. Often, you will have an urge to urinate, you go to the bathroom, and once there, you fail to void. And then, after you get up and leave, the urine will then dribble out involuntarily.

VARICOSE VEINS

Comments: This woman has had a history of varicose veins during her pregnancy. In the later years of her life, these varicose veins may be problematical for her.
Physical Symptoms: The varicosity has itching, soreness, and a stitching pain.

❀CHAMOMILLA❀

Origin: Made from the German chamomile plant.
Comments: It has fern-like leaves and delicate daisy-like flower heads of white petals with a big yellow center. Hippocrates used this herbal medicine for strengthening a woman's uterus during childbirth, and for asthma, eczema, and insomnia. Juice from the whole, fresh plant is used to make the homeopathic version.

ACUTE ANXIETY OR PANIC ATTACKS

Comments: Anxiety attacks are brought on by being angered by an event or person, from drinking too much coffee, or from taking narcotics (including medical drugs). The attacks can occur around 9 a.m. or 9 p.m. or 11 p.m., on an almost cyclical basis. You are hypersensitive to pain (emotional as well as physical) and this can translate into rage, fury, and at the very least, irritability. Anxiety is triggered in you during this disgruntled state.
Mentals: During an attack, you do not want to be spoken to, touched, or even looked at. You do not want to talk to anyone, either, and there is a haste or hurriedness to your every action. If someone approaches you, you can fly into a rage. You do not want anyone trying to console you in any way; it just makes you more miserable.
Physical Symptoms: You have a feeling of great uneasiness and you will find dissatisfaction with everything and everyone in order to cover your anxious state. There may be an ineffectual urge to urinate even though there isn't much liquid in the bladder during an attack. A unique feature is that you have a fear of wind blowing, or during a windy period your anxiousness will increase or return.

You feel as if every nerve in your body is screaming and on edge, which is the reason for your increased irritable state. There is heat in your face and eyes, and one cheek may be red and the other white.
Modalities: WORSE – from anger, at night, in cold, damp air, or from the wind blowing. BETTER – from warm, wet weather, heat, sweating, and walking.

❀CHENOPODIUM❀

Origin: Made from the seeds of the Jerusalem oak. The oil in the seeds creates the remedy.
Comments: Oil of chenopodium was used to remove hookworms and roundworms from people in the nineteenth century.

HEARING DIFFICULTY

Physical Symptoms: One of our excellent remedies for hearing loss simply due to old age. Buzzing sounds in the ears can be heard. You cannot hear voices very well or discern high-pitched sounds, but you are sensitive to the sound of a passing car or airplane overhead.

❀CHINA OFFICINALIS❀

(CHINA OR CINCHONA BARK)

Origin: This remedy is made from the bark of the cinchona tree, which grow in the Andes Mountains of South America.

Comments: This remedy has an illustrious history and has long been used, even in the 1800s, as a quinine remedy for malaria epidemics in Europe. It was the first remedy proven by Samuel Hahnemann, the founder of homeopathy. It is a powerful remedy to use whenever there is hemorrhaging, whether acute (short-termed) or chronic (long-termed).

A keynote of this remedy is that one of your hands will be icy cold and the other will be warm. You may also have blue rings beneath your eyes, or have hollow-looking eyes and a feeling of pressure within them. Your complexion may turn sallow or yellow looking.

FLOODING DURING MENSES

Physical Symptoms: This is a flood that just doesn't stop, and eventually, you can become apathetic, listless, and weak after losing your body fluids. Your abdomen is very bloated and you have dark clots and profuse bleeding with pain. There is a heavy feeling in the pelvic region.

The pains accompanying this flow can be labor-like—very severe. An unusual keynote for this remedy is that this flooding may be accompanied by ringing in your ears. You may want to fan yourself with something to keep air circulating around you. The flooding has a very definite cycle or periodicity to it, usually getting worse at midnight or every other day.

The heaviness that predominates in the abdominal region may extend to your anal region, as well. There is complete exhaustion due to the loss of blood, and you may feel faint along with an incredible sense of fatigue. Your skin may be cold feeling, but perspiring.

Due to the loss of blood, you toss and turn at night and insomnia may pursue you. Hard pressure applied to the abdomen may lessen the flooding for awhile, but light pressure (such as massaging the area) will aggravate it and the flooding will increase markedly. There may also be a sensation of coldness within your abdomen or stomach.

Modalities: WORSE – from the slightest touch, being in a draft, at night, after eating, and leaning forward. BETTER – the flooding may ease up slightly if you bend double, apply hard pressure (with your hand) to your abdomen, are out in fresh air, place a warm cloth across your abdomen, or take a warm shower or bath.

HEARING DIFFICULTY

Physical Symptoms: For those who experience roaring, humming, or ringing noises in their ears. You are sensitive to noise in general. The external ear is also sensitive to touch, and the lobes are red.

❀COFFEA CRUDA❀

(COFFEA)

Origin: Yes, this homeopathic remedy is made from unroasted coffee beans.

Comments: Coffee has been around since the fifteenth century. Caffeine, which is the main ingredient, has been used as a painkiller, stimulant (remember how it keeps you awake?), and diuretic. This remedy's sphere of action is on the central nervous system. It has helped many an insomniac to get some sleep.

MENOPAUSAL HEADACHE

Comments: This remedy is for women who get migraine headaches from drinking CAFFEINE-containing products—regardless of whether it's coffee, soda pop, tea, or other food sources.
Mentals: You are hypersensitive to EVERYTHING and as a result, your "screaming nerves" cannot handle noise or strong odors of any kind. Your mind runs like a squirrel's cage. There are so many thoughts, millions of them, crowding into your brain, and you can't turn them off. If you drink tea or coffee, your headache intensifies.
Physical Symptoms: The headache comes on, little by little, in the morning after you wake up. There can be a burning sensation within your head. Any movement, touch, or bright light (sunlight or indoor lighting) makes the pain increase markedly. Your scalp and head feel supersensitive. There is a crushing pain, as if your brain is being torn apart, or a nail is being smashed into your head. A sensation of the head being too small may be present.

Some women may hear a cracking sound at the top of their head. Your temples may throb and there is a burning sensation present in your eyes.
Modalities: WORSE – in the evening and if you can get to sleep, you will suddenly, without reason, wake up at 3 a.m. The least sound or noise will exacerbate your pain. You cannot stand the thought of food. Nausea and vomiting are possible. The headache worsens with any excessive emotions (joy or happiness brought on by a surprise, for instance), taking narcotics, from being around strong odors (perfume, cigarette smoke, etc.), any noise, open air, or cold, windy conditions. It is worse from any sort of mental exertion, overeating, or consuming alcohol. Touch of any kind (even if you'd like to rub your head, your scalp's too sensitive to do it) increases your headache pain. BETTER – with warmth after lying down, consuming a cold drink, putting some ice in your mouth, or going to sleep.

SPASMS IN THE VAGINA (VAGINISMUS)

Mentals: The Coffea woman has a highly keyed nervous system. She can be fun, delightful, changeable, and easily excited. She is somewhat child-like in her actions and reactions. Because she's easily impressionable, her nervous system cannot take a beating. She can be hit broadside by good news as well as bad news—and be knocked over by it. Overstimulation is the key here. She's extremely restless; she can't sit still. Drinking any caffeinated substance (coffee, tea, soda pop) will make her glow like a million-watt light bulb because it jolts her nervous system. Her past menses history is one of being too early and lasting too long. Large, black clots of blood are passed during menses.
Physical Symptoms: The vulva and vagina are hypersensitive. Only, this time, there is a pleasurable sensation of itching with burning, that comes and goes. You can scarcely stand the fabric of your panties rubbing against your supersensitized area; even that contact can set off painful and pleasurable sensations. The type of pain you experience in the vaginal tract is like a toothache or nerve-like pain that is sharp, jabbing, and intense. The vagina is hot and sensitive, which may prevent penetration.
Modalities: WORSE – from any motion during this time, and there is a bearing-down sensation in the vaginal area if you walk or move. You'd like to rub yourself, but the area is too sensitive to do so.

❁CONIUM MACULATUM❁
(CONIUM)

Origin: This is made from the common hemlock tree.
Comments: The tree grows not only in Europe, but in most major areas of the world. The juice is taken from the leaves and stems of the tree. However, when the juice is potentized homeopathically, there are no molecules of this highly toxic substance left and it is harmless to take in this form. Poison hemlock has a prestigious history. In Greece, it was considered the state poison and it was used to kill criminals! Socrates, unfortunately, was forced to drink it. What a loss!

During Roman times, it was used by Pliny and Dioscorides for many medical conditions such as breast tumors, cancer, as a painkiller, for nervous system complaints, and for skin ailments. Homeopathically speaking, Conium is one of our chief cancer remedies and it has been known to cure breast cancer.

BREAST CYSTS AND FIBROIDS

Physical Symptoms: There is a maddening type of itching within your breasts. Sometimes, you may want to simply put pressure on your breast with your hand. Stitching pains can be felt in the nipple region.
Modalities: WORSE – the itching and pain are always worse just before and during your menses.
Other: Stop wearing a bra for 2 weeks. There is plenty of evidence that wearing a bra stops lymph gland drainage, and cysts and fibroids may result, as well as breast cancer. Take it off and see what happens!

BREASTS SWOLLEN OR PAINFUL

Comments: This remedy may be thought of when you are in the first trimester of your pregnancy and your breasts are undergoing changes due to your hormonal condition. Stop wearing a bra for two weeks and the pain and swelling will reduce on their own without a homeopathic remedy.
Physical Symptoms: See the same physical symptoms for breast cysts and fibroids. When you touch your breasts, there is a great tenderness to them.
Modalities: WORSE – when lying down, turning over in bed, or from becoming cold.
BETTER – when expressing your emotions, and allowing your arms to hang down.

GALACTORRHEA

Physical Symptoms: Your breasts are hard and painful to touch, with secretion from the nipples. There can also be itching within the breast or shooting pains around the nipples. Also, stop wearing a bra for two weeks. There is plenty of evidence to support that wearing a bra stops lymph gland drainage, and cysts and fibroids, as well as breast cancer, may result. Take it off and see what happens!

MEMORY LOSS

Comments: This is one of our great memory remedies, particularly as we age. It takes too much energy to think, and you do not as a result. If there is confusion over ideas, and your brain feels drowsy or sleepy, then Conium may help. This remedy is often of great service to women who have been broken down by the harsh brutality of life.
Mentals: You feel tired, discouraged, and dissatisfied with your surroundings. If someone tries to give you sympathy, it only makes things worse. There is a feeling of guilt weighing you down.

There is fear of being alone, but at the same time, you dread strangers or having company during your menses.
Physical Symptoms: You are readily forgetful, and are unable to sustain mental efforts for very long. There is difficulty or inability of fixing your attention on something that occurs because there is a lack of energy to focus long enough and remember. Often, there can be slowness of comprehension to what is being said or explained to you. Worse, there is excessive difficulty in remembering things that were said an hour ago, much less a week ago.
Modalities: WORSE – from drinking alcohol, before and during menses, in the Spring of the year, or living in a dry, hot climate. BETTER – during a food fast, walking about, or being out in sunlight.

❀CROTALUS HORRIDUS❀
(CROT. HORR.)

Origin: This remedy is made from timber rattlesnake venom.
Comments: A wonderful remedy for women who cannot keep their legs still. You might sit across from a totally composed Crotalus woman during a meeting, but if you peeked under the table, you'd see her feet were jiggling a mile a minute! An important menopause remedy.

If, while menstruating, you had a sensation of pressure in your cervical or vaginal region, or felt pain extending down your thighs—and medical problems have been ruled out—this remedy could work for you during menopause.

HOT FLASHES

WARNING: Any acute or persistent symptoms such as pain in the chest or pelvic region should be immediately evaluated by a physician. After serious problems are ruled out, you can safely proceed with your non-hormone, non-drug homeopathic treatment.

Physical Symptoms: Hot flashes may occur in one specific area of your body, and can resemble what is known by dermatologists as "urticaria"—and by the rest of us as hives! Those red, bumpy spots on the skin are hot to the touch and infernally itchy.

MEMORY LOSS

Comments: This remedy is for women who cannot express themselves and they end up making silly mistakes.
Physical Symptoms: You cannot hold your focus or thoughts on a topic, and your perceptions become clouded as a result. You can go into a shop and then forget what you have gone in there to purchase. You can forget phone numbers, names, and places. At other times, you may talk or mutter out loud to yourself, and when speaking to others, you may stumble over your words.
Modalities: WORSE – with the consumption of alcohol (even a little bit), in the morning and evening, during the Spring with warm weather coming on, or during damp, cold, rainy weather. BETTER – if you get rest, or are in open air.

❀CUPRUM METALLICUM❀
(CUPRUM MET.)

Origin: Made from copper.
Comments: Long ago, copper was used as an ointment on wounds. The men who worked on copper discovered how poisonous this metal was as they ended up with mineral deficiencies and

coughs. If ingested in its crude state, it can cause convulsions and later, death. Happily, in its homeopathic state, the copper is neither poisonous nor lethal and is an excellent remedy for severe muscle cramping of the worst order. It is also one of our best epilepsy and upper respiratory remedies, especially asthma.

LEG CRAMPS

Physical Symptoms: There are vicious spasms that begin in the toes and move *upward*. There is a violent, intermittent, contractive cramping. The cramps usually involve not only the calves, but the feet as well. Your legs will feel weary and the only thing that will make these cramps go away is to get up, walk around, and put warmth (a heating pad or warm cloth) on the affected region.

These assaults usually occur around 3 a.m., the cramping is brutal and convulsive (almost like a seizure), and there can be bending or flexion of the toes.

❁DULCAMARA❁

Origin: Made from the woody nightshade, this plant is a member of the Solanum family.
Comments: From Roman times onward, this plant has been used as an herbal cure for many ailments, including pneumonia, rheumatism, and asthma, among others. Your symptoms come on swiftly after enduring cold, damp, or wet weather conditions, or a sudden change in temperature (we see this all the time in Arizona in the summer when a thunderstorm comes along and drops the temperature 30 or 40 degrees in a few minutes!) Or, if you are sweating and you cool down too quickly—like being outdoors, perspiring, and then walking into an air-conditioned home or office—you will catch a cold. If your symptoms come on shortly after any of these episodes, Dulcamara may be just the remedy you are looking for!

ALLERGIES

Comments: If the allergies come on with cold or damp weather, this is a keynote, and Dulcamara should be thought of. For instance, if walking out of doors and being caught in the rain, or if fog rolls in, or if sitting on damp ground, and then the allergies pop up—consider Dulcamara.
Physical Symptoms: Your eyes will have profuse watery discharge, and may ache when you read. There can be twitching of your eyelids in cold air—even in an air-conditioned home or office.

Your nose stops up completely when there is a cooling rain or storm. Any type of cold air will do it, too. The mucus may be thick, yellow, and bloody looking.
Modalities: WORSE – in the open air. Just walking from the summer heat into an air-conditioned office or vice versa can bring on your allergies. The worst time for your allergies is in the Autumn, when there are warm to hot days and cool to cold nights—and then your allergies manifest promptly and powerfully. BETTER – from moving around, being kept warm, and enjoying dry weather.

❁EUPHRASIA❁

Origin: Made from the plant, eyebright.
Comments: This very delicate looking plant has white, pale lilac, or purple flowers. It has been used since 1305 as an herbal medicine for the eyes. Euphrasia was named after one of the Three Graces of Greek mythology, Euphrosyne, which means "gladness" in that language. Some think the plant was named after this particular Grace because having one's sight would indeed make one glad or happy!

ALLERGIES

Comments: One of the great keynotes of this remedy is that the watering of your eyes causes a hot, acrid, burning sensation while the discharge from your nose is bland!

Physical Symptoms: A unique symptom is yawning during a walk in open air. Interestingly, this remedy for allergies improves if one is outdoors or in open air—instead of being inside a house. The eyelids may have a burning sensation to them and swell, and more blinking than usual may occur. There is a feeling of pressure within the eyeballs, along with soreness, if pressed with your fingertips.

Photophobia, or problems enduring bright light or sunlight, will cause your eyelids to spasm or twitch. There may be pressure-like pain around and in your eyes. Many times, you may end up with granular lids and thick, yellow mucus that you must constantly remove from the corners of your eyes.

Modalities: WORSE – in the evening. Mucus increases in the evening and is "hawked up" by coughing as it slides out of your sinus cavities and down the rear of your throat. The allergies worsen in sunlight, in wind, or in a warm, stuffy room, and in the evening, if indoors. Cold wind (even air conditioning) causes the eyes to water profusely. Your allergies are worse after sleeping. BETTER – when in open air and wiping your eyes.

EYES DRY, BURNING, OR ITCHING

Physical Symptoms: This remedy helps with discharge of acrid matter or mucus from the eyes. The discharge is thick and burning. The eyelids are burning, with pressure in your eyes. There is a frequent desire to blink the eyes. The eyes water all the time, which is a keynote.

❅FLUORICUM ACIDUM❅
(FLUOR. AC.)

Origin: Made from distilling fluorspar, which is calcium fluoride, into a very fine powder. This eventually yields hydrofluoric acid.

Comments: This acid is used to clean metals, and also for etching and cleaning glass. Hydrofluoric acid's main ingredient, fluorine, is added to water supplies to halt tooth decay.

Modalities: WORSE – warmth, the heat of a room, drinking alcohol in any form, consuming red wine, eating sour foods (citrus, vinegar, etc.) and consuming warm drinks. Symptoms are always worse at night and in the morning. BETTER – cold weather, walking, taking a cooling shower or bath, rapid motion (hard work, cardiovascular or aerobic-type exercises), short sleep or naps, bending the head back, or eating.

VARICOSE VEINS

Comments: This remedy is especially good for ulcerated varicose veins. It works very well on the elderly or for young women who look older than they really are.

Physical Symptoms: The varicose veins are distended. There may be little blue collections of varicose veins in small spots anywhere on your body. Poor circulation of the lower legs is a keynote of this remedy.

Varicose veins start shortly after pregnancy. They tend to ulcerate easily with bleeding and they have a burning pain. There can be a burning sensation to the area along with incessant itching.

❀FOLLICULINUM❀

Origin: Made from a synthetic form of estrogen in the 1940s.
Comments: Since that time, millions of European women have used this potentized form to help them through all phases of menopause—without any other treatment, and happily, without hormone replacement therapy!

Your symptoms include being hypersensitive to heat, noise, or physical contact (tight-fitting clothes around the throat or waist). You cannot stand to have anyone touch your throat, and you prefer loose-fitting clothes that leave your neck free.

HOT FLASHES

WARNING: Any acute or persistent symptoms such as pain in the chest or pelvic region should be immediately evaluated by a physician. After serious problems are ruled out, you can safely proceed with your non-hormone, non-drug homeopathic treatment.

Physical Symptoms: This remedy prevents any type of hot flash including night sweats—if you fit the symptom picture. Your face may become red or just the opposite—pale. Heart palpitations may occur with the hot flash, and you may feel faint. There may be a feeling of a band around your heart, with this sensation spreading to your left arm.

The hot flash will make you want to rush to the nearest window to get fresh air. After you've opened a window, you will take huge, deep breaths, and after the hot flash has passed, you may sigh a great deal.

The hot flashes can occur anywhere on your body and in any form (spots, splotches, streaks, etc.). When they strike, you may sweat considerably. You may move more slowly, or feel mentally or emotionally "spacy" during the hot flash itself. The bulk of your hot flashes occur in the evening or at night.

❀GELSEMIUM❀

Origin: Made from the fragrant yellow jasmine plant.
Comments: Most of us know this remedy as the fragrant, climbing Carolina or yellow jasmine that scents the night air so beautifully. This plant, despite its wonderful odor, has deadly and poisonous yellow flowers. The homeopathic remedy is made from the yellow-colored roots, which also have an aromatic fragrance. Unlike the flowers, the root has a highly bitter taste, and is toxic, despite its pleasant odor.

In the 1840s, a farmer in Mississippi accidentally chewed on the root of this plant and it cured the fever he had. Luckily, he didn't consume enough to be killed, and the result was the 'discovery' of Gelsemium as a powerful remedy to cure not only fevers, but flu (epidemic types, too) and debilitating migraine headaches, to name a few ailments this remedy can tackle.

DIARRHEA

Comments: This is an ideal remedy for diarrhea brought on by sudden emotions such as grief, good news, bad news, from being shocked or frightened or traumatized in some way, from stage fright—such as having to go before a group to give a talk or perform in some way (as an actress), to receiving exciting news. Your nervous system is not 'hard-wired' and you cannot handle a lot of ups and downs emotionally speaking, in your daily life—and if they happen, and they always do, diarrhea is your response to it.

Physical Symptoms: The stool is copious and may be clay colored, chalk-like, or cream colored, tea-green or yellowish in appearance. The diarrhea is involuntary and painless, and can look like gruel or pabulum, or have a milky consistency. There is no thirst with the diarrhea, and there can be a sensation of emptiness in the stomach region or a heaviness, as if a stone is lodged in it.

A gnawing pain can be present across the middle of your abdomen with spasms that may make you cry out. There are rumbling sounds in your abdomen, followed by flatus or a release of gas.
Modalities: WORSE – in the evening, although it can come on at any time due to the above reasons. It is worse with damp, humid weather, in the Spring, in fog, in the heat of the sun, at 10 a.m., and before a thunderstorm. The diarrhea becomes worse if you think about your condition. BETTER – with copious urination, sweating, drinking alcohol, consuming stimulants (coffee, soda pop, tea), using the mind in some way (reading, working, etc.), being in the open air, bending forward, or reclining with the head held high.

EYE STRAIN

Physical Symptoms: For eyes that feel tired and overworked. Your eyelids may even droop or look like they're at half mast (what we term "bedroom eyes"). One pupil is dilated and the other is contracted, a keynote. Your eyes feel painful, and there is a twitching to the muscles. Vision may become blurred or smoky. Double vision is a keynote, as well.

MENOPAUSAL HEADACHE

Comments: This remedy addresses the "pre-jitters" type of headache or migraine that can be experienced when having to speak out in public, take a school test, act in a play, or do anything that places you in an uncomfortable, unsure situation, which equals DISTRESS to you. This is a stress headache–migraine remedy of note for women who possess a highly sensitized nervous system and who cannot handle the extra stress.
Physical Symptoms: There is a full feeling in the head, as if the brain is swollen and too large for the skull. A band-like sensation may occur. Many times the headache or migraine settles in the rear of your head, known as the occiput. It will include tension in the neck and shoulder muscles as well. There can also be pain in either temple which extends to your ear, a keynote of this remedy. If touched, your scalp is exceedingly tender and sore.

When it is a migraine, your eyes will dilate, and there is a feeling of heaviness and a bruised sensation to them. Your eyesight may dim before the migraine strikes fully. Your face will turn red or purple, become flushed, or appear congested looking. Your expression is dopey looking, and your eyes are half closed. The eyes will appear dull or lackluster. Your mouth may hang partly open (and you will not care).

You do not want to move when this migraine strikes, and you will sit like a lumpy couch potato, lacking the strength to move. You can feel extremely weak (which is why you sit like a round mound) and may even feel shaky or trembly.
Modalities: WORSE – upon receiving good or bad news, any type of emotional excitement, shock or trauma, smoking a cigarette or being around secondary tobacco smoke, or from being caught out in damp, humid weather. This type of headache worsens in the Spring of each year, before a thunderstorm, and when thinking about how miserable you feel. BETTER – in the afternoon, with profuse urination, sweating, consumption of an alcoholic drink, stimulants such as coffee, tea, or soda pop, mental efforts such as reading a book, being out in the open air, continued, gentle motion, or reclining with your head held high.

HEARING DIFFICULTY

Physical Symptoms: Loss of hearing for a short duration (usually due to a highly stressful condition). Rushing, roaring sounds in the ears. Loss of hearing due to middle ear infections (even from childhood and you are 50 now!) Deafness due to an overstressed central nervous system, or nervous strain.

❁GRAPHITES❁

Origin: This remedy is made from black pencil lead. And, of course, pencil lead comes from charcoal, not the metal, lead. Graphites is actually a soft, natural form of carbon; it also contains traces of iron and silica.
Comments: This remedy works well on women whose typology is somewhat overweight, dark-haired, and pale looking. Even more important, if a woman has a history of late menses with constipation, this may be her remedy—despite the above typology. Other symptoms of a Graphites woman are nosebleeds, weight gain, scanty periods, or cutting pain in the lower abdomen (remember any persistent abdominal pain should also be evaluated first, by a physician).

BREAST CYSTS AND FIBROIDS

Physical Symptoms: The breasts in a Graphites woman are usually large and thick. They can be swollen. The nipples are not only sore, but may be cracked or bleeding as well. Small, corrosive-like blisters can also encircle the nipple. There can be pain under the left breast during menses. The breasts may feel, quite literally, like hardened rocks.
Modalities: WORSE – with movement of any kind.
Other: Stop wearing a bra for 2 weeks. There is plenty of evidence that wearing a bra stops lymph gland drainage, and cysts and fibroids may result, as well as breast cancer. Take it off and see what happens!

HEARING DIFFICULTIES

Physical Symptoms: Cracking sounds can be heard in the ears when eating or moving your lower jaw. You hear better when there is background or white noise. Hissing, whistling, tinkling, singing, buzzing, or rumbling like thunder sounds can be heard. The sound of a gun going off near your ear is another symptom. A beating sound is heard in the ears. Your left ear may have the sound of water in it. Hearing improves with movement such as walking or driving a car.

HOT FLASHES

WARNING: Any acute or persistent symptoms such as pain in the chest or pelvic region should be immediately evaluated by a physician. After serious problems are ruled out, you can safely proceed with your non-hormone, non-drug homeopathic treatment.

Physical Symptoms: You get hot flashes only in your face, not the entire body, a keynote symptom.

❁HAMAMELIS VIRGINICA❁

(HAMAMELIS)

Origin: Made from the witch hazel tree.
Comments: The Native American medicine people used this tree's bark to treat hemorrhoids and varicose veins. Later, in traditional medicine, it was used for bites by insects, burns, and skin

rashes. Dr. Hering, one of our most famous U.S. homeopaths, used the potentized version for varicose vein cure in the mid-1800s.

Hamamelis is one of our most powerful remedies to stop hemorrhaging anywhere in the body. It will cure hemorrhoids, too.

Mentals: It acts well on women who are nervous, sensitive, and highly excitable.

Modalities: WORSE – in warm, humid, moist air.

EYE "FLOATERS"

Physical Symptoms: If an ophthalmologist or eye specialist has told you that you are experiencing bleeding within your eye, this remedy should be considered to stop that bleeding.

VARICOSE VEINS

Comments: One of our major varicose vein remedies, it acts chiefly upon the coat of the vein and strengthens it accordingly. If the veins are too relaxed, they engorge with blood, and this remedy will stop that from occurring.

Physical Symptoms: The varicose veins may be hard, knotty, swollen, and painful. Your ankles may also be swollen and have a purplish color around them. There is an uncomfortable feeling to the veins and they are inflamed.

This remedy is used on ulcerated varicose veins that bleed dark or black-colored blood. Otherwise, the area surrounding this varicosity appears dark purple (like a bruise) or dusky purple. The varicose veins are sensitive to pressure and are painful, sore, and stinging.

❋HYDROCOTYLE❋

Origin: Made from Indian pennywort (gotu kola), a small plant that grows in India and southern Africa.

Comments: This little-known remedy of today was used in the nineteenth century to cure vaginal itching. Its sphere of importance is as a skin remedy.

VAGINAL ITCHING

Comments: One of the villains that can cause this itching is candida. Check with your gynecologist to rule out this possibility, before taking a remedy. Other villains can be spermicidal creams, vaginal deodorants, soap used to clean the vaginal area, soap residue on your panties, tampon use, napkin rubbing and irritating the skin, or use of any powder, to name a few. You may be allergic to one of these products and this could be the source of the itching. After you have made sure that none of these are the culprit, then match your symptoms against the remedies presented below.

If you have been diagnosed with candida, it can be dealt with homeopathically; so can the other conditions listed above, but the use of the remedy below is not recommended, if this is the case. Work with your homeopath because the vaginal itching is only a minor symptom to an overall larger picture that needs to be addressed on a constitutional level and not an acute level.

For minor relief from itching, you can use a NON-ALCOHOLIC tincture, such as calendula. Wash three times a day with it. Or try urtica ointment, and apply lightly to the area where the itching is located. Both products are used only topically and not internally. If there is no relief after 2 days, then stop using it and see your homeopath.

Physical Symptoms: There is a deep-seated heat felt in the vagina along with shooting pains and itching at the external opening. There is heat along with redness to the vagina and labia region.

Discharge is profuse. At the same time, there can be inflammation at the neck of the bladder, the urethra. If itching has gone on long enough, the skin in the labia becomes toughened and thickened. In an extreme case, the skin is thick and tough, like elephant hide, and continues to have an intolerable itching.

❀IGNATIA AMARA❀
(IGNATIA)

Origin: Made from the St. Ignatius bean.
Comments: This is a tree found in the Philippines. Its seeds are used to make the homeopathic version of Ignatia. Your previous menses picture would be premature with a violent onset. Menses occurs every 10 or 15 days, not the normal 28-day cycle. There is flooding (black blood) and cramping, but the cramping is relieved to a high degree if you lie down on your back.

The cramping can be so bad that you become hysterical or faint. There is always anxiety, heart palpitations, and tiredness with your menses. In fact, it can be said that Ignatia's menses is completely predicated upon her emotional response to Life, in general. If she's under terrific strain, her menses will reflect it directly insofar as the intensity of the symptoms will be worse. On months when she's not under such emotional strain, the menses will be better and less troublesome.
Mentals: The Ignatia woman has a highly changing mood structure, with confusion—her mind goes in 20 directions all at once. It is one of our chief remedies for hysteria, in general, from over-excitement. There is an erratic quality to this woman, who is emotionally changeable at a second's notice. If she drinks coffee, her delicate nervous system crashes, and she becomes like a highly agitated thoroughbred in the starting gate before a big race.

DEPRESSION

Warning: If your depression is more than 3 months old, you are considered a chronic case. Do NOT take the homeopathic remedy indicated below. Instead, seek out constitutional homeopathic treatment from your nearest homeopath. See the appendix for the phone number of the National Center for Homeopathy (NCH).
Comments: This wonderful depression remedy is to be used in cases where depression appears after experiencing the loss of a loved one, a divorce, the loss of a beloved pet, a move, or the loss of a job. In other words, when any major lifestyle change occurs and sadness or grieving is the result. Considered one of the major grief remedies. If you have experienced anger and humiliation with grief as the result, Ignatia can help.

Ignatia is particularly useful in the first year after the trauma that induced your grief response. The key to utilizing this remedy is whether you have been able to cry. If you are still easily moved and SHOW your grief in some demonstrable way (such as crying when thinking about the event), then Ignatia will be of immense benefit. Do not be dissuaded by time, either. I've seen clients who have grieved for 20 years or more, and the feelings and tears are just as fresh, just as painful now as they were shortly after the traumatic event occurred.

However, if you have jammed your grief down into repression or denial and you are not in touch with your feelings or tears from that event, then the remedy to consider is not Ignatia, but Natrum Muriaticum (see below).
Modalities: WORSE – in the winter, in the morning, in open air, after meals, when experiencing warm weather (or a warm room), drinking coffee, or smoking. BETTER – while eating, after a change of position, and during the summer months.

IRRITABILITY

Mentals: In a depressed state, you are highly sensitized to getting your feelings hurt and you are easily offended in general. It could be nothing more than a look or body movement, not necessarily what someone said to you. When feeling in this space, you can become very defensive and touchy and you spurn consolation. You'd rather go off by yourself, struggling not to cry or become emotionally overwrought in front of everyone—but that may not always happen, and you will burst into tears, anyway.

There is a definite passive-aggressive facet to you, and you can manipulate others through your sometimes hysterical emotional states. You can laugh and cry in the same breath, change moods quickly, joke with others and then hours later, be plunged back into a pit of melancholy. If disturbed while in this state, you may scream, strike out, or be tearful. You can rage, tear at your clothes, and become tearful and uncontrollable. When irritable, your are inconstant, impatient, irresolute, and quarrelsome. The least contradiction will throw you into this state. Because your nervous system is so highly sensitized, Life brutally affects you much more than other people. Hysteria—the type that can paralyze, create numbness, or trigger an out-of-control emotional behavior—responds beautifully to this homeopathic remedy.

ANXIETY

Mentals: You may constantly cycle in and out of anxiety. The anxiety is accompanied by sleeplessness and feelings of despair. There is dread of every trifle, fear of robbers, and when in this state you do not want to talk, and you want to be left alone. Your anxiety is that something terrible has happened and you cannot speak of it. The anxiety has hurry, fear, and terror alternating with a sense of helplessness and inability to make decisions. Your anxiety may become so deep that you quite literally shriek out for help.

Physical Symptoms: You may experience heart palpitations, loss of appetite, and constipation.

SLEEP

Physical Symptoms: Your sleep pattern is disrupted by any of the above, and insomnia is the result. Sometimes, you will have dreams of water, with stormy waves crashing over you to symbolize your chaotic emotional state. (Symbolically, water represents our feelings.) Or sleep may be interrupted by "starting"; your arm or leg jerks or twitches spasmodically. You may "start" with fright just as you fall asleep. Another keynote of this remedy is yawning and sighing a great deal. Yawning is a way to get more oxygen into the body, not necessarily a sign of being tired or sleepy. The sighing, for Ignatia, is a way to relieve herself of those awful, burdensome feelings of depression that she carries around on her shoulders like a well-worn blanket.

MENOPAUSAL HEADACHE

Comments: These headaches aren't the type that are due to menopause or major life changes, or the type that evoke a sense of grief or sadness in you. This headache may have a root cause of grief or suppressed anger.

Ignatia is one of our premier grief remedies, and it is used in cases involving the loss of a loved one, job, or relationship, a divorce, a separation, a move to another neighborhood or state (or country), or loss of self-identification.

Physical Symptoms: The symptom is a congestive type of headache. There can be a sensation of a nail being driven through your skull and out the other side. Smoking, or the secondary odor of cigarette, pipe, or cigar smoke, will manifest this headache instantly. Your head may have a hollow

or heavy sensation to it. The pain is always worse if you stoop or lean down. The pain is cramp-like and centers over the root of your nose and the center of your forehead. There can be a tight band sensation around your brow.
Modalities: WORSE – if you smell secondary cigarette smoke, from worrying, from being frightened, angered, or grieving, from being in the open air, or from coldness (draft, air, weather, air conditioning). Yawning, stooping, or moving around also make the pain worse. The headache deteriorates in the morning hours. BETTER – when eating something, from changing your position, from pressure being applied to the painful region, or by taking deep, slow breaths of air, eating sour foods (citrus fruit, vinegar), or standing near a warm stove.

SPASMS IN THE VAGINA (VAGINISMUS)

Comments: If there is bad news that involves grief of any kind (particularly a love affair that is broken up, or the death of a loved one—human or animal), this remedy may help with vaginismus.
Physical Symptoms: The spasms consist of tearing, shooting pains that travel upward through the vagina and reach the belly button region of your abdomen. There are lance-like pains in the vagina that become worse if touched. A keynote is that you will sigh a lot (sighing is another way to get extra oxygen into your body). There is an intense soreness to the vagina if it is penetrated that can take you into a frantic, sometimes weeping state.
Modalities: WORSE – in the evening, especially after a meal. BETTER – the pains alleviate to a degree if you lie on your back.

❁IODUM❁

Origin: Made from iodine that has been extracted from seaweed or saltpeter deposits in Chile.
Comments: In the early days, iodine was used as an antiseptic. Most of us remember our mothers putting iodine on our scratches and lacerations—and the resulting smarting pain! But, the wound stayed clean. This remedy is wonderful for hypo or hyperthyroid difficulties. Today, potassium iodide is added to our salt so that we get a constant source of iodine; a "small" mineral that our bodies cannot live without. Before the advent of adding iodine to our salt supply, there was a lot of goiter (a thyroid condition) in our country, particularly in the Midwest where few folks ever got to eat ocean fish, which contains iodine. There is a constitutional type of Iodum person: She can have dark hair and complexion, or dark or yellow, tawny skin, and she is constantly busy, restless, and highly talkative.

Many women who have had a baby experience a problem with their thyroid never returning to normal functioning and the extra weight is not shed as a result. Instead, this gland remains borderline low. Often this remedy can be used to nurture your thyroid back into full function—and you can lose the weight you kept on after having the baby.

BREASTS SWOLLEN OR PAINFUL

Physical Symptoms: There can be nodosities on the skin that have black points. Your breasts may dwindle or shrink in size and they may have blue-red lumps on the skin, instead. When nursing, your breasts felt heavy and as if they were falling. There can be a burning and shooting pain in your breasts.
Modalities: WORSE – from touch or pressure, warmth, and lying down. BETTER – when sitting up.
Other: Stop wearing a bra for 2 weeks. There is plenty of evidence that wearing a bra stops lymph gland drainage, and cysts and fibroids may result, as well as breast cancer. Take it off and see what happens!

❁KALI BICHROMICUM❁
(KALI BICH.)

Origin: Made from potassium dichromate.
Comment: Originally used in dye when manufacturing calico material, for electric batteries, and in photography; the orange particles of potassium dichromate have had many uses in industry. Kali Bich. was used in the 1800s as a homeopathic remedy for mucus conditions, ranging from chronic sinus drainage to pneumonia.

ARTHRITIS

Comments: A useful keynote symptom is that the arthritis will improve for awhile in alternation with bouts of diarrhea.
Physical Symptoms: The pains move from place to place and are characterized as "wandering pains." These pains are felt in your bones, which feel sore or bruised. With the pain, there is swelling, stiffness, and cracking of your joints. A peculiar keynote is that you will experience soreness in your heels when walking.

Your Achilles tendon can become swollen and painful. There can be pain experienced in small, localized spots. Your arms and legs can become very weak. There may be left-sided sciatica along with the arthritis symptoms.
Modalities: WORSE – in the morning hours or at 1:00 a.m. It has a unique ability to appear and then disappear from time to time. BETTER – the arthritis is always better with motion and heat.

❁KALI BROMATUM❁
(KALI BROM.)

Origin: This remedy is made from bromide of potash, or what is known as potassium bromide.
Comments: Used in photography, this white crystal salt substance has a fascinating background. Historically, it was used by traditional medical practitioners in our country for a number of conditions. It was given in huge doses for epilepsy! And men who had gross sexual desires or who were prisoners, were forced to take potassium bromide to halt their sexual urges. When made into a homeopathic form, it addresses epilepsy and nervous system complaints, and is one of our great acne remedies.

MEMORY LOSS

Comments: This remedy can be thought of when medical drugs have caused an impairment of your memory.
Physical Symptoms: The memory is spotty because you have overworked your brain and are mentally fatigued as a result. You cannot recall names or words. It would seem that you have completely lost your memory. You may forget how to talk, or have to be told the word before you can speak it. Words may come slowly; you may hesitate a great deal, and omit or mix up the words in writing or speaking.
Modalities: WORSE – if you are angry or emotionally upset and then try to complete a mental task, and from becoming frightened, worrying, or experiencing grief. The new moon creates havoc with remembering things. BETTER – from remaining busy mentally as well as physically.

❁KALI CARBONICUM❁

(KALI CARB.)

Origin: This remedy is made from two major homeopathic families—the kalis and the carbons. It is made from potassium carbonate.
Comments: Kali Carb. is also known as salt of tartar, salt of wormwood, and carbonate of potassium. Kali Carb. is called the "vegetable alkali" because it originally came from the ashes left after burning wood and vegetable structures. And from that, the homeopathic version was made. Historically, the Egyptians used potassium carbonate to make glass.
Mentals: Women who respond best to this remedy are opinionated, inflexible, and sometimes rigid in their outlook on life. They have impeccable morals, values, and integrity. Their sense of duty to others, particularly to their family and employer, is powerful and unchanging. If you are a Kali Carb. woman, you are a very hard worker and are often conservative in nature.

ACUTE ANXIETY OR PANIC ATTACKS

Comments: Anxiety or panic attacks will surface after experiencing long recuperation from an illness, such as pneumonia or the flu. Women who need this remedy will say, "I haven't been well since …" and this is a red flag to look closely at this remedy. Also, catching a cold or being under stress for too long will cause attacks. Kali Carb. types have an inflexibility and rigidity toward themselves and their world. You are one-pointed; your world and existence focus on duty. You are stoic and accepting about responsibilities and the loads you carry (which are considerable), and you will not complain about them.

The world is black and white to you, with no gray areas in-between. Anxiety will build up simply because you carried too much for too long—but you are the last to realize that about yourself. Your family and friends will see your Herculean efforts and wonder when you will snap and break under the tremendous burdens you carry because of your duty and honor-bound nature.
Mentals: Anxiety can manifest because of any change in your schedule, concerns regarding your children, fear of the future, or disorientation from being jolted out of the safety of your rut in life. Because you are so fixed and dogmatic in nature, this inflexibility creates its own potholes for you and anxiety is the result.
Physical Symptoms: You first feel anxiety in the region of your stomach and you have no idea why you are feeling this way. It is felt most deeply when you are alone, and you may begin to cry and think you are getting a serious illness instead of realizing that stress is bringing this condition on. There can be violent heart palpitations that shake your entire body. Usually, your anxiety reaction comes on between 2 a.m. and 4 a.m., always in the morning hours, and it can wake you out of a deep sleep.
Modalities: WORSE – from being out in cold air, experiencing cold weather, drinking too much water after overheating, and during the winter and early morning hours. BETTER – with moist, warm weather conditions, during the day, while moving about (puttering), remaining warm, and being out in the open air.

ARTHRITIS

Comments: This remedy can be considered if your arthritis is right-sided.
Physical Symptoms: Your arthritis has stiffness, stitching, and sharp, cutting pains. A keynote is that the pains are always worse from 3:00 a.m. to 5:00 a.m. and it will awaken you. If there is deformity to this arthritis, Kali Carb. should be looked at when there's great pain in the joints and

sensitivity to the soles of the feet along with it. There can be throbbing, along with swelling and edema. Sweating, backache, and weakness may also be present.

The pain seems to originate from within the joint or bone—and then it spreads outward. Stinging pains in the muscles are frequently felt.

Modalities: WORSE – intolerance to cold weather or a dip in temperature greatly affects your arthritis condition. BETTER – it's always better with movement.

HOT FLASHES

WARNING: Any acute or persistent symptoms such as pain in the chest or pelvic region should be immediately evaluated by a physician. After serious problems are ruled out, you can safely proceed with your non-hormone, non-drug homeopathic treatment.

Physical Symptoms: You usually get night sweats or hot flashes around 3:00 a.m. to 5:00 a.m. Furthermore, you may feel very nervous and get heart palpitations along with your hot flashes.

❀KALI MURIATICUM❀
(KALI MUR.)

Origin: This remedy is made from chloride of potassium and is a well-known Schuessler's cell salt.

Comments: The woman who needs this remedy has a history of mothering and mother issues—with her mother or the mother-figure in her life being at the core of her symptoms. You carry a great deal of psychic weight regarding emotional wounding by your mother. Later, as an adult, this unresolved issue may transfer to you as you struggle to be a dutiful mother to your own children. The Super Mom image is taken to heart by a Kali Mur. woman. Usually, she is the oldest daughter in the family and is therefore saddled with a lot of responsibility beyond her years, so she grows up with this added psychic weight, this sense of being an overly conscientious mother herself.

FLOODING DURING MENSES

Physical Symptoms: Your symptoms include a heavy, bright red blood with dark red clots or clots that are black and tarry looking and large (the size of a nickel or quarter). The blood can also be tough and stringy, and can be dark red or black in color. Along with the flooding, there is an extreme tenderness to your vaginal area, and this soreness increases markedly if you move around.

Modalities: WORSE – in the morning, upon waking. There can be insomnia and waking up around 3 a.m. A strong keynote is that you flood even more if you move around just a little bit. Your condition is worsened by the warmth of the bed, from getting caught in a draft, from experiencing rainy or foggy weather, or by consuming fatty or rich foods or pastries. BETTER – your flooding lessens by remaining still.

❀KALI PHOSPHORICUM❀
(KALI PHOS.)

Origin: This is made from potassium phosphate.

Comments: Potassium phosphate is one of our brain foods and we cannot do without it, chemically speaking. It is traditionally given intravenously as potassium phosphate. It has been found to be useful for people who have chronic fatigue syndrome, but go to your homeopath for constitutional treatment to confirm the use of this remedy for that condition.

MEMORY LOSS

Comments: This is a wonderful remedy for those who have acute "brain burn-out" from tests, or stress and pressure that demand overtime from our flagging brain cells. Anyone doing any type of mental work for a living can use this remedy from time to time when the overworked brain goes into an exhaustion phase and they need a pickup.

I've used this remedy over the years, probably twice a year, because the bulk of my work is mental as a homeopath and as a writer. I can take one 30C pellet, one time only, and within an hour, my brain has been put back on track (do not abuse the privilege of this remedy. If you take it more than once a month, then you need to see a homeopath for a constitutional remedy, instead). I feel great afterward and I can once again jump into my usual mental routines, completely recharged and refreshed.

Physical Symptoms: The mind becomes sluggish, with partial loss of memory. Exhaustion sets in even after a moderate mental effort (and this includes creative efforts, too). You can hardly articulate and speak. The tongue feels thick when you struggle to talk and express yourself.

Modalities: WORSE – your memory is worse with pain, getting cold, enduring dry air, experiencing too much excitement, worrying, or trying to work in the early morning hours. BETTER – your memory improves markedly with a good night's sleep, from eating, when your menses comes, and with rest.

❁KREOSOTUM❁

Origin: This is made from distilled wood tar.

Comments: Every ranch and farm uses this material, called creosote, as a wood preservative for their fences. It also stops range animals from chewing on the fences.

If your menses stops when you sit or walk, and then reappears when you lie down, this remedy may be for you.

HOT FLASHES

WARNING: Any acute or persistent symptoms such as pain in the chest or pelvic region should be immediately evaluated by a physician. After serious problems are ruled out, you can safely proceed with your non-hormone, non-drug homeopathic treatment.

Physical Symptoms: For burning hot flushes and night sweats.

❁LAC CANINUM❁

Origin: This remedy is made from a female dog's milk—a mongrel bitch's milk. Also known as bitch's milk.

Comments: Pliny the Greek used dog's milk to expel a dead fetus from women back in ancient times. Sextus, another physician, used this remedy for inner ear infections and intolerance to light (photophobia).

MEMORY LOSS

Physical Symptoms: This remedy is excellent for those who make mistakes while writing. When reading you may change the meaning, omitting or adding words. At times, you find it difficult to read anything that requires true mental effort. You cannot concentrate. As soon as you start a task, you want to stop it. When talking, you substitute the names of the object seen for what you thought it was. In writing, you use too many words or not the right ones.

Modalities: WORSE – your memory is worse in the morning of one day, and the evening of the next day (a very cyclic keynote to use this remedy). The memory lessens at night, from cold winds or "sharp" air. BETTER – from experiencing fresh air, from consuming cold drinks, and from a nosebleed.

❁LAC HUMANUM❁

Origin: Made from a mother's breast milk.
Comments: This is a recent proving on a very important remedy that has many far-reaching ramifications—among them, women with eating disorders, problems with the breasts, and changes in weight. This remedy was proven by two women in England, Halahan and Houghton.

BREASTS SWOLLEN OR PAINFUL

Physical Symptoms: Breasts are swollen, with stitching pain in them. There is a sensation as if milk is coming out of the nipples, but it is not.
Modalities: WORSE – before menses and consuming alcohol. BETTER – from having sex.
Other: Stop wearing a bra for 2 weeks. There is plenty of evidence that wearing a bra stops lymph gland drainage, and cysts and fibroids may result, as well as breast cancer. Take it off and see what happens!

❁LACHESIS MUTA❁
(LACHESIS)

Origin: Made from the venom of the South American bushmaster snake.
Comments: In minute doses and used homeopathically, the venom is no longer toxic and it's completely safe to take. Interestingly, a day before this woman's menses starts, she gets very busy, has high energy, wants to work or be outside all day, and is very active.

Her menses is always scanty, late, and irregular. Some women have nosebleeds before their menses. The face may take on a blotchy appearance, the cheeks and nose may be reddish purple, and the lips have a slight purple cast to them. She cannot sleep on her left side.

With the exception of Folliculinum, Lachesis is probably one of the best remedies for menopause symptoms of every variety. Another indicator for this remedy is a tendency to lick your lips a great deal.
Mentals: Women who need this remedy are intense, dramatic, and eloquent. They can be extremely envious, passionate, intense, and emotional. They can be highly assertive, even aggressive, and in touch with their anger. If you are a Lachesis, you are probably highly talented and display your passion for life in some form of artistic expression.

FLOODING DURING MENSES

Physical Symptoms: The blood is black-appearing and thick, possibly with an offensive odor to it. The cramping pains occur before your menses. There are colic-like, sharp, shooting sensations in your abdomen. Pain is also experienced in the lower back and the sacral-tailbone region. Usually, there is more pain on the left side, and the left ovary is particularly problematic.

The pain may start in the left ovary, and move to the right ovary, and then back to the left one, a keynote of this remedy. As the flooding begins, the pains will disappear. Your menopausal menses will have a pattern of coming every 2 or 3 months, and when it does appear, the blood is lumpy, black, or acrid in appearance.

Modalities: WORSE – from the least touch (you cannot stand clothes against your abdominal area), being in direct sunlight, experiencing hot temperatures (inside or outside the house), intolerance to tight clothing around your throat or waist, and upon waking. BETTER – by going outside into fresh air, experiencing moderate temperatures (in the 70s), and warm applications, such as a bath, shower, or heating pad to the abdomen. You will even throw open the windows and doors to allow fresh, cooler air to flow into the house.

HEART PALPITATIONS AND SHORTNESS OF BREATH

Physical Symptoms: A feeling of faintness or fainting with a constricting feeling across your chest, along with anxiety. You hate anything tight around your neck and waist. The palpitation may be hard, then soft. A feeling of trembling may be felt around the heart itself, or stitches through the organ accompanied by anxiety.

HOT FLASHES

WARNING: Any acute or persistent symptoms such as pain in the chest or pelvic region should be immediately evaluated by a physician. After serious problems are ruled out, you can safely proceed with your non-hormone, non-drug homeopathic treatment.

Physical Symptoms: Like Folliculinum women, Lachesis types may not be able to tolerate tight clothing, especially around the neck or waist. Perspiration appears with the flush, and there may be a violent headache that centers on the vertex, or top of your head.
Modalities: WORSE – in the morning hours and after sleeping. You 'sleep' into your symptoms and awaken worse rather than feeling better.

MEMORY LOSS

Comments: If time seems deranged to you, this remedy may help.
Mentals: You experience a sad feeling in the morning when you get up.
Physical Symptoms: You forget what you have said as soon as you start to speak. You have a very weak memory regarding anything you have heard. Mistakes are made in speaking and writing, as well as in the hours of the day and the days of the week. Confusion as to what time it is. Or what day it is.
Modalities: WORSE – in the morning, from being in a room that's too hot, during menopause, or from consuming alcohol or hot drinks. BETTER – with the appearance of discharges of any kind from any orifice of the body, including your menses, from warm applications, being out in open air, consuming cold drinks, and eating fruit.

❃LYCOPODIUM❃

Origin: Made from the pollen dust of club moss.
Comments: The spores from this plant are gathered in the summer and then potentized. This is one of our great "dry" remedies. In the seventeenth century the yellow pollen dust from this plant was sniffed as a cure for gout and retention of urine. Later, traditional Western medicine used it as an herb for stomach ailments and to remove kidney stones. Homeopathically, Lycopodium is one of our greatest remedies with broad application in many areas. This remedy is for women who, after menses, have their vagina become dry, another key symptom. There may also be the condition of varicose veins around the vulva.

Mentals: She is very intelligent, but has low-self-esteem problems, although she may not show it at all. Rather, she puts on a good offense and will look as if she has everything and everyone under control. She does not, but it appears to be that way! If put on the defensive, this woman may verbally attack, or try to bluff her way out of a situation. Highly conservative, introverted, and usually shy, she is quite self-possessed and has an emotional air of detachment about her. Upon waking, she's very grumpy the first hour.
Modalities: WORSE – from 4 p.m. to 8 p.m., from an overheated or warm room, in bed, and from warm applications. BETTER – with motion, after midnight, from warm food or drink, from getting cold, and from being uncovered.

ACUTE ANXIETY OR PANIC ATTACKS

Comments: If feelings of low self-esteem and a constant fear of breaking down under stress haunt you, then this remedy may be for you. Your anxiety will manifest when you undertake anything new. For example, you're no longer in your life role as a mother, and are now free of child-bearing responsibilities, and you are frightened to face the next cycle of your life.
Mentals: Your anxiety may manifest in a deteriorating memory, even with dyslexia symptoms such as spelling or writing the wrong words. Sometimes, you may not be able to read what you have written. When anxiety strikes you are afraid to be alone, apprehensive, and exceedingly sensitive. You can weep at a moment's notice over small things, such as the thoughtfulness of a friend doing something for you. Another fear is of men, or of strangers approaching you. Yet, while you hate having people around, you cannot stand being alone, either. Music strongly affects you—it can make you sad or uplift your spirit.

As the anxiety appears, you can become spiteful, hateful, and cranky. A lot of irritability and anger will surface, surprising even you. At other times, you can feel melancholy. The vulnerability you always feel can be masked by suddenly appearing haughty and domineering. You become highly critical and fault-finding toward others. In this mode, unconsciously, you feel the best defense is a good offense, and you can come across as someone that no one would dare question.
Modalities: WORSE – around 4 p.m. to 8 p.m. or 3 p.m. to 7 p.m., from eating, from wet, stormy weather, before your menses, from becoming too hot, from being in a hot, stuffy room, or from warm applications of a cloth. BETTER – with motion, after midnight, with cool applications from a cloth, or from being uncovered and cooling off.

CONSTIPATION

Comments: One of our great digestive remedies of all time, Lycopodium may help the constipation that occurs when you are away from home. Any type of traveling, long or short distance, or being a road warrior, binds you up, quite literally.
Physical Symptoms: Your stools are incomplete, hard, and very difficult to pass. And when you are able to expel them, the first part of the stool is hard, and the last half of it is soft and is either thin in appearance or literally shoots out of you. Constipation difficulties may alternate with bouts of diarrhea. These two states will exist, never a normal bowel movement to be seen. Regardless, there is a raw sensation to your anus.
Modalities: WORSE – constipation is always worse between 4 p.m. and 8 p.m., on the right side or from right to left, from pressure of clothes around your waist or abdominal region, shortly after awakening, from eating too much, from consuming oysters, from getting wet, experiencing stormy weather, before your menses or from a suppressed menses, from consuming milk, and eating cabbage, beans, or pastry. You are always worse in a warm, stuffy room, in hot air

(temperature-induced), or in bed. BETTER – with motion such as exercise or taking a nice, long walk, after midnight, on getting cold from being uncovered, from cold applications (shower, bath, swim in a pool), consuming warm food or drink, burping or belching, and urinating.

INDIGESTION

Comments: This remedy is for women who experience bloating after eating only a few bites of food. Digestion is imperfect. You can experience hunger, eat a few bites, and feel full when you really are not.

Physical Symptoms: There can be sour-tasting belching that rises to the top of your throat (known as waterbrash or reflux), or foods may taste sour. You will awaken at night, starving to death! You are the type who goes to the refrigerator in the wee hours of the morning to snack. A few bites and you feel stuffed and back to bed you go!

There is a dislike of bread, but a desire for sweets and pastries, instead. Foods that give you plenty of gas are cabbage, beans, oysters, and onions. You prefer liquids and foods that are hot. You have what is known as "canine hunger"—as if starved, you gulp down food and a little later, you are starving again. Of course, eating only a few bites and feeling full will drive you to eat many small meals, as a result.

Later, there can be a band-like feeling around your waist, and there's a lot of noisy passing of gas. Pains can shoot across the lower abdomen, right to left. The abdomen will bloat and swell immediately after eating, a keynote of this remedy.

Modalities: WORSE – on the right side of your body, between 4 p.m. and 8 p.m., from the pressure of clothes, during wet or stormy weather, from suppressed menses, drinking or eating any of the foods mentioned above, from heat, being in a warm, stuffy room, a warm bed, or any warm application (a heating pad, warm cloth, etc.). BETTER – with motion, after midnight, from consuming hot foods or liquids, on getting cold after having the blankets tossed aside, belching, or urinating.

MEMORY LOSS

Comments: There is an underlying fear of breaking down under mental stress. An excellent remedy to consider for Alzheimer's.

Physical Symptoms: You have a weak memory, confused thoughts, and you constantly spell or write the wrong words and syllables. You feel as if you have a failing memory or loss of brain power. You cannot read what you write. Fatigue from mental exertion leads to incapability of further devotion to your mental tasks. Inability to express yourself as you want; the word you are searching for is there—you know it, but you cannot verbalize it. So, you use another word that might be close, or explain around the word to describe what you are seeking to say, instead.

Speech may become confused. There may be confusion about everyday items but you can still converse intelligently on more abstract ideas. You are unable to retain or remember what you have read. The wrong word is used. For instance, you meant to say ankle, but you said elbow, instead. Gradual dullness of mental faculties.

SKIN ITCHING

Physical Symptoms: This remedy is for women who have clammy feeling dry skin, along with a feeling of ants crawling across it (formication). Your skin is pale looking and may be liberally sprinkled with freckles. You do not perspire properly.

VAGINA DRY OR POOR LUBRICATION

Physical Symptoms: Your vagina is dry and intercourse is painful. Burning sensations are experienced in the vagina after making love. Dryness with itching is present. One of the key symptoms to use this remedy is that you can expel flatus (gas) from your vagina.

VARICOSE VEINS

Comments: Another "elderly remedy," it acts well upon varicose veins that are swollen. Your varicosities are usually right sided. The valves in the veins are imperfect or they do not operate properly and Lycopodium can strengthen them accordingly.
Physical Symptoms: Varicosities are inflamed, and there is usually a spider-like network of them. They are painful, with a stitching-like pain. Often used in varicose ulceration in the elderly.

❁MELILOTUS❁

Origin: This remedy is made from the sweet, yellow clover that you find in a farmer's field.
Comments: The first provings on this remedy were made in 1851 and both the yellow and white flower varieties were used.

MENOPAUSAL HEADACHE

Comments: This is an excellent remedy for a congestive or sick type of headache. Melilotus is one of the top migraine and menopause-caused headache remedies. Interestingly, either a nosebleed or the onset of your menstrual flow will relieve your headache.
Physical Symptoms: The headache attack is violent and congestive, with vomiting and throbbing pain present. A pressure is felt in your eyes, and there may be black spots dancing before them. There can be blurred vision, and your eyeballs will feel heavy and all you want to do is close them to get some relief.

Your face takes on a pallor and there is an undulating or wave-like feeling inside your brain from this headache. A fullness will be felt inside your head, the scalp is sore and tender to the touch, and there are neuralgia (nerve-like) pains around and over the right side of your head and neck. There is a feeling of blood rushing into your brain. The continual throbbing pain completely debilitates you.
Modalities: WORSE – in changing weather conditions, during rainy weather, with the approach of a storm, with motion of any kind, walking, and around 4 p.m. BETTER – this type of headache improves with profuse urination.

❁MURIATICUM ACIDUM❁
(MUR. AC.)

Origin: Made from hydrochloric acid, this is known as the "spirit of salts" by alchemists.
Comments: Typologically, homeopaths regard women (or men) who have black hair and dark brown eyes as suited for this remedy. Nowadays, we don't put as much stock in this, as we do in whether a person fits the symptoms of the remedy.
Mentals: You are an introverted person by nature, and are considered sad or taciturn. You suffer eloquently in silence; we'd never hear you complain about the pain you carry. One of the keynotes is that you mutter out loud, to yourself, and you may make loud moaning sounds. When not feeling well, you are irritable and restless.

Modalities: WORSE – sitting, being around people who are talking, damp weather, before midnight, after sleeping, and after eating (you get diarrhea). BETTER – from being in motion, warmth, drinking, and lying on the left side.

URINARY INCONTINENCE

Physical Symptoms: This is a remedy to consider if your incontinence is due to weakening of the muscles surrounding the urethra. There are involuntary emissions of urine. Also, another keynote is that you pass gas (or have flatulence) along with the incontinence episode.

❀NATRUM MURIATICUM❀

(NAT. MUR.)

Origin: Made from sodium chloride, common table salt, this is one of our driest and most powerful constitutional remedies.

Comments: Salt has played a large and significant part in our world history. This mineral was once used instead of money to pay soldiers. This remarkable remedy is especially good for dried-out skin involving the mucosa layer, which makes it a specific remedy for vaginal dryness. You may crave salt, a keynote for this remedy.

Your menstrual history is one of being irregular. Usually it's too early and then it's profuse, or it's retarded and scanty. Your emotional and mental outlook is the key to giving this remedy.

Mentals: You possess a reserved demeanor, appearing emotionless to outsiders, although you really feel very deeply and hard. Conservative and introverted by nature, you are unable to display your feelings. Before your menses starts, and the flood begins, you get irritable and morose. As the bleeding begins, you become sad and you withdraw. Consolation from others only makes your symptoms worse.

ALLERGIES

Physical Symptoms: Allergies create a dryness in you—from your mouth, nose, and throat region. The discharge from your nose is acrid and usually thick, white or clear, and may turn watery. One of the keynotes is sneezing at the outset of your allergy attack, followed by a profuse, watery discharge.

The mucus looks like albuminous egg white. Your nose can be completely blocked up, causing mouth breathing. There is a loss of smell and taste. Ulcers may form within the nostrils and nosebleeds may occur if stooping or coughing at night.

Your eyes are supersensitive to sunlight or any type of bright lighting (photophobia). There is itching and burning present in your eyes and you must constantly wipe them. There are many tears and your eyes will look red-rimmed, with swollen lids. A keynote is that tears will continuously stream down your face.

Your vision may become blurred or wave-like lines may appear in front of your eyes. When reading, writing, or doing close work, your eyes may give out. There is pain if you look DOWN. Reading by any kind of indoor lighting is nearly impossible for you. Your eyelids will feel heavy and weighted.

Modalities: WORSE – in the morning, in sunlight, during a thunderstorm, or when visiting the ocean. BETTER – if you're in the open air, around 10 a.m., cold bathing, going without regular meals, and lying on your right side.

BREASTS SWOLLEN OR PAINFUL

Physical Symptoms: Your breasts are large or engorged due to edema or excessive water being retained in them. Stitches of pain beneath the nipples.

Modalities: WORSE – in the morning, at full moon time, from touch or pressure, or when walking. BETTER – lying down, rubbing them gently (massaging type motion), and wearing a snug-fitting bra.

Other: Stop wearing a bra for 2 weeks. There is plenty of evidence that wearing a bra stops lymph gland drainage, and cysts and fibroids may result, as well as breast cancer. Take it off and see what happens!

DEPRESSION

Warning: If your depression is more than 3 months old, you are considered a chronic case. Do NOT take the homeopathic remedy indicated below. Instead, seek out constitutional homeopathic treatment from your nearest homeopath. See the appendix for the phone number of the National Center for Homeopathy (NCH).

Comments: This is one of the most profound and deep-acting depression remedies. Nat. Mur. is a possible candidate for anyone, regardless of gender, who suffers from PTSD, post-traumatic stress disorder (and you do not have to be a military warrior who was exposed to and wounded by actual combat to qualify in this category). Unfortunately, PTSD is alive and well in the families and homes across America where there is mental, emotional, or physical child or spousal abuse going on daily. The family home has become the latest battleground and the children and women find themselves caught in a daily, ongoing war that sends their vital forces into a survival reflex mode that will create the PTSD symptoms.

Mentals: This remedy is for reserved, responsible women who have armored themselves against their feelings and become disconnected, or who are in a state of denial about whatever they are feeling—be it rage, humiliation, grief, or any other emotion. These individuals bottle up their feelings and they cannot stand anyone's pity or even consolation—pushing them away, if need be.

You will never see this woman cry openly or in public. She battles back the tears every time and if she cannot stop them, she will go off by herself to cry where no one will see them or find her—the bathroom, a closet, or some other closed, private space. At the same time, she has a quiet, strong dignity about her; she always seems to be able to take Life on the jaw and stand even the severest of blows—and remain upright and functional.

In reality, the depressed Nat. Mur. woman may appear very perfectionistic and picky, controlling not only herself, but her home and office space, as well. Along with this reserved demeanor is an unspoken "stay away from me and do not touch me" kind of body language that emanates from her. Only when certain types of music are played will the carefully concealed and suppressed reservoir of feelings come tunneling up through her for powerful emotional release and expression. At that time, there may be tears in her eyes no matter how much she battles them back—and one or two tears will fall before she can throttle off her powerful surge of emotions.

This woman always feels a certain bittersweet sadness that she wears like a shawl around her shoulders. She suffers in a dignified, eloquent silence; the wounded warrioress who never complains about her own inner pain.

At the same time, the introverted Nat. Mur. appears too serious or overly responsible toward everything in her life. She cannot play or be childlike at all; such is her controlled reserve. As a matter of fact, many Nat. Mur.'s never HAD a childhood, at least, not one where they could experience being a carefree child. There were always responsibilities heaped upon her in some major way and she was too young to take them on.

When wounded by a word or action, this woman will dwell on that injury for a long, long time—she doesn't forget or forgive. Noise and music can aggravate her irritability. If she's asked what is wrong, she may become hostile and attacking.

Modalities WORSE – her depression worsens in the morning hours (and continues to slowly improve throughout the day), during the summer heat, from 10 a.m. to 11 a.m., during the full moon, when experiencing heat of any kind (stove or weather), after sleeping, and after breakfast. BETTER – her depression improves if she visits the ocean, takes deep breaths of air, eats irregular meals, and perspires.

ANXIETY

Mentals: Her anxiety is expressed as dread that something will happen. It doesn't, but the pervading threat is there, lurking around at the edges of her consciousness. The smallest blemish on her body becomes a mountain out of a molehill. She worries that the mole might be skin cancer, for instance. Hypochondria is strong when she is in this anxious mode. Her anxiety and irritability explode just before her menses. For her, control of a situation will lessen her anxiousness. She becomes fastidious, compulsive, and perfectionistic during that time frame.

Few would recognize her anxiety except that she becomes far more controlling during these episodes. She will never ask for help, simply retreating even more deeply within herself, but sooner or later, this wall of control will shatter, and when it does, she goes into uncontrollable bouts of deep, hard weeping that can become hysterical in nature.

IRRITABILITY

Mentals: Many times the depression is worse before her menses, along with more irritability and keyed-up nervousness than usual. She wants to be left alone and she will not seek out the company of others for help, or ask for or need consolation.

She becomes offended at every word, avoids company in general, and hates the person who offended her. If you try to comfort her, then the irritability and anger are fully displayed. She becomes hasty as well as impatient when in this irritable state.

SLEEP

Physical Symptoms: Sleep patterns for a Nat. Mur. woman consist of great drowsiness during the day, with lots of yawning. When she does get to sleep, she is extremely hard to wake up the following morning. There is excessive drowsiness, even lassitude. If she awakens during the night, then it's hard for her to drop back to sleep. Her dreams can be anxious, vivid, or disturbing.

EYES DRY, BURNING, OR ITCHING

Physical Symptoms: There's a bruised feeling to the eyes. The eyelids feel heavy. Letters may run together. Tears stream down her face on coughing, a keynote. Her eyes appear wet with tears, and there is a burning and acrid feeling in them. There may be a fiery zigzag appearance around objects, as well. A burning sensation occurs along with pain in her eyes when looking down at something.

EYE STRAIN

Physical Symptoms: It hurts to move the eyes downward or to look upward or sideways; there is an aching sensation to them.

FLOODING DURING MENSES

Physical Symptoms: When she floods, there is a distinct bearing-down pain or pressure in her uterine and vaginal region. She is always hot during her menses, but cool, otherwise.
Modalities: WORSE – flooding is heaviest in the morning hours. Her flooding is made worse from noise, listening to music, being in a warm room, lying down, performing any type of mental exertion, experiencing too much heat, or having to talk. It is especially bad around 10 a.m. BETTER – if she is out in the open air, enjoying cool bathing, going without regular meals, lying on her right side, placing pressure against her lower back, and wearing snug-fitting clothing around the abdominal area.

UNWANTED HAIR

Physical Symptoms: Far too much hair on the upper lip.

URINARY INCONTINENCE

Comments: An excellent remedy to consider in stress incontinence situations.
Physical Symptoms: Dripping may occur involuntarily if you laugh, sneeze, cough, or walk. Incontinence will occur more often at night. There is a burning, drawing, or cutting sensation in the urethra and itching in the region after voiding or dribbling. There can be an aggravation of incontinence at 10 a.m. You are thirsty for drinks that are ice cold.

VAGINA DRY OR POOR LUBRICATION

Physical Symptoms: Dryness of the vagina; it just will not become lubricated. Burning and smarting pain is experienced during intercourse. Pain after making love. You do not want to make sexual contact. The skin around or within your vagina may be withered, dried-out looking, and itchy.
Modalities: WORSE – you do not want to be consoled (which makes you worse). Heat is not tolerated in any form. Symptoms worsen around 10 a.m., in heat (sun, temperature, and summertime), in a warm room, or lying down. BETTER – affected area becomes better in open air and with cold bathing.

VAGINAL ITCHING

Comments: One of the villains that can cause this itching is candida. Check with your gynecologist to rule out this possibility, before taking a remedy. Other villains can be spermicidal creams, vaginal deodorants, soap used to clean the vaginal area, soap residue on your panties, tampon use, napkin rubbing and irritating the skin, or use of any powder, to name a few. You may be allergic to one of these products and this could be the source of the itching. After you have made sure that none of these are the culprit for the itching, then match your symptoms against the remedies presented below.

If you have been diagnosed with candida, it can be dealt with homeopathically; so can the other conditions listed above, but the use of the remedy below is not recommended, if this is the case. Work with your homeopath because the vaginal itching is only a minor symptom to an overall larger picture that needs to be addressed on a constitutional level and not an acute level.

For minor relief from itching, you can use a NON-ALCOHOLIC tincture, such as calendula. Wash three times a day with it. Or, try urtica ointment, and apply lightly to the area where the itching is located. Both products are used only topically and not internally. If there is no relief after 2 days, then stop using it and see your homeopath.

Physical Symptoms: Itching includes a loss of hair in that region and in your pubic area. Pimples appear on the pubic region. Discharge is profuse, acrid, and greenish colored, and it increases with walking. Other types of discharge may be transparent, whitish, and thick. A scalding, burning, and smarting itch may be present.

❁NUX VOMICA❁

Origin: This remedy is made from a tree known as the poison nut.
Comments: This tree grows in Southeast Asia as well as in Australia. The green, fist-sized fruit yields dried seeds that are shaped like round buttons. The seeds are also known as Quaker buttons. They are ground down and used to make the homeopathic remedy. They contain the poison, strychnine. During the Middle Ages, the poison was extracted from these seeds and used as an antidote for the Plague (or Black Death). In its homeopathic form, it is not poisonous, but aids many modern-day complaints, such as indigestion.

CONSTIPATION

Comments: This type of constipation comes on because the woman has a lifestyle where she must sit for a good part of her day and she gets little exercise as a result. This is also an excellent remedy for women who have abused herbal laxatives, enemas, and other mechanical means to achieve a daily bowel movement. Nux Vomica is a major addiction remedy, generally speaking, and if the body has become lazy and addicted to having bowel movements created mechanically with herbs or other laxative forms, this is a remedy to consider to break that cycle and get the body totally involved in moving the stools along on a timely basis on its own once again.
Physical Symptoms: There is a bruised, sore feeling to the abdomen along with an urgency and spasm to defecate—but you cannot, or very few stools are passed as a result. Stools can be dry, scanty, knotty, ball or dung-like, or large, dry, and painful. Often, there is mucus coating the stool. There can be cramping and painful spasms in the rectal region. Constipation may be tied up with anger as a root cause and may be the real reason that the constipation is occurring in the first place. Who are you angry with?

Along with the lack of bowel movement is great irritability. Constipation occurs in the early morning hours. The urging is ineffectual and there's a feeling that part of the stool has remained behind. A feeling of uneasiness is always present in the rectal region. There may be "blind" hemorrhoids (they are inside your rectum and you cannot see them—they don't hang out like the other type of hemorrhoids). Your hemorrhoids itch a lot.
Modalities: WORSE – from experiencing cold temperatures (air conditioning included) or weather, from drinking too much coffee or alcohol, and after "brain-fag," which means you have overstressed your mental faculties with too much study or work. Sitting too long at one's desk and doing mental work for long periods at the computer are good examples of this. Mental strain and exhaustion equals constipation for a Nux Vomica type. BETTER – bowel movements improve with heat, in the evening, and after taking a nap.

HEART PALPITATIONS AND SHORTNESS OF BREATH

Physical Symptoms: Heart palpitations come on after eating too much rich food or overeating. They will also manifest after drinking alcoholic beverages. Stress can produce this symptom, and you are usually highly irritable and nervous. Nux's are known as Type A individuals
Modalities: WORSE – palpitations may also manifest upon lying down.

INDIGESTION

Comments: You always crave stimulants of some kind, such as lots of coffee on a daily basis, a few glasses of wine or beer, or caffeine-bearing or spicy foods in general. You may smoke cigarettes to keep going at Mach 3 with your hair on fire! Nux women are doers and accomplishers of major proportions—they walk fast and talk fast, and worse, they eat fast. Indigestion springs up from being too high strung, too pressured with Type A behavior, and not being able to slow down and eat healthy food instead of junk.

This is a remedy to use if indigestion comes on after hearing sudden, shocking, or upsetting news, being angered or disappointed, or feeling humiliated or embarrassed. The old saying that one shouldn't eat when one is upset applies to you.

Mentals: With heartburn comes major irritability and being snappish and impatient with people around you. If you get grouchy with indigestion, this may be your remedy.

Physical Symptoms: You will experience heartburn 30 minutes after eating your meal (on the run, or at a fancy restaurant replete with rich foods). Hiccups may occur after drinking hot or cold liquids. The morning after eating too big or rich a meal, there will be a sour taste in your mouth, as well as nausea. A sensation of a painful weight will be felt in the stomach region, and it's made worse by eating. After eating, your stomach will become severely bloated for many hours. It is difficult for you to belch or to pass gas to get rid of this swollen feeling. If you have nausea, you will feel better after vomiting—but, often you cannot vomit, which compounds your misery, tenfold.

The food, quite literally, lies like a Gordian knot in the bottom of your stomach. If you drink coffee, heartburn attacks you 30 minutes later. And if you can belch, which isn't often, there is always a sour taste to it.

Modalities: WORSE – in the early morning, in cold, dry air, from drafts, wind, or being uncovered. Mental fatigue, becoming irritated or angered, enduring too much noise, inhaling noxious odors, or wearing clothes that create pressure around the waist, all help produce indigestion. BETTER – if you can grab a quick nap, rest during damp, wet weather, apply pressure (massage) to your bloated stomach, consume a hot drink or milk, or inhale moist air.

❀OLEUM JECORIS ASSELLI❀
(OLEUM J.)

Origin: This remedy is made from cod liver oil.

Mentals: This woman is typically introverted and reserved and never shows her feelings—although she's in touch with them.

UNWANTED HAIR

Physical Symptoms: This is a specific remedy for women who have too much hair on their chin or upper lip.

❀PHOSPHORICUM ACIDUM❀
(PHOS. AC.)

Origin: This is potentized phosphoric acid.

Comments: In its crude state, phosphoric acid is in daily use by our pharmaceutical drug companies, in our soaps, and by our farmers who use it as a fertilizer. In the nineteenth century, traditional medicine used this crude form to stimulate digestion. Nowadays, traditional medicine uses it to bring down calcium levels for people who have cancerous and benign tumors in the parathyroid gland, which is located in the neck.

Homeopathically, this remedy is wonderful for children who grow too fast and experience that crippling pain that comes with the muscles being stretched too far, too quickly. It is a major adult-onset of diabetes remedy of remarkable proportions.

ITCHING SKIN

Physical Symptoms: You have sensitive, clammy skin. You will also get the sensation of insects crawling across your skin (formication), along with not being able to perspire properly. There can be red, burning spots on your arms and legs, as well.

❀PHOSPHORUS❀

Origin: Made from the element, phosphorus.
Comments: This is a non-metallic solid that is yellowish white in color. Phosphorus was discovered in 1669 and was found to ignite quite well. The only problem was, it was also highly poisonous, so it was replaced with red phosphorus, which isn't. It glows in the dark and is exceedingly flammable. One of the most valuable minerals in our body, it is found in our genetic code, teeth, and bones.

Homeopathically, this is one of our great constitutional class remedies. It is used for many symptoms, including respiratory problems, pneumonia, and hemorrhaging, to name a few. It is also one of our main remedies for panic attacks, anxiety, and fears.

ACUTE ANXIETY OR PANIC ATTACKS

Comments: If you are the type of woman who feels that you are without some type of inner core or center to cling to when things get rough, this premier anxiety remedy may be for you. Because there is no anchoring core in you (and constitutional treatment can give this back to you), people that are a part of your life become your external core. This core essence is about being grounded, or centered—and you are not. Your friends call you effervescent, extroverted, bubbly like champagne, and possessing a star-like quality that you expend lavishly upon those who care about you. Anxiety strikes when you are alone, during a thunderstorm, while sleeping, after eating, or during dinner. Often, there is fear about the future regarding your state of health.
Mentals: The anxiety may make you a hypochondriac about health matters. There may be this feeling that "something" is going to come creeping out of the darkened corners and get you. This makes you timid and unable to go about your daily tasks and responsibilities. You cannot work, study, or talk, which just isn't like you. Any type of sympathy, just a touch on the shoulder, instantly makes you feel better. When anxiety hits, which is in the morning, upon waking, or at dusk or twilight, you rely heavily on the support of your company (spouse, children, or friends) to make you feel more stable and you can also lean on them for support during such a crisis.
Modalities: WORSE – during thunderstorms, in cold, windy weather, or from an expenditure of emotions. BETTER – with company, sympathy, being out in the open air, washing with cool water, or getting rubbed or massaged.

EYE "FLOATERS"

Physical Symptoms: If your eyesight has a misty quality to it, this is a remedy to consider for that condition. Your vision will have a veil over it, and there may be black points that cross your vision. Also, a green halo may be seen around a candle and letters appear red in color.

HEARING DIFFICULTY

Physical Symptoms: Difficulty in hearing human voices, especially if there's background noise. A re-echoing of sounds, with vibration, is felt in your head. The types of noise you hear in your ears are murmuring, roaring, ringing, and buzzing sounds. Frequent, unceasing tinnitis can occur. Aching or itching in the ears is also a symptom.

❁PHYTOLACCA DECANDRA❁
(PHYTOLCACCA)

Origin: Made from the plant, pokeweed.
Comments: This plant's berries, a dark purple color, are highly poisonous if eaten. A number of children every year in the United States die from ingesting this plant's berries. Back in the old days, the young shoots, however, when first appearing in Spring, were picked and eaten like asparagus without any poisonous effects.

In the last century, Phytolacca was used for breast cancer with great success. It is also one of our premier homeopathic breast remedies—especially for new mothers who want to breast feed their babies. Inflammation of the breast, including mastitis, can usually be cured by this marvelous remedy.

BREASTS SWOLLEN OR PAINFUL

Physical Symptoms: The lymph glands in your armpits are usually sore, swollen, or hard, and they in turn affect your breasts. There is heat and swelling in the breasts, with burning pain in them. Breasts may feel hard and stony as well as tender. Your breasts may turn reddish purple. Cracks and ulcers may be found about your nipples. There can be a bloody, watery discharge from the nipples (see a gynecologist about this right away). There can be hard nodes in the breast. Your nipples may also be inverted.
Modalities: WORSE – breast swelling along with pain is worse just before and during your menses. BETTER – breast pain and swelling go away or markedly reduce after your menses.
Other: Stop wearing a bra for 2 weeks. There is plenty of evidence that wearing a bra stops lymph gland drainage, and cysts and fibroids may result, as well as breast cancer. Take it off and see what happens!

❁PLATINUM METALLICUM❁
(PLATINUM or PLATINA)

Origin: Made from the rare, precious metal, platinum.
Comments: There is an interesting correlation between platinum's value in the world as a monetary exchange form, and how this woman values herself. This mineral was discovered in South America in the eighteenth century. Spanish for this mineral is *platina*, which means "like silver," hence its name. In the nineteenth century, it was used by traditional medicine as a cure for syphilis (it didn't). Today, homeopathically, its sphere of use is for women with reproductive difficulties. Typologically, Platina is said to suit women with dark hair who are thin and have a sanguine complexion.

The menses pattern for Platina is that it's too early and profuse with dark clots. She experiences spasms of the uterus accompanied with a bearing-down sensation. The menses is short in duration. She may be so exquisitely sensitive that she cannot wear a napkin against her delicate skin. She is extremely chilled and there is a sensitiveness to her vaginal area as well as to her ovaries. She will have a burning sensation in that region of her abdomen. There may be problems more with the left ovary than the right one.

There is an unusual keynote feature to Platina: she feels as if a part of her body is growing larger or longer than the rest of her. It is usually a limb, but can be some other part of her body, too.

Mentals: There can be an extreme arrogance or haughty disposition to her. She's very proud, she thinks that she knows best, and she rarely asks for advice—but is always giving it. There is a sureness and powerful confidence to this woman and it may or may not border on arrogance. She knows what she knows and she's sure of what she knows. Platina women are nonstop talkers, too—rarely allowing anyone else to voice their opinion. Usually, Platina men and women are very sexual beings, and they can carry this desire to an uncontrolled extreme of sexual excess. An interesting symptom is that Platina feels as if she does not belong to her own family, a keynote to watch for.

SPASMS IN THE VAGINA (VAGINISMUS)

Physical Symptoms: This includes a cold feeling in the vulva and the pubic hair region, although the area is terribly sensitized and touch is aggravating. There is spasm and constriction of the vagina, and it remains tender and hypersensitive. The spasms may occur during love making. A tingling sensation starts in your vagina and moves up into your abdomen. Pressure can be felt in the pubic hair region and vaginal area.

❁PLUMBUM METALLICUM❁
(PLUMBUM)

Origin: This is the metal, lead.

Comments: In ancient times, lead was used by the ingenious Romans to make pipes for plumbing necessities in their expensive villas, as hair ornaments for their women, and as an exchange for Roman citizenry to enter the circus maximus and watch such events as chariot racing and gladiator events. Unfortunately, lead pipes create lead poisoning. Physicians in the later centuries realized that weakness of the muscles, abdominal pain, and colic were all part of the lead poisoning symptoms generated by drinking water from lead pipes.

Homeopathically, lead is safe and is considered one of the great spasm remedies. It is especially noteworthy in cases of vaginismus that will not respond to any other homeopathic remedy. Your menses history includes a tendency toward miscarriages (spontaneous), excessive bleeding, and a sensation of a string pulling from the abdominal region back to your spine. During pre-menopause, your menses may be filled with dark, black clots of blood.

Mentals: A Plumbum woman may be depressed. She may suffer from high blood pressure, or may feel very weak in a muscular sense. People around her may feel that she's mentally slow in her perception or understanding of something. She may complain about a loss of memory and it tires her out too much to think.

MEMORY LOSS

Comments: This is an excellent remedy to consider after amnesia aphasia (loss of memory after a stroke).

Physical Symptoms: Weakness or loss of memory. Slow grasp of perception along with increasing apathy. You struggle valiantly for a long time and are unable to find the right word while talking. Dementia. Slow mental perception.

SPASMS IN THE VAGINA (VAGINISMUS)

Physical Symptoms: This includes severe spasm with intense pain within your vagina. Constriction of the muscles of your vagina are voluntary and involuntary. Pains may be violent and nerve-like in their manifestation. There is a pulling, contractive, and tearing sensation within your vagina. There is a marked hypersensitiveness to the vaginal region, in general. This remedy should be thought of in stubborn cases of vaginismus when nothing else will cure the condition.

❁PULSATILLA NIGRICANS❁
(PULSATILLA)

Origin: Made from the windflower or pasqueflower.
Comments: Found in Scandinavia and Russia, this purple-black flower with a bright yellow and black center has been used since the eighteenth century. A very delicate looking plant; if chewed when fresh, it creates a burning sensation in the mouth and throat region.

Homeopathically, this is one of our great constitutional remedies. Typologically, this woman is usually thin and willowy looking, perhaps even ballerina-like, and she is never still! The other type of Pulsatilla woman can be overweight and plump looking. Movement is a constant with her. Her emotional structure parallels a ride on a roller-coaster—her feelings change from one moment to the next. Pulsatilla women also tend to have a history of varicose veins.
Mentals: You may also be inclined to be oversensitive, you cry easily, and you are touched emotionally by everything in your world. Sometimes you can cry at the drop of a hat, but not always. The key here is that you are remarkably sensitive to all external events; at times you are like that wind-whipped flower on the tundra—always in constant movement, feelings-wise.
Modalities: WORSE – in the evening, when left alone, when walking about, from heat, standing for long periods of time, eating fatty or rich food, toward evening, in a warm room, lying down, or when allowing your feet to hang down below the rest of your body. BETTER – in open, fresh air (a window is always open wherever you live), from motion, being in the company of others, cold applications on the affected part, or cold food and drink. You are a thirstless individual and drink very little fluid (and you should drink more).

ACUTE ANXIETY OR PANIC ATTACKS

Comments: If you are a flighty, bubbly, extroverted woman who is well known for your changeable moods (which is referred to as an "April Day" by homeopaths), your anxiety can strike at any time. It's as changeable and flexible as you are.
Mentals: The anxiety resembles a razor-like panic that funnels up through you, leaving you shaking and nearly frozen in its wake. Another time, it can be there, but you can busy yourself and it will only eat at the edges of your daily tasks or attention. No two anxiety attacks are exactly the same for you—and this is a keynote to use this remedy.

These attacks frequently have no cycle or periodicity to them and will hit you day or night. An attack may come while you are in bed, in the dark, stimulated by a fear, from being in the house, or upon going to sleep. There can be suicidal anxiety along with a sensation in the pit of your stomach. You can suffer an extreme anguish—a feeling as if you are about to die.

This anxiety can leave you weepy, easily moved over the slightest trifle, easily offended, and fearful for your spouse, your marriage, or your job. There is a history of abandonment issues with this type of anxiety and you may be afraid that your spouse will leave you (he will not) and just thinking about that possibility may bring on an anxiety reaction. At the other end of the anxiety

spectrum, you can be irritable, almost vicious at times, very touchy, easily slighted, and suspicious. If your menses is suppressed, as it can be during menopause, then mania, such as the sudden highs and lows of emotions, may occur.
Modalities: WORSE – in a stuffy, overheated room, at twilight, from eating too much rich food, before your menses, or if you rest, sit, or lie down. BETTER – if you can get up and move around, walk outdoors, find a cooler room with a breeze from an open window, sip a cold drink or eat cold foods, get a massage, or sit with an erect posture.

ARTHRITIS

Comments: This remedy should be thought of if the arthritis is better in the morning, but as the day moves on, you become more stiff. By evening, the arthritis is at its very worst. There are always wandering pains with this type of arthritis. A keynote to use this remedy is that the pains are never in the same place twice!
Physical Symptoms: The major pain can settle in your hips and knees, although it will migrate without reason or logic! A unique symptom is that the tension and pain you carry will release suddenly, with a "snap." Swelling comes and goes with irregularity, but swiftly. There can be pain in your heels toward evening. Pains can have a drawing or tearing sensation to them. The veins in your forearms and hands swell. Your feet can be red, inflamed, and swollen. The legs may feel heavy and weary. The pains will make you restless and sleepless—and you will be very cold. There can be numbness in specific areas, such as in the elbows.
Modalities: WORSE – pain intensifies with movement, but if the movement is continued, the pain is relieved. Pain worsens with warm applications. If you allow your arms or legs to hang down, it will always be worse. BETTER – your pain improves with cold applications.

BREAST CYSTS AND FIBROIDS

Mentals: The pain you feel in your breasts will make you cry.
Physical Symptoms: The level of pain experienced in your breast is never the same twice, nor will you feel it in that region again. Typical of your constitutional trademark: never the same, or in the same place. This goes for the pain you may experience in your breasts—it is different every time and this is a keynote to consider the use of this remedy.

BREASTS SWOLLEN OR PAINFUL

Comments: This remedy should be thought of if the breasts swell before the menses; a classic keynote for this remedy. The engorgement of the breasts is due to hormonal fluctuations in your body at menses.
Physical Symptoms: Usually this condition exists with PMS-like symptoms and the breasts temporarily engorge with excess water or edema. Pain can be shooting along the side of each breast. They can be sore and aching. Secretion of milk before your menses is possible.
Modalities: WORSE – before your menses, during the evening hours, and from becoming too warm. BETTER – after your menses, from gently massaging your breasts, placing a cold cloth on them, sitting up, or gentle movement.
Other: Stop wearing a bra for 2 weeks. There is plenty of evidence that wearing a bra stops lymph gland drainage, and cysts and fibroids may result, as well as breast cancer. Take it off and see what happens!

DEPRESSION

Warning: If your depression is more than 3 months old, you are considered a chronic case. Do NOT take the homeopathic remedy indicated below. Instead, seek out constitutional homeopathic treatment from your nearest homeopath. See the appendix for the phone number for the National Center for homeopathy (NCH).

Comments: This is for women who seem to roller coaster up and down out of depression, especially the manic depressive or what is known as a bi-polar state. One moment, Pulsatilla feels like she's in hell, the next, in heaven, with all the attending euphoric feelings being turned up in volume.

Depression for this woman is never periodic or cyclical. It comes and goes at a whim, without seeming rhyme or reason. It will stay 5 minutes, and at another time, an hour, and then, for a day. There is an erratic quality to her depression—from the duration of it, to the intensity of it.

Physical Symptoms: There is much weeping with this kind of depression, and the least thing, such as music playing, will send you into nearly hysterical bouts of crying and sobbing. You can watch something on the television that spirals you into gloom or tears. If you read something upsetting in a newspaper or magazine, the effect and reaction is the same—tearfulness.

Modalities: WORSE – in the evening, particularly in a stuffy room, at twilight, when left alone, long after eating a meal, before your menses, before a thunderstorm, or from being out in hot sunlight. BETTER – if you are out in the fresh air or have a window open, in the company of others, receiving sympathy and attention from others, when drinking or eating cold condiments, and with gentle motion such as walking or puttering about.

ANXIETY

Mentals: Your type of anxiety is generally sudden, powerful, and without any pattern or periodicity. And ANYTHING can set it off. The anxiety is as changeable as the weather. When there is a known fear, it is of ghosts, of being abandoned, of some unrequited grief that has never been worked through, or some spiritual or religious melancholy.

There can be fear of losing your mind or of taking your life (and you really do not want to do this awful thing), and you may cry incessantly as a result. If you are of a religious nature, you may see the devil coming to get you, or believe the world is on fire. Your anxiety deepens around the beginning of your menses. You may be afraid of everyone, and consider everyone your enemy, with an internalized feeling of dread and distrust and outwardly, being tearful.

Physical Symptoms: Anxiety is felt in the stomach region along with a general sense of foreboding, or an impending disaster. You may have heart palpitations along with your teeth chattering during an anxiety reaction.

It is easy to see anxiety on your face: there is a disturbed quality to it, and you are suspicious of others, and more reserved than usual. The anxiety attack may make you gasp for breath.

IRRITABILITY

Mentals: If you are not pampered, paid attention to, and being cared for by another or several people, your irritability can manifest. You may cry angrily that you are not loved anymore, and often you can resort to using tears as a way to manipulate those around you. If your family does not respond appropriately to your needs, your moods can change like the wind. Becoming peevish, sulky, pouty, and tearful in order to get that needed attention is all part of your irritability mode. You can become touchy, disgusted with everything, and suspicious, and you will answer abruptly: yes or no. And then you may pout.

SLEEP

Mentals: Your mind is crowded with ideas and it keeps you awake; you cannot turn off these errant thoughts in order to sleep. If in an anxious state, you will have a sleepless night due to a known or unknown fear haunting you. At night, you are restless, tossing and turning endlessly about in bed. Your thoughts while in bed are about despair of ever recovering, of a religious or spiritual nature (your soul will never be saved, you think); you suffer melancholy or have a fixed idea of some kind. After you fall asleep, usually after 2 a.m., the soundest sleep is in the morning when it is time for you to get up.

Physical Symptoms: Sleepiness always strikes you in the early afternoon, and if you can nap at that time, you awake unrefreshed, languid, and confused (you may feel frightened or not know where you are). And come evening, you are wide awake.

When you go to bed, your sleep is restless, and frequently you will talk or chatter in your sleep, even whining or screaming. A lot of anguish can be experienced during your sleep state, including agitation, tossing, and jerking of the limbs. Many times, you don't get to sleep until 2 a.m. There is no regularity to your sleep pattern; it is different every night.

DIARRHEA

Comments: You have a type of diarrhea where *no two stools ever look the same*, a keynote of this remedy. Diarrhea will strike you after eating fatty meat or food containing a lot of fat, or eating rich foods, more than your fair share of butter or ice cream (all high in fat), or after eating too much fruit, eggs, pork, or pastry.

Physical Symptoms: There is soreness just above the belly button area of the abdomen, along with pulsating or cutting pains in that same region. It can be accompanied by loud rumbling sounds and abdominal swelling. There may be a sensation of a stone resting in your abdomen, and possible numbness with pains extending into your groin area.

The diarrhea is rumbling, watery, and always worse at night. The stools are a bile green color, sometimes white or yellow, but not as often. It is a noisy, spluttering expulsion along with a lot of gas. There is no debilitation from this type of diarrhea. However, there can be shredded, stringy, or membrane-like scrapings from the intestinal wall present. Undigested food may be present.

Modalities: WORSE – if you are taking iron supplements, allow your feet to hang down below the rest of your body, drink tea, are out in direct sunlight, consume hot food, remain in a warm, stuffy room, or lie down on your left side or the painless side. The diarrhea worsens toward evening, or before your menses. BETTER – from cool, open air (such as having a window open or walking outside), gentle motion or movement, application from a cold cloth, or consuming cold food or drinks. And, chances are you will not be thirsty. If you move around, rub or massage your abdomen, uncover the affected area, or lie down with your head high, the diarrhea will improve.

MENOPAUSAL HEADACHE

Comments: This is one of our premier menopause-headache remedies. The headache may come on because you ate too much rich food, or simply ate too much of a good thing.

Mentals: When this headache strikes, it will make you feel like you are on an emotional roller coaster. It is not unusual to become over-emotional and tearful, and possibly want to cry. You will desire company and want to be pampered (fussed over) and cared for by others.

Physical Symptoms: There can be nerve-like pain in the right temple region, with scalding tears in the right eye. Pains can also occur in the forehead and around the bones of your right eye.

One of the keynotes of this remedy is wandering pain—it does not remain static or stay in the same place time after time. There can be a feeling of pressure on the top of your head, with stitching pains about the head that may extend into your face and even into your teeth. Your head may feel heavy, as if you cannot hold it upright. It may be accompanied by profuse sweating on your scalp. The pain is always a bursting, burning, or pulsating type.
Modalities: WORSE – from being in a warm room or in stuffy, stale air, wearing too many clothes, getting your feet wet, or going to bed. With beginning motion (such as getting up from a chair) the headache worsens temporarily, but with continued motion, it improves. Approaching storms, eating fats, ice cream, pork, or eggs, eating hot food, or being out in the sun, also intensifies the symptoms of your headache. If you allow your limbs to hang down, it worsens. The pain is worse at twilight and through the evening and night time hours. BETTER – if people pay attention to you, by remaining near an open window and fresh air, from a cold cloth, from consuming cold food or drink, from uncovering, sitting up straight, constantly moving around, rubbing or massaging your head, or lying down with your head held high.

HEART PALPITATIONS AND SHORTNESS OF BREATH

Physical Symptoms: For women who experience up and down, roller coaster emotional states, this could be the remedy of choice. Heart palpitations can be brought on by eating fatty or rich foods or experiencing too much heat (indoor or outdoor temperature), in general. A "catching" of one's breath, which becomes better or lessened if your hand is pressed against your chest or if you walk around.

HOT FLASHES

WARNING: Any acute or persistent symptoms such as pain in the chest or pelvic region should be immediately evaluated by a physician. After serious problems are ruled out, you can safely proceed with your non-hormone, non-drug homeopathic treatment.

Physical Symptoms: They can occur day or night, and they have no pattern, no rhythm to them, which is a keynote to use this remedy. Further, like Folliculinum women, you will often need fresh air, and will run for an open window during a hot flash—even in the middle of winter or the middle of the night!

INDIGESTION

Comments: This remedy is useful for indigestion that is caused by eating too many rich foods, products high in fat, ice cream, pastries, and desserts. Onions disagree strongly with you. Usually, there is a desire for foods that are sour, such as lemonade, berries, vinegar, or other "refreshing" kinds of food (things that have a zing to them, such as bubbly soda pop). Sometimes, food tastes too salty to you. You are nearly always thirstless and will not drink water or other liquids with your meals.
Physical Symptoms: Indigestion comes on 2 hours after eating, along with heart palpitations and a bitter taste in your mouth. The symptoms worsen in the evening. It may be accompanied by a headache that centers around your eyes, nausea, and possible vomiting. You will also feel highly emotional at such times of discomfort, perhaps even tearful.

Pain may be felt in the stomach an hour after eating. There is swelling and you must loosen your waistband to get relief. Upon rising in the morning, you may feel a weight or stone sensation in your stomach. There is a feeling of pulsations in the stomach. If you are a tea drinker, there may be an "all-gone" feeling in that region. If you smoke cigarettes, you may get hiccups.

Modalities: BETTER – if you're out in cool, fresh air, near an open window, and experiencing gentle motion or movement. Rubbing or massaging your stomach or abdominal region makes you feel better. Lying with your head high helps too. Consuming cold food or liquids improves your symptoms, but you still have no thirst. WORSE – if you remain in a warm, stuffy room without ventilation, before menses, allowing your feet to hang down, consuming tea, or if you are out in bright, hot sunlight. Hot food may make you vomit immediately, and your indigestion is always worse at twilight and into the evening hours.

LEG CRAMPS

Comments: For those who experience cramps in differing parts of their legs, calves, or feet—a wandering kind of cramping that is never the same two nights in a row.
Physical Symptoms: The cramps have a drawing, tension-like or stretching pain with restlessness. The cramping can shift rapidly and the tension in the leg will let go with a "snap." There may be a boring pain felt in the heel of your foot. The cramps worsen significantly if you allow your legs to hang down (and they are improved markedly if legs are supported slightly above the rest of the body).
Modalities: WORSE – from heat of any kind, including the covers of the bed at night, and you may stick your feet out from beneath the covers because they are too hot. The cramps become worse with heat application, being in a warm, stuffy room, and lying on the painless side. BETTER – with movement, fresh air being available (a window open or going outdoors), or placing a cold cloth over the cramping region.

URINARY INCONTINENCE

Comments: This is an especially good remedy for women who are pregnant and suffering from incontinence. However, this remedy should be carefully considered by a homeopath before taking, as Pulsatilla is known, through various literature, to cause miscarriage if there are pregnancy problems—so do not take this without consulting a professional homeopath first!
Physical Symptoms: There is loss of urine if you cough or pass gas, particularly at night. This is also a remedy for young girls who have problems with incontinence while in bed at night. This is one of our premier bed-wetting remedies for any and all ages, regardless of gender.

VARICOSE VEINS

Comments: This remedy may help those who acquired varicose veins during their pregnancy. Pulsatilla is used frequently on leaky varicose vein ulceration. The varicose veins may come and go, and move around on any part of your body, a keynote of this remedy.
Physical Symptoms: There is a bluish color to your veins, and they are highly inflamed and swollen. They itch and they are distended along with a stinging sensation.

Your ankles and feet may swell and feel very heavy and painful. If this condition occurs, your varicose veins will also swell, a keynote of this remedy. The varicosity may be hard, knotty, and intensely painful if touched. It can also be a deep crimson color, swollen, dull, aching, and tender.

❃RHODODENDRON CHRYSANTHEMUM❃
(RHODODENDRON)

Origin: Made from Siberian rhododendron or the yellow snow rose.
Comments: This wonderful herb was used in Siberia, where it grows naturally, for gout and rheumatism complaints. Later, it was introduced to England. The fresh leaves are used to make the

homeopathic equivalent to the herbal preparation. It was proved in 1831, and is used primarily as an arthritis and muscle injury remedy.

ARTHRITIS

Comments: This remedy has an interesting keynote for those who have arthritic symptoms: If your arthritis gets WORSE before a storm or front comes through—then this is your remedy! Sometimes this remedy is confused with Rhus Tox., but remember, Rhododendron is always influenced strongly by passing weather fronts and storms and Rhus Tox. is not.

Physical Symptoms: Rheumatic pains may occur simultaneously with gout. The joints are swollen. Gout inflames the big toe joint in either foot. There are tearing pains in all your limbs, but the arthritis is usually more right-sided. Pains in bones are in spots, and reappear after a change in the weather.

There is stiffness in the neck region. The sufferer cannot sleep unless her legs are crossed—an important keynote of this remedy. The arthritis symptoms will always strongly reappear with stormy weather and the symptoms improve after the storm passes. Nodosities can be associated with this remedy and there is pain in your heels.

Modalities: WORSE – your arthritis symptoms are always worse at rest and during stormy weather. BETTER – walking improves your arthritis condition. You feel better when awake. Pain is also improved if exposed to warm water, such as a bath or shower, and by eating.

MEMORY LOSS

Physical Symptoms: You experience sudden loss of ideas. You leave out whole words when writing. While speaking, you forget what you were talking about.

❁RHUS TOXICODENDRON❁

(RHUS TOX.)

Origin: Yes, that's right. This remedy is made with poison ivy leaves.

Comments: This remedy grows throughout North America—chances are, most of us have unwittingly run into some! In the eighteenth century, a physician noticed that a man with herpes on his wrist cured his own condition with poison ivy leaves. Traditional medicine has used poison ivy for rheumatism. Most of us have had poison ivy and we know what it can do to our skin—not to mention the awful itching that accompanies it!

Homeopathically, this remedy will not give you poison ivy, as there are no molecules of the plant left in there. It is used primarily for arthritis-type conditions as well as—yes, you guessed it—skin conditions!

ACUTE ANXIETY OR PANIC ATTACKS

Comments: These anxiety attacks can make you restless, with a feeling of helplessness and fear for your children or your family. You may fear that you could kill someone or that someone was poisoning you—which are earmarks to use this remedy. Your mind leaps from topic to topic; sometimes, it feels as if your mind runs a million miles an hour and you cannot stop it. You lie awake at night, your legs moving involuntarily as you toss and turn incessantly.

Mentals: You feel great apprehension at night, and there may be suicidal impulses, as well. Forgetfulness about recent events can occur, along with confusion. You can also become depressed, and consider drowning yourself to escape the driving intensity of the anxiety attacks. Do not do it—seek homeopathic help.

Modalities: WORSE – during cold, wet weather, being in a cold room, being jarred, finding yourself uncovered in bed, in the evening, around twilight, or after midnight while in bed. You cannot remain in bed. BETTER – with warm, dry weather, with constant movement about the house or outdoors, taking a warm bath or shower, or being in a heated room.

ARTHRITIS

Comments: This is one of our great arthritis remedies. If you overwork yourself, the result can be "restless legs" syndrome, which means you cannot keep your legs still—you must move them in some way. And it worsens during the night.

Physical Symptoms: These women have very hot, enlarged, swollen joints with shiny red skin across the affected area. The joints are hot to the touch; indeed, they may feel like a small furnace radiating heat! The pain is tearing in the tendons, ligaments, and fascia.

Limbs are stiff-feeling, and there can be paralysis later on. Sciatica can also flare up with the arthritis symptoms, and it's a tearing pain down the thigh. Numbness can be experienced in the extremities. Formication, which is a sensation of ants or bugs crawling over your skin, can be present. There is always tenderness around the knee joints. A loss of power in the forearms and fingers may be present. In the fingertips, there may be tingling or a feeling of formication. The feet may also be tingling, hot, and swollen.

Modalities: WORSE – fresh air, particularly cold, damp weather, makes your symptoms worse. The pain and restlessness are always worse at night. The pain is worse before a change in weather or a storm, but not to the degree of someone who might consider taking Rhododendron. BETTER – you are always better with motion, although you may experience stiffness upon rising—the more you move around, the less the stiffness and the better you feel. This kind of arthritis does well with a form of *mild* exercise, when lying on something hard like a bed or couch, after taking a hot bath or shower, or placing a warm application over the area (a cloth or heating pad). You inevitably improve during dry, hot weather.

EYES DRY, BURNING, OR ITCHING

Physical Symptoms: You experience pain on moving your eyes or pressing on them. There can be profuse tearing, with a scalding sensation upon opening them. Photophobia (inability to stand bright lights) along with a profuse flow of yellow mucus will occur. Intense itching. Eye symptoms become worse in the wind, or in dry, cold weather.

LEG CRAMPS

Comments: One of the premier remedies for restless legs, Rhus Tox. is also excellent for curing cramping conditions.

Physical Symptoms: These are rheumatic pains; a tearing, rending sensation announces the cramps. Cold air isn't tolerated and your skin may become painful. A tingling in the feet can accompany the cramping of your calf or foot. If the cramping is severe, there is a numbing sensation along with it.

Modalities: WORSE – This type of cramping becomes stiff and worsens if you rest in one position too long. BETTER – any type of pressure against the cramp, such as kneading it or massaging the area, always makes it feel better. Movement and walking eases the cramping, and so does applied warmth (blanket, heating pad, bath, or shower), a change of position, or stretching out your limb.

MEMORY LOSS

Physical Symptoms: There is the sensation of emptiness in your brain. Your memory simply blanks out. You have difficulty in thinking and speaking. It is very hard for you to collect your ideas at all, much less communicate them adequately. When you mean to write the number 2, you write the number 1. There is an error of the senses and you are forgetful of the recent past. Your brain feels like an empty vacuum as if there are no longer any words, thoughts, or ideas left in it!

SKIN ITCHING

Physical Symptoms: This remedy helps women who experience a cold feeling to their skin. When it itches, scratching makes it worse. You can also experience the crawling of insects over your skin (formication), and it tends to be red colored or flushed looking all the time. Chilblains, which is redness of the hands and feet accompanied by burning and itching, is addressed with this remedy.

❁RUTA GRAVOLENS❁
(RUTA GRAV.)

Origin: Made from the plant known as rue, which has pretty yellow flowers with dark brown centers.
Comments: During the Middle Ages when Black Death or the Plague killed hundreds of thousands of people throughout Europe, rue was used to hopefully ward off getting the deadly disease. Why? Because the plant has such a noxious odor to it! Just touching the plant's sap will irritate the skin!

The great Italian painter, Michelangelo, put great faith in rue, as did many other Renaissance era painters. They believed that rue would improve their eyesight. Homeopathically, Ruta Grav. is used today in eye, skin, and arthritis conditions.

EYES DRY, BURNING, OR ITCHING

Physical Symptoms: There is heat, redness, and pain while reading or performing close work with your eyes. A deep pressure sensation is felt within your eyeballs. Pressure may occur over the eyebrows. Eyestrain is followed by a headache. Your eyes become weary if reading.
Modalities: WORSE – your eye symptoms become worse with too much motion. BETTER – your eye symptoms always improve if you close them.

EYE STRAIN

Physical Symptoms: This remedy is used when your eyes burn and there is a straining sensation felt in them. It is usually caused by too much close work such as sewing, or other detailed types of work. Too much reading will also make your eyes feel strained. Eyeball pain is worse on movement, better on rest. A good computer screen remedy.

❁SABADILLA OFFICINALIS❁
(SABADILLA)

Origin: Made from cevadilla seeds. It is also known as Asagraea officinalis.
Comments: This plant grows in Mexico, South America, and the United States. As an herb, sabadilla has been used since the sixteenth century for killing intestinal worms and getting rid of

lice. The seeds are used to make the homeopathic remedy nowadays. It is considered one of the great allergy remedies in our pharmacopoeia.

ALLERGIES

Comments: Allergy sufferers who have a continual runny-faucet nose may do well with this remedy. Those who are labeled with hay fever may also be helped.

Physical Symptoms: There is constant, spasmodic sneezing along with nonstop nasal discharge. It is watery in nature and profuse. If around flowers of any kind, your allergies worsen. You are oversensitive to odors in general. Fluent discharges with pain from the nose and redness of the eyes may occur. Your nostrils are dry and itchy feeling. One nostril or the other is always plugged up. You cannot tolerate the odor of garlic. Mucus drainage from your sinus cavity that is "hawked up" may contain bright red blood.

Your eyelids have a distinct burning sensation and watery lachrymation from them becomes worse if coughing, sneezing, or yawning. There is a sensation of pressure in your eyeballs, especially if you look UP. The margins of your eyes are red. Blue circles may appear beneath your eyes.

Modalities: WORSE – from odors, drinking wine, in the morning hours, and at the new and full moon. BETTER – from standing near a warm stove, wrapping up in clothes or a blanket, consuming warm liquids or food, open air, and eating.

❁SABINA❁

Origin: This is made from an evergreen shrub from the juniper family, Juniperus sabina, or savin. It is found in Europe.

Comments: This is a wonderful woman's remedy because of its special affinity for the uterus, especially when it involves hemorrhaging of any kind, whether during pregnancy, your menstrual period, or menopause. A keynote of this remedy, and for the woman who would best respond to it, is that she has suffered one or more miscarriages in the third month of her pregnancy. Some of these women will have warts in the vaginal region that itch and bleed easily.

Mentals: A unique keynote is that music is intolerable to you and places you into a highly nervous or agitated state.

FLOODING DURING MENSES

Physical Symptoms: There are pains in your uterus that extend into your thighs, a keynote of this remedy. Knife-like pain begins in the sacral area of your lower back and extends into the vaginal area. The blood is a pale or bright red color and partly clotted, or it's very thin, discolored, and offensive smelling. The flooding comes and goes, almost spasmodically, like the ebb and flow of an ocean tide.

Modalities: WORSE – when you are in a warm room or the temperature soars. The least movement causes the flooding to increase. If you stand up, clots will discharge.
BETTER – from being in open air, placing a cool cloth across your abdomen, or indulging in a cooling bath or shower. You get relief when in a cooler, air-conditioned environment. Taking a walk reduces the flooding. One of your best positions is lying flat on your back with your legs slightly elevated by a pillow; the flooding symptoms will then abate.

❀SANGUINARIA CANADENSIS❀
(SANGUINARIA)

Origin: Prepared from the bloodroot plant, this lovely white-flowered plant grows quite close to the ground in richly wooded areas of North America.
Comments: This herb has big, round, umbrella-shaped leaves. Next time you see one in the early spring, break a stem and squeeze it. You will see from the red-orange sap how the plant got its name.

ALLERGIES

Comments: Sometimes your allergies are known as a "rose cold" without the asthmatic symptoms being present.
Physical Symptoms: Those who need this remedy for their allergies have profuse yellow discharge from their nostrils. The membranes of your nose feel dry and congested. There is pain at the root of the nose. There may be a loss of smell—or odors seem out of proportion to what they would be like without the allergies. There may be a smell of roasted onions in your nostrils.

Your eyes have a burning, dry sensation to them, followed by heavy tearing or lachrymation. There is swelling over your eyebrows, and the tears from your eyes feel hot. There is redness in your eyes during the morning hours. There may appear to be a mist or veil before your eyes. The eyes feel extremely painful upon moving them. The sclera, or the whites of your eyes, are yellow or jaundiced looking.

HOT FLASHES

WARNING: Any acute or persistent symptoms such as pain in the chest or pelvic region should be immediately evaluated by a physician. After serious problems are ruled out, you can safely proceed with your non-hormone, non-drug homeopathic treatment.

Physical Symptoms: Specifically for hot flashes or night sweats that settle mostly in your head and chest. These also create burning sensations in the palms of your hands and the soles of your feet.

❀SECALE CORNUTUM❀
(SECALE)

Origin: This fungus, made from the black, hornlike spur found in rye just before harvest, is known as ergot of rye.
Comments: In the nineteenth century, there were many reports of ergot's poisonous nature. It was noted in the old homeopathic materia medicas by observant homeopaths that pregnant cows aborted their calves if they ate ergot-infected grasses. Even worse, farm people who accidentally mixed the ergot fungus with flour they were grinding created ergotism epidemics. Many people died of this fungus when they unknowingly ate it in their flour-made products. The spurs, which have the fungus on them, are collected and then potentized. Known as Secale Cornutum, this is another remedy whose sphere of influence is well known for women's reproductive difficulties. In the homeopathic form, it is harmless.

Your menses is irregular, but when it comes, the blood is thin and black, with black clots or lumps, or brown fluid that may continue to ooze watery blood until your next period, which is a keynote symptom of this remedy. Another symptom is black liquid blood flowing with the slightest of movements accompanied by a tingling sensation in your legs and a feeling of great fatigue. Between menses, the discharge from your vagina can be brownish colored and so offensive smelling that it has been known to make a woman vomit. It has a rotting meat, road kill, or dead animal odor to it.

Even though you may feel like part of your body is burning up, if the area in question is touched, it feels cool or cold, not hot. Your skin will feel cool or cold, and yet, you cannot stand covering up, and you improve in a cool or cold environment—a unique keynote for this remedy.

FLOODING DURING MENSES

Physical Symptoms: This is a passive type of hemorrhage that just keeps leaking day after day, even though your menses ends for that month. You will continue to dribble a blackish blood discharge that smells very bad, right up to your next period. Another symptom is that during your menses and flooding, you may experience formication (a sensation of a bug crawling over your skin). Your vagina will feel either cold or hot to the touch.
Modalities: WORSE – all your symptoms are worse if you are in a hot room, exposed to high temperatures, or covered up. BETTER – if you are exposed to colder temperatures (weather or air conditioning) and are uncovered. The pain is a burning sensation—like embers—and will rapidly improve if a cold application is used, or if you move to a cold room.

❁SEPIA❁

Origin: Made from the ink of the cuttlefish, which is related to the squid family.
Comments: The cuttlefish is a soft mollusk that squirts a cloud of ink to hide in from its predators. (Wouldn't it be nice if women could also have such a cloud to nestle away in?) The ink has been used since the time of Dioscorides, a Roman doctor, for hair loss. Later, it was used by artists as an ink pigment.

Hahnemann discovered Sepia by observing a painter friend. The paintbrush was loaded with the raw, crude ink. He observed that his friend developed an illness, by licking the brush with his tongue, which was directly related to the previously unknown poisonous qualities of the ink. In 1834, Hahnemann potentized the ink and it's now known as Sepia, one of our greatest constitutional remedies and certainly a standout for women's reproductive problems at any age.

Typologically, a Sepia woman's complexion is usually sallow with a yellow cast to it. Generally speaking, women who respond best to this remedy are dark-haired with olive complexions and dark eyes (African Americans included). Some blond, blue-eyed women can also use this remedy.

This is one of the best menopausal remedies in our homeopathic pharmacopoeia. This powerful remedy influences the entire endocrine system of a woman, which includes the pituitary, pineal, thyroid, thymus, pancreas, adrenals, and ovary glands. It helps women who are pushed beyond their limits (Super Mom Syndrome), or who are exhausted mentally, physically, and emotionally, or are feeling spiritually bankrupt.
Mentals: The Sepia woman may have a feeling of emotional isolation or disconnection from those she loves as she moves through menopause. There is a general fatigue that accompanies everything she does, with no sense of joy or hope connected with it. She is pessimistic about everything in her life, personal as well as career. This remedy is for the woman who can no longer cope with all the demands placed upon her. A general sense of emotional numbness is felt toward everything in her life (these are also classic signs of depression, so you may consider asking your doctor's advice).

Modalities: WORSE – in the afternoon and evening, with high humidity, after perspiring, when experiencing cold air, or before a thunderstorm. BETTER – with exercise, pressure, the warmth of the bed, hot applications or cold bathing, drawing your legs upward as you rest in bed, and after sleeping.

DEPRESSION

Warning: If your depression is more than 3 months old, you are considered a chronic case. Do NOT take the homeopathic remedy indicated below. Instead, seek out constitutional homeopathic treatment from your nearest homeopath. See the appendix for the phone number of the National Center for Homeopathy (NCH).

Comments: This is a premiere menopausal depression remedy for women who are passing through this stage in their lives. The depression is usually acute and may come and go for seemingly no reason at all. *Those who need this remedy do not experience anxiety with their depression.* The depression experienced, however, is deeper and darker than any hole you have ever imagined; a black blight sends you spinning into a hellish pit where you think you will never get out of it or resurface.
Physical Symptoms: You may experience a low or nonexistent sex drive coupled with your depression. During depression, the Sepia woman is chilly.
Mentals: Women in the work force who are being forced into balancing not only their jobs but also family obligations, can utilize Sepia in the sense that their depression comes on from being, literally, worked to death. After awhile, trying to be a good parent, provider, and spouse catches up with you, and this is when the hopelessness and detachment begins.

Sepia can intervene beautifully and stop this deteriorating dance and put you back on track and get rid of the depression that is dogging your heels. You want nothing to do with anyone; you no longer want to be a mother, wife, friend, or relative, and you no longer have any feelings toward your family or spouse. You experience a freezing emotional disconnect in your state of depression. Indifference to everything and everyone in your life is a keynote symptom.
Modalities: WORSE – just before or during your menstrual cycle and then all these symptoms are exacerbated to a high degree, from being in cold air (air conditioning included), experiencing dampness, when a cold north wind is blowing, being exposed to snow-laden air or snowfall, and just before a thunderstorm. You dislike any company, morning and evening, performing dull, drudgery housework, or having to work at a boring job, and you feel worse after sex. BETTER – when you are left alone, exercising, dancing, performing an aerobic-type workout, being in a warm bed, consuming cold drinks, taking a cooling shower or bath, and being in the open air.

IRRITABILITY

The hallmark of Sepia's depression is red flagged with tremendous irritability and indifference—even to her own suffering or problems. It is not unusual that when a Sepia woman is in her depression she will, at first, scream and yell at her spouse and children. Later, as she dives deeper into the morass of depression, she no longer has feelings with which to respond and stops reacting to those who place demands on her. The screaming and yelling stop. That is Sepia's indifference—an awful feeling of loss and detachment, a huge void that no one can fill and no one can even begin to understand her struggles.

She can become sharp-tongued, with a biting, hurtful edge to her words. She may suddenly burst into tears and not know why she's crying. As the depression deepens, Sepia feels that she will never recover from it; there is a sense of surrendering to the hopelessness of the situation.

SLEEP

Physical Symptoms: The Sepia woman in depression would much rather sleep during the day. There is a powerful, almost overwhelming urge to take a nap. If she makes it through her day, then she will surely nap in the early evening hours, if she gets a chance. This sets up the cycle, then, of staying up late as a result. She is worse upon awakening in the morning, and sleepily trudges through the morning hours, barely coherent. If she goes to bed late, then inevitably, she awakens at 3 a.m.! And then she can't get back to sleep again.

In deep depression, her sleep may be muddled with agitation, anxiousness, or frequent 'starts' of screaming. And then, she awakes in the morning completely unrefreshed, which only makes her feel worse.

FLOODING DURING MENSES

Physical Symptoms: Your flooding is accompanied by a sensation that your reproductive organs are going to fall out of your vagina. Consequently, you cross your legs repeatedly to prevent this (it won't happen, so don't worry about it). A violent, stitching pain starts in your uterus and moves up to your belly button region. Your menses is either too late and scanty or it is early, with profuse bleeding.

There is a sensation of heaviness in the abdomen and there can be a burning, cramping pain within the uterus. The blood is dark and slimy, and flows more heavily at night, when you are in bed. When you awaken the next morning, there can be stitching symptoms in the vagina that move upward.

HEART PALPITATIONS AND SHORTNESS OF BREATH

Physical Symptoms: Your heart palpitations are violent and can awaken you out of deep sleep. It feels as if there is a pulsating or beating occurring in all of your arteries. Palpitations can be violent and intermittent. Nervousness and stress can also bring on the above symptoms. Sometimes, there can be a single, hard thump of the heart that scares you half to death.

HOT FLASHES

WARNING: Any acute or persistent symptoms such as pain in the chest or pelvic region should be immediately evaluated by a physician. After serious problems are ruled out, you can safely proceed with your non-hormone, non-drug homeopathic treatment.

Physical Symptoms: You may at times have flushes or night sweats followed by a chill. The heat may occur anywhere on your body, with no specific region targeted. Heavy, profuse sweat may occur after the flush.

SKIN ITCHING

Physical Symptoms: For women who have cold-feeling, itchy skin that cracks in the winter. The itching has a burning sensation to it. Formication, or the insects crawling over your skin sensation, is another symptom covered by this remedy.

UNWANTED HAIR

Physical Symptoms: Dark-colored hair can exist anywhere on your body—face, abdomen, thighs, etc. This remedy is of use for hair found in regions that didn't have any before.

URINARY INCONTINENCE

Comments: This is a spectacular menopausal incontinence remedy.
Physical Symptoms: Involuntary dribbling may occur when you are sneezing, laughing, or coughing. Night-time emissions are a keynote. Many times you will be awakened out of sleep and have to go urinate.

VAGINA DRY OR POOR LUBRICATION

Physical Symptoms: You can experience a soreness and redness of the labia region with extreme dry conditions of the vulva and vagina, especially after menses. A greenish yellow discharge, which is smelly and irritating, contributes to the dry condition of your vaginal tract. There can also be an internal and external heat to this region of your body. Pain is in the form of a violent stitching, which moves upward from the vagina, through the uterus, to the belly button region of your abdomen. Intercourse is painful, and is followed with great tenderness and possible bleeding. Soreness and redness exists in the labia region and between your inner thighs. There is a definite loss of interest in sex.

VAGINAL ITCHING

Comments: One of the villains that can cause this itching is candida. Check with your gynecologist to rule out this possibility, before taking a remedy. Other villains can be spermicidal creams, vaginal deodorants, soap used to clean the vaginal area, soap residue on your panties, tampon use, napkin rubbing and irritating the skin, or use of any powder, to name a few. You may be allergic to one of these products and this could be the source of the itching. After you have made sure that none of these are the culprit, then match your symptoms against the remedies presented below.

If you have been diagnosed with candida, it can be dealt with homeopathically; so can the other conditions listed above, but the use of the remedy below is not recommended, if this is the case. Work with your homeopath because the vaginal itching is only a minor symptom to an overall larger picture that needs to be addressed on a constitutional level and not an acute level.

For minor relief from itching, you can use a NON-ALCOHOLIC tincture, such as calendula. Wash three times a day with it. Or, try urtica ointment, and apply lightly to the area where the itching is located. Both products are used only topically and not internally. If there is no relief after 2 days, then stop using it and see your homeopath.
Physical Symptoms: There is redness, swelling, and itching on your inner labia. Pimples may surround the vulva area. There is severe itching of the vulva, and your labia is swollen with moist eruptions. There is a burning pain to this itching. Your vagina may be a reddish brown color.

❁SILICEA❁

Origin: Once this remedy was made from quartz crystal or pure flint, as homeopathic sources. Nowadays, it is made and prepared chemically; the part being used is the silicea.
Comments: Found in abundance in nearly every mineral in the world, including the sand on our beaches, silicea lends a strength and hardness to every rock. Within our body, silicea helps keep our connective tissue strong and is the glue that holds many other structures in our body together, too—like our bones.

This is an excellent remedy to consider for osteoporosis, as well as for women who lack true grit and determination to go after their goals, dreams, or visions. This remedy lends one a backbone of steel and the stick-to-it-iveness to not only meet one's goals, but exceed them. A very powerful, far-embracing homeopathic constitutional remedy in our pharmacopoeia.

CONSTIPATION

Comments: This is an excellent remedy for women who are continually constipated before they have their menses, a keynote of this remedy.

Physical Symptoms: The anal area may feel paralyzed, as if nothing is ever going to move in there again. There is great straining, and a stinging sensation is felt in the rectal area. If a stool tries to pass, your anus instantly closes up in response.

There is another keynote phenomenon with Silicea: This woman has what is known as "bashful stools." This means that the stool will begin to protrude from the rectum, but just as quickly, it will slide back up into the rectum and is not completely expelled. The stool may be consciously kept in the rectum because of the great pain it can cause if it is passed. There can be exceedingly painful spasms of the sphincter, very cutting and cramping in nature.

If you have hemorrhoids, they will always protrude when you have a bowel movement. If there is a fistula, or fissures in your rectum, this is an excellent remedy to help relieve these conditions.

Modalities: WORSE – during the new moon, in the morning, uncovering, lying down, becoming damp, lying on the left side, or becoming cold. BETTER – by being in a warm room, wrapping up the head in the summer (wearing a hat), and during wet or humid weather.

HEARING DIFFICULTY

Physical Symptoms: You hear sounds that are like a report of a pistol going off. A roaring, tinkling, clucking sound, or the fluttering of a bird's wing near your ear, may occur. Deafness is always worse around the full moon, a keynote of this remedy. You are hard of hearing WITHOUT noise in your ears. Large amounts of earwax buildup can happen. Hearing loss may disappear after blowing your nose or hearing a loud noise.

❀SQUILLA MARTIMA❀
(SQUILLA)

Origin: This remedy is made from the squilla onion.

Comments: This plant grows on the shores of the Mediterranean Sea, and has been used since ancient times. The tincture is made from the red variety of what is known locally as the sea onion.

Homeopaths of the nineteenth century noted that people who needed Squilla would have black teeth. Squilla was a cure-all for horses that had hooves that cracked and split, as well.

Modalities: WORSE – in the early morning, with motion, uncovering, drinking cold water causes coughing, exertion, being caught out in cold air, or having to climb stairs. BETTER – from rest, sitting up, or wrapping up warmly.

URINARY INCONTINENCE

Physical Symptoms: The keynote is loss of urine when you cough. The urine will literally spurt out with a cough. It is an excellent remedy for the elderly, in particular.

❀STAPHYSAGRIA❀

Origin: Made from stavesacre, a plant of the Ranunculacea family.

Comments: From Roman times onward, this plant has been used as a purgative to cause vomiting, and has also been made into an ointment to soothe insect bites or stings. This is a pre-

eminent remedy regarding sexual disorders and symptoms involving the reproductive region in both males and females. Nowadays, it is of great use in treating incest and rape survivors.
Mentals: The Staphysagria woman is usually shy, sweet, and sensitive to anything said to her. Her feelings are easily hurt. One of the keynotes of this remedy is that if she becomes angry, she rarely shows it; instead, she represses it. The harbored negative feelings smolder for weeks, months, or even years before resurfacing. She will instead put on a sweet expression, smile a lot, or be exceedingly helpful with no trace of the anger present.
Modalities: WORSE – by pressure, with movement, at night, during the new moon, or from drinking cold water. BETTER – with rest, during the daylight hours, and from warmth placed on that region of the body.

VAGINA DRY AND POOR LUBRICATION

Physical Symptoms: Vaginal dryness includes a supersensitivity to this region, making it impossible for you to have intercourse. There is even painful sensitivity when you sit down, a keynote of this remedy. There can be spasmodic pain and a stinging sensation to your vulva and vagina. Warts in the genital area may also contribute to the overall dryness of this region.

❃SULPHUR❃

Origin: Made from the chemical, flowers of sulphur.
Comments: This is one of the greatest of all skin remedies. Yes, it's the stuff that smells like rotten eggs! A keynote for Sulphur is redness coupled with irritation around any orifice of your body, whether it is your mouth, vagina, or anus.

Oddly enough, in the Middle Ages, this mixture was diluted and used as a gargle and mouthwash. Full strength, it's a strong acid that is considered a hazardous material. But homeopathically, of course, it is safe and effective because none of the actual chemical is left in the remedy.

If you have had a past history of late, short, scanty, or difficult menses, along with thick, black blood, this can be an ideal remedy for you during menopause.
Mentals: This woman is extroverted and optimistic, and cherishes her mental abilities as well as what she knows. She's usually highly educated or dives into life, getting a hands-on education. She can be extremely messy, not only in her clothing, but her home looks like W. C. Fields's office where there are stacks of items teetering everywhere! A tornado coming through her office could not make it look any messier! She will wear the same pair of shoes until they wear out, proclaiming them to be "old friends" and "I just cannot bear to part with them!"

She can be vain about her intelligence, and she loves to discuss the philosophical nature of things—ad infinitum. There's also a rigidity and inflexibility in her belief system and of course, it is the ONLY system that works and she tries to convince everyone else of that, generally through erudite discussions. Why shouldn't we all embrace her all-knowingness!
Modalities: WORSE – the itching worsens when she stands still, washes the area with water (the itching is much worse after she dries off), around 11 a.m., and the heat of the bed at night intensifies the itching problem. The humid, warm weather of summer makes her itching almost intolerable. This region of her body is moist and smelly, anyway, and it's doubly irritated by hot weather. BETTER – her itching is much improved by perspiring via exercise, in the morning hours, by motion, and from dry weather.

HOT FLASHES

WARNING: Any acute or persistent symptoms such as pain in the chest or pelvic region should be immediately evaluated by a physician. After serious problems are ruled out, you can safely proceed with your non-hormone, non-drug homeopathic treatment.

Physical Symptoms: This is an outstanding remedy for any kind of heat condition, which automatically includes hot flashes and night sweats. Sulphur people are hot-blooded in general, and will always wind up with one foot thrust out from under the bedclothes in an attempt to cool off during the night. Her face flushes a bright, beet red, a keynote for this remedy.

Women who need this remedy during menopause are always throwing off sweaters or layers of clothing (while the rest of us may be adding some!). This remedy is for hot flashes that occur during the day, as well as for night sweats. A keynote is burning sensations in the feet during the hot flash or night sweat. Her hot flashes are most prominent at night.

MEMORY LOSS

Physical Symptoms: There is a great loss of memory for names of people, places, or things—particularly for people's names. Mistakes in time are made and you may think it's earlier than it really is. You misplace or cannot find the proper word when you speak. There is difficulty in understanding what someone says. You do not answer the question correctly. Worst of all, you forget what you were going to say.

SKIN ITCHING

Physical Symptoms: For women with cold-feeling skin that cracks easily, especially during the winter. You always have dry, highly sensitive skin, and experience the crawling ants sensation (formication) over it. The itching increases tenfold after a bath or shower.
Modalities: WORSE – itching is made worse by scratching the area or taking a bath or shower, at night, in bed (heat makes the itching much worse), in the morning, or being out in cold air.

VAGINAL ITCHING

Comments: One of the villains that can cause this itching is candida. Check with your gynecologist to rule out this possibility, before taking a remedy. Other villains can be spermicidal creams, vaginal deodorants, soap used to clean the vaginal area, soap residue on your panties, tampon use, napkin rubbing and irritating the skin, or use of any powder, to name a few. You may be allergic to one of these products and this could be the source of the itching. After you have made sure none of these are the culprit, then match your symptoms against the remedies presented below.

If you have been diagnosed with candida, it can be dealt with homeopathically; so can the other conditions listed above, but the use of the remedy below is not recommended, if this is the case. Work with your homeopath because the vaginal itching is only a minor symptom to an overall larger picture that needs to be addressed on a constitutional level and not an acute level.

For minor relief from itching, you can use a NON-ALCOHOLIC tincture, such as calendula. Wash three times a day with it. Or, try urtica ointment, and apply lightly to the area where the itching is located. Both products are used only topically and not internally. If there is no relief after 2 days, then stop using it and see your homeopath.

Physical Symptoms: The Sulphur candidate has a red circle around her vagina or her vulva is a bright red color. The skin can become so raw that it burns, cracks, and bleeds. There is almost always a burning sensation to it. And it can become so bad that she cannot bear to sit still. This itching includes the clitoris as well as the vaginal area. There may be pimples around the vulva area along with a papular or reddish colored rash.

VARICOSE VEINS

Comments: This remedy is often used when varicose veins begin to rupture and bleed. Itching, burning, and aching always accompany this situation.
Physical Symptoms: There may be blue spots around your ankle. Itching is one of the keynotes of this remedy. There is soreness and a stitching pain to the varicosity. There may be blue spots and smaller varicose veins on the legs themselves (other than just around the ankle).

❁SULPHURICUM ACIDUM❁

(SULPH. AC.)

Origin: This remedy is made from sulphuric acid, which is also known as vitriol.
Comments: During the Middle Ages, vitriol was a favorite of the alchemists. When diluted, it was used widely as a treatment for cancer, venereal ulcers, gum disease, diphtheria, and other skin conditions—as well as for mouthwash! It was also known as the "mineral lemonade" and was given to a person who was known to have lead poisoning.

HOT FLASHES

WARNING: Any acute or persistent symptoms such as pain in the chest or pelvic region should be immediately evaluated by a physician. After serious problems are ruled out, you can safely proceed with your non-hormone, non-drug homeopathic treatment.

Physical Symptoms: For women whose hot flashes are followed by perspiration (a clammy, sticky type of sweat) and trembling. This is an inner trembling from the center of the body, a shaking sensation. It is not an external trembling of the hands. There are more hot flashes at night than during the day. You may flush a deep, red color in the facial region only.
Modalities: WORSE – in the evening, after exercise (particularly aerobic or cardiovascular exercise), and if you are feeling more fatigued than usual after your daily activities.

❁TARENTULA HISPANIA❁

Origin: Made from the wolf or Spanish spider, this is a powerful reproductive remedy in many ways. Its Latin name is Lycosa tarentula.
Comments: Do not confuse the Latin name for the wolf spider with the tarantula (a Southwest desert dweller). This wolf spider remedy comes from an insect found in Tarentum, Italy! It has a fascinating history in Italy because it was legend that if you were bitten by the wolf spider, "tarantism" would affect you. Once bitten, you would dance wildly, shrieking and gesticulating, and move with maniacal behavior, or you would fall into the pit of melancholia. This was how the wolf spider got its reputation!

The Tarentula woman has an interesting keynote: she gets highly agitated or nervous around the colors black, green, or red. She will not wear these colors and usually has a disgust of them.

She is, by nature, a highly sexed individual, sometimes bordering on nymphomania. Having intercourse does not relieve her appetite for sex. Another keynote is that she's able to expel gas or flatulence from her vagina. If she sits or lies down, her legs are constantly jerking or twitching; she cannot keep her legs still for any amount of time.
Mentals: The woman who fits this picture is constantly on the go, mobile, and with extreme restlessness. Emotionally, she is a mass of contradictions—one moment joyful, the next dashed into the depths of sadness.
Modalities: WORSE – she's highly annoyed by sad events or news, by wet, cold, weather, and by physical contact with the area where the itching or symptoms are located. Noise of any kind aggravates her greatly at night and there is great dryness to the skin in the affected area. BETTER – her symptoms always improve with music that has a strong beat or rhythm to it (think of bass guitars and heavy drum beats) and by walking outdoors, providing it's not cold weather.

VAGINAL ITCHING

Comments: One of the villains that can cause this itching is candida. Check with your gynecologist to rule out this possibility, before taking a remedy. Other villains can be spermicidal creams, vaginal deodorants, soap used to clean the vaginal area, soap residue on your panties, tampon use, napkin rubbing and irritating the skin, or use of any powder, to name a few. You may be allergic to one of these products and this could be the source of the itching. After you have made sure that none of these are the culprit, then match your symptoms against the remedies presented below.

If you have been diagnosed with candida, it can be dealt with homeopathically; so can the other conditions listed above, but the use of the remedy below is not recommended, if this is the case. Work with your homeopath because the vaginal itching is only a minor symptom to an overall larger picture that needs to be addressed on a constitutional level and not an acute level.

For minor relief from itching, you can use a NON-ALCOHOLIC tincture, such as calendula. Wash three times a day with it. Or, try urtica ointment, and apply lightly to the area where the itching is located. Both products are used only topically and not internally. If there is no relief after 2 days, then stop using it and see your homeopath.
Physical Symptoms: Itching symptoms include formication (the sensation of ants crawling over one's skin), and intense, unbearable itching that extends up into the vagina. Your vulva is hot, dry, and itchy.

❁THLASPI BURSA PASTORIS❁

(Thlaspi)

Origin: Made from shepherd's purse; this lowly herb is considered a weed by many a gardener, but is a boon to the herbalist and homeopath.
Comments: Thlaspi is a premier uterine remedy that has many spheres of action, among them prolapsed uterine conditions, uterine hemorrhage (with cramps and clots), and fibroids. Herbalists of old used it to stop bleeding in any part of the body. The shape of the seeds even looks like a uterus, and it was used in mother tincture form to stop uterine hemorrhages.

UTERINE FIBROIDS

Physical Symptoms: Uterine hemorrhage that has profuse, dark-colored blood that is clotted. There is severe pain (colic type) in the abdominal region, which may cause vomiting. This type of bleeding just won't stop. Your menses may be extremely light the first day, and the bleeding comes on slowly and gradually grows worse until the second day; there is hemorrhaging with clots—this condition has been reported to last up to 15 days if not stopped homeopathically or via gynecological procedures. Your menses may be fine one month, but the next month, it is like the above symptoms, so there is a periodicity to it.

Vaginal discharge is smelly, dark, and bloody looking before and after the menses. The cramping is so severe that you may feel better if you bend over.

Modalities: WORSE – the bleeding is always worse in the morning. The cramping pain is felt in the uterine area, but there may be an overall feeling of being bruised (bruising as if you were in a major car accident). There can be a sensation of needles or electrical shock felt from your sternum down to your belly button.

VAGINAL ITCHING

Comments: One of the villains that can cause this itching is candida. Check with your gynecologist to rule out this possibility, before taking a remedy. Other villains can be spermicidal creams, vaginal deodorants, soap used to clean the vaginal area, soap residue on your panties, tampon use, napkin rubbing and irritating the skin, or use of any powder, to name a few. You may be allergic to one of these products and this could be the source of the itching. After you have made sure that none of these are the culprit, then match your symptoms against the remedies presented below.

If you have been diagnosed with candida, it can be dealt with homeopathically; so can the other conditions listed above, but the use of the remedy below is not recommended, if this is the case. Work with your homeopath because the vaginal itching is only a minor symptom to an overall larger picture which needs to be addressed on a constitutional level and not an acute level.

For minor relief from itching, you can use a NON-ALCOHOLIC tincture, such as calendula. Wash three times a day with it. Or, try urtica ointment, and apply lightly to the area where the itching is located. Both products are used only topically and not internally. If there is no relief after 2 days, then stop using it and see your homeopath.

Physical Symptoms: The discharge from your vagina produces itching, a keynote to use this remedy.

❀THUJA OCCIDENTALIS❀
(THUJA)

Origin: This remedy is made from the cedar tree or the arbor vitae. The parts used are the fresh green twigs.

Comments: Another general, all-around remedy for endocrine disorders.

Mentals: For the woman with a chameleon type of personality—who strives to fit into every situation instead of standing out in the crowd.

UNWANTED HAIR

Physical Symptoms: This remedy is for hair in unwanted places anywhere on your body.

❀USTILAGO MAYDIS❀
(USTILAGO)

Origin: Made from corn smut.
Comments: This is a premier homeopathic remedy for hemorrhaging in women, whether it be during their menstrual cycle, after their pregnancy, or during the menopause phase of life. The smut is actually a fungus that grows on the corn. One observant homeopath saw that cows that ate grass sprinkled with smut would abort their calves. Further, he saw that these unlucky bovines shed their hair and sometimes, even their teeth fell out!

This also occurred in humans unlucky enough to unknowingly consume the corn smut. Hens who ate the smut laid eggs without shells around them, and mules would lose their hooves as a result of ingesting smut-laden grass.

There are some important keynotes to this remedy: loss of hair (on your head as well as any other part of your body), and loss of your fingernails or toenails. You can experience pain up under the left breast, in the rib cage area between your periods. (If you stop wearing your bra for 2 weeks, this pain will disappear).

This remedy is excellent when nothing else seems to stop the hemorrhaging or flooding. The bleeding just goes on and on, without letting up.
Modalities: WORSE – with the least movement, which increases hemorrhaging, turning over in bed, rising, or walking. Warm rooms make you feel faint. Riding in a car or any type of vehicle also aggravates your bleeding.

FLOODING DURING MENSES

Physical Symptoms: Your menses comes and goes, almost in a vicarious fashion. The ovaries will burn with pain, particularly the left one. There is a sensation of pressure across the pelvic region. With the least movement, your flooding increases. It is bright red blood, partially clotted, or there is oozing of dark blood which is clotted, but it forms in dark strings. It is a passive type of bleeding.

❀VERATRUM ALBUM❀
(VERATRUM)

Origin: Made from a plant known as white hellebore that grows in the mountains of Europe.
Comments: Hippocrates cured a case of Asiatic cholera with this herb. The fresh root is used. At one time white hellebore was also used to treat epilepsy, mania, and depression. Hahnemann proved this herb between 1826 and 1830, for use as a homeopathic remedy. Even as an herb, this plant is highly poisonous—even when dried! However, in the homeopathic state, it is harmless. The root reminds me of a many-legged spider with light brown tentacles, or perhaps a many-armed octopus!

DIARRHEA

Comments: This is a well-known diarrhea remedy when there is a picture of total collapse characterized by a dangerously high loss of electrolytes from the diarrhea.
Physical Symptoms: Cramping pain extends into all of your extremities, including your abdomen. There, the pain is knotting and colicky and you may feel faint, or lose consciousness. In such a case, get to your doctor or emergency room and take this remedy on the way there—providing your symptoms fit this remedy.

Causes for this type of diarrhea are emotional excitement or fright, drinking cold liquids on a hot day, or experiencing hot weather in general. There is a cold feeling in the abdomen and stomach region, along with a sinking or empty feeling. You always experience severe pain in the abdomen before the attack of diarrhea. It feels as if your intestines were being twisted in two, the pain is so great. There is violent release of gas, and if held in too long, it is hard to expel.

During the evacuation, you break out in a cold sweat, become nauseated (and may vomit), and experience a burning sensation in the anus. Afterward, you look pale, shiver, and feel anxious. You may FAINT during the evacuation, a keynote symptom.

The stools are shaped like flat, thin ribbons. They are watery, thin, green, odorless, or colorless ("rice water"). They may appear to be flaky green stools that remind you of spinach. Or you will have large, massive amounts of diarrhea, with intense straining that leaves you exhausted and in a cold sweat afterward.

Stools can also be black, fermented, flatulent, and noisy with a spluttering explosion, known as "projectile" diarrhea. A keynote is involuntary diarrhea while urinating. The "attack" of diarrhea hits like lightning and you must move quickly to get to the bathroom in time or else.

Modalities: WORSE – at night, during cold, wet weather, from exertion, consuming cold drinks, experiencing a change in the weather, or before and during your menses. You do not want your abdomen touched or any pressure applied to that region at all. BETTER – from walking, warmth being applied to your abdomen, warmth in general (wrapping up in a blanket or using a heating pad), consuming hot drinks, lying down, eating meat, or drinking some milk.

❁XANTHOXYLUM❁

Origin: Derived from the prickly ash.

Comments: This tree was also known as the "toothache tree." Its roots were used by Native Americans for ulcers, colic, and other painful conditions. The bark was used to relieve toothache. Chew it a while, and the pain would disappear. Prickly ash is considered a large shrub, rather than a tree, and grows in the northeastern United States.

This remedy is recommended for women whose typology is thin and nervous, and whose menstrual history includes pain behind and down the legs. Menstrual blood was often thick and black, along with severe ovarian pain. (To rule out any serious causes of pain, however, it's a good idea to see your physician.)

HOT FLASHES

WARNING: Any acute or persistent symptoms such as pain in the chest or pelvic region should be immediately evaluated by a physician. After serious problems are ruled out, you can safely proceed with your non-hormone, non-drug homeopathic treatment.

Physical Symptoms: You may wake up at night, particularly around 4 a.m., your face red and hot feeling, with pain in your heart region that makes you go pale—a keynote of this remedy. Your face may feel flushed or feverish. The flush may have a prickly, almost electric feeling to it as it spreads.

❀ZINCUM METALLICUM❀
(ZINCUM)

Origin: Made from a blue-white metal; the source is zinc sulfide.

Comments: Found in the United States and throughout Asia, Australia, and South America, this white metal is homeopathically potentized. It is a trace mineral found in our bodies that is essential for growth. Insulin, a hormone in our body, also needs a good supply of zinc. From a traditional medical application, zinc is used topically as an ointment for ulcers and fissures. From a mineral supplement viewpoint, it is used and taken orally for many conditions, such as slow sexual growth (from puberty to adulthood), convulsions, and neuralgia.

MEMORY LOSS

Physical Symptoms: You repeat a question before answering it—a keynote for this remedy. Many times, you will forget what you have accomplished during the day. Difficulty in grasping concepts and an absence of ideas.

APPENDICES

A. PROFESSIONAL HOMEOPATHIC ORGANIZATIONS

B. HOMEOPATHIC COURSES

C. HOMEOPATHIC "NATURAL TRANSITIONS" KIT

D. HOMEOPATHIC COMPUTER SOFTWARE

E. HOMEOPATHIC JOURNALS

F. RECOMMENDED READING ON HOMEOPATHY

G. NATURAL FLOWER AND GEM ESSENCES CATALOG

H. JOIN ATHENA—THE ALTERNATIVE MEDICINE LIST

I. SEMINARS BY EILEEN NAUMAN

J. BOOKS BY EILEEN NAUMAN

APPENDIX A

PROFESSIONAL HOMEOPATHIC ORGANIZATIONS

To find a homeopath near you:

1. The National Center for Homeopathy (NCH), 801 North Fairfax St., Suite 306, Alexandria, VA 22314. Phone: (703) 548-7790. Brochures and a directory of homeopaths in the United States and Canada for sale at a reasonable price. The Net address to the directory is http://healthy.net/nch/find.htm. Homeopathic books for sale. Summer courses available for consumers and professionals. Information on homeopathic study groups in the United States. Monthly newsletter available to members.

2. Classical homeopaths are listed by state in the United States at http://homeopathy-cures.com. Canadian resources as well.

3. The Council for Homeopathic Certification, Directory of Practitioners, 1709 Seabright Avenue, Santa Cruz, CA 95062.

APPENDIX B
HOMEOPATHIC COURSES

The British Institute of Homeopathy, Registrar, 520 Washington Blvd., Suite 423, Marina Del Rey, CA 90292. Phone: (310) 306-5408. Fax: (310) 827-5766.

The British Institute of Homeopathy, Cygnet House, Market Square, Staines, Middlesex TW18 4RH, England. Phone (if calling from the U.S.): 011-441-784-440-467. Fax: 011-441-784-449-887.

APPENDIX C

HOMEOPATHIC "NATURAL TRANSITIONS" KIT

This kit is available through one of the finest homeopathic pharmacies in the United States, the Hahnemann Pharmacy. It has been especially created to include most major menopausal homeopathic remedies written about in this book. It has 50 remedies in the 2-dram size, and is $119.95, plus shipping and handling.

This pharmacy also sells other types of kits (the Traveler's Kit for acute epidemics for Eileen's book, *Poisons That Heal*, and the Advanced First Aid Kit for her book, *Help! And Homeopathy*), as well as single remedies. Ask for their free catalog.

Hahnemann Pharmacy, Michael Quinn, R.Ph., 1940 4th Street, San Rafael, CA 94901. Mail order only. Toll free number to order: 1-888-427-6422.

E-mail: MQREMMAKER@aol.com

Web address: http://www.hahnemannlabs.com

APPENDIX D
HOMEOPATHIC COMPUTER SOFTWARE

CARA Software, Miccant Ltd., 14 Mulberry Close, West Bridgford, Nottingham, England NG2 7SS. Phone/Fax: (calling from the U.S.) 011-44-115-945-5289.

CARA HELP!, software based on Eileen's book, *Help! And Homeopathy*, is for first aid and emergency medicine and how to use specific homeopathic remedies for such situations. They also have many other types of homeopathic software available. If anywhere in the world, other than the U.S. and Canada, Miccant Ltd., 14 Mulberry Close, West Bridgford, Nottingham, England NG2 7SS. Phone/Fax: (calling from the U.S.) 011-44-115-945-5289. E-mail: dwitko@miccant.co.uk. Website: http://www.miccant.co.uk.

APPENDIX E
HOMEOPATHIC JOURNALS

New England Journal of Homeopathy, 356 Middle St., Amherst, MA 01002. Published quarterly. $40.00 USA, $45.00 Canada and Mexico and $55.00 outside of the USA.

Simillimum, The Journal of the Homeopathic Academy of Naturopathic Physicians, HANP, PO Box 69565, Portland, OR 97201. Quarterly, $35.00 a year in U.S., $40.00 Canada and Mexico, $45.00 outside North America.

APPENDIX F
RECOMMENDED READING ON HOMEOPATHY

BEGINNERS:

1. *Homeopathic Medicine Today*, Trevor M. Cook, Keats Publishing, Inc., Connecticut, 1989.
2. *Homeopathic Medicine at Home*, M. B.. Panos, MD and J. Heimlich, J. P. Tarcher, Inc., Los Angeles, CA, 1980.
3. *The Family Guide to Homeopathy*, Dr. Andrew Lockie, Simon & Schuester/Fireside books, New York, 1989.
4. *Women Ripening through the Menopause*, Melissa Assilem, MNCHM, RSHom, FBIH, Idolatry Ink Publisher, Berkeley, CA 1996.
5. *Homeopathic Methodology–Repertory–Casetaking, and Case Analysis*, Todd Rowe, MD(H), North Atlantic Books, Berkeley, CA, 1999.

ADVANCED HOMEOPATHY:

1. *Divided Legacy*, Harris L. Coulter, North Atlantic Books, Berkeley, CA, 1973.
2. *Organon of Medicine* (6th edition), Samuel Hahnemann, J. P. Tarcher, Inc., Los Angeles, CA, 1982.
3. *Homeopathic Medical Repertory*, Robin Murphy, ND, Hahnemann Academy of North America, Colorado, 1993.
4. *The Science of Homeopathy*, G. Vithoulkas, Grove Press, New York, 1980.

SERIOUS STUDY OF HOMEOPATHY:

1. *Desktop Guide to Keynotes and Confirmatory Symptoms*, Roger L. Morrison, MD, Hahnemann Clinic Publishing, California, 1993.
2. *Psyche and Substance*, Edward C. Whitmont, MD, North Atlantic Books, California, 1982.
3. *The Alchemy of Healing Psyche and Soma*, Edward C. Whitmont, MD, North Atlantic Books, California, 1993.
4. *A Dictionary of Practical Materia Medica*, John Henry Clarke, MD, Vols. 1–3, Jain Publishers Pvt. Ltd., New Delhi, India, 1984.
5. *Homeopathy in Paediatric Practice*, Hedwig Imhauser, MD, Haug Publishers, Heidelberg, Germany, 1988.
6. *Homeopathic Medica Viva, Vols. 1–3*, G. Vithoulkas, Health and Habitat, Mill Valley, California, 1992.

APPENDIX G

NATURAL FLOWER AND GEM ESSENCES: HOW TO ORDER

To order a free catalog detailing and listing 100 flower and gem essences, please write: Blue Turtle Publishing, PO Box 2513, Cottonwood, AZ 86326. Or Email: docbones@sedona.net

APPENDIX H

JOIN ATHENA—THE ALTERNATIVE MEDICINE LIST

You are invited to be one of our many subscribers. Weekly topics are rotated on a bi-monthly schedule. Topics include homeopathy, flower and gem essence proving information, herbs, soul recovery and extraction (a healing method), metaphysics and spirituality, and medical astrology. Free articles are given each week on one of these topics. Visit our Library of Health and find educational health information for yourself and your pet. Eileen Nauman is the owner of this list and frequently fields questions from her women subscribers on women's health issues, including menopause. Please join us. To subscribe, go to **www.medicinegarden.com** and point/click on Athena Email.

APPENDIX I

SEMINARS BY EILEEN NAUMAN

Eileen gives 5-day seminars in Sedona, Arizona on a yearly or bi-yearly basis on the following topics:

1. Flower and Gem essence training; Levels 1, 2, and 3
2. Beginning Medical Astrology

If you have an interest in these topics, simply go to her website, www.medicinegarden.com, and point/click on the seminar and workshop heading. If not on the Internet, write to her for a brochure at Blue Turtle Publishing, PO Box 2513, Cottonwood, Arizona 86326.

APPENDIX J

BOOKS BY EILEEN NAUMAN

HOMEOPATHY

Beauty in Bloom: Homeopathy to Support Menopause, $24.95, Blue Turtle Publishing, Cottonwood, AZ, 1999.

HELP! and Homeopathy, $16.95, Blue Turtle Publishing, Cottonwood, AZ, 1998.

NATIVE AMERICAN

Soul Recovery and Extraction, $9.95, Blue Turtle Publishing, Cottonwood, AZ, 1985.

Path of the Mystic, $11.95, Light Technology, Sedona, AZ, 1996.

Colored Stones and Healing, $4.95, Blue Turtle Publishing, Cottonwood, AZ, 1988.

ASTROLOGY

Medical Astrology, $29.95, Blue Turtle Publishing, Cottonwood, AZ, 1980.

GLOSSARY

Acute Illness: A set of symptoms or a complaint that has a beginning, middle, and end to it; usually 3 weeks or less in duration. An example would be a cold or flu. However, acute ailments can kill, such as Ebola, which kills in 10 days.

Agoraphobia: Fear of being out in open spaces. The Greek word, "agora," means public square and "phobia" means fear. Many times agoraphobia is confused with claustrophobia (fear of enclosed spaces, such as elevators, etc.). A woman with agoraphobia will remain within her home, for fear of stepping out into the wide open spaces of her yard or neighborhood block, as an example.

Alopecia: Losing one's hair. Baldness.

Anorexia Nervosa: Losing one's appetite. Usually seen in younger women, who have an extreme aversion to eating.

Anxiety Attack: A feeling of worry or panic that may be accompanied by physical symptoms such as perspiration, heart palpitations, pain, suffocating, or a lump in the throat. Usually there is a combination of psychological as well as physical symptoms to anxiety attacks. Also known as panic attacks.

Bulimia: Known as canine hunger, this is the inability to stop eating or to control one's appetite.

Candida (Candidiasis): A yeast infection that inflames one's mouth, intestinal tract, or vagina. The culprit is Candida albicans, and a nosode of this miserable set of symptoms can cure it.

Case Taking: A step-by-step questioning by the homeopath of the client about their unique set of symptoms. Generally speaking, it takes at least an hour to take a case, perhaps up to 3 hours, depending on the individual's symptoms. Also known as constitutional homeopathic treatment. One remedy is found to closely match your set of symptoms, and this is given one time only. There is generally a 4 to 6 week waiting period, and then you will see your homeopath, who will at that time retake your case. This is known as practicing classically—one remedy, one time and then wait. Six-week check-ins are normal, and you may or may not receive another dose of your remedy, depending on many criteria that your homeopath must determine at that time. Treatment will last at least a year, up to 3 years, to cure a set of symptoms.

Cell Salts (Schuessler's): Twelve mineral compounds that are homeopathic remedies that were created and used by Dr. W. H. Schuessler in the 1870s. He saw that poor diet and malnutrition were part of the reason for disease, and his 12 cell salts addressed this issue on the cellular level, where all of these nutrients were needed to keep a cell healthy and strong. They are part of our modern-day pharmacopoeia. They should NEVER be taken unless authorized by your homeopath.

Chief Complaint: The most important complaint of the client to the homeopath taking the case.

Chilblains: If you have ever gotten your fingers or toes frostbit, this is chilblains—there is redness and pain experienced due to cold.

Chronic Illness: A set of symptoms or a complaint that is ongoing for more than 3 weeks, and although there may have been a beginning, there may be no middle or end in sight. Chronic illness requires a homeopathic case to be taken and should never be treated with acute homeopathic remedies or means. This is a deep-seated illness in the Vital Force of a human being that can, in some cases, cause death. Examples are cancer, multiple sclerosis, asthma, diabetes, and heart disease.

Classical Homeopathy: Giving one remedy, one time to the client and waiting 4 to 6 weeks until the check-up time; it is also known as a unicist approach to homeopathy. The homeopaths in the directory from the National Center for Homeopathy are all classically trained homeopaths, and are recommended. For chronic ailments, always get to a classically trained homeopath. Do NOT take combination tablets, as this can create more harm than good in your Vital Force and will not necessarily cure your dis-ease as a classically given remedy can.

Climacteric: A phase of our lives when our ovaries and endocrine systems go through many changes. This is a period of roughly 20 years, including the menopause years. Often, these two separate functions are combined, but they are individual. The climacteric usually occurs at age 40 through 60.

Combination Therapy: Also known as mixology, pluralistic therapy, and polypharmacy. The opposite to treatment done classically or from a unicist mode, which is one remedy, one time and then wait. Combination therapy is the use of more than one homeopathic remedy in a tablet (usually 4 to 12 homeopathic remedies), usually in low potency form, placed into a tablet to address a specific condition in the body, such as a cold or flu. This type of treatment is NOT recommended. To take a combination remedy for a long-term set of symptoms or ailment is asking for problems (such as proving—you will get your old symptoms back worse than when you had them originally!). See your homeopath, instead. Do not self-treat with combination remedies. See: Classical Homeopathy.

Constitutional Homeopathic Treatment: See: Case Taking.

Constitutional Remedy: There are 60 homeopathic remedies out of about 4,000 worldwide that have deep-acting applicability and wide-reaching abilities to put us back into a state of health. These remedies are known as constitutionals or polycrests.

Hering's Laws of Cure: Healing occurs in a natural order: from the most important organs of our body to the least important (heart and brain to the skin), from the top of the head downward to the feet, and re-experiencing illness or sets of symptoms from the most recent going back chronologically to when you were a baby. I call this retracing. For example, you're 50 now, and at 45 you broke your foot, at 30 you had ulcers, and at 15, you had terrible acne. Taking a homeopathic remedy will stimulate your body, over a period of time, to 'clear out' any residue from any of these conditions that are left in the memory of your body. Perhaps, 6 days after taking a constitutional remedy, you might have a mild aching in the foot you broke, and then a month later, your stomach symptoms of the ulcer come back (not for as long and not as bad as the first time you had ulcers), and then perhaps many more months later, your face will break out in the acne you had at age 15. All of these symptoms will appear and then disappear—for good—once they are pushed out by the Vital Force with the help of the homeopathic remedy—so don't despair! Any old condition will come and go, quite quickly.

Homeopathic Consultation: See: Case Taking.

Homeopathic Dentist: Dentists who have learned homeopathy use remedies before and after dental surgery, to relieve toothaches and treat certain mouth disorders.

Homeopathic Veterinarians: The use of homeopathic remedies to treat large and small animals in the same way as we treat humans—through observation of symptoms.

Homeopathic Remedies: There are 1,400 remedies approved for use by the FDA in the United States, and about 4,000 worldwide, that are made from the vegetable, animal, and mineral kingdoms. They are made in homeopathic pharmacies that have been approved by the FDA.

Hot Flash: A symptom of menopause. Scientists and doctors aren't sure what causes it, but it is harmless and will eventually disappear after menopause (a 2 to 5 year cycle).

Law of Similars: Samuel Hahnemann's principal of *simmila similibus curentur*—like cures like—that is the foundation of all homeopathic principles. Example: if stung by a bee, homeopathically we would take your case, note the symptoms, and match it to the closest remedy that had the same symptoms and give it to you; most likely, Apis Mellifica, crushed honeybee. Your symptoms would disappear in minutes!

Limits of Homeopathic Treatment: Not every dis-ease can be treated homeopathically. Sometimes, it has to do with the strength of a person's Vital Force—the less there is of it, the less energy it has with which to react to a homeopathic remedy given to you. Or, your age may be a deterrent. For instance, it's easier to treat babies and children because their bodies haven't taken the wear and tear that our older ones have. In some cases, age or the erosion of our Vital Force from disease may disallow homeopathic treatment. Similarly, those with a psychosis, such as schizophrenia, are almost impossible to treat and cure. Only your homeopath will be able to evaluate your potential to be treated with a homeopathic remedy. Homeopathy cannot 'fix' any organ or system in the body that is already dead. For example, in a heart attack, some of the muscle of the heart dies. Homeopathic treatment cannot resurrect the dead muscle. It can, however, work to prevent another heart attack. Similarly, it cannot resurrect scarred liver tissue, but it can work to support full functioning of what is left of your liver.

Materia Medica: A compilation of symptoms ranging from characteristics to properties for each homeopathic remedy. The book(s) that hold this information are known as materia medicas—medical material.

Menopause: The ceasing of a woman's menstrual cycle. You are considered to be in menopause if you have not had a period in one year. Menopause, the cessation of our menstrual cycle, takes between 2 and 5 years, and peri-menopause begins at age 40–49, with menopause from 49–54, roughly speaking. A number of different symptoms occur to a woman, such as hot flashes, as an example, but not all women get them. Pre-menopause means before the onset of peri-menopausal symptoms.

Modalities: Conditions that make your symptoms better or worse; they can include time of day, temperature, weather conditions, and so forth. For example, your hot flashes are better in fresh air than in a stuffy, hot room. The modalities here are better fresh air and worse stuffy room.

Nosode: A homeopathic remedy made from the disease material, then potentized and given to a person who has similar symptoms. For example, a woman with a vaginal yeast infection could take the homeopathic nosode, Candida Albicans, and cure her problem—once and for all!

Panic Attacks: See: Anxiety Attack.

Potency or Potentization: The way a homeopathic remedy is made. Repeated dilutions of the original substance are successed (by repeatedly shaking or jarring the solution). The original substance of the remedy is transformed or "dynamized" into an energy representing the original substance.

Provers or Proving: To discover the properties of a homeopathic remedy, volunteers in good health will take a remedy and keep a detailed diary of any spiritual, mental, emotional, and physical symptoms it creates in them. After a certain period of time, the diaries of the provers are collected and the rubrics or symptoms are noted and compiled. This information is then placed into our repertory as well as our materia medica. For example, I recently took part in a proving on wolf's milk, Lac Lupus. There were 20 volunteer provers, in good health, who maintained a diary for 2 weeks while on the remedy. Melissa Assilem, who headed this proving project, then collected the information and is writing a book on it. Eventually, this remedy will become available for use to people who exhibit Lac Lupus symptoms.

Repertory: A homeopathic index that contains, in detail, all the symptoms and attributes of the many homeopathic remedies in our pharmacopoeia. These rubrics or symptoms were found by doing provings on healthy people who took the homeopathic substance and noted, in detail, the symptoms that manifested in them. These rubrics were then placed into a repertory.

Rubric: Another word for a symptom. For example, my head feels like it's going to burst open. That is a rubric or symptom.

Simillimum: Applying the Law of Similars (like cures like); although there may be several remedies that closely approximate your symptom picture, there is one that most closely fits better than the others. This is the simillimum.

Symptom: A person's reactional expression mode of their body to get rid of a dis-ease. The homeopath collects all of the symptoms during case-taking to determine which homeopathic remedy is best to treat them and effect cure. See: Rubric.

Tincture: Also known as a "mother" tincture. A liquid vegetal extract that is placed in a solution of alcohol. For example, tincture of hydrangea is the root of the hydrangea bush, which has been washed off, macerated and shredded, and placed in alcohol. The alcohol then leaches out the chemicals and nutrients of the root. The root is allowed to sit for a specified period of time and is strained off; what is left is the mother tincture.

Typology: Classification of a person's personality and psychological characteristics, as well as the color of their hair, eyes, and skin, and their build. Typology was very popular in the early 1900s, but has since been relegated to a minor observation and more emphasis is now placed on a person's symptoms. For example, a woman who was blond haired, blue-eyed, and had a fair English complexion would be typed as a Pulsatilla constitutional remedy.

Vaginismus: The spasmodic contraction of the vagina, which can make intercourse painful or impossible.

Vital Force: The unseen energy that is the foundation of a person's health. In Chinese medicine, it is known as "chi." Our Western counterpart would get wordy and refer to it as our immunological defense mechanism!

BIBLIOGRAPHY

Al-Azzawi, F. Endocrinological aspects of menopause. *British Medical Bulletin* 48 (2), 262–275, 1992.

Allen, S.H. Primary osteoporosis. Methods to combat bone loss that accompanies aging. *Postgraduate Medicine* 93 (8), 43–46, 49–50, 53–55, June 1993.

Aloia, J.F., et al. The influence of menopause and hormonal replacement therapy on body cell mass and body fat. *American Journal of Obstetrics & Gynecology*, March 1995, pp. 896–900.

Andrews, W.C., MD. The transitional years and beyond. *Obstetrics & Gynecology* 85 (1), 1–5, 1995.

Archer, D.F., MD, et al. Bleeding patterns in postmenopausal women taking continuous combined or sequential regimens of conjugated estrogens with medroxprogesterone acetate. *Obstetrics & Gynecology* 83 (5), Part 1, May 1994.

Armamento-Villareal, R., and Civitelli, R. Estrogen action on the bone mass of postmenopausal women is dependent on body mass and initial bone density. *Journal of Clinical Endocrinology and Metabolism* 80 (3), 776–782, 1995.

Axel, R. The molecular logic of smell. *Scientific American*, October 1995.

Ballinger, C.B. Psychiatric aspects of the menopause. *British Journal of Psychiatry* 156, 773–787, 1990.

Barlow, D.H. Hormone replacement therapy and other menopause associated conditions. *British Medical Bulletin* 48 (2), 356–367, 1992.

Barrett-Connor, E. Hormone replacement and cancer. *British Medical Bulletin* 48 (2), 345–355, 1992.

Barrett-Connor, E. Estrogen and estrogen-progesterone replacement: Therapy and cardiovascular diseases. *American Journal of Medicine* 95 (5A), 405–435, 1993.

Barrett-Connor, E. and Kritz-Silverstein, D. Estrogen replacement therapy and cognitive function in older women. *Journal of the American Medical Association* 269 (20), 2637–2641, 1993.

Beard, M., MD and Curtis, L., MD. *Menopause and the Years Ahead.* Tucson, Arizona: Fisher Books, 1991.

Beattie, J.H. and Peace, H.S. The influence of a low-boron diet and boron supplementation on bone, major mineral and sex steroid metabolism in postmenopausal women. *British Journal of Nutrition* 69, 871–884, 1993.

Berkow, R., MD, Ed-in-Chief. *The Merck Manual, 16th Edition.* Rahway, NJ: Merck Research Labs, 1992.

Bernhard, L.A. and Sheppard, L. Health, symptoms, self-care, and dyadic adjustment in menopausal women. *Journal of Obstetric, Gynecologic, & Neonatal Nursing* 22 (5), 456–461, 1993.

Bernstein, L., et al. Relationship of hormone use to cancer risk. *Monographs of the National Cancer Institute* 12, 137–147, 1992.

Berkow, R., MD. *The Merck Manual of Diagnosis and Therapy.* Rahway, NJ: Merck Research Laboratories, 1992.

Bloomfield, S.A., et al. Non-weightbearing exercises may increase lumbar spine bone mineral density in healthy postmenopausal women. *American Journal of Physical Medicine & Rehabilitation* 72 (4), 204–209, August, 1993.

Boericke, William. *Boericke's Materia Medica and Repertory*, 9th ed. Philadelphia, PA: Boericke & Runyon, 1927.

Bolognia, J.L. Dermatologic and cosmetic concerns of the older woman. *Clinics in Geriatric Medicine* 9 (1), 209–229, February, 1993.

Boman, K. et al. The influence of progesterone and androgens on the growth of endometrial carcinoma. *Cancer* 71 (11), 3565–3569, June 1, 1993.

Bonnick, S.L., MD. Intensive healing for brittle bones. *Prevention Magazine*, p. 92, June 1994.

Bowen, C., MD, BA. *Hand-Book of Materia Medica, Pharmacy and Therapeutics*. Philadelphia, PA: F.A. Davis, 1888.

Breely, B., L.Ac. *Menopause Workbook.* San Rafael, CA: Brenda Beeley, 1993.

Brunner, E.J., et al. Gender and employment grade differences in blood cholesterol, apolipoprteins and haemostatic factors in the Whitehall II study. *Atherosclerosis* 102 (2), 195–207, September, 1993.

Burnett, J.C., MD, FRGS. *Curability of Cataracts with Medicines*. London: Homeopathic Publishing, 1880.

Butler, R.N., MD, et al. Love and sex after 60: How to evaluate and treat the sexually-active woman. *Geriatrics* 49 (11), 33–42, November, 1994.

Calle, E.E., et al. Family history, age, and risk of fatal breast cancer. *American Journal of Epidemiology* 138 (9), 675–681, November 1, 1993.

Carson, C.A., et al. Coffee consumption: Relationship to blood lipids in middle-aged women. *International Journal of Epidemiology* 23 (3), 523–527, November, 1993.

Casper, R.F. and Chapdelaine, A. Estrogen and interrupted progestin: A new concept for menopausal HRT. *American Journal of Obstetrics & Gynecology* 168 (4), 1188–1194, April, 1993.

Cauley, J.A., et al. Prevalence and determinants of estrogen replacement therapy in elderly women. *American Journal of Obstetrics & Gynecology* 163 (5), Part 1, 1438–1444, November, 1990.

Chappell, P., RSHom, BSc, FSHom. *Emotional Healing with Homeopathy, A Self-Help Manual.* Dorset, England: Element Books, 1994.

Christiansen, C., MD. What should be done at the time of menopause? *American Journal of Medicine* 98 (suppl 2A), 56S–59S, February 27, 1995.

Clarke, J.H., MD. *A Dictionary of Practical Materia Medica.* New Delhi: B. Jain, 1984.

Clarke, J.H., MD. *A Clinical Repertory to the Dictionary of Materia Medica.* N. Devon, England: Health Science Press, 1979.

Cleghorn, D.B., et al. Fracture rates calculated from fracture histories in normal postmenopausal women. *Journal of Epidemiology & Community Health* 46 (2), 133–135, April 1992.

Colditz, G.A., MB, BS., et al. The use of estrogens and progestins and the risk of breast cancer in postmenopausal women. *New England Journal of Medicine* 332, 1549–1593, Number 24, June 15, 1995.

Cole, E, and Rothblum, E. Commentary on "sexuality and the midlife woman." *Psychology of Women Quarterly* 14, 509–512, 1992.

Cole, T.G., et al. Differential reduction of plasma cholesterol by the American Heart Association. Phase 3. Diet in moderately hypercholesterolemic, premenopausal women with different body mass indexes. *American Journal of Clinical Nutrition* 55 (2), 385–392, February 1992.

Coleman, P.M. Depression during the female climacteric period. *Journal of Advanced Nursing* 18 (10), 1540–1546, October 1993.

Compston, J.E. HRT and osteoporosis. *British Medical Bulletin* 48 (2), 309–344, April 1992.

Coney, S. *The Menopause Industry.* Alameda, CA: Hunter House, 1994.

Coney, S. A beginner's guide to menopause. *Ms. Magazine* 5 (4), Jan/Feb 1995.

Corley, D., et al. Postmenopausal bleeding from unusual endometrial polyps in women on chronic tamoxifen therapy. *Obstetrics & Gynecology* 79 (1), 111–116, January 1992.

Cramer, D.W., MD, et al. Does "incessant" ovulation increase risk for early menopause? *American Journal of Obstetrics & Gynecology* 172 (2), Part 1, 568–573, February 1995.

Crighton, I.L., et al. The effect of a low-fat diet on hormone levels in healthy pre- and postmenopausal women: relevance for breast cancer. *European Journal of Cancer* 28 A912, 2024–2027, 1992.

Daly, E., et al. HRT: An analysis of benefits, risks and costs. *British Medical Bulletin* 48 (2), 368–400, 1992.

Dawson-Hughes, B. and Harris, S. Regional changes in body composition by time of year in healthy postmenopausal women. *American Journal of Clinical Nutrition* 56 (2), 307–313, August 1992.

Davis, D.L. and Bradlow, H. Can environmental estrogens cause breast cancer? *Scientific American*, p. 165–172, October 1995.

Demirovic, J., et al. Menopause and seru cholesterol: differences between blacks and whites. The Minnesota Heart Survey. *American Journal of Epidemiology* 136 (2), 155–164, July 15, 1992.

Dennerstein, L., et al. Menopausal symptoms in Australian women. *Medical Journal of Australia* 159 (4), 232–236, August 16, 1993.

Derby, C.A., et al. Correlates of postmenopausal estrogen use and trends through the 1980s in two southeaster New England communities. *American Journal of Epidemiology* 137 (10), 1125–1135, May 15, 1993.

Diamond, T., et al. Cyclical etidronate plus ergocalciferol prevents glucocorticoid-induced bone loss in postmenopausal women. *American Journal of Medicine* 98, 459–463, May 1995.

Ellerington, M.C., et al. HRT: Developments in therapy. *British Medical Bulletin* 48 (2) 401–425, 1992.

Ettinger, B., MD, et al. Cyclic hormone replacement therapy using quarterly progestin. *Obstetrics & Gynecology* 83 (5) Part 1, 693–700, May 1994.

Facchinetti, F., et al. Psychosomatic disorders related to gynecology. *Psychotherapy and Psychosomatic* 58 (3–4), 137–154, 1992.

Falkeborne, M., et al. Hormone replacement therapy and the risk of stroke. *Archives of Internal Medicine* 153 (10), 1201–1209, May 24, 1993.

Fayazuddin, M. *The Woman at Menopause.* Kakinada, India: Sripathi Press, 1988.

Fishbein, E.G. Women at midlife: The transition to menopause. *Nursing Clinics of North America* 27 (4), 951–957, December 1992.

Fisher, P., Dr., et al. Fibrosistis. *British Medical Journal* 299, 365–366, 1989.

Frederick, L. and Hawkins, S.T. A comparison of nutritional knowledge and attitudes, dietary practices, and bone densities of postmenopausal. *Journal of the American Dietetic Association* 92 (3), 299–305, March 1992.

Freedman, R.R. Biochemical, metabolic, and vascular mechanisms in menopausal hot flashes. *Fertility and Sterility* 70 (2), 332–337, August 1998.

Frock, J., and Money, J. Sexuality and menopause. *Psychotherapy and Psychosomatics* 57 (1–2), 29–33, 1992.

Gambrell, R.D., Jr. Update on hormone replacement therapy. *American Family Physician* 46 (5, Suppl.), 875–965, November 1992.

Gaby, A., MD. *Preventing and Reversing Osteoporsis.* Prima Publishing, Rocklin, California, 1994.

Gavaler, J.S. and Love, K. Detection of the relationship between moderate alcoholic beverage consumption and serum levels of estradiol in normal postmenopausal women: Effects of alcohol consumption quantitation methods and sample size adequacy. *Journal of Studies on Alcohol* 53 (4), 1992.

Gibbons, John H. *The Menopause, Hormone Therapy, and Women's Health.* Background paper, OTA-BP-BA-88, U.S. Congress, Office of Technology Assessment. Washington, DC: U.S. Government Printing Office, May 1992.

Grismaijer, S. and Singer,S.R. *Dress to Kill: The Link Between Breast Cancer and Bras.* Avery Publishing, 1995.

Guzick, D. Premenopausal determinants of menopausal estrogen use. *Preventative Medicine* 20 (3), 343–349, May 1991.

Hallberg, L. Iron requirements. *Biological Trace Element Research* 35 (1), 25–45, October 1992.

Handley, R. *Homeopathy for women.* London: Thorsons, an imprint of HarperCollins, 1993.

Helson, R., and Wink, P. Personality chance in women from the early 40's to the early 50's. *Psychology & Aging* 7 (1), 46–55, March 1992.

Hu, J.F., et al. Dietary calcium and bone density among middle-aged and elderly women in China. *American Journal of Clinical Nutrition* 58 (2), 219–227, August 1993.

Hemminki, E., MD and Sihvo, S., MPH. A review of postmenopausal hormone therapy recommendations: Potential for selection bias. *Obstetrics & Gynecology* 82 (6), 1021–1028, December 1993.

Hemminki, E., et al. Selection to postmenopausal therapy by women's characteristics. *Journal of Clinical Epidemiology* 46 (3), 211–219, March 1993.

Hoyer, G., and Lund, E. Suicide among women related to number of children in marriage. *Archives of General Psychiatry* 50 (2), 134–137, February 1993.

Hulka, B.S., MD, MPH. Links between hormone replace therapy and neoplasia. *Fertility and Sterility* 62, 168s–175s, Supplement 2, December 1994.

Hussain, R.C., et al. Effects of oral gamolenic acid from evening primrose oil on menopausal flushing. *British Medical Journal* 30, 501–502, February 19, 1994.

Kaminski, P. *Flower Essence Repertory.* Nevada City, CA: The Flower Essence Society, 1984.

Kato, I., et al. A case-control study of breast cancer among Japanese women: With special reference to family history and reproductive and dietary factors. *Breast Cancer Research & Treatment* 24 (1), 51–59, 1992

Kent, J.T., MD. *Lectures on Homeopathic Materia Medica.* New Delhi, India: B. Jain, 1921.

Khaw, K.T., editor. *Hormone Replacement Therapy.* London: Churchill Livingston, 1992.

Kim, J.W., et al. Estrogen and progesterone receptor assay in carcinoma of the cervix with monoclonal antibodies. *Gynecologic Oncology* 47 (3), 306–310, December 1992.

Kirchengast, S. Relationships between fertility, body shape and menopause in Austrian women. *Journal of Biosocial Science* 24 (4), 555–559, October 1992.

Koespell, T.D., et al. Non-contraceptive hormones and the risk of rheumatoid arthritis in menopausal women. *International Journal of Epidemiology* 23 (6), 1994.

Krieger, N., et al. Dietary factors and fracture in postmenopausal women: A case-control study. *International Journal of Epidemiology* 21 (5), 953–958, October 1992.

LaRosa, John C. Has HRT come of age? *Lancet* 345, 76, January 14, 1995.

Lessell, C.B., MB, BS, BDS, MRCS, LRCP. *The World Travellers' Manual of Homeopathy.* Essex, England: C.W. Daniel, 1993.

Levine, D., et al. Simple adrenal cysts: The natural history in postmenopausal women. *Radiology* 184 (3), 653–659, September 1992.

Lindgren, R., et al. Hormonal replacement therapy and sexuality in a population of Swedish postmenopausal women. *Acta Obstetricia et Gynecologica Scandinavica* 72 (4), 292–297, May 1993.

Lindheim, S.R., et al. Behavioral stress responses in premenopausal and postmenopausal women and the effects of estrogen. *American Journal of Obstetrics & Gynecology* 167 (6), 1831–1836, December 1992.

Lockie, A., MD. *The Family Guide to Homeopathy.* New York: Simon & Schuester/Fireside Books, 1989.

Lockie, A., MD, and Geddes, N., MD. *The Complete Guide to Homeopathy.* London: Dorling Kindersley, 1995.

Lockie, A., MD, and Geddes, N., MD. *The Women's Guide to Homeopathy.* New York: St. Martin's Press, 1994.

London, S.J., et al. A prospective study of benign breast disease and the risk of breast cancer. *Journal of the American Medical Association* 267 (7), 941–944, February 19, 1992.

Loprinzi, C.L., MD, et al. Megestrol acetate for the prevention of hot flashes. *New England Journal of Medicine* 331 (6), 347–352, August 11, 1994.

Lovering, A.T., MD. *Hints In Domestic Practice and Home Nursing.* Boston: Otis Clapp & Son, 1896.

Maclennan, A.H., et al. The prevalence of hysterectomy in South Australia. *Medical Journal of Australia* 158 (12), 807–809, June 21, 1993.

Mais, V., MD, et al. The role of follicle-stimulating hormone in the depletion of follicular reserve: Menopause in a Woman with hypogonadotropic hypoestrongenic amenorrhea: A case report. *Fertility and Sterility* 63 (3), 669–672, March 1995.

Marsh, M.S. and Whitehead, M.I. Management of the menopause. *British Medical Bulletin* 48 (2), 426–457, 1992.

Martin, M.C., et al. Menopause without symptoms: the endocrinology of menopause among rural Mayan Indians. *American Journal of Obstetrics & Gynecology* 168 (6), Part 1, 1839–1845, June 1993.

Mason, M. Facing Hirsutism. *Essence Magazine*, p. 26, April 1994.

Matthews, K.A., et al. Influences of natural menopause on psychological characteristics and symptoms of middle-aged healthy women. *Journal of Consulting and Clinical Psychology* 58 (3), 345–351, June 1990.

Mathur, K.N., MD. *Principles of Prescribing—Collected from Clinical Experiences of Pioneers of Homeopathy*. New Delhi, India: B. Jain, 1981.

Meade, T.W. and Berra, A. Hormone replacement therapy and cardiovascular disease. *British Medical Bulletin* 48 (2), 276–308, 1992.

Moen, M.H. Is Endometriosis a disease? Why do women develop endometriosis and why is it diagnosed? *Human Reproduction* 10 (1), 8–12, 1995.

Mones, J., et al. Influence of the menstrual cycle and of menopause on the gastric emptying rate of solids in female volunteers. *European Journal of Nuclear Medicine* 20 (7), 600–602, July 1993.

Montero, I., et al. Social functioning as a significant factor in women's help-seeking behavior during the climacteric period. *Social Psychiatry & Psychiatric Epidemiology* 28 (4), 178–183, August 1993.

Morrison, N.A., et al. Contribution of trans-acting factor alleles to normal physiological variability: Vitamin D receptor gene polymorphism and circulating osteocalcin. *Proceedings of the National Academy of Sciences of the U.S.A.* 89 (15), 6665–6669, August 1, 1992.

Morrison, R., MD. *Desktop Guide to Keynotes and Confirmatory Symptoms*. Albany, CA: Hahnemann Clinic, 1993.

Murkies, A.L. Common problems with HRT. *Australian Family Physician* 21 (3), 217–218, 222, 225, March 1992.

Nabulsi, A.A., et al. Association of hormone-replacement therapy with various cardiovascular risk factors in postmenopausal women. The Atherosclerosis Risk in Communities Study Investigators. *New England Journal of Medicine* 328 (15), 1069–1075, April 15, 1993.

Nachtigall, L.E., MD and Heilman, J.R. *Estrogen*. New York: HarperCollins, 1995.

Naldoni, C., et al. Association of cyst type with risk factors for breast cancer and relapse rate in women with gross cystic disease of the breast. *Cancer Research* 52 (7), 1791–1795, April 1, 1992.

Naessen, T., et al. Hormone replacement therapy and the risk for first hip fracture. A prospective, population-based cohort study. *Annals of Internal Medicine* 113 (2), 95–102, July 15, 1990.

Noord, R.A. *Selenium and the risk of postmenopausal breast cancer in the DOM cohort.* Dept. of Epidemiology, Rijks University at Utrecht, The Netherlands, 25 (1), 11–19, 1993.

Nordin, B.E, et al. The nature and significance of the relationship between urinary sodium and urinary calcium in women. *Journal of Nutrition* 123 (9), 1615–1622, September 1993.

Ojeda, L., Ph.D. *Menopause Without Medicine.* Alameda, CA: Hunter House, 1989.

Oldenhave, A., et al. Impact of climacteric on well-being. *American Journal of Obstetrics & Gynecology* 168 (3), Part 1, 772–780, March 1993.

Padus, E. *The Woman's Encyclopedia of Health and Natural Healing*. Emmaus, PA: Rodale Press, 1981.

Palmer, J.R., et al. Reproductive factors and risk of myocardial infarction. *American Journal of Epidemiology* 1136 (4), 408–116, August 15, 1992.

Paranzzini, F., et al. Oral contraceptive use and risk of uterine fibroids. *Obstetrics & Gynecology* 79 (3), 430–433, March 1992.

Pathak, D.R. and Whittemore, A.S. Combined effects of body size, parity, and menstrual events on breast cancer incidence in seven countries. *American Journal of Epidemiology* 135 (2), 153–168, January 15, 1992.

Popay, J., et al. Gender inequalities in health: Social position, affective disorders and minor physical morbidity. *Social Science and Medicine* 36 (1), 21–32, January 1993.

Pazsko, Z., et al. Estrogen and progesterone receptor status in breast cancer in Kuwait female population. *Neoplasma* 40 (2), 127–132, 1993.

Perlmutter, C. Triumph over menopause. *Prevention Magazine*, p. 78, August 1994.

Plunkette, E.R. and Wolfe, B.M. Prolonged effects of a novel, low-dosage continuous progesti-cyclic estrogen replacement program in postmenopausal women. *American Journal of Obstetrics & Gynecology* 166 (1), Part 1, 117–121, January 1992.

Posner, B.M., et al. Diet, menopause, and serum cholesterol levels in women: The Framingham Study. *American Heart Journal* 125 (2), Part 1, 483–489, February 1993.

Pulte, J.H., MD. *Homeopathic Domestic Physician.* Cincinnati, OH: Moore, Wilstach, Keys, 1856.

Ramin, S.M., et al. Sexual assault in postmenopausal women. *Obstetrics & Gynecology* 80 (5), 860–864, November 1992.

Raz, R., MD, Stamm, W.E., MD. A controlled trail of intervaginal estriol in postmenopausal women with recurrent urinary tract infections. *New England Journal of Medicine* 329 (11), September 9, 1993.

Rees, Margaret. On menstrual bleeding with hormone replacement therapy. *Lancet* 343, 250, January 29, 1994.

Reeve, J. Future prospects for hormone replacement therapy. *British Medical Bulletin* 48 (2), 458–468, 1992.

Reginster, J.Y., et al. A double-blind, placebo-controlled, dose-finding trial of intermittent nasal salmon calcitonin for prevention of postmenopausal lumbar spine bone loss. *American Journal of Medicine* 98, 452–458, May 1995.

Riechenberg-Ullman, J., ND. Menopause naturally. *Natural Health*, March/April 1992.

Ringsbert, K. Muscle strength differences in urban and rural populations in Sweden. *Archives of Physical Medicine & Rehabilitation* 74 (12), 1315–1318, December 1993.

Russo, F., et al. Endogenous sex hormones and cholesterol gallstones: A case-control study in an echographic survey of gallstones. *American Journal of Gastroenterology* 88 (5), 712–717, May 1993.

Ryan, P., et al. Compliance with HRT after screening for postmenopausal osteoporosis. *British Journal of Obstetrics & Gynecology* 99 (4), 325–328, April 1992.

Sachs, J.S. Hormone-replacement therapy: Overprescribed? *New Woman,* p. 144, July 1993.

Sachs, J. *What Women Should Know About Menopause*. New York: Dell, 1991.

Salaman, M. *Foods That Heal.* Menlo Park, CA: Statford, 1989.

Samanta, A., et al. Is osteoarthritis in women affected by hormonal changes or smoking? *British Journal of Rheumatology* 32 (5), 366–370, May 1993.

Schweiger, U. Depressed to the bone ... *Science News* 146, 360.

Seeley, D.G., et al. Is postmenopausal estrogen therapy associated with neuromuscular function or falling in elderly women? *Arch Internal Medicine* 155, 293–299, February 13, 1995.

Sharan, F., MDMA, ND. Natural treatment of menopause using herbs. *Alternative & Complementary Therapies* 1 (3), 146–153, April/May 1995.

Shaver, J.L., et al. Sleep quality subtypes in midlife women. *Sleep* 14 (1), 18–23, 1991.

Standing, T.S., RN, and Glazer, G., RN. Attitudes of low-income patients toward menopause. *Health Care for Women's International* 13, 271–280, 1992.

Smith, L.G., et al. Postmenopausal uterine bleeding due to estrogen production by gonadotropin-secreting lung tumors. *American Journal of Medicine* 92 (3), 327–330, March 1992.

Smith, P. Estrogens and the urogental tract. *Acta Obstetricia et Gynecologica Scandinavica* 157 (Suppl.), 1–26, 1993.

Smith, T., MD. *Homeopathy for the Menopause*. Worthing, England: Insight Editions, 1994.

Smith, T., MD. *Homeopathic Medicine for Women*. Rochester, VT: Healing Arts Press, 1989.

Souter, K. *Homeopathy and the Third Age*. London: C.W. Daniel, 1993.

Stevens, J.C., et al. Conditions associated with carpal tunnel syndrome. *Mayo Clinic Proceedings* 67 (6), 541–548, June 1992.

Stewart, D.E. and Boydell, K.M. Psychotic distress during menopause: Associations across the reproductive life cycle. *International Journal of Psychiatry In Medicine* 23 (2), 1576–1562, 1993.

Sturdee, D.W. Is the timing of withdrawal bleeding a guide to endometrial safety during sequential oestrogen-progestagen replacement therapy? *Lancet* 344, 979–982, October 8, 1994.

Swartzman, L.C., et al. Impact of stress on objectively recorded menopausal hot flushes and on flush report bias. *Health Psychology* 9 (5), 529–545, 1990.

Svendsen, O.L., et al. Effect of an energy-restrictive diet, with or without exercise, on lean tissue mass, resting metabolic rate, cardiovascular risk factors, and bone in overweight postmenopausal women. *American Journal of Medicine* 95 (2), 131–140, August 1993.

Tarbell, J.A., MD, AM. *Homeopathy Simplified; Or, Domestic Practice Made Easy.* Boston: Otis Clapp & Son, 1890.

Taylor, M.A., and Reilly, D.T. Is homeopathy a placebo effect? Hay fever trial. *Lancet* 2 (8512), 8881–8886, 1986.

Thomas, C.L., MD, MPH. *Taber's Cyclopedic Medical Dictionary*, 13th ed. Philadelphia, PA: F.A. Davis, 1977.

Thorogood, M., et al. Fatal stroke and use of oral contraceptives. *American Journal of Epidemiology* 136 (a), 35–45, July 1, 1992.

Ubell, E. Don't get embarrassed—get help. *Parade Magazine*, September 10, 1995.

Ushiroyama, T., et al. Plasma lipid and lipoprotein levels in perimenopausal women: Clinical research in 1198 Japanese women. *Acta Obstetricia et Gynecologica Scandinavica* 72 (6), 428–433, August 1993.

Udvardy, M. The fertility of the post-fertile: Concepts of gender, aging and reproductive health among the Giriama of Kenya. *Journal of Cross-Cultural Gerontology* 7 (4), 289–306, 1992.

van den Brandt, P.A., et al. Alcohol and breast cancer: Results from the Netherlands cohort study. *American Journal of Epidemiology* 141 (10), 1995.

van Beresteijn, E.C., et al. Perimenopausal increase in serum cholesterol: A 10-year longitudinal study. *American Journal of Epidemiology* 137 (4), 383–392, February 15, 1993.

Wallis, C. Estrogen: Is it for you? *Reader's Digest*, p. 94–98, December 1995.

Weed, S. *The Menopausal Years: The Wise Woman Way.* Woodstock, NY: As Tree Publishing, 1992.

Wheatly, D. Correspondence. *British Journal of Psychiatry* 158, 431–32, March 1991.

Wilkes, H.C. and Meade, T.W. Hormone replacement therapy in general practice. *British Medical Journal* 302 (6788), 1317–1320, June 1, 1991.

Wolf, P.H., et al. Reduction of cardiovascular disease—Related mortality among postmenopausal women who use hormones: Evidence from a national cohort. *American Journal of Obstetrics & Gynecology* 164 (2), 489–494, February 1991.

Wolfe, B.B., and Huff, M.W. Effects of low dosage progestin-only administration upon plasta triglycerides and lipoprotein metabolism in postmenopausal women. *Journal of Clinical Investigation* 92 (1), 456–461, July 1993.
Wren, B.G. The effect of oestrogen on the female cardiovascular system. Medical Journal of Australia 157 (3), 204–208, August 3, 1992.
Wysowski, D.K., et al. Use of menopausal estrogens and medroxyprogesterone in the United States, 1982–1992. *Obstetrics & Gynecology* 85 (1), 6–10, January 1995.
Yu, H., et al. Risk factors of fibroaedeonma: A case-control study in Australia. *American Journal of Epidemiology* 135 (3), 247–258, February 1, 1992.

SOFTWARE

Amr'ta, IBIS Software . Portland, OR, 1993.
Warkentin, D.K., MACREPERTORY software. Fairfax, CA: Kent Associates, 1991.
Warkentin, D.K., REFERENCEWORKS software. Fairfax, CA: Kent Associates, 1992.

INDEX

G